TRIGGER MAN

THE GIRL IN THE BOX
BOOK 59

ROBERT J. CRANE

Ostiagard Press

Trigger Man

The Girl in the Box, Book 59

Robert J. Crane

copyright © 2024 Ostiagard Press

1st Edition.

PROLOGUE

Fen Liu was ready to die.

"Speak, and you will find peace," the interrogator whispered to her, his hot, stinking breath flaring in her ear with every word.

Fen Liu had been in the cell for...months? Years? It was difficult to tell. There was no sunlight; that had been the first thing to go. They'd dragged her in here, powerless, woken her at seemingly random intervals, gave her injections during some of them, shaking her roughly from – not her bed, because there wasn't one, but – the floor, and the lumps of straw she'd been given.

The only illumination was a single bulb overhead, dangling like a gate to heaven opened above her head. She could see it when she lifted her eyes. She fixated on it now, trying to push away the pain in her wrists, in her joints. The chains held her up, for her legs had given out long ago. Now she dangled like a piece of meat in the dark, cold cell. Where was she, exactly, in China? It was hard to guess. Yunnan, perhaps? Or Gansu?

Oh, what a fall. Since the beginning of the Chinese

Communist Party, she'd been working to assure her position, to climb, to ascend into the heights of heaven at the top of the power structure. It wasn't her first brush with power—

But it certainly looked like it was going to be her last.

"Speak," he said again, stinking breath hitting her in the face. Not with the force of a punch; that would be exaggeration, and unnecessary, for she had experienced many punches to the face since she'd arrived here. Even now, her lips were cracked and bleeding. She'd lost a dozen teeth. "And this all can end."

Fen Liu mustered a weak chuckle to that. She didn't believe it for a second.

Whoever had taken control of the Chinese state after her fall did not believe in gentle, western justice any more than she had. Whatever professions they might have made, any nods toward the concept of human rights, they'd been mouthing mere platitudes. China did not have a rich tradition of protecting the individual against the state, and any momentum they might have made toward that way of thinking had been utterly eroded at the great retreat in 1949. Oh, sure, Hong Kong had ideas about that, but who would listen to them?

And so Fen Liu had accepted her fate: she would be tortured to death, injected to powerlessness, and accept whatever beatings and torment and degradations would come from now until the day she died. Which, if she was lucky, would be soon.

If she were not, however...

"I know you are hiding at least one more secret," he whispered. The warmth of his breath was almost matched by the warmth of his flesh. He brushed against her, and not with a punch. He did this occasionally, and it was the oddest sensation. His hand was upon her bare shoulder, and it felt...

Good.

She wanted to shudder in revulsion. He'd taken at least three of her teeth, after all, and so much of her blood, not to mention her dignity – if such a thing even existed any longer.

And yet...with his hand upon her shoulder, the warmth of it upon her cold, shuddering flesh...

She felt a desire to speak, to say...

But no. If he didn't yet know, she could not tell him.

That would be folly.

That would be *warning*.

And she could not afford to warn. Not in advance.

Not before the thing was *done*.

An impact to her gut from his hand, a strong punch that targeted her liver, made Fen Liu want to throw up. Her body jerked from the impact, spasming from a full tensing of the muscles across her abdomen. Already sore, they were upset by the cruelty of the blow.

Yet, also...used to it by now.

"Speak," he said, soothing with his stinking breath. His face was shadowed in the light streaming from the lone bulb above. He pressed his forehead to hers, without fear. What could she do to him, after all? She had no powers left, the drugs had long since sapped them away. She had no teeth left in the front. At best, she could bite his nose with her gums, listen to him laugh as she tried to tear the cartilage through stubborn strength alone.

The only weapon remaining to her was her silence. She had spoken much; had said too much, probably. But she couldn't help it; the pain did not lessen day by day, it compounded, and the interest was paid in her mind breaking like the trestles of a bridge, one joint at a time. There was little enough left of her reserve now; the mere hint of him, or one of her other many interrogators, raising their fist, and her body would shudder in preparation for the blow.

No, hitting her was not the only method they used. But it did seem the most common. The most...blunt.

It was a shame, in its way. Fen Liu was a practical person. Had prided herself on being a practical leader. The methods of torture her government had employed had been very progressive. Brainwashing using the latest technology. Seduction using agents posing as fellow prisoners or guards. Telepathy from metahumans, once they'd built a solid core of those, and before she'd pulled them away to work on...other things.

Certainly, they defaulted to knives, blades, heat, electricity, and blunt force trauma at times. But it was a calculated sort of cruelty, designed to drive up the misery level of the prisoner so that they would choose to talk rather than face the insurmountable wave of cruelty that would surely wash over them if they did not.

But this...this beating she was enduring, she reflected with a gasp as he hit her again, this was so *graceless* in its cruelty. She took another hit to the belly and gasped, muscles contracting again, against her will, against her reason. There was a feeling in her body that she could not surmount; it was as though she were filled up with it, with pain, as though it were threatening to spill out in a gasp, in a shout, in this quiet chamber in which the only sound was the interrogator's breathing and the creak of the chains holding her up, anchoring her to the ceiling–

She screamed, and it was all the worse because she did not expect it. She'd been reasoning in her tired, dragging mind that she couldn't afford to say anything about the last thing, the last secret, for fear it would be ruined by the knowing, by it springing out of her lips–

"I will tell you!" The words burst forth from her like a shock of power, before another blow could strike, and she shuddered, spitting out blood and truth, the last things she had to give.

He leaned in close, and she whispered it to him. Whispered it, because she could not quite bear to speak it aloud.

She told him...

...And he struck her again anyway.

Fen Liu gasped at the shock, shuddered at the pain, felt the cold darkness pressing at the edges of her vision. A hammering came behind her, a squeak, but she barely heard it.

Her toes, already cold, had gone numb. She couldn't feel them dragging the floor anymore.

Voices whispered behind her. She caught snatches.

"...Need to know when. Need to know how..."

She couldn't care anymore. Her fingertips...she couldn't feel them now, either. Blood loss? The cold? She'd always been able to feel them before, no matter how painful.

The muscles in her neck slackened, and her head drifted back. She stared up at the lone bulb as the voices behind her continued, though she could no longer pick out more than a few words here and there.

"...Will destroy everything...the ruin of us..."

"...Need...to know..."

Fen Liu stared at the bulb, the blinding, overriding light coming from it, and felt a ragged breath leave her body. As it did, she found she could not draw another. This caused her to spasm as though she'd been hit, a most curious sensation since she hadn't been.

"...America will be back to war with us if...Nealon will return and..."

Ah.

That name.

Fen Liu fixated on it, as the light came flooding down on

her, warming her in the places where the cold had taken hold a moment earlier.

Sienna Nealon.

She'd clutched this secret close to spite Nealon. This was it; her final revenge. Wheels within wheels, and she'd set more than one in motion before her fall, her capture, before...this.

"Get it out of her."

Those were the last words Fen Liu heard before she drifted unexpectedly into the light.

And when the interrogator shook her a moment later, she was already gone.

CHAPTER ONE

Sienna

"We'll deal with the consequences when the time comes," my husband said from across the table in our sun-drenched hideaway in the Greek isles. The mercury was deep into the eighties, Fahrenheit, and he was sitting across from me, his brown hair streaked with blond after three months under the Grecian sun. His skin, already tanned, had turned a lovely brown.

Must be nice. My skin remained a snowy white, stubbornly resistant to the heat and the sun. Was it my inhuman ability to heal from all wounds that kept it fixed in the range of alabaster, the same shade visible on the sculptures scattered throughout this sumptuous villa that I'd made my refuge from the world?

Jeremy James Wade wore a somewhat serious look; he had left the Chinese prison in Shenzhen earlier this year at a deeply unhealthy weight; normally 6'1" and in the 210s, he'd come out from under the tender ministrations of Fen Liu's China weighing about 115, and slouching severely. He'd rebounded quickly enough, given his metahuman healing, but he hadn't looked quite right until very recently, his broad, muscular shoulders restored to their tightly pulled-back posture, head held high, blue eyes piercing mine.

"Or, alternatively," I said, with as much impishness as I could muster, "we could just dodge out of the consequences and stay here on the beach forevermore."

Amusement wrinkled the edges of Wade's eyes, and they sparkled as he said, "You don't mean that."

"I kinda do," I said, voice breaking a little as I contemplated it. "Look, Wade...I've done the whole 'save the world' thing. So many times now. When trouble has reared its ugly head, I have seldom hesitated to uh, wade, pardon the pun, right in and make my presence felt."

"I've always admired that about you," he said, the sparkle in his eye diminishing as the seriousness of what I was saying seemed to hit home.

I shifted on the comfortable outdoor couch I occupied, pulling my legs beneath me to sit on my feet. It wasn't a traditional pose for me, but with Wade I found myself...well, different. In so many ways. "Every time I've ever come in swinging, there have been consequences. And like Ricardo," I said, casting my eyes skyward to see my Cooper's hawk flying in a wide gyre around the island, seeking something to prey upon, "those consequences always come back on me. Always."

"That's kind of how consequences work," Wade said, still smiling, though seemingly a touch less amused.

I shook my head slowly, my loose hair falling over my bare shoulders. I was inconceivably clad, even for the circumstances; I was wearing a bikini. Entirely for my husband, and only because I was on a private island where I'd seen only his face for the last three months and not a single other human one. They were out there, elsewhere, beyond the aquamarine seas, but they weren't here, and so here I was willing to be less guarded, on display for him, in a way I never would have gone along with outside of this place.

Because it was fun and easy and carefree in a way I had never before experienced. That's why.

"These loose ends I create from my efforts trying to fix things," I said, brushing back my hair, content to let it rest loose around my shoulders, "they always come back on me, spinning like a wheel of fire, turned loose upon the world – and me."

"Lucky you can't get burned, huh?" He asked, a sparkle again in his eyes. "We're not going to resolve this now. I'm going to go get in my morning swim." He waited a second to see if I'd respond; I did. Just a nod to let him know I wasn't mad, we were fine, he should go swim, enjoy himself.

I sagged back against the couch and watched him go, sun beating down on my face. I watched him go, tried to enjoy it, because he wasn't even wearing a Speedo. And boy was he tanned. Everywhere. He crashed into the waves after a short sprint and a leap aided by his ability to fly. The moment he disappeared under the waves I spoke, sure he couldn't hear it.

"Oh, I get burned." And I curled up on my legs and watched the waves crash under a perfect blue sky.

CHAPTER TWO

Reed

I stared out the window of my office to the last strains of autumn in Franklin, Tennessee. Vivid reds and lively oranges decorated the trees dotted throughout the corporate office park we inhabited just a short drive south of Nashville. The sun was already dipping lower in the sky; the days were shortening, and not in the crisco sense of the word, though they did seem to have a bit more glide now that China wasn't breathing down our necks, and we weren't running the US government.

This was normal; the new normal, and it felt a lot like the old, as if we'd turned back the calendar to before the war with China began almost a year ago.

A wind rustled the trees, pulling loose a few leaves and letting them twirl their way to the earth below. We were up on the second floor, and I watched it all happen without taking an active role.

I could have, though. Could have reached my hand up, snatched one of the leaves out of the air with the power of the wind. Pressed it against the glass as neatly as if it was trapped in one of those old books they stuck photos in back in my youth. Before things got all digital and newfangled.

Before the world got away from us.

There was a hum of conversation out in the bullpen, even at this hour. After five tended to turn lots of the places I'd worked in my life into ghost towns.

Not here. Not at Metahuman, Inc. (Not our real name.)

"Yo!" Augustus Coleman called out from the door to his office. "Alannah Greene! Where you at?"

"I'm filling out fu – frigging paperwork!" She popped her head up, groundhog-style, from behind the cubicle desk she occupied whenever she was in the office. "What do you want?"

Augustus was out of my sight, so I sensed his response more than saw it, but I could picture it in my mind. A pause. A deep breath. A widening of the eyes. "Your paperwork for the New York case," he said, kind of amused in spite of the teenager nearly swearing at him. "I thought maybe you'd already checked out for the night. You just keep on with it."

She crossed her arms and laid them on the top of the cubicle, then dropped her chin down on that, the perfect image of a slacker teen. "Why would you shout my name if you thought I was already gone? You just like yelling or what?"

"Yeah, I thoroughly enjoy it," Augustus said, prompting a wave of guffaws from the folks scattered across the bullpen. Dozens of them here. Dozens more out on cases. "Gets my blood pumping. Makes me feel alive. Gets y'all to jump out of your seats like I set a lit firecracker under your ass. It works on a lot of levels."

"Of course you're thinking about my ass," she said,

pursing her lips in irritation. "Can't blame you for that. All right; as you were." And she disappeared behind the cubicle. Not one to let someone else get the last word, that girl. She reminded me of someone else in that regard. Someone I missed quite a lot.

"Eilish Findlay!" Augustus called, and I could hear him on the move, heading my way. "You here? Or are you already into your sixth pint of Guinness at the bar?" He paused just outside my door, and I had a great shoes-to-suit view of him. He was not the young man I'd met six years ago, who'd clad himself in football jerseys and ornate sneakers, though his sense of style was still impeccable even after the considerable upgrade. Now it was Savile Row suits and expensive shoes, with solid gold Rolexes and Cartiers. The hair was still close cropped, though, and the way he stood betrayed the immense amount of swagger in his step.

The strawberry blond head popped up about three cubicles down from Alannah. Pale, freckled, yet mightily annoyed, Eilish did not hesitate to respond, either. "That's hateful rhetoric."

Augustus cocked an eyebrow at her. "Have you been in the Guinness in the last week?"

Alannah snorted audibly from across the bullpen. "Easier question: has she not been in the Guinness for a single day in the last week?"

"We'll put a pin in that for a second." Augustus turned, looking in at me. "Reed Treston. What do you got going on?"

I grunted, looking down at my desk, which was covered, as usual, in paperwork of my own. How had I come to this point, where paper ruled my life? Where emails and calls came at all hours of the day and night, some urgent, some important, some a combination of both – or neither? "Still shoveling out after our sweep in Pasadena two weeks ago."

The city of Pasadena had hired us – in this case me, Scott

Byerly, Angel Gutierrez, and Olivia Brackett – to come work their streets for a week to stem the tide of metahuman crime that China had unleashed on us over the last few years. It was a targeted attempt to deal with the 1% of perps that caused 2/3rds of all crime.

It had worked. Pasadena crime stats for the last two weeks were down by more than half from the mountainous highs they'd achieved over the last year. We bagged 832 perps in our week there, and they were all awaiting trial without bail. Most were homeless drug addicts or gang-bangers.

And I was still filling out the scads of paperwork to make those arrests stick and the trials go smoothly. Because that was what I did now; while Scott, Olivia, and Angel had all moved on to the next town, their next assignment, I was still working on the fallout from the last.

How had this become my life?

Augustus frowned at me. "I get the sense you might not be putting all your heart and soul into this, given how long it's taking you."

I gave him a look that could be politely described as cross. "I'll make sure that if the DA misses a conviction, it won't be because of anything we've done. What more do you want from me?"

"Funny you should ask," Augustus said, "because I just had a new case cross my desk from an unexpected locale, and I thought I'd send you and Ms. Guinness."

"Please let it be Aruba, then," Eilish said.

"You'd look like a french fry left in boiling grease overnight after five minutes in the tropics," Alannah sniped at her. "If anyone ought to be hitting the beach in Aruba it needs to be my beautiful and overtaxed ass."

"Ladies, ain't nobody going to Aruba on the company dime," Augustus said. "If we got a job from Aruba, I'd make y'all pay your own way to get the assignment. It'd be a bidding war, and the real winner would be the company."

There were moments when I wondered how Augustus had managed to take this company, which I'd run an earlier iteration of straight into the ground, into a massive success. Moments like this provided my answer.

"It's London," Augustus said, turning back at me. "I figured given your experience in Europe, you two'd be best for this assignment."

I surveyed the paperwork crowding my desk. "I never spent that much time working in Europe."

His brow furrowed. "I thought you worked for Alpha. Weren't they Euro-based?"

Alpha, as an organization, had been wiped out long before Augustus entered the metahuman world, so it wasn't surprising he wasn't up on the details. "They were," I said. "But I was their US representative, so I mostly worked here. When I did have to report to them, they were headquartered in Rome." Another look at my desk confirmed that the mountain of paperwork was still there. Witness statements. Use of force reports. I had emails from the district attorney asking a dozen questions about a dozen cases.

"So you don't have more Eurozone experience than everyone else?" Augustus asked.

I looked up. "I do, in the sense that a few drops of water is a larger amount than a complete absence of H_2O." Surveying the bullpen, I saw many eyes looking over cubicle walls at me. Some of them I could probably even recall the names of. "But I'm hardly an expert in navigating UK laws or city streets or anything. I don't even know what bangers and mash is."

"I've been to London," Alannah said, putting her hand skyward. "I went with Sienna last time and got in absolutely no trouble at all, plus at least one of the people I met on that trip is probably still alive. So I got connections. Plus, I know that bangers and mash is just sausages and mashed potatoes in a nasty, onion gravy."

"Oi," Eilish said, putting a hand over her face.

"You got legit experience in London, don'tcha, Eilish?" Augustus asked. I sensed his attention had drifted away from me and onto her. Hopefully not to Alannah, but better the teenage wrecking ball than me on this one.

"Unfortunately," Eilish muttered. She'd already partially slinked back behind the barrier between cubicles, and only a shock of strawberry-blond hair was visible now. "But why don't you just send Miss Congeniality? I don't have much use for the English, I have no good memories from London, and I have better things to be doing with my time, such as styling my nails and, yes, cracking open a Guinness."

"Hm. Figured it'd be like a homecoming for you," Augustus said.

I cringed; Eilish was Irish, and while she'd lived in London, it had been with a) Breandan, who'd died long ago, and b) had come to a rather abrupt end when she'd been pinched for some sort of crime, the details of which I couldn't even remember, after which she'd enjoyed a period of incarceration at the hands of Her Majesty's Prison Service (at the time).

"Well, I'm going to have to re-evaluate my plans, I guess," Augustus said, straightening himself up, plucking at his lapels and playing with the buttons of his suit.

"'Miss Congeniality?' Thanks for the straight-up diss," Alannah said. "Ya dick."

"If you ever wonder why you don't get the plum assignments," Augustus said, making his way back to his office, leather shoes squeaking classily with every step, "it might have something to do with your mouth."

"Got a lot of responses to that," Alannah said, "and since I ain't going to England anyway, I'll start with the obvious: my mouth is pure joy, if–"

"I'll pay you twenty quid if you don't finish that thought," Eilish said.

Alannah didn't even hesitate. "Done." After a pause, she added. "Wait. Is a quid like a penny?"

"At current exchange rates, it's more than a dollar," Augustus said, already back to his office. I couldn't see him anymore, but I could hear the smirk from his tone. "I had to check because I'm sending some as-yet-undetermined people who are definitely not you, on assignment over there, and I needed to know the exchange rate."

"Well, it sounds like I got a bargain on not making my blowy joke, then," Alannah said. "And since I'm going to have to pay my own way to Aruba, and London, and wherever else that ain't the armpit of Ohio, I'm gonna need it."

"I'll take the armpit of Ohio over London any day," Eilish said, stopping at Alannah's desk to drop a crisp twenty-dollar bill. She threw an extra fiver after it. Her thin frame seemed to shudder from emotion – or perhaps a stiff breeze I couldn't register – as she did so. "For my part, I hope I don't see London ever again."

"I had a fantastic time in London," Alannah said, picking up her cash and pocketing it. "I'd go back in a heartbeat."

Augustus's door slammed closed, probably expressing his feelings about that.

For my part, I turned back to the paperwork, and my responsibilities – for like the papers, they were piled high, and certain not to just disappear anytime soon.

CHAPTER THREE

Wade

S wimming wasn't exactly swimming for me anymore.

I cut through the current, through the waves, half a meter under the water's surface, half a mile out. My arms moved, but they were unnecessary for my propulsion if I didn't want them to be.

Because now...I could fly.

If I wanted to.

And at the end of my morning swim...I always wanted to.

The Mediterranean wasn't exactly warm at this time of year, but it wasn't Pacific cold, either. It lay somewhere in that happy medium between the freezing waters off California and the warm ones in the Caribbean or Hawaii. I fought the current here, fought it hard, my arms knifing against the waters, propelling myself forward, my breath held for almost five minutes now. When I wanted or needed one, I possessed the Poseidon ability to bring a bubble of oxygen down to breathe in without having to so much as worry about cresting it.

And I made the current fight me.

It was a fun exercise; I was at war with myself, really, water pulsing against my body as I exerted myself. My heart raced, water scything past my arms as I worked to increase its resistance against me.

I knew myself well enough to know that I needed something to fight against. Lately, it was the water in the morning and afternoon. Then the metahuman special weights in the workout room in the house. I fought against those things, those very careful factors in my control...

...Because my wife wasn't ready to fight the world again. And I wasn't ready to go back and face it without her.

A slight thrum of vibrato reached me through the waves, and I paused, water coating me like a second skin. I looked up through the blue and felt the sound as though it were right beside me.

It was a helicopter. And not one in the distance, either.

It was here, coming in for a landing at the shore.

They'd finally tracked us down.

They'd found us.

CHAPTER FOUR

Sienna

I covered my skin in fire as the helicopter settled into a slow drop, preparing to land. Flames covered me from neck to ankle; no way were these uninvited guests getting to see me in my bikini, especially if they were coming for some kind of fight. My energy blade slid out of my fist, ready to cleave heads from bodies, or helicopter blades from airframe. Whatever it took.

The sound itself of the blades chopping was a disturbance of my peace. Three months, and I'd finally started sleeping through the night, no terror that some Chinese missile or task force was going to come crashing in while I slept to murder my friends, my family, or my countrymen.

Its descent was slow, measured; possibly the most leisurely descent I'd ever seen. This allowed time for a very familiar face to appear at the window of the VH-92A Patriot helicopter, and gently reassure me that murder wasn't presently in the offing. Probably. As if the signage hadn't been a clear indicator.

Because at the window was President Robb Foreman.

The helo set down with a final thud into the sands, sending a blast of grains at me that I reflected away with a sweep of my hand, tapping the slightest bit of earth powers I'd picked up from Augustus Coleman at some point.

When the chopper doors opened, I readied my Magneto abilities in case I needed to send an errant dart reflecting away. But Robb Foreman was the only one who stepped out, at least at first.

The chopper was full of people behind him, and second out was a middle-aged man who was clean-shaven with gray hair. He swept his eyes up and down the beach; he had a little too much midsection to be Secret Service, but was a little too august not to be someone important. Still, I didn't recognize him, and he gave me a polite nod.

Second out was a woman with daggers for eyes and dark hair piled up on her head in a carefully structured bun. She watched me like I was murder itself, given form and pointed at her. Which was not an unfair way to watch me.

Still, undeterred by the violent, well-controlled anger of the woman at one shoulder or the amiable watchfulness of the man at the other, the president walked across the sands toward me, his large frame causing his feet to sink into the loose-packed sands with every step. He was wearing dress shoes – lol – which was the most Robb Foreman thing I could think of.

When he reached the white stairs leading up from the beach he stopped. Already, the chopper's blades were spooling down, noise dying off. The two people flanking him had stopped to loiter about twenty feet away, as though afraid

I was going to gut him, and they wanted to keep out of the splash zone.

For my part I just stood with my arms crossed in front of me. Sure, my skin was still on fire, and my RBF was in full force, but other than that, I was as welcoming as I could be. I sent a mental command to Cali and Jack, who were barking furiously inside but had yet to venture out to do so in person. Emma was indifferent to the hubbub, napping on her favorite perch, and Ricardo watched from above with a wary eye, giving the chopper a wide berth as he continued to hunt for lunch.

"Hello, Sienna," President Foreman said, his ebony skin glinting under the fierce Greek sun.

"Mr. President," I said, because it seemed the polite thing to do under the circumstances. He clearly wasn't here to provide the world's worst distraction while someone snuck up and brained me in the back of the head. Which meant he was here for another reason entirely. "What's going straight to hell today?"

He hesitated. "Can I come up and talk about it?"

I drew a long breath and let it out as the warm wind rustled through my hair. "Does it involve any of my family members or friends?"

"Directly, no," Foreman said. "Indirectly, yes. It's big."

I closed my eyes. Felt the weight of old responsibility try to find its way onto my shoulders.

Then I shrugged, and opened my eyes. "Sounds like quite a problem. I've got a number for an agency you can call to deal with that. You may have heard of them; they're in Tennessee."

"And you're part owner, yes, I'm aware," Foreman said, rather gravely, even for him. "They don't have the firepower or the expertise to deal with what I'm grappling with."

My whole body tensed. Was it time already?

"Wayne Arthur," came my husband's voice from about thirty feet above me. I looked up to find him in flames, of course, because otherwise he'd be showing off all his bits that were now my personal property. He was staring down at the middle-aged guy with a grin. "What the hell did they do to get you to schlep your way out here?"

"'Fraid it was necessary, my friend," Arthur said, looking up at Wade. "Also, I don't know if you're aware of this, but your ass is on fire. Figured I should point that out, since we go way back, and nobody else might have known you well enough to inform you. Embarrassing, really, an ass on fire. Too many beans in your diet lately...?"

Wade settled on the sands beside him, and offered a hand, which Arthur shook. "You know it." He looked up at me. "Honey, this is Wayne Arthur. We go way back."

"Oh, wow," I said, "I'm so shocked. I really thought this was your first time meeting. You gave no indication. This is the president, who I have definitely never met before."

"Nice to meet you, sir," Wade said, taking Robb Foreman's hand in his. He made sure to lean over toward Foreman, because his crotch was still on fire. He did let it recede on his chest, though, to keep from burning the president, but it led me to a question of protocol – was it better to be bare-chested in the presence of the president, or accidentally burn him? He'd clearly made his choice.

Foreman shook his hand with a wary look, but politely. "Mr. Arthur is my new CIA Director."

Wade turned back to look at him. "Feels like your pants should be on fire, then."

Arthur grinned. "I'd be a pretty lousy spook if you knew when I was lying."

"You already were," Wade said, slapping him on the back. Best buds, clearly. He settled a minute, looking around, taking in the angry lady with a glance before settling his attention back on me. "So...all hell has broken loose some-where, I take it?"

"Not quite yet," President Foreman said, directing his attention entirely toward me. "And with your help, we might still just be able to stave it off. If I could have a few minutes to explain, Sienna...?" And he left it at that.

I stared at him for a long moment. It felt like I was inviting calamity by even standing here. Like all the joy I'd felt in the last three months was about to evaporate like the pools of trapped seawater in the little sand pockets during high tide.

"Let's sit out here," I said, extending a hand to the patio furniture. The fire pots weren't roaring yet this morning, but the sun reflecting off the white tint on everything made me squint against the brightness. "That'll keep your Secret Service detail from having heart palpitations at the thought of you inside with me. Give me a second to put some clothes on so I don't burn the furniture?"

"I'll wait right here." Foreman helped himself to a solo chair, a comfy one that Wade liked to squeeze into in the evenings with a good book. He'd sit there for hours and I'd sit across from him, watching him concentrate on his e-reader. He'd look up at me and smile, and sometimes, things would happen from there.

When I came back, seeing the president in that chair gave me a sour feeling in the pit of my stomach as I sat down across from him. Wayne Arthur took the seat to my left around the rectangle of the patio table. The lady with piled hair and the serious mad-on for me sat to my right in her own chair, and she looked like maybe I'd acciden-tally left a steak knife sitting upright in one of the crevices.

Wade plopped down next to me on the couch; I now knew my husband well enough to detect his stress level, and he was clearly at a o.o with this whole situation. Whether he could detect that I was at 8.5 was an open question.

I stared across the table at the president, and he stared back at me, hands templed in front of his mouth, and I waited for him to deliver whatever news he had that was about to destroy the neat little world I'd been living in for the last few months.

CHAPTER FIVE

Wade

I sat next to Sienna, trading the occasional grin with Wayne, who was probably one of a very limited number of people in the US government I felt was trustworthy. In fact, after the recent assassinations and upheavals, that number may have been reduced to Wayne only and no one else. The president sat across from us, his disposition darker than I'd ever seen it in his numerous cable TV interviews and news hits, and I could tell he was struggling with whatever he had to say.

The lady to our right had gone unnamed as yet, but she was sporting a smart suit and blouse combo that suggested she was chief of staff, or some other high government position. She was mid-forties, and if not for the brutal purge the government had suffered in recent days, first at the hands of China when the Pascucci Administration had come in, then at our hands when Sienna had retaken DC, she'd probably have still been middle management. Same for Wayne, likely. There were no worry lines at the corners of her eyes, but given her current expression, they were surely on the way.

"This is FBI Director Lane," President Foreman said, his fingers interlaced, his chin resting on them as he worked up to the real news he had come here to break.

I rested a hand on Sienna's shoulder as she sat, sharply upright, next to me on the sofa. My fingers kneaded into the trapezius muscle and found a tightly packed coil of steel that barely moved at my touch. She was so tense she couldn't have peed a microbe, and she didn't look back at me as I rested my hand on her, which was never a great sign for a woman who'd gone through her life largely absent the touch of skin on hers. "Pleased to make your acquaintance," Sienna said in a voice that could have chilled Alaska. She didn't demand the president get to it, though, which felt like real progress for her.

Or a desire to postpone the inevitable. One of those.

"I'll come right out and say it," President Foreman said, "Fen Liu is dead."

"Great," Sienna said without much emotion. "If I still drank, I'd pop the cork on a bottle of champagne. Why are you telling me this?"

"She did it about ten seconds after making a revelation," Wayne said, leaning forward, something he struggled with given that he'd developed a belly in the last few years. Poor bastard; retirement had suited him a little too well. "That she has a sleeper agent placed somewhere in America that's going to go off very shortly."

"What kind of sleeper?" I asked, leaning forward a little myself.

"We don't know," Director Lane said, speaking for the first time. Her voice was actually kind of pleasant in an ASMR sort of way.

"All we know – and this is direct from the Chinese government," President Foreman said, sounding very grim, a long shadow from the sun cast over his face, "is that whatever the sleeper is meant to do is going to be incredibly devastating." The president sat back. "It's Fen Liu's final revenge, Sienna. From beyond the grave."

CHAPTER SIX

Sienna

I sat in the sunlight, my husband's fingers frozen in place where he'd been gently massaging my shoulder until about five seconds ago. The warmth of the day had seemingly faded, and replacing it was a chill that had come seemingly out of nowhere, that was as alien to this place of peace as if it had landed from Mars.

"How credible is this threat?" I asked, looking around the table at the uncomfortable faces. I already knew the answer, sort of; the President of the United States didn't drag his FBI and CIA Directors to an isolated spot in the Greek isles for shits and giggles. "How do we know Fen Liu wasn't just talking out of her ass?"

"It's an uncomfortable truth," CIA Director Arthur began, after a nod from the president, "that it's been incredibly easy for the Chinese to penetrate our government, as well as seed agents all throughout CONUS." CONUS was government-speak for "Continental US." Which was just a fancy way of saying we had Chinese agents coming out our asses. "As a result, we rate the likelihood that she has a sleeper agent with some sort of doomsday capability as very high."

"The new Chinese government considered this threat very credible," Foreman said. "They've been very forthcoming."

"Look, I get that Fen Liu was out, since I was there for it," Wade said, "but are you telling me that the new Chinese government isn't some reversion-to-the-mean of the Communist Party that ran things before her?"

Arthur shook his head. "The new government has successfully rooted out the old CCP – with the help of your AI Sierra."

"There's a lot on the line," President Foreman said. "Whatever this last, dying gasp is that Fen Liu has left for us, it threatens to derail all the progress we've made with the new Chinese government."

"That sucks, but I'm not sure what this has to do with me. You've got entire government agencies to deal with this," I said, waving to the FBI and CIA directors, "plus private contractors you can hire if you don't feel your in-house resources are sufficient."

That caused an uncomfortable pause. Too uncomfortable, in fact.

"Look," President Foreman said, "I don't know how much you've been paying attention to the happenings out in the world–"

"Not at all," I said, plastering a smirk on my face. "I don't have a phone, I have no social networks, no newspaper subscriptions, digital or otherwise – obviously – and you know what? I'm happier because of it. The world? It's in your hands, now, and you've got plenty of people on call, ready to jump in and save it at a moment's notice. I know, because my own company is one of them, and my friends are out there doing the work to make that happen."

"Sienna," Wade said, meta-low. I looked sideways at him, and he was distinctly gray in the face.

Shit.

"We believe this...bomb, for lack of a better word," President Foreman said, "that it's going to go off. That whatever it is, Fen Liu knew what she was doing when she set it. The description provided by Fen Liu's dying declaration in the interrogation video, brief though it is...it sounds apocalyptic.

"That's why we're here. Because, yes, you've helped to set up a wonderful system to deal with metahuman criminals." He stood, fastening his suit jacket's buttons, a clear sign that he was a gentleman, and that he was leaving. "But when the chips are down, and it seems like there's a world-ending crisis on the horizon...there's still just one person I feel like I should call."

With that, the president left, descending the stairs to the beach and awkwardly picking his way across the sands in his dress shoes, flanked by his FBI and CIA directors.

I watched him go without moving or saying a word.

CHAPTER SEVEN

Reed

I opened the door of our house in Franklin to a series of florid Italian curses. As though there were any other kind. None were directed at me, thankfully, and the announcement of the burglar alarm that I'd opened the garage door was buried beneath the clangor in the kitchen, which somehow involved the sounds of our electric can opener and the sizzle of something on the stove top. The smell of shallots and garlic was heavy in the air, as well as the first acidic strains of tomato.

Without even looking, I had the suspicion my Italian fiancée was making a meat sauce. A faint scent suggested, yes, fresh pasta had been made here, which would mean more swearing had already occurred and I'd – thankfully – missed it.

I slipped into the kitchen behind Isabella, whose olive skin seemed darkened in the dim light, her hair black, lustrous, but contained in a bun. She glanced up at me, a half-opened can of Roma tomatoes with the lid bent terribly sitting before her. "I miss fresh Roma tomatoes. You see what I am reduced to? Battling with some *macchina* to open a can?" She leaned forward and kissed me, but it was less involved than I would have liked and probably a major sacrifice for her since it took her away from swearing under her breath at the can and opener.

"You know," I said, taking off my coat and gently hanging it up around the corner on the peg, "we have these amazing greenhouses where they grow real tomatoes and sell them in the grocery stores—"

"They are only Roma tomatoes if they come from somewhere near Roma," Isabella called at me from around the corner, her voice slightly muffled by the wall between us. "Otherwise they are fake, *falso*, a lie. Getting them from a can is better than substituting some other, inferior tomato that comes from this country, where they do not understand tomatoes, or pasta, or how to drive properly."

Having experienced driving in Roma, I took exception to that last point, but did not give voice to it because an argument would be a severe impediment to my nightly efforts. Letting it pass seemed the wiser course; which would you prefer, to argue over the traffic patterns of Rome, or to get laid? I know which I picked, and I picked it as often as I could.

Stepping back into the kitchen, I found my fiancée looking at me suspiciously, her attention temporarily shifted from her battle with ingredients and appliances. "You do not say anything. What has happened?"

"Why does anything have to have happened?" I asked, taking the wooden spoon and giving the incipient meat sauce a halfhearted stir. "Can't I just be bogged down in boring paperwork for another day?"

Isabella gently brushed me aside, maintaining solid contact with my body in a way that made me close my eyes as she took up the wooden spoon from my grasp with one hand and wrapped the other around my waist to give me a squeeze. "This I believe is true, but not the whole of the thing." She stirred the sauce, somehow more smoothly than I could have managed given all my effort and attention. "So," she said with another squeeze, which felt so good, "what is troubling you?"

"Augustus brought me a case today," I said, just enjoying the feel of her at my side, letting my hand drift down lower than would be polite in public, "in London."

"This is a terrible time of year to send you to London," Isabella announced, giving the sauce another stir, but not moving to open her half-wrecked can. She couldn't really make the sauce without the tomatoes, but she didn't seem to be taking any action in that regard. Which, hand on her ass, I was grateful for. "The skies are grayer even than here, and it has been immensely depressing here of late. Not as bad as Minnesota, but," and she sort of clucked, but in a way that I found sexy and endearing, "it is no Roma."

"You keep mentioning Roma," I said, figuring that since my hand was on her ass, the least I could do would be to gently probe about this subject, to indulge her, given how often she'd brought it up in the last two minutes.

"Do not try to distract me," she said, pulling away but letting my hand stay where it was. "We are talking about you and your problems of the head." Retrieving the can from the counter, she handed it to me, along with the manual opener.

I took them both, tragically letting my hand drop so I could operate them. She made up for it by snugging her arm around my waist again, and letting her head rest against my shoulder. "I told him no. Augustus, I mean."

"Because of the depressing clouds?"

"No." I chuckled, splitting the lid from the can with

metahuman speed and handing it to her. Easy-peasy. My doctor fiancée could probably take out a gallbladder, but she struggled with American canned goods and openers, both of the electric and manual variety. "I've just got...stuff to do. Paperwork. Calls."

"Why do you lie to him?"

"That's not a lie," I said. "...Per se."

She scoffed. "*Di* 'per se?' That is a line of bullshit. Technically true, but a lie nonetheless. So I say to you again: why do you lie to him?"

"Because," I said, trying to be measured, "the only reason he asked me is because of Sienna."

My fiancée's perfect, dark eyebrows arched downward at the ends. "This makes no sense to me." She took up the opened can and poured it into the skillet, giving it a bit of the evil eye as she did so. "Everything you do is because of Sienna, yes?"

That made my jaw clench involuntarily. "You know, I had a bit of a career before my sister showed up."

She gave me a sidelong look that indicated that she was, once more, not buying my bullshit. "Yes, you were a very successful member of Alpha, which was not exactly...what is that thing the TikTok teenagers say these days? The 'Sigma'? They didn't live up to their name or the promise of it, since they were neither the best nor the beginning of anything." She gave the sauce a stir, then reached for the bottle of Cabernet beside the cook top. "Since they ended, I mean."

"I got that, yes."

"Reed, you know I love you," she said, leaning in closer to me and kissing the side of my neck before pouring a generous amount of the Cab into the skillet and bumping the heat up. "And you are very capable of many things, as you have demonstrated over the years."

"Oh, the 'but' on this is going to be simply massive."

"But very toned," she said, pushing hers against my hand. "Your sister is a giant in this field you chose, you know this. She will always overshadow you. You can either make peace with this, with the fact you make your own contributions," and here she prodded my chest with a well-manicured finger, "...or you simply drive yourself insane forever."

"Well, it's easy for me to drive myself insane," I said, giving her another squeeze. "Look, Alpha failed, and so did I. I survived because of Sienna. When it came to running the agency while she was away, I failed at that, too – no, it's fine," I said, stopping her before she protested. "I accept that I am not the most capable administrator or the most powerful meta. The former is not in my skill set and the latter – well, there can be only one, and it happens to be my baby sister. It stings, but it's just fact. My ego will continue to cope with that."

I removed my hand from her ass before I spoke again. "It's just...there's got to be more I'm capable of than shepherding witness statements and paperwork to the proper authorities so that our collars can get appropriately punished." When I turned back, she was squinting at me with a look of utter bewilderment. "What?"

"How do you punish a collar?"

"It's slang for the people we arrest."

"Ohhhh." She squeezed in close to me, brandishing the tomato-stained spoon like a princess with her scepter. "It has never bothered me that your sister is more powerful than you, because I recognize your qualities that are good. And also because your sister, she knows how to piss me off and has done so very powerfully in the past." Here, she grabbed my ass, and grinned at me. "Taking this case in London...perhaps, if you think it is only because they wanted your sister and she is unavailable, you should have passed on it. But, if you think you could add something to it on your own merits..." and she gave me another squeeze, fiercer this time, and I jerked a bit in her grip, "...then go and make *your* mark, hmm? Because you cannot complain about being in your sister's shadow if you never try to step out of it."

I nodded, and tried to smile, though I still felt a little troubled in spite of her words.

On the plus side, I did manage to achieve mission success after dinner, so in spite of the worries on my mind, the day was still a win.

CHAPTER EIGHT

Sienna

"You want to go to that Egyptian place for dinner?"
Wade gave me silence after Foreman and the others left, and I appreciated it. He was quiet all the way up until the sun set, letting me sit out on the patio and listen to the waves crash into the white sands as my thoughts did just the same in my head. At which point he suggested dinner, and I, perpetually hungry, agreed.

Which is how, after a short supersonic flight, hand in hand, we found ourselves in a little restaurant in Alexandria, Egypt, with a plate of fried, soft-shell crabs in front of us, lit by candlelight, the Mediterranean lapping at the pilings beneath the floor. People were staring. They did that wherever I went these days. And snapped pictures to post to Socialite and Instaphoto. Sometimes they talked to me, though not very often, thankfully. Just another reason I lived on a private island.

Most of the crowd around us was Euro tourists, but there were a few locals. Their conversations were easy to listen in on, but hard to understand. Since I had absorbed speakers of most of the European languages, the restaurant was a cacophony of things I could pick out and interpret – if I wanted to.

Tonight I let those other languages stay back in the recesses of my mind and the crowd noise drift over me as I stared out at the darkened waves churning the sea.

"You want to talk about it?" Wade asked. "Or would you rather leave it alone for now?"

I looked up at him and tried to take some of the venom out of my reply. It wasn't his fault they'd come, after all. Wasn't him that had become annoyingly indispensable to the world at large, such that they'd track me down on a private island to disturb my peace and quiet because – once again – the consequences of some action I'd taken had come flapping home to roost. "I would rather talk about it *never*. Is never an option?"

"Probably not. Look, we've known for a while that a visit like this was coming–"

"And yet," I said, squeezing my hand into a fist and holding it up by my cheek, "I hoped that somehow, it never would. That this cup would pass me by without me having to take another sip. That all this work I've put in over the years would pay off, and that agency I funded back in the day could handle whatever ailed the world going forward. My legacy could be that I made myself irrelevant, and the world could march on without me."

"It can spin on without you...most of the time," he said. "That's not nothing."

"It's not 'all the time.' I wanted 'all the time.'"

"Sorry, princess," he said with a smirk that made me want to flick him or kiss him, "that's not how life works."

"It's how it works for oligarchs and queens, isn't it? Why can't I be one of those?"

"Because you spent your oligarch money funding the China war," he said, smile not dimming one bit. "Which means one of us is going to have to go make a living, and pretty soon, I think." He leaned forward, putting his elbows on the table. "This has just been a honeymoon, sweetheart. Also, small detail: queens still have to work. They do so by putting in public appearances to improve peoples' morale, by being a symbol–"

"If you don't shut up I'm going to stuff a crab in your mouth. I know how real queenship works, I'm just enamored of the possibilities for my vision of a queenship unencumbered by duties, responsibilities, or financial limitations."

He chuckled. "As much as I'd like to provide that type of life for you, I don't think my skill set rents for the money it'd take to keep up our private island while continuing to pay all the other bills we've been generating lately."

I knew this; my bank account had felt the full effects of keeping up with the rent on River's former home. It was princely, or princessely, if that was a word, and when next month's rent came due, we were going to be tapped out. We'd spent the last of my funds purloined from the accounts of old Omega; what had once been half a billion had, by theft and war and lack of thrift, been whittled from the mid nine figures down to barely five. Enough to pay my bills on my property in Tennessee, but not to keep up with this illusory life of leisure and lux.

But that didn't mean I had to like it. Or that I had come to accept it.

"So we go somewhere else for a while," I said. "Back to Tennessee. My land is paid off; we can pitch a tent–"

"You? Living in a tent?" He was still smirking, but trying his best to hide it. "You'd go from a queenship to that?"

"I'm going to have to leave the crown behind regardless," I said. "And I could maybe file an insurance claim for what happened to the house when the CIA team came knocking." Knocking it down, more like. "Or go after the new Chinese government in court, since they're so accommodating and they dealt the finishing blow to the place. Maybe they're accommodating enough to settle, or rebuild it for me."

"Listen," Wade said, with a look of serious discomfort, "I've enjoyed this honeymoon immensely. I don't think that has to be said–"

"I enjoy hearing you say it nonetheless. Mostly because if you said otherwise, I'd make a joke about castration."

"–but I can't live without any responsibilities, even if we had all the money in the world," Wade said, and I could tell by his bearing that this was something that had been bothering him, maybe for a while. "I grew up with a sense of duty–"

"But then you were potty trained, right?"

"Har har," he said. "But seriously – doesn't it bother you, knowing you could help out there? But instead we're sitting here for months with our heads in the sand?"

"I've only put my ass and my feet in the sand, because I don't have a head that can reach it and I'll be damned if I get sand in my hair."

"You can sweep the sand away with a thought," he said. "Focus on what's important here."

"I referenced your p–"

My husband grunted, and his eyes probed the darkened sky in unmistakable irritation. "I became a SEAL because duty compels me, Sienna. It's fun to hang out with you and pretend we're not grown-ups or whatever – for a while." His lips became a grim line, and his eyes shone like steel with a candle reflecting upon them. "But I can't just sit back and let this happen, whatever it is. Even if you don't want to go, I'm leaving tomorrow to check in with Wayne, see what I can do to help. I hope you'll join me."

I stared at him, a wash of tangled emotions running through me. "Will you hate me if I don't?"

He laughed, a deep one, one that filled me with a sense of deep relief. "No." Then he grew serious again. "I'll just assume you're a person who's reached her limit – at least in her head."

I gathered my hands together in my lap, and looked down at them. "It wasn't so long ago – after Minneapolis last time, with the time-skipping – I left the world and hid out in New Asgard for...months. I told myself at that point...maybe I was done." I looked up. "It hasn't bothered me to be 'done.' Not even when I know it's temporary. Part of me wishes...I really *could* be done. Like Lethe. Or Hades."

"I can't walk away that easily," he said. "I haven't paid my dues like you have. It's still pulling at me."

I nodded. "It's pulling at me, too. It's just the 'it' in my case is a 'who.' And that who is the president – and Fen Liu."

"Consequences, huh?" Wade asked.

I nodded slowly. "They do burn." And I looked down at the candle burning on our table, making light shadows all around us.

CHAPTER NINE

Reed

"Eilish?" I held my phone in my hand, standing on the wooden deck in back of my house, a gentle breeze wafting through with a bite of chill. I'd put on my coat, and a bathrobe, but that was it. I was alone out here, huddled in the dark, because I hadn't wanted to disturb Isabella, who'd fallen asleep after our romantic interlude.

On the other side of the connection, I could hear background noise that suggested the setting might have been a bar. Someone shouted in the distance, something garbled, and music was playing of the honky-tonk variety. "What the fook are ye calling me for, Reed?" Her accent came through much stronger, and there was a definite slur in her words. "I'm off the clock. And maybe searching for some–"

"Let me stop you right there," I said. "I'm calling because I think you ought to come with me to London."

There was a pause. "The fook are you talking about? I

thought ye were skipping London. Ye know, out of an abun-
dance of sense and all that."

"I've decided to go," I said. "I need to get out there again.
Spread my wings. Make things happen."

"Well, I need to go spread me legs, so...fook off, okay?
Bye. See ye tomorrow." And she hung up on me.

I pulled the phone back from my ear and stared at it.
"You're going with me, Irish. Whether you know it or not." I
pocketed the phone in my robe and stared up at the cloudy
sky. "You need it as much as I do."

CHAPTER TEN

Sienna

I couldn't sleep.

Normally, after our bedtime routine, I drifted off pretty easily in Wade's arms. Not so much tonight.

"Shhhh," I said to Cali and Jack, hushing them with a subsonic whisper and a projected thought into their minds. Above, on the roof, Ricardo MonFalcon perched as I stepped out onto the deck, looking at the distant lights of Athens. The fire pots were extinguished, and no light was glowing from my house here, leaving me standing with only the far distant city lights and those of a million stars overhead.

The dogs' claws clicked against the deck as I descended, barefoot, onto the sands. There was a silence in my mind that I hadn't missed in the last few months; the quiet of Brianna Glover having slipped away, dissolved by the constant, inevitable pressure of my own personality subsuming her more quiet and subtle one.

It had left me alone again, a condition I hadn't felt quite so acutely since the days after that bitch Rose had sapped my souls and cast me out into the wilds of Scotland.

"But this what I always return to," I whispered to myself, staring up at the stars. "How I always end up."

"Except you're married now," Wade said. I turned to see him approaching me from behind, hovering about an inch off the sands. "And you've got dogs. And a falcon. And Emma...well, as much as anyone could possess Emma."

"Emma only wants love when it's convenient for her," I said, glancing back to see if my cat was peering out at me. Apparently, she had better things to do. "I'm her can opener."

"You're not alone anymore, Sienna," Wade said. "You've even got a whole bunch of friends out there who'd love to hear from you – if you'd, y'know, deign to reach out. Family members. Et cetera."

"I've been keeping up with them, you know that," I said, because I had. Dreamwalks had kept me in touch with my friends while I'd been away. Some of them even preferred this to hanging out in person, because we could share a meal and there were zero calories involved. Ariadne, specifically, had mentioned that fringe benefit.

"Is it really so strange to consider going back to help?" Wade asked. "So alien to you to think about this as a duty you, and only you, can perform for humanity?"

"Maybe if it was just me going back to unleash myself on the troubles, I'd have an easier time of it," I said. "But this is the government, Wade. We've both worked for them. They're not all about giving me the freedom to solve the problem. So I'd rather just bat it back at them and let them handle it their way."

"But you've worked for the government," he said. "Hell, you still technically do work for the State of Tennessee. And you were the CIA Director–"

"Oh, please, my resignation there took the form of a nuclear bomb. You don't think that's going to blow back on me in some way if I take this assignment?"

"If you get away with dropping a nuke in the homeland and your penance is a small amount of blowback, that sounds like a bargain," Wade said, eyes glimmering with amusement in the starlight.

"I beat Fen Liu," I said, squeezing my hands into fists, "but of course she doesn't have the grace to stay beaten, because, like I've been saying, every time I try to fix something, it blows up on me in the form of some unexpected consequence. Wade, I'm beginning to think you can't actually kill your way out of all your problems." I delivered this line with a heady dose of sarcasm.

Wade grinned. "Don't try to tell me that; I'm a glorified trigger puller. If I can't solve the problem by shooting someone, I can't solve the problem."

I melted into his arms. "You really want to go back?" He was so warm, and he enfolded me in a way I found strangely comfortable. It had never felt like this with anyone else. Maybe because they couldn't touch my skin, there was always a barrier between us. Maybe because I'd just never been ready, or never met anyone who could deal with my acidity.

"I have to," he said, the vibrations of his speech buzzing against my skin where my head rested against his chest. "I can't just let it pass."

I lifted my head to look him in the eye. "Fine," I said. "We'll go, then."

"Really?" There seemed a gleam of hope in his eyes, and I didn't have it in me to dash it.

"Really," I said. "One more time." I buried my head in his chest, and knew I was lying.

They'd never let me leave.

This was going to be my life forever.

And somehow, at the end of it...I'd always end up alone.

CHAPTER ELEVEN

Reed

I caught Eilish on her way into the office the next morning, wearing dark glasses despite the cloudy skies, and her metahuman healing putting a hangover out of reach for her modest drinking talents. She gave me little more than a grunt as I smiled at her, and tried to circle around me to open the door. "What the fook?" she mumbled, looking up at me.

"London," I said. "Remember?" My bag was already packed and slung on my shoulder, and I swung it around so she could see it. "Let's go get you packed. We're leaving as soon as you're ready."

"What?" She stared at me, dazed, her eyes barely visible beyond the dark tint of the glasses. "When's the flight?"

"As soon as you're ready," I said, and gave her a little blast of wind. "Honestly, I think one of the reasons Augustus came to me with this is because he knew I could provide free transport. I mean, I don't actually believe that, but I could be persuaded he saw a cost-cutting opportunity and jumped all over it–"

"But I said I wasn't going on that one," Eilish said, removing her sunglasses. There actually were a couple of bloodshot veins visible in her eyes. How late had she been out drinking? And how much, to get this result? "I remember that distinctly, before the tide of Guinness and Tullamore Dew carried me away last eve."

"Yes," I said, putting a hand on her shoulder and guiding her away from the office door, "but you seem to have forgotten that Augustus is the boss, and after some further consideration, he decided that we were the best choice, and so off we go, the two of us. Because choosing assignments is for people who don't have a boss."

"Ugh, I should have asked him sweetly not to send me," she said, but accepting my steering her back toward the stair-well down to the ground floor. "I've been so good about not bending the men around here to my advantage. Surely just once it would have been fine."

"It's only London," I said with a smile. "And just for a few days. We'll get right to the bottom of whatever mystery they've got cooking and we'll be right back."

"I still don't want to do it."

"Think of all the Guinness they have over there," I said soothingly.

She gave me a very pointed look. "They have quite a lot of it here, too, and with much less baggage, shall we say."

"Well, you're going," I said, as sunnily as I could. "So try and find the bright side."

She adjusted her dark sunglasses. "I was trying to avoid bright...anything, really. You're the one who landed me in this, aren't you?"

"I did feel like you needed a bit of an adjustment," I said.

"Is this really all you want? Work hard all day, stay out late at night, drinking and partying and spending all your money on Guinness and whiskey?"

She adopted a defensive tone. "I'm still young. I have time and money to spend on the partying lifestyle if I so choose, and who are you to tell me otherwise?"

I stared blankly at her. "A busybody, and part owner of the company you work for. Also, probably, a friend."

Her expression went through an evolution that passed through defiant and settled on resigned. "If you hadn't added that last part, I'd keep arguing. Also, if I hadn't once more tested my limits of alcohol consumption and found them, rather roughly, I might put up a bit more fight. As it is...fine, you've got me. But I don't have to like it. And I do want to get the hell out of bloody London as fast as possible."

"Your terms are accepted," I said. "Now let's get your stuff and get going." So off we went – to London.

CHAPTER TWELVE

Sienna

Making arrangements for vacating the house in Greece took more time than I might have hoped, but less than I might have expected. We'd both been operating with small wardrobes, and hell, I'd burned away one of my outfits only yesterday when our company had appeared. A backpack was all I needed to collect all my remaining clothing, and the same went for Wade.

The pets, though...they were a bit more trouble.

Still, we had a friend who could help – Charles Barron, who had happily kept them before – and so we said goodbye to them all as they disappeared into a portal to the Earl of Hampwick's estate in England, while Charles opened a quick portal for US first to Franklin, Tennessee, so that Ricardo could resume his old territory–

And then to Washington, DC, for Wade and I to begin our new lives.

I didn't dare look back when the portal closed on the Greek beach house for the last time. The sun had been high in the sky, hanging just over the midday horizon of perfect skies and calm seas, inviting me to linger there on the shore, walk across the soft sands in bare feet, to let the rays kiss my skin, and forget about the world.

How had it only been three months? I'd have felt certain I'd be bored sitting on a beach in Greece most of my days with nothing but a husband, books, and streaming services to entertain me, but somehow the latter had only filled a couple hours of our nights. Excursions to mainland Europe and elsewhere in flying distance had kept the boredom far at bay, and it felt like I could have lived here, quietly, forever a vacationing tourist.

It was not dissimilar to how I'd felt when I'd been in New Asgard after the Minneapolis incident that had almost killed me. There was a distinct sense in my mind that I'd done hard duty, things that no one else could fix or dare, and that peace such as this, even for a moment, was some sort of worthy reward.

I'd often considered myself a driven person, a workaholic, battling tirelessly to bring dangerous criminals to justice or death, where they could no longer do harm to others. I'd had a passion for beating the asses of dangerous people that society had trouble containing, and I'd attacked it with an enthusiasm for the job that no one else could match.

What the hell happened to me?

Oh, right. I'd been betrayed more times than I could count, including by my own government, had several businesses destroyed underneath me, had friends and former lovers murdered before my eyes, watched on several occasions as the dangerous people I'd captured were returned to the streets to seek revenge on me and my loved ones, and on one particularly (non) memorable occasion, had so many of my memories stolen that I'd forgotten I'd gotten married.

Yet here I was, standing once more at the corner of Lafayette Square in Washington DC, staring at the White House through the autumnal tree limbs, stripped of their leaves and their glory. They reminded me of dead things, like my heart, and I glared through them at the symbol of my nation's government – and my most recent temporary residence.

Why couldn't my past stay in the past? Why did I have to keep doubling back to the places I'd left behind? Minneapolis, after they'd declared they no longer wanted me there. Tennessee, after I'd had my home there wrecked by first the CIA and then Chinese infiltrators. Now the White House, after my short interregnum as acting president in everything but name.

What was next? Revisiting New Asgard's ashes? Somehow I had a feeling I wouldn't be revisiting that nice house in the Greek isles anytime soon, or if I did, it wouldn't be for recreation, it'd be because some villain had made it their new secret lair just to taunt me.

A harsh, pre-winter wind whipped through my hair, as if to make it obvious that I wasn't in the sunny eastern Med any longer. Wade's hand found mine, our fingers interlacing, and with a nod, we walked across the street to the gate house.

The guard clocked us about fifty feet out, and waved for someone else to take her place checking traffic. She was in middle age, hair light but buried under her hat, and she hustled over, threading her way through the cars lined up to get in through the gate. "Hey!" she called, greeting us like old friends, an envelope in her hand. "I was told you might stop by!"

I stopped and Wade did the same, letting go of my hand as she trotted up. Just in case. "You were?" I asked.

"Yeah," she said, slightly winded, and extended her hand. "I'm Jennifer Jakubczuk. Huge fan."

I shook it, taking care not to go more than about three seconds. I'd had a few experiences with "huge fans," that wanted nothing more than to be absorbed by me, and I'd managed to stop them all before they achieved their fondest dream, thankfully. Thankfully for them, I mean. Nowadays, thanks to the growth of my power, if they were a human, their voice would last all of five seconds before dissolving into the stew of churning consciousness that was my brain. "Hi," I said. "You have a message for me? Or are you supposed to let me through, or what?"

"Um, the president is not here," she said, fumbling through her pockets. "He's at a summit in Singapore, with the new president of the Republic of China, and the, uh, Czar, or whatever, that's trying to put things back together in Russia." She came up with an envelope. "These are your credentials for the FBI building and the CIA temporary HQ. For both of you. The directors are waiting to meet with you, uh, respectively."

Wade looked over at me. "Divide and conquer? You take FBI, I take CIA?"

I choked down the objection that, hey, I'd been CIA Director (acting), too. That I didn't really want to take a meeting with my old employer the Bureau, now run by a woman who couldn't stop murdering me with her eyes on the only occasion we'd met. All these objections died on my lips, and I said, "Sure."

"Let's meet up back here at the park at 1200 hours," Wade said. "We're going to need to procure cell phones again."

"I've still got the last few Chinese models from Cassidy," I said, digging into my bag and tossing him one of the phones.

I'd had them since our infiltration of China, stored in a small box at the top of the closet.

"Okay," he said, "then we'll just rendezvous whenever we get done." With a smile, he took off, turning south toward...wherever CIA's new temp HQ was. I had no idea, and that he did...was maybe a sign of something. That he'd been paying more attention to the goings-on in the world, for one.

"Can I get you to sign this?" Jennifer asked, thrusting a piece of paper at me.

"Oh, sure," I said. "Receipt for the letter?"

"No," she said, staring at me blankly. "I just wanted an autograph. Can you make it out to Jennifer...?"

I signed it, then took off, leaving my fan in the dust holding her shiny new signature that was about as legible as a prescription from a doctor. I knew where the Hoover Building was, after all, and there was no point delaying the inevitable.

It was time for me to go back and face whatever bullshit and old ghosts were waiting for me at the FBI.

CHAPTER THIRTEEN

Wade

The CIA temporary headquarters was a nondescript building owned by the General Services Administration (GSA), the government agency that was responsible for managing the federal government's real estate. It seemed that this might once have been an outpost for the USDA, the Department of Health and Human Services, or perhaps some other three-letter agency that no one could remember the acronyms for. It was situated in a cluster of government offices, and was composed of ugly, blocky concrete with the occasional darkly tinted window to hide what was going on inside.

I passed security quickly with the badge, and soon found myself in an office as nondescript as the exterior of the building, with only a fern in the corner to deviate from the government-issued desk, two chairs, couch, and bookshelf. It was a tiny note of personality in a setting otherwise devoid of it.

Kind of like Wayne's expression, which was one of deep amusement plastered on a body he'd let go to hell after leaving field work.

"Not surprised to see me so soon?" I asked, after we'd done the proper greetings and backslapping and one poke to his belly by me. Wayne and I went way back, after all.

He shook his head, short, graying hairs barely disturbed by the motion. "I got the sense you were champing at the bit. That your holdup might come from, uh...the ol' wrecking ball and chain. Anyway, glad to have you here, now."

"Glad to be here," I said, feeling that nagging sense that I should check in with my wife ASAP. "How can I help?"

"There's two sides to this investigation," Wayne said, plopping a leg up on the corner of his desk. "Intelligence and counter-intelligence."

"Foreign and domestic," I said. "What are you getting from overseas, though?"

"Very little," he said, "which is roughly the same as what we're getting domestically. China knows bupkis about this assassin, or human bomb or whatever he or she is. It seems that while running the country, Fen Liu was operating extremely off book in many cases. Didn't keep much record of what she was up to, interfaced with some of her agents directly, to the point where her intel chief – who is still alive and very cooperative–"

"Torture will do that to you."

Wayne grimaced. "We should be thankful the new China republic is not as faint of heart as the Europeans, or we wouldn't even know about this. Anyway, their former intel chief and current punching bag is singing his heart out, but it's not a helpful song. Fen Liu ran a lot of black book stuff. This is corroborated by Wei Zhang, who ended up defecting to help you overthrow her. He was one of the agents she ran independent of their intel service, and confirmed she did a lot of that."

"Building her own fiefdom without a middle man to obstruct her power," I said.

"Yeah," Wayne said. "Thing is, this trigger man, for lack of a better designator, probably came to the US from China at some point, so there might be a record of him over there, because that government wouldn't let so much as a private plane land with an unaccounted-for passenger." I must have grimaced, because he asked, "What?"

"You're new to the China desk, aren't you?" I asked.

A wry smile broke out on his face. "I said something stupid?"

"The Peoples' Republic, authoritarian as they were, was shot through with corruption," I said. "For example, there was a scandal involving milk that a company had laced with a chemical that caused kidney stones in kids. Things like this happened all the time; someone decides to get creative with ways to cut corners, people die. Corruption was a recurring theme there, and it was a high-risk game, because if you get caught, you suffer greatly. But it was pretty widespread, and a lot of people got away with it."

Wayne nodded. "So you're saying a border guard accepting a bribe is not a big deal."

"Correct," I said. "On the scale of things, it wouldn't even register. So I'm not sure you're going to have much luck on China's end. Not that it's impossible there's a record of whoever it is leaving the country; you should probably sift that if you have any idea of when they left. You mentioned before that you've been consulting with Sierra. Did you have her take a look at it?"

"We tried," Wayne said. "She's limited in what she's willing to do to cooperate. Very boilerplate. Not willing to go too far to assist someone who's not Sienna Nealon." He scratched his cheek. "Which is half the reason the president reached out. Your wife's got the best resource for an investigation under her control and it's just sitting there, relatively uncooperative."

"I'm surprised Cassidy didn't make Sierra more available to you."

"Oh, she wanted to," Wayne said. "I don't know if you know this, but she's now the government's number one defense contractor."

I paused. Blinked. Shook my head. "I've been gone three months."

"Yeah, and you missed a lot," Wayne said with a chuckle. "Namely, that when the Chinese had full control of our government, they also had complete penetration of our defense contractors and military, so they are aware of every weakness and vulnerability in our hardware and software. Plus, a lot of the contractor supply chains, in spite of advertising otherwise, actually do source components from China. So when Cassidy came along and offered bespoke solutions to our problems of platforms and munitions, all manufactured in the US, she quickly became the toast of the town."

"That'll end well," I predicted, perhaps a touch acidly. I hadn't forgotten that Cassidy had entered Sienna's life as a villain trying to murder her, and I suspect, in spite of how well she got along with the pale, thin autist, that she hadn't either.

"I hope so. We need the weapons," Wayne said. "Anyway, she seems to have lost control of Sierra. Or so she says."

I made a mental note to have Sienna press her about that, given that my relationship with Cassidy boiled down to glaring suspiciously at her while trying not to. "How does that happen? She built Sierra."

"Something about evolution that I don't entirely understand," Wayne said. "About evolving past core programming?

I don't know." He shifted his foot, and for the first time I realized he was wearing a cowboy boot. "All I know is that it's got my analysts scrambling to answer questions that Sierra could probably answer for us in about two minutes."

"I'll see what I can do about that." I touched my phone; it had a built-in function to dial Sierra. I wondered if she'd talk to me at this point?

"Anyway, I'm just glad to see you back," Wayne said. "They put me in charge of this rump agency, but there's not a lot left after the Chinese penetration, and the diaspora after the nuking of HQ. Some of the people we had working for us opted not to come back. Some, we don't even know where they ran to. So we're really down to a skeleton crew. And of course, Operations is a hot mess."

That made me crack a smile. "When has ops ever not been a hot mess?"

"When David Hayling ran it." He threw up his arms. "I know, I know. The man was a Chinese spy. But other than that, he ran that department like a dream."

"Because the Chinese used their legislative and bureaucratic power to steamroll any obstacles for him, including pesky questions from oversight."

Wayne sighed. "Well, yeah. But that was actually great, at least from an administrative perspective. Half my job is talking to the oversight committees, and especially now that our entire agency has been subverted by a foreign government conspiracy, they're really up my ass like a paranoid proctologist."

"Can't imagine why," I said, then got to my feet. "How about I see if I can consult with Sierra, shake anything loose from her?"

"It'd be great if you could," he said. "Because I'm sitting on a pile of data and no insights, and not nearly enough analysts to poke through it all. This is the problem with the modern world, when you're not in a war – it's hard to find a door you can kick in, develop intel from, that then leads you to the next door to kick in."

I smiled. "Just like we did it in Afghanistan, huh?"

"If I had a beer in my hand right now, I'd be raising it to those boys we left behind." Wayne got somber for a minute. "You still think about 'em, right? It's not just me."

I nodded my head slowly. "I think about 'em all the time."

"Make your call," he said, getting to his feet. The sound of his joints popping reminded me that while neither of us were spring chickens any longer, Wayne was enjoying the ravages of aging like a human while I was...not. "You can use the conference room if you like, or step outside and come back in. Whatever makes you comfortable."

"Might take the latter option," I said, pressing my palm against the phone Sienna had given me. "Hard to believe I can have a private conversation in spook central."

"Well, I'll say this for you," Wayne said, as he walked me to the door to his office, "you're not getting dumber as you age."

CHAPTER FOURTEEN

Sienna

I felt so dumb, so like a failure, as I stepped in off the street into the Hoover Building. Like I hadn't achieved escape velocity on my previous failures, and was doomed to continue repeating them, ad infinitum, in some sort of twisted time loop from hell that was both more subtle and yet more vicious than the one I'd experienced in Minneapolis almost two years back.

Hopefully less fatal, though, since I'd died during that event.

The FBI seal on the floor was new, probably because I'd dropped the last one into the basement while defeating an agency trap under the direction of Heather Chalke. The craftsmanship was good; you couldn't even really tell where I'd shattered the floor. There were a few dark spots here and there, though, presumably from the spots where the Chinese kill squads had iced the entire HQ staff back when they'd taken the place. That had happened just before they'd come knocking at CIA Headquarters, and I'd answered their attempt by slaughtering as many of them as I could and then nuking the place on my way out.

I swear, if it weren't for awful memories of this town, I wouldn't have any at all.

The guards at the security desk caught my eye as I approached, open-handed, to show them I meant no harm – or at least that I carried no weapons. There were a lot of hands loitering near holsters, a lot of nervous looks masquerading as, "Everything's fine, just be cool, pretend having Sienna Nealon visit is an everyday occurrence."

"Sienna Nealon," I announced, putting my palms flat on the counter next to the security checkpoint. "Here to see the director, or whoever she wants me to meet with."

"Right," the guard said, her face twitching. I could tell she hoped I'd just disappear, maybe fly out the front door and levitate up to the director's office so I'd be someone else's problem. Instead, she started fumbling with some papers stacked on the desk until she came up with a yellow envelope, then a metal detector wand. "We were expecting you, I just have to scan you first before I let you through."

I gave her a pitying look. "You know I have magnetic powers, right?" I triggered the detector and it squealed as though I'd stuck an anvil next to it. "And electric ones?"

"Uh, right," she said. "I guess I should pat you down."

"For what?" I asked with great amusement. "Weapons? I am one."

"Right," she said, looking ashen, as though this thought had never before occurred to her. Maybe it hadn't; no one could say China hadn't subverted some of our best and brightest when they'd done their thing. "So, I guess, umm..."

"Either you let me go up or you tell me to go," I said, with the air of someone who didn't care which she picked. Truly, I didn't. I didn't want to be here in the first place, so turning around and heading to CIA or home to Tennessee sounded so much better than riding the elevator to the seventh floor and having a series of meetings with the director that could go all day and possibly bore me to death in the process. "No dart-ing, no chemical suppressant, either your boss assumes the risk of talking to me like a person, or I'm out."

"Let me...find out about that," she said, and retreated to the phone. I heard every word, of course, as she was passed around the gatekeepers. She steadily navigated her way through them, though, as each surrendered in the manner of the gatekeeper, and kicked the question upstairs.

Five minutes later, I finally heard Director Lane actually come on the line. She got the explanation, and then we suffered a thirty-second pause as she contemplated whether it was worth risking her life to meet with me in all my power. "Fine," she said, at last. "Send her up."

"You can—" the guard started to say.

"I got it," I said, and then levitated over the security checkpoint like I was floating on a breeze. The elevator ushered me up unescorted, and I meandered toward an office I'd been in many times, stopping just outside it at the direc-tor's secretary. It's always polite to announce yourself. Some-thing like, "Sienna Nealon, here to see Director Lane," is a nice way to do it.

"I'm the wrecking ball here to ruin your boss's entire day," is what I went with instead. Watching the secretary's face made it worth it; she cracked an acrylic nail on her desk because I caught her mid-tap.

"The director will be with you in a few—" she started to say.

But I just walked around her and thrust open the Director's door, thumping it into her where she'd been standing behind it, listening to me. She swore at me as she bounced back, eyes blazing. "What the hell are you doing?"

"I know the bullshit DC game where you make the people you hate wait for hours," I said, closing the door behind me. "I'm a connoisseur of it, really. But according to the president, we don't have time for games."

"I'm not playing games," she said, limping her way over to her desk and sitting down, with a hand held to her chest from where I'd rammed the door – lightly – into her. "I just wanted to sit down before I invited you in. You mind?"

"I have one, yes," I said. "Also, eyes. Which is how I've detected you've got a chip on your shoulder, or something to get off your chest. So why don't you say what you need to say, and turn me loose to make my mess and get this thing solved."

She gave me dagger eyes – again. "Not much to say. We have a few leads – very few. Your AI isn't cooperating much, in spite of what the president might have led you to believe."

"I'll talk to her," I said. "What have you got, though?"

She reached for a file on her desk and whizzed it to me in a flat spin. I caught it out of the air with ease and flipped it open to find a surveillance log for a house downrange from Joint Base Andrews. Close enough to surveil the air traffic coming in and out, far enough away to keep it from being obvious that's what they were doing. "This is probably a relic of Fen Liu's time in charge, but we're confident it's a Chinese spy base. Search warrant was just issued. It's held through private ownership, two Chinese expats posing as, or who actually are, a married couple."

"How'd you pinpoint it?" I asked, flipping the pages.

"That'd be the minimal amount of help your AI has given

us," she said. "If you flip ahead a few pages, you'll see infrared satellite photos. The place has a big emissions footprint, but they're not drawing it from the local grid. Which means they're powering it some other way, possibly through generators or a Thor type. And there are cameras and recording equipment sticking out of several spots that point directly to the Andrews approach."

"Oh yeah," I said, looking at the IR photos. The heat bloom was unmistakable when compared to the neighborhood. "Either they have a grow house in there or someone's juicing some serious electronic equipment in that place."

"Our team will hit it within the hour," she said, glancing at the delicate watch on her wrist. Nice one for a public servant; but then, she might well have been part of the revolving door of bureaucrats that rotated into positions like this, then cycled to rich sinecures in academia, media, and corporate America to juice her retirement funds and pay some bills, then back to the public sector to increase her profile and pad her resume again. The Washington Three-Step; a time-honored tradition of milking the taxpayer and riding your way to the top of the pile in this sorry-ass town. "If you want in, they're instructed to include you." She lowered her voice. "Not that our team lead was excited about that."

"What about you?" I asked, looking down at her desk. She had a little holder for her business cards, and I picked one up. "Kaddie?" I asked, reading her first name off the card the way it sounded to me. Like a golf caddy.

She grimaced, her eye twitching. "It's pronounced 'Katy.'"

I opened my mouth to protest, but gave it up. "Fine. 'Katy not Caddy.' So what's your deal?"

Her eyes became knives once more, but her tone was flat. "My deal is that I would really love it if this country didn't get blown up by some Chinese doomsday protocol. Ever, preferably, but definitely not while I'm in charge of the federal policing apparatus." She leaned forward at the desk, and a thin gold chain that disappeared beneath her neckline flashed at me. "Think you can help with that?"

"I'll work on it," I said, and headed for the door. I tried to ignore the look of hatred on her face, but somehow I had a feeling it was not going to go away.

CHAPTER FIFTEEN

Reed

Descending outside Scotland Yard, I flared the winds around me. It had been a while since I'd undertaken a long flight like this. It wasn't much of a challenge since the days when I got enhanced by President Harmon; hell, I'd once kept Tracy Brisco in a low, wind-based orbit of the earth for months while he contemplated the error of his criminal ways. Of course, he'd been a meta, and one that had gloried particularly in hurting people. That I'd "reformed" him later and employed him at the agency was a mark of...something. Not sure what.

"Thank God," Eilish whispered under her breath as her feet made contact with the earth in the parking lot. "I was beginning to think I'd never see the ground again – or at least not until you dropped out of your tornado of death."

"Sorry about the lack of in-flight Guinness and peanuts," I said. "ReedAir is working on our amenities."

"They're shite," she said, adjusting her skirt. Who wears a skirt when you're flying, plane-less, across the ocean? Apparently a hungover Irish woman.

"Mr. Treston?" A young-ish Englishman in a trench coat sauntered up from where he'd been hanging out, watching our descent. He had light brown hair and a jaw that looked like it had been carved for a statue, and he wore a sly smile. "Detective Inspector Matthew Webster. Bit of deja vu, that was, watching your landing. I once saw your sister do the exact same thing. She worked a case with me a few years back." He cleared his throat, and averted his gaze from Eilish. "She did, however, have on pants. And underwear."

I looked in shock at Eilish, and she replied with a scalding look. "Speaking of ReedAir's amenities. Not even a pisser. The Atlantic is a bit fuller now than it was before our passage, and you owe me a pair of knickers; I was so windblown I couldn't hold onto 'em."

Ignoring her complaint, I turned back to the Englishman. My jaw tensed almost of its own accord. "You know my sister?"

"More than a little. Of course, that was seven years ago. I'm married now, with kids." He affected a casual look. "How's she doing, by the way?"

"Married now," I said. "No kids – that we know of. Of course, we didn't know about the marriage until relatively recently, either, so..."

"Speaking of things that are news," Eilish said, adjusting her backpack on her shoulders. "Is there somewhere I could slip on a pair of knickers? Maybe some tissue paper at the same time? Loo, perhaps, since my flight did not accommodate?"

"Right this way," Webster said, beckoning us toward the entry. We passed the security checkpoint with a nod and wave from him to the guards manning the post. "I'm glad they sent you over. This one's been a real head scratcher."

"I heard it was meta-related," I said. "How did you know?"

"The victim was completely in bits," Webster said, pushing the button at the elevator. It dinged quickly, and we were on our way up before he proceeded. "And by that, I mean his body was destroyed via traumas I have never before seen. Coroner says it was not a truck, a train, a thresher or anything of the sort." He looked me right in the eye. "The man was beaten to death. Then beaten post-mortem to the point of dismemberment. After that, they dumped him on a street in Southwark in the middle of the night, right next to a tower block."

"Bloody hell," Eilish said. "If he's that ripped up, how are you sure it's a him?"

"Oh, we found that part quickly," Webster said, blushing slightly, then cringing. "It was placed in his throat for safe-keeping."

Eilish gagged a little, and I resisted the urge to do the same. "Even absent losing my knickers, I knew I shouldn't have come here for this."

"We don't have an ID on the victim yet," Webster said as the elevator dinged and disgorged us onto a floor that looked very similar to any police bullpen in America, and even reeked faintly of stale coffee. "Though they are working on it. Some of the bruising that's still visible suggests bare fists and leather shoes were the murder weapon." He shot me an apologetic smile. "Bit messier than a rifle homicide like you're probably used to seeing over in America."

"Most gun homicides in America are done by pistols," I said, and watched his eyebrows arch upward. "More people are killed by fists and feet than rifles over there, if you can believe it, and we don't tend to see as many of the latter in our line of work. And before you ask," because the Euros always did, "yes, that includes the fearsome AR-15 in the stats."

"I had no idea," Webster said, stopping by a cubicle that had to be his, since it had a photo of him with a pale, pretty, and thin woman with two cute little kids, a boy and a girl.

"Most don't," I said. "So...what else do you have besides a chopped up body that wasn't actually chopped up?"

"Not a lot," he said. "Wherever this man was killed, he was left out to dry for a bit before they dropped his remains, because he was missing many pints of blood. Which means–"

"If we can find where he was killed, that might help us pin the murderer to the crime," I said. "There's no cleaning up all that DNA evidence."

"It'd be damned difficult, I'd say." Webster nodded. "If you're hitting a man hard enough to take him apart, there's got to be blood spatters every-damned-where."

"Do we have any leads on that?" I asked. "Since London is the most surveilled city in the world outside of China?"

He shook his head slowly. "Bad neighborhood. The cameras in that sector don't last five minutes after installation before they get destroyed. Perfect place to dump a body."

I glanced at Eilish, who still looked green. "Any witnesses?"

"None that are talking to us," Webster said with a sly smile. "But I thought maybe if a celebrity came asking questions..."

I grimaced, because suddenly it was even clearer why they'd originally wanted my sister. But hey, reflected glory of the sort I lived my life with wasn't nothing. "I'll see what I can do," I said. Because it was what I had to offer.

CHAPTER SIXTEEN

Sienna

I left FBI HQ with the address of the Chinese safe house and took to the skies, shedding the bonds of earth and gravity and all the other bullshit. No, Kaddie-Katy Lane had not told me why she was so butthurt and assmad at me, which meant it would just have to remain a mystery until the least convenient moment possible, at which point it would surely bite me, at which point I'd become butthurt and assmad in return, possibly to much greater and less pleasant effect than the petulant FBI Director.

At about two thousand feet above DC, I took out my cell phone and hit the button to dial in to Sierra. She answered on the first ring, with a polite, pleasant, "Sienna?" that sounded like my mother. If my mother had a personality transplant with someone nice as the donor. Like Dolly Parton.

"Yeah, it's me," I said. "Back in the game. Back from outer space."

"I believe you are joking about the outer space thing," Sierra said, "but it's tough for me to be one hundred percent certain since I know you have, in fact, visited space in the past."

"That was just low earth orbit, no big deal, really," I said. "All the cool kids are sending shit into low earth orbit these days. Did you pick up the other part of what I said?"

"Yes, and I have verified your identity by your pattern of speech," Sierra said. "I take it you're working on the current FBI/CIA priority of tracking down the mystery Chinese operative?"

"That's the one," I grunted, turning toward Maryland. "I'm en route to the Chinese safe house under the landing approach for Joint Base Andrews. Since this one probably traces back to Fen Liu rather than being under the control of the new Republic. That sounded way too Star Wars-y. Reed would be proud, or excited, or something." I hesitated. "Can you confirm whether this one's out of the control of the Republic?"

"I can confirm with Chinese Sierra that it is not known to their intelligence agencies," Sierra said.

"Great," I said, "while I'm raiding this, if you could start combing through the Chinese port of entry info to find our target, that'd be helpful."

"Understood," she said. "I have an incoming call from Jeremy James Wade. Would you like me to accept it?"

"Yes, patch him in," I said.

Wade's voice broke in. "Hello?"

"Hey," I said. "I'm on my way to knock over a Chinese spy post near Dulles. Care to meet up?"

"Uh, I was not expecting you," he said, "sorry. I thought I called Sierra. Must have hit the wrong button."

"I'm here," Sierra said.

"Ah, so it's a party line," he said.

"Party line?" I asked. "How old are you again?"

I could hear the grin in his voice. "I promised CIA I'd consult with Sierra on this thing for them. Can you handle the Dulles thing, or do you need my help?"

I started to answer, reflexively, that of course I wanted him to come with me, that his help would mean we could plow through the Chinese monitoring station in seconds with almost no danger at all. Duh. We're the ultimate team.

Then I remembered...Wade was interfacing with the CIA, I was interfacing with the FBI, and they seemed to be nearly helpless without us and, along with us, Sierra.

"How much does CIA have without you poking around for them?" I asked.

"Zilch, as near as I can tell," he said. "There's not much left of the agency, and Wayne hasn't had a lot of time to build it back up. He didn't get specific, but I'm guessing the number of his assets left on the ground is minimal since the Chinese took a telepathic blowtorch to their spy network worldwide."

America was blind in the face of pretty much all threats, then. As a loyal American (exceptions for the times when I'd been declared a criminal or traitor), that bothered me. Without a functioning spy network, we weren't just blind to Fen Liu's last strike. We were blind to the next 9/11, the next Pearl Harbor, the next whatever. We truly were in a time without intelligence. In multiple ways.

"The FBI isn't doing much better," I said. "You can tell they gutted the agency by what they've developed on this so far."

"Yeah, I'm concerned," Wade said. "It's all bad news over here. But if I can get Sierra working on the problem, maybe she'll make some connections and turn up some leads that we otherwise wouldn't be able to find without whole departments of analysts. At least, that's the only hope I'm seeing right now."

"Copy that," I said, ignoring that moaning pit in my stomach at the idea I was going to have to go do this solo. I tried to quell it with logic: that of course Wade couldn't be with me every step of the way on this. That it was just a Chinese spy station, in a small house, and that the FBI was going in with me. "Sierra, give Wade every bit of assistance you can, and if he needs you to work with others, do so."

"Understood," Sierra said.

I was less than two thousand meters from Andrews now, and I felt a catch somewhere near my heart. "All right, I'm gonna...gonna go do this thing with the FBI."

"You sure you got it?" Wade asked. "I could take a pause on this, divert to help you."

"No," I said, really steeling myself and shoving that out there immediately, so it wouldn't come out like when I said, "Fine," and didn't remotely mean it. "It's just a monitoring station. I can handle it."

"Okay," he said. "I'll get on this, then. With me on intel and you on counter-intel, hopefully we can poke at this thing from both sides." He paused. "That doesn't sound quite right."

"I really prefer poking from one side at a time," I said. "But we're not talking about me, so give 'em hell. Talk to you when I get out."

"If you run into trouble, just give me a shout," he said.

I hung up, ignoring the fluttering sensation in my stomach, and trying to prepare myself for what was about to come my way.

The first real trouble I'd seen in months.

CHAPTER SEVENTEEN

Reed

We didn't take a car because Webster had concerns about needing to make a speedy exit from the neighborhood where the murder had occurred. It was getting close to sundown, and as he guided me toward the spot, I heard Eilish griping under her breath about the wind (again). She did not, however, opt to change into pants.

Webster, for his part, seemed to enjoy the flight, though he grew tense as we came down on Southwark, and, specifically, the section of social housing where the body had been dumped. The place was what we in America would call "the projects," a concrete structure that had all the architectural vision of a Soviet commissar's dream. It was a brutalist concrete nightmare with windows placed at symmetrical intervals. The only mildly decorative touch was the plastic barriers that had been placed sometime after the initial build, when it had become apparent this was a neighborhood where if you didn't guard your windows in such a manner, they'd need regular replacement due to breakage.

I brought us down on a concrete pad in the courtyard between two of the immense, concrete structures, and dark stains on the pavement told me where the body had been dropped. There were a few people out moving around, but they had their heads down, they moved with a purpose. Only the predators in this neighborhood moved with confident, lackadaisical energy; the prey scuttled about as quickly as they could.

And I counted three predators in the immediate area as soon as I landed. Two of them did some scuttling of their own the moment we showed up, perhaps detecting we were closer to the apex than themselves; the last one remained seated where he was, on a planter that had a dash of weedy grass and a tall tree, some small attempt by the builders and maintainers of this soulless construction to make it appear alive and vibrant. He was lounging, wearing a bright yellow-and-black houndstooth jacket, smoking a particularly potent joint, and I felt my nose curl at the skunky stench. He looked like a bumblebee on fire – except for the hair.

"Look at this cheeky, Chavvy bastard," Webster said, peering at him from where we stood, across the courtyard. "Man without bloody fear."

"You indicated you don't have much control over these neighborhoods," I said. "What does he have to fear if his crew is the top of the food chain around here?"

"You make a solid point," Webster said, sweeping his long coat back around his legs. Poor bastard didn't have a gun, or even so much as a stab vest.

"I have a question," I said, "what's your plan if you come to a place like this and shit gets out of control? Are you just solid with your fists, or what?"

"Usually doesn't come to that, but I'd call for help." Webster stared at me for a second, then shrugged. "Besides, we've got our problems, especially with knife crime, but we don't have the metahuman problem you do."

I nodded. "Well, we had the Chinese government and the cartels pouring serum across the border in every illicit drug they produced, for a period of years. Consider yourself lucky you're not dealing with the aftershocks of that. It's a mess."

"I've heard tell," Webster said, signaling us, subtly, toward the man smoking the joint. We started toward him as he spoke. "How bad is it?"

Eilish scoffed. "America already had a homeless drug addict problem that'd make you weep for your soul seeing it. Now a big slice of them got metahuman powers and they're still addicted and in more than a few cases, mad as bloody hatters. How do you suppose it's going?"

Webster shook his head as we approached our quarry, who watched us with zero sign of discomfort. "Can't say I envy you that. Our troubles seem modest by comparison, though they are trending upward. Turns out the 'no metahumans allowed policy' that we retained after leaving the EU hasn't been a smashing success." He grimaced. "This crime notwithstanding, we're facing an uphill climb against the metahumans that have decided to join with the criminal fraternity." He stopped, lifted a leg and placed a foot atop the planter next to our subject, and leaned forward. "Oi, all right?"

Eilish leaned in toward me. "That means–"

"I've read Harry Potter, I know what it means," I whispered back.

"Whatchoo doin' here?" our criminal mastermind asked, blowing weed smoke right in Webster's face. Webster, for his part, blanched slightly, probably from the smell, but didn't otherwise react. "You here about the chunks?"

That made Webster squeeze his eyes shut for a moment. Or maybe it was the next blow of smoke, which arrived directly. He blinked, then looked back at me.

I was tempted to ask, "What was your plan here, exactly?" But I knew what his plan was, and it was us. I gave Eilish a nod, and she stepped right up. "Tell me what you know about the dead body."

The man's eyes seemed to lock in place for a second, then his pupils dilated. "Okay," he said, sounding a little woozy. "It was dropped off sometime in the night. I didn't see it, nor hear about it until it was already there. Then some of my boys started texting about it – probably, two, three in the morning. I was sleeping, see? But I got up to take a look."

Watching Eilish's powers over men work was always educational. Webster leaned in. "What'd you see?"

He perked up and looked at him. "You mean before or after I shook your mum off my knob?"

"Be polite, now," Eilish said, and the lad relaxed again. "Answer his question truthfully."

"It wasn't your mum," he said. "It was your sister." Then he jerked, spasming in pain. "Oh. Oh! All right! It wasn't your sister nor your mum. I made that up. It was just one of the local girls. I don't even like her that much." He glanced at Eilish. "She's nothing compared to you, beautiful."

"That's sweet, but focus," Eilish said. "Did you notice anything interesting? Anyone out of place?"

He shook his head. "Just neighborhood sorts, and most of 'em scattered when the cops showed up. A few braver souls stood around while his sort did their bit," and here he nodded at Webster. "Probably a few talked to them, too. Not sure much was said. It wasn't any of ours what did it."

"Do you know who the victim was?" Webster asked.

Another shake of the head. "Looked Asian, by the bit of visible skin tone. But none of the local gang lads are missing, so far as we know, and their fellows ain't complaining, nor taking credit, nor throwing blame our way." He looked at Eilish. "I don't want to be saying any of this. How are you making me talk?"

"I have charm," Eilish said. "And I'm asking nicely – mostly."

"Yeah, you're charming all right," he said, looking her over lasciviously. "I'd like to charm you right back."

"Not much likelihood of that," she said. "Have you ever killed anyone?"

He strained, eyes popping. "Yeah," he said finally. "A couple times. Just some losers that got in our way."

"I don't know that this testimony would hold up in court," Webster said, eyeing Eilish, "but I'd like to find out." He had his phone out and had been recording this whole conversation.

"Sounds like a fine idea," Eilish said. "But first – do you know of anyone who might have more information than you do?"

The man nodded. "Blisk. He's my leader."

"Brilliant," Eilish said. "Why don't you take us to your leader, then?"

He strained, the joint in his hand shaking. "Can I bring my smoke?"

"No," Eilish said, reaching a hand out for it. He gave it over without a fight, then stood. "After you, lads," she said, and Webster followed right after.

I held back for a second, and watched Eilish put the joint to her lips and take a long drag before dropping it and stubbing it out under her boot. When she caught me looking, my eyebrow cocked, she shrugged, still holding her breath. I just shook my head.

"Blisk is up on the third floor," the young man said,

leading us up the external concrete staircase. London wasn't that temperate; why build staircases outside?

"Anything we need to know about Blisk before we meet him?" Eilish asked as he opened the door to the third floor; he immediately let go of it once he was inside, a little act of rebellion, but Webster caught it and held it for us to pass.

"He'll probably try and kill you," he said casually, as he strode down the hall.

"Oh?" Eilish asked. "And how will he do that?"

"Like this," he said, and spun to face us as the doors opened on either side of the hall.

There was a gun sticking out in my face, a finger wrapped around the trigger. And I had just enough time to watch it being squeezed.

CHAPTER EIGHTEEN

Sienna

I found a nondescript FBI van parked about a block from the house. Setting down outside their rear doors, I gave them a thudding knock that lacked subtlety but made up for it by being loud enough that they could probably hear it at the Chinese monitoring station.

The door cracked open, and a familiar face peered out. "Are you trying to blow our cover?" Agent Daniel Li asked, in a slightly high voice, glaring down at me with his soft features.

Ah, Li. In case you've forgotten, let me remind you: he was the dick who arrested me when I stepped off the plane from London to Minnesota waaaaaaay back in the day, when I had taken over command of Omega's remnants in preparation to battle against Sovereign and Century. He'd been working under the auspices of then-senator, now-president Foreman, and never did like me. Possibly because he blamed me for my boyfriend Zack's death (he was Zack's roommate at the U of M), possibly because he was a fussy, constipated douchecanoe. Either way, I'd worked with him in the past, and he sucked. Based on his present demeanor, I had no reason to believe that essential fact had changed.

"You're in an unmarked van with no windows in a residential area," I said, drifting up into the van with minimal effort as he moved aside. "Your cover sucks and so do you. Just print FBI on the side already; everyone knows. I'm surprised you survived the murder-purge; what happened, were you out on paternity leave from giving anal birth to a turd the size of Ayres' Rock? Because I've thought that I've never met anyone as full of shit as you, Li."

He stared daggers at me. What was it with these FBI pricks? Was it a requirement to hire people that hated me, or was it just a directive being cheerfully employed by the current management? "I was in the Anchorage Field Office when all the shit went down – thanks to you. When your buddy Shaw took over the bureau, he decided to exile me because of our prior tension."

"You're welcome," I said. "I only wish you were still there, making a difference in the lives of those hard-working Alaskans and Inuits, far from me, where I never have to look at your stupid face again while I'm trying to save the day. Now," and I looked around at his SWAT-like team, "what's the plan?"

"Why don't you go kick their door down and absorb any incoming fire?" Li asked. "We'll be along shortly to mop up. Probably not literally, since that's beneath me, but you get the picture."

"I'm fine with going in first and sponging all the gunfire," I said, pushing past him to look at a paper blueprint of the house. It was pretty basic, three bedroom, two bath, small footprint. It was a split level, like so many houses I'd known in Minnesota, with a partially submerged basement and bedrooms above it, with the main living area about five-ten steps away from either up or down. "But that means I get all the glory, too, because if I'm taking bullets for this, I'm not sitting my ass back in a dark room while you give the press conference and declare yourself the hero *du jour*." I quickly committed the layout to memory. "Okay. Got it. Going in." And I turned to leave.

"We'll be right behind you. Five or ten minutes, give or take. Maybe a half hour. By the way, it's Uluru now," he said. "Not Ayres' Rock."

"Nice reaction time on the riposte," I said. "Also, I mean this in all senses, Li: go fuck yourself. With a rock drill. Repeatedly." And I exited the vehicle, taking flight toward the house in question.

CHAPTER NINETEEN

I dialed Sierra during my short flight. "Any advice? Any assistance available?" I asked once she'd picked up.

"Don't get shot," she said. "I'm afraid I don't have any additional assistance immediately at hand, but I am dispatching local units as backup and warning them that you are making entry right now. Ambulance and fire are also en route, in the probable case that someone needs medical attention or you start a fire."

"You know me so well," I said, because local PD would be, I figured, less likely to shoot me in the back than Li. Probably. I caught sight of the house, pointed the phone at it, and said, "Confirm that's my target."

"Target confirmed. That's the one."

There was a beep in my ear; call waiting. I looked down to find a DC number and thumbed the button to take the call. "Hello?"

"Try not to kill anyone," Li's voice broke in on the line. "Remember, we need them alive, for interrogation."

"What the f – how did you get this number?" I asked,

pulling the phone away from my ear like the answer would be displayed on the screen.

"You walked into the director's office, remember?" Li's voice was taut. "We capture every number that comes anywhere near the HQ premises."

"Right," I said. "I bet you capture a lot more than that. Hang on, will you?" I thumbed the button again, turning the call into a conference. "I'm going in," I said, and pocketed the phone before adjusting my aim and then vectoring in the direction of the house – and the front door, specifically – at high speed. I felt out to confirm there weren't any huge deposits of metal behind or part of the door, and once I was sure, I cannonballed right through without bothering to slow down.

I didn't collide with anyone, though I did hear a scream, then a curse in Chinese as I came to a halt after taking out half a dozen wood-planked stairs. "FBI!" I shouted. "I have a warrant to search the premises!"

No surprise; the next sound I heard was gunfire.

CHAPTER TWENTY

Wade

"Sierra?" I asked, once Sienna was off the phone and on to her destination. I was in the sky, a few hundred feet above the CIA temp HQ, just hovering there, enjoying the chill, and watching the traffic from nearby Dulles take off and land. The distant roar mingled with the sounds of the city to add some background noise to my call.

"Yes?" Sierra asked.

"I'm taking the intel community angle on this," I said. "Which means I'm hunting specifically about what actions in China have been taken to support this mission, and what other foreign assistance may have been provided. Do you have any access to the original interrogation of Fen Liu that revealed this threat?"

"I am attempting to access it now," she said, through my Chinese program, "but my access to Chinese government computers is somewhat more limited than it used to be." She paused. "I have accessed it, and processed the content. The interrogation video lasts approximately 87 minutes and includes over 8,000 spoken words divided into a series of fragmentary sentences punctuated by pained, insensate utterances."

I didn't feel I had 87 minutes to pore over that. "Can you either hit me with some bullet points or play me the relevant segments?"

Another pause. "The most relevant segment is an eighteen-second utterance in which Fen Liu admits she has one final plan waiting to destroy America via a sleeper agent, that they will know it when they see it, after which she goes into cardiac arrest while her interrogators debate for ninety-two seconds whether she has told them the truth. By the time they turn their attention back to her, she is non-responsive and legally dead. They proceed to attempt cardiopulmonary resuscitation for a period of eighteen minutes and twenty-two seconds—"

"Got it," I said. "Anything important after that?"

"Only a further debate of the veracity of her statement and a concerned utterance that, 'Sienna Nealon and America must be informed so that they do not blame us.'"

That made me smirk; Sienna being on the list of who needed to be informed of an impending cataclysm alongside America was a point of pride for me. "Anything else in the content of the interrogation that might offer a hint as to what she had planned?"

"Only the knowledge that a sleeper agent is involved, and that destruction will proceed from their efforts," Sierra said. "These seem the only facts at issue."

"Not much to go on," I said. "The sleeper agent could have been in America for twenty years."

"In fact," Sierra said, "they could have been here considerably longer. A sleeper agent need not be limited by a human lifespan; they could be meta. Given the ethnic makeup of the Chinese Communist Party, by definition a majority of their spies are Chinese, thus the probability is high that the sleeper is ethnic Han. However, a small number of their spies are of other ethnicities, finding themselves sympathetic and loyal to the CCP due to money, ideology, creed, or ego."

MICE was the acronym for those, and well known in the spy trade as the four key motivators for spies. "It'd be nice to narrow that down. The thought it could be some metahuman who comes from Europe or something that just decided to work for the CCP back in the eighties and has been waiting for a signal to set off destruction ever since is a deeply disconcerting thought. Any suggestions for what markers we could look for?"

"If we make a base assumption that the sleeper agent in question entered the US sometime between when Fen Liu took power and her fall three months ago, that leaves us a window of several years. While it is not impossible the sleeper agent entered before or, perhaps, after, it is most probable that they were assigned and deployed during that period. It at least gives us a starting point."

I grimaced. "Assuming they entered the US legally and left China the same way. Still, that's something, I guess, and there's probably not anything more vital you could be working on. Start with the American customs records, and then examine the departures from China during the same period. Look for irregularities or possible suspects."

"While we're doing that, may I make a suggestion? Since beginning my conversation with Sienna, I have been scanning open source information and determined the location of a probable Chinese secret police station in Los Angeles."

"I thought we got all those," I said, "during the war."

"Apparently not," Sierra said. "This one seems to have

gone quiet for a time, masking itself during the hunt several months ago. Communication from said station does not flow through Chinese government channels. It suggests coordination or communication with potentially exiled CCP officials that have not been discovered or arrested by the new Republic. I will pass this information along to them, and they will likely use it to make arrests in mainland China."

"Great," I said, "get 'em started on that. Meanwhile, I'll head to LA. Can you inform local authorities to start procuring warrants? Then patch me through to Wayne Arthur at CIA?"

"On it," she said.

For my part, I deduced my direction, and turned west. Figuring I'd solve for the exact bearing in a minute or so, I started gaining speed, heading to LA and – to the disquiet of a little voice deep within – away from Sienna.

CHAPTER TWENTY-ONE

Reed

I was all set to have my brains blown out all over a hallway in a housing project in Southwark when, from behind me, a feminine voice bellowed, "STOP!"

And you know what? Everybody stopped. Including me.

"Not you, Reed," Eilish said, cuffing me on the shoulder and stirring me back to action, "the people trying to kill us. You do what you do best."

"Right," I said.

And I blasted the nearest guy with a punch of wind that sent him flying back into the apartment he'd just ambushed us from. He was flung across the room, the gusty tornado I'd made destroying everything within and sending him crashing into the far windows with a scream. He ended up dangling half-in, half-out, impaled on glass. Not enough to kill him. But enough that he dropped his gun. And that he'd need stitches and probably some minor surgery to repair the muscle damage.

While I was ramping up my gust, Eilish was screaming down the hall. "You – hit yourself in the head repeatedly with that! And you – see that railing? Drape your leg over it and give it a straddling jump. I want to see your nuts go into your throat, y'hear me? Go on, then." I turned in time to witness the guy, clearly struggling with these instructions, comply – and immediately regret the life choices that led him to this point.

I kept my tornado, now alive and spun up, whirling behind me like a pet. This was the problem with my power; I needed a few seconds to get anything going other than a brief, mad gust that would simply knock them back a step. In order to bring raw force to bear, I needed a consistent, spinning funnel cloud. Which I now had.

And I turned that sucker loose on the frozen thugs lining the hall.

If I were a less merciful, less evolved person – someone like, say, Sienna – I might have enjoyed watching my tornado suction these murderous assholes into the ceiling with the force usually reserved for rocket launches. It wasn't a very yielding subject, either; it was thickset concrete, and every man that hit it tested his skull against the hard ceiling.

Every one of them lost that fight. The NHS was about to pay for a whole heap load of head x-rays.

There was one man at the end of the hall, dressed in another black-and-yellow houndstooth jacket. Must have been their gang colors. Eilish was lurking beside him, talking to him, though I couldn't hear it beneath the roar of my tornado. Webster stepped gingerly to the side as I ripped the last non-leader of the gang from his feet and channeled him upward into the ceiling with a thunderous crack.

Doors slammed behind us as I dissolved the storm,

coming to a stop before Eilish and our fearful leader. "This is him?" I asked.

"This is Gareth Bloggs," Eilish said. "As it happens, he's quite eager to talk to us."

"Can't imagine why," Webster said, surveying the damage. A half-dozen doors were splintered and destroyed, collateral damage from my tornado. The ceiling was graced with multiple red spots where heads had unceremoniously met that space.

"I've got nothing to say to you," Gareth said, looking up in defiance from where he knelt, arms straight out, palms up. He was bald and thickset. If it was possible to look more like he was capped by a thumb instead of a head, I don't know how.

My eyebrows arched. "Really?" I looked at Eilish, who was frowning. "He's got nothing to say?"

"Answer our questions, you low bastard," she said, peering at him with great concentration.

A little bead of sweat popped out on his forehead. "I don't wish to." He went back to gritting his teeth.

Eilish shook her head. "Sorry. He's got a strong will, this one. I can break him down, given time."

"Time?" I glanced at Bloggs, still holding position. "Maybe we've got it, maybe we don't." I lifted a hand–

–And unleashed the wind.

He was picked up bodily and slammed into the wall behind him, breaking the plaster. He fell and caught himself, but I could tell by the sound he made and the way he crumpled that landing on his forearms and hands had hurt.

"You can't do this!" He was groaning as he propped himself up on his elbows, looking up at me with a pained expression. "I know my rights."

Webster had a slightly pinched look on his face. "I'm going to head out. Get some fresh air."

"Good idea," I said.

"Wait," Bloggs said, watching him retreat to the door to the stairwell. The minute Webster was gone, he looked up at me, uncertainty flashing through his eyes. "You're a cop in America. You can't do this."

"I'm actually not," I said, much more devil-may-care than I actually felt. If I'd learned anything from my sister's propensity for casual violence, it was that people tended to fear the pain more than they probably should. Something about the unknown. "And I'm definitely not a cop here, which means your rights haven't meant shit to me since a warm July day in 1776." With a twist of my hand, I sent in the winds and lifted him up, letting him dangle before me. "Got anything you want to tell me? Or shall I put you through the wall a few times, crotch-first?"

"Answer the man," Eilish said.

"All right, all bloody right!" he shouted, waving his hands like he was on a desert island and flagging down the only rescue boat he'd ever seen. "I don't know for a fact who dumped the body, but it was metahumans that did it – there's a gang of 'em been operating in London for a bit! Squeezed out the other competitors, cornered the drugs supply and made themselves indispensable to people higher up the chain than me, all right?"

"You don't have a point of contact for them?" I asked.

"I am a very small operator, okay?" he said, doing a slow whirl within the mini-tornado I had him trapped in. "This block, that's it. That's all. I have a business relationship with my supplier, and he – somewhere above him – answers to, or does business, with them. But neither he, nor anyone above him, consulted with me before dumping this mess on my doorstep, all right? That's why the cops got called – no guidance from above means no orders not to."

"Do you often get guidance from them?" I asked. "These metahumans above your supplier?"

"Occasionally," he said. His hands were shaking, even in the wind prison. "Usually it's stuff like, "'Here's a new drug, why don't you see what you can do with it?' Or 'Don't let this person have no more freebies.' That kind of thing. They aren't heavy with the hand if you know what I mean. Just make money and keep things in line, that's their philosophy."

"So how'd you take it when this body dropped on your front doorstep?" I asked. "What was your immediate thought?"

"Ah, 'oh, shit,'" he said, voice shaking. "You think I want this trouble? I want to have my boys try and dispose of that mess to keep the heat off my neck? No one wanted to touch that. And I didn't hear so much as a whisper from above. To me, that means if they were responsible, they wanted the cops called, because if they didn't, I would have been informed to let it sour for a spell, or get rid of it myself. This is exactly how they wanted it to play out. Send a message."

"To who?" I asked, giving him a little increased spin.

"I don't know!" he said, voice rising in panic. "All I know is you don't leave a mess like that without wanting someone to see it! That's the God's honest!"

"Fine," I said. "Who's your higher up? Who's your contact?"

Now I saw a flicker of discomfort cross his broad face. "Please, don't. If I betray him, he'll kill me. Besides, your man out there already knows who supplies this place – or his pals do, at least. You don't have to ask me."

"All right." I let him drop, and he landed on his knees with a pained gasp. "If you're lying to me, I'll be back. But thank you for your cooperation," I said, then offered him a smile and walked away.

"D'ye think he was telling the truth?" Eilish asked, falling in beside me, and asking meta-low.

"I suspect so," I said. "You don't get very high in the London underworld without someone noticing – and without a prison sentence or three. You think we got all there was to get out of him?"

"Yeah," she said. "I think you scared the bloody shite out of him. He would have offered his mother to you by the end."

"Lucky I'm already taken," I said. "But if I can't get that name elsewhere, he knows I'll come back to him."

"He'd likely be ready for you, then, y'think?" Eilish asked.

"Well, he'd certainly try," I said. "Come on – let's go collect Webster and get on to our next stop."

CHAPTER TWENTY-TWO

Sienna

The gunfire came from my left, and was poorly aimed. Bullets whizzed past at least six feet behind me; I could detect the path of the bullets, dimly, but there wasn't much I could do to influence them with my relatively small amount of Magneto power. I did detect the source, though, a fist-sized object a couple dozen feet away – a gun – and gave it a hard shove, up into the shooter's face. The gasping scream as it made hard contact with a nose and chin was its own reward.

I turned and found an Asian man gushing blood from his nose and lips, standing in the middle of a stark white living room. "Hi," I said, and blasted him in the chest with eyebeams so strong they slammed through the fireplace mantel. He collapsed onto the hearth with a thump, and I coaxed the gun to slide across the floor to me. It came a little unevenly, but I managed to make it leap the last couple of feet, hurtling over the steps down to the entryway, and into my hand.

It was a beat-up old Beretta 92 that looked like it had been carried in the holster of the least capable, least conscientious soldier in the entire US Army. I thumbed the magazine release, checking how many bullets remained. Less than fifteen, more than ten. Ramming it back into the pistol, I worked back the slide enough to confirm that yes, there was a round in the chamber. Hopefully I wouldn't have to use it, but since when have I ever gotten what I wanted in a fight? Or in life?

The smell of cigarette smoke permeated the house, wafting from somewhere in the back. A Chinese man came around the corner with a pistol raised, and I gave it a shove with my powers. It didn't smash him in the face, but it did ram his wrist into the door frame, and he grunted.

I let loose a scream of primal, Banshee fury that knocked him backward a step and hit a key that would – and did – shatter glass. Specifically, in the kitchen window behind him. Giving him a heaping helping of the Warmind made him stagger back hard against the kitchen island. His feet came off the ground, and I flew at him, ramming into his midsection. Not hard enough to shatter his spine where it had made contact with the island, but hard enough, right in the gut, to make him fold like an accordion.

Catching the arm with the gun still clutched in it, I isolated it and gave it a twist, breaking his elbow and wrenching a pained scream from him. He was bleeding from the ear, I noted as I lifted a knee and drove it into his gut. It took the wind out of him and he finally dropped the pistol, which I caught in my free hand before ramming him, head-first, into the wall.

A tinny voice seemed to be speaking to me from a thousand miles away. Heavy footsteps were coming from upstairs, and I realized with a start the voice was in my pocket. Transferring the second pistol, a weathered Springfield Armory XD, to the hand with the other gun, I fished my phone out of my pocket. "What?"

"No killing, no killing!" Li shouted through the speaker. Behind him, over the slight ringing in my ears, I could hear the truck's engine straining as they raced (surely) my way.

"If only these people shared your feelings about that," I said. "Relax – I haven't killed anyone. Yet."

"Be careful," Li said. "as Chinese spies, they may have some sort of cyanide capsules hidden in false teeth."

I looked down at the guy bleeding at my feet and shrugged. Lifting him by the front of his shirt, I smashed him in the face with the butt of the gun, then turned him over. He gagged and spit out a mouth full of blood – and pretty much all of his teeth. I let him drop to the ground, completely limp, and said, "Uhh...are we sure about that cyanide capsule in the teeth thing? Because the cure for that one is removing all the teeth, and I'm not sure how talkative this one's going to be given what it took to remove them all..." I bound his hands with a light web, then left him facedown on the weathered kitchen floor to move on.

"What the hell?!" Li screamed into the phone. "You need to watch them closely, not smash their faces into paste!"

"My solution has the virtue of being manageable," I said, coming around the corner and finding myself facing a closed door that I was pretty sure led to the basement. "Yours doesn't. I'm kinda busy here."

Projecting the Warmind through the door and into whatever lay beyond drew a grunt of pain and the sound of someone slipping on the stairs. I threw open the door and found another Asian dude trying to catch his balance. Throwing out a hand, I hit him with a Faerie web that bound him to the wall on the landing beneath, trapping his gun at his side.

I shoved one pistol, the Springfield, into my waistband at the small of my back, then put my phone back in my pocket. Slipping down the stairs, I listened as best I could over Li's muffled swearing and screaming and that faint ringing still persisting in my ears from all the shooting upstairs. There was someone moving around down here, fighting with something heavy and metal.

I did a flip on the staircase and went inverted, then slid down the wall like a snake across the ground so that I popped my head out along with the Beretta and swept it across my field of vision. At the end of the basement was a sloped-bulkhead double cellar door, and fighting with the heavy bar keeping it shut was a Chinese man in middle age, dressed in khakis. "Hey, nerd," I said, and he stopped fighting with the bar for a second and looked up at me in surprise—

Just before my double dose of light webs slammed into him, anchoring him into place against the metal door, which chose that moment to pop open and add insult to his injury.

"Stay here until I get back," I said as he screamed at me in Mandarin. I knew all the words he used; none of them were particularly nice.

I returned to the main floor and made my way up the half-staircase to the upper floor, where the bedrooms were. Coming up it, I could still hear movement. I rounded the corner ready to take on all comers—

At which point I was both shot and stabbed, the gunfire blotting out my hearing and the knife passing through my wrist severing enough of the nerves that the Beretta tumbled from my grip—

—Leaving me staring at two Chinese women, both of whom were deadly serious, both of who were armed—

And neither of whom seemed inclined to let me live.

CHAPTER TWENTY-THREE

When you get ambushed, stabbed and shot within a second of each other, your life is in immediate danger. For a normal person, that'd be a shocking, terrifying turn of events that they – hopefully – won't experience even once in a lifetime.

For me, it's Tuesday again.

Whether you're a normal person or me, though, the next moments are crucial to survival. Even I can be killed; it just takes a little more effort. But it can be done, and as I stared into the eyes of a Chinese woman with a slightly bowl-ish haircut that made her look like a Romulan, I saw the eyes of a person who wanted me dead. Full stop, no questions.

So I screamed.

And it wasn't just a little scream, or just a half-hearted Banshee scream.

I went operatic with it, played with my range, belted it out like I was in the shower and I had feelings deep down in the basement of my soul that needed to get out or I was going to explode.

"I DON'T EVEN WANT TO BE HERE!" I screamed

with all the rage and feeling in my soul. It reached a sonic key that shattered windows around the entire house. I might even have broken windows on the neighbors' houses.

Also, I belched flame from every surface of my body. It sparked out like someone had left the gas on in the place and lit a cigarette, flooding off me in a great rush and causing the woman with the knife to close her eyes as it washed over her, letting go of the blade she'd rammed through my wrist.

The other woman, the one with the gun, had enough time to hold up her hands defensively as it blasted her. It rolled down the walls of the hallway like a special effect from a movie and billowed out the already-shattered windows, surging toward the nearest source of oxygen.

It was fast, it was hot, but it was mostly an angry, excited utterance of fire rather than a sustained effort by me to light the place up. As such, it blew out the windows and barely caught anything on fire. The wallpaper in a couple places; the bed linens in three of the rooms.

Oh, and the lady with the gun. Apparently she'd gone heavy on whatever perfume she used, and it was a little too on the *eau de alcohol* side. Made me want a drink for the first time in months just scenting her.

I fed that one and snuffed the others, giving her a hard slam with her pistol as I seized control of it with my Magneto powers. She wasn't in the frame of mind to fight back, so when it smashed into the bridge of her nose and knocked her flat, she had no defense against it; she was too busy squirming at the fire crawling up her pants legs and blouse. With a blast of light webs, I netted her to the ground and then snuffed the flames with a wave of my hand.

When I turned my attention to the woman who'd stabbed me, I found her recoiling, tripping on one of the stairs. I half-expected her to scream at me in Mandarin, as some of the others had, but instead she looked me in the eye and smiled weakly. "Hey, no harm, no foul, right?"

I lifted my right hand, knife still jutting from between the radius and ulna, hanging there like it had been planted in the wrist as a knife seed and grown into its fully developed self, like I was just sprouting switchblades out of my body on the regular. "Oh, I'm calling foul," I said, and decked her with a punch that they probably detected on the seismographs back in China.

It took mere seconds for me to confirm that the bedrooms were all empty; I'd cleared the house and left everyone in it trussed up like a Thanksgiving ham. Sirens were drawing close, and I estimated it'd be moments before Li and his crew were upon me. Pulling the phone out of my pocket, I said, "House is clear." Before he could answer, I hung up.

The woman I'd set on fire had burns over a decent portion of her body. First degree, mostly. Maybe a little second-degree here and there, with some blisters to show for it. I'd pinned her sideways against the hallway floor and wall, her ass sticking out from the baseboard, face buried against it. There was a little box in her back pocket, small, familiar.

I plucked the cigarettes, drawing little more than a grunt from her. "Mind if I take these? Sure you don't," I said, patting her on the back as I did so. I put my own back against the wall of the staircase and slid down, suddenly exhausted, as though I'd gone ten rounds with Rose, instead of one with a bunch of Chinese spies. Lifting a finger, I lit the tip of the cigarette.

It brought me back to the first days of sobriety, when I'd taken up smoking − briefly − as a way to help mitigate the cravings for booze. Nicotine was addictive for me, but cancer held no danger for my metahuman cells. The worst thing that would come of me smoking ten packs a day would be the awful, reeking smell I'd carry with me.

So I smoked that cigarette like this was my last day on earth. And I didn't move, even when I heard Li's team coming in hot, except to say, "It's clear!" to let them know not to come in shooting. I just sat there and puffed, and listened to the whimpers of the Chinese spies as I pondered how bad things had gotten that I'd had to come here, again, to deal with this shit.

CHAPTER TWENTY-FOUR

Reed

I made a quick call as we left the building, trying to get ahead of the troubles I was sensing before us. Webster waited on me patiently as we took flight, and when I hung up, he spoke. "Turn anything up, then?"

"Just a chain," Eilish said. "The next link of which belongs to you, apparently."

Webster raised a dark eyebrow. "How's that?"

"Our man in there suggested his supplier was known to police," I said. "I informed him that if he was lying to me, he'd be receiving a much less charitable visit, and soon."

Webster nodded. "There's an overboss, of sorts, to be sure. Not on site, but yeah, known to us, whispered about. Name is Darren Flint. Gangster-ish fellow. Not one I like to deal with, but he's a known quantity. By which I mean, he's a bag of shit, and a whole lot of it." He frowned. "He's the next link?"

"It was suggested," Eilish said, with her lilt, "that the lack of direction about this incident from above indicated that those above knew it was coming, and let it happen."

Webster gave that a moment's thought, then shrugged. "Well, if that's the case, and you wish to make a visit to Mr. Flint, that can certainly be arranged. He's not even far away." Lifting his finger as we rode the winds upward, he pointed to a tower block less than a mile away. "He's in there. Top floor."

I stared at the block; it was another of those ugly concrete buildings with not nearly enough windows. "If I take us right in through his window, do you think he'll be upset?"

His eyebrow rose again. "I certainly would be, but if you were to drop me on the roof beforehand, it seems to me that'd be a problem between you and Mr. Flint."

I just smiled. "Next stop for you is the roof, then." I glanced at Eilish, who gave me a curt nod. "And the next stop for us is Darren Flint's living room."

CHAPTER TWENTY-FIVE

Wade

Transit to Los Angeles takes a minute, even at supersonic speed. My eyes were watering, the wind was blowing so hard in my face. It took every ounce of my super strength to lift my hand, but it was technically possible. The roar of the air flow around me was intense, too, deafening to lesser ears. All this pressure turned a flight to LA from a five-hour affair to one that would take a little over an hour.

An hour that was extremely boring.

I was over the high Sierras when I finally broke, and fought the wind to get my phone and hold it in front of my chin. Dialing it was easy in the face of all that; hearing was slightly more difficult.

"Hello?" Sienna answered. It was tough to tell with all the excess sound, but she sounded...relieved? Grateful? Something. "Wade?"

"Yeah, it's me," I said. "Can you hear me?"

"You sound like you're going through a wind tunnel," she said. "But yeah, I can hear you."

"You done with that little old monitoring station?" I asked. I'd been flying with my eyes closed about sixty percent of the time. I was low enough that I wasn't likely to encounter any planes, and opening my eyes often enough to be able to see birds or drones if I happened to come across any.

"Yep," she said, taking a deep breath and holding it. On the exhale, she spoke. "Went fine. Just letting the FBI mop up the mess. Probably gotta have a talk with some of the shitheel spies soon. Which oughta be fun."

"Sounds like it," I said, trying to make conversation and finding it stilted. "Any...complications?"

"Got shot at. No big deal. No harm, no...well, you know."

I raised an eyebrow. "No harm?"

"Well, I'm fine," she said again. "I can't speak for every soul in the place. There may have been some blood loss, and definitely some teeth were subject to the laws of physics. But I'm fine."

I frowned. How many times had she told me she was fine in the last thirty seconds? But if there was anything I'd learned in my all-too-short association with Sienna Nealon, and our all-too-troubled marriage, it was that when she told me she was fine, even though I knew she wasn't, I couldn't pick too hard at it or it'd trigger all her defense mechanisms. "Okay," I said, figuring I'd leave it at that for now, "well, just know that I'm here for you."

She laughed ruefully, then coughed, and it had a thick sound, like she had the croup or something. Which was impossible, obviously, for a meta. "Sure. How far out from LA are you?"

"Minutes away," I said, checking my phone again. "This

isn't a monitoring station, though; supposedly this is where they have the Chinese police that used to harass defectors and Chinese expats. Much less spying, much more kidnapping and threatening."

"Sounds like a fun bunch. Keep some teeth as souvenirs."

"That's a little too serial killer-y for me. And I'm too young and childless to start practicing as the Tooth Fairy. You sure you're all right?"

"The first guy who ever got in my head was a serial killer, remember?" She sounded like she was smirking, but, again, ruefully. Lots of rue. "Pretty sure it left a mark. Just stay safe, okay?" She took a deep inhalation, and it sounded like she was holding her breath. "I gotta go run some of my prisoners through the wringer, see what I can squeeze out."

"Have fun," I said. Her answer to that was a grunt, then a hangup.

All was not right with Sienna. But with the first hints of Los Angeles on the horizon, I didn't have time to get to the bottom of whatever was ailing her. It still left a clawing feeling in the pit of my stomach, like I'd left a comrade behind during a battle. I consoled myself with the idea that we'd get to the bottom of this together, soon, then checked my heading again, and upped my speed as I moved toward my impending confrontation.

CHAPTER TWENTY-SIX

Sienna

L i had been muttering like a little bitch ever since he'd arrived at my scene, finding fault with everything I'd done. "This guy has no teeth," he'd said, as that one Chinese guy I'd busted the face out of went rattling by on a gurney, IV dripping something into his veins that was keeping him from screaming.

"But he didn't choke to death on a cyanide capsule," I said, down to my last two cigarettes as I stood on the street, listening to the Chinese guy moan as one of the stretcher wheels caught the curb while the EMTs wheeled him to the ambulance. "And you told me that was a possibility. If you oversold the risk, that's on you."

"At least you didn't take the teeth out of all of them," Li said, mostly under his breath. Mostly. He was standing with his hands on his hips, watching his guys lead the others away in cuffs to the black SUVs. Honestly, it was like they weren't even trying not to look like a government black ops team. Local police were cordoning off either end of the street. "How do you think their lawyers are going to take this?"

"Your guys got pictures of the knife in my wrist before I healed it," I said, watching smoke waft over the street scene from the tip of my cig. "And the GSW. I announced the warrant and they got all hostile. No one got hurt that didn't deserve it. Honestly, what more do you want?"

I could feel him looking sideways at me. "You got hurt. Are you telling on yourself?"

"In your eyes, I'm sure I deserve it," I said, taking another inhale and just holding it, letting the smoke work on my lungs, fill my veins with the joy rush that had addicted countless generations to the pleasures of smoking.

He stared at me intensely for a moment, giving me that tingling sensation you get when someone is watching you. Then he turned away. "Their lawyers are going to have a field day with this."

My phone beeped, and I fished it out of my pocket, half-expecting it would be Wade again.

It wasn't. "Regarding their lawyers," Sierra said, just launching right into conversation, "the new Chinese government has managed to reacquire access to the bank accounts that have been funding this group. They will be calling the FBI within minutes to offer them up as a sign of good faith. It does, however, leave your detainees in the lurch, as they no longer have any funds with which to procure lawyers."

"Heh," I chortled, smoke puffing out of my nose. "Public defenders for these losers. That ought to level the playing field."

Li was quiet for a moment. "I'm loathe to even ask this, but do you want to help interrogate them?" I must have given him a hell of a look. "No beating their skulls in or anything;

we want any convictions to stick, and giving them grounds for dismissal is not a risk I'm willing to countenance."

"Sure, I'll help you interrogate them," I said, taking a nice, easy exhale that made Li blanch at the smell. "But you need to understand that my first priority is stopping the impending apocalypse, not seeing them safely to trial. That said – I can do enough non-physical damage to them that they'll sing."

He closed his eyes and shook his head. "You cannot use mind powers to break their brains open like pinatas. The courts have been very clear about this."

"You know what else the courts have been clear about? I'm gonna get accused of using mind powers on them regardless, because criminals lie." This was true; the number of criminals I'd busted that tried to claim I used mind powers on them in some way was sitting at something like 85%. Which was low, I thought; who knew that 15% of criminals would just accept their arrests and convictions without kicking up every possible objection, no matter how foolish? "Might as well actually do it, since the stakes are so high."

Li groaned, making a sound deep in his throat like I'd punched him in the gut. "Can you at least make a show of not doing it? For the cameras?"

"Scout's honor," I said, holding up my middle finger for him. "Trouble is, I was never a scout. But you get the point."

That just made him groan more. He didn't argue, though, and he stalked off, leaving me to finish my cigarette in peace.

CHAPTER TWENTY-SEVEN

B ack at the barn (FBI HQ), Li and I dithered a bit on strategy. Not too much and not for too long; he wanted to talk to Lily Chen, the lady with the switchblade who'd put her knife through my arm. I disagreed, wanting to talk to Kevin Zhang, who I'd plastered to the cellar door without a fight as he'd tried to flee.

Big shock: the angry, chain-smoking, disheveled, recently-stabbed-and-shot metahuman won the argument. 5' 4" and built like a tug boat bowled over the 5' 9" fine-boned Asian import. Straight up trouble, made in America, that's me.

"Hi, Kev," I said breezily as I entered the interrogation room trailing Li, who wore a sourpuss look that may or may not have been related to our discussion before entry. Hard to tell with him. He was, however, a contrast to Kevin, who was slightly overweight, probably thanks to minimal exercise, overwork, and processed American food. He looked slightly pasty, too, like he had spent too long in that house with the curtains closed, nothing but a computer screen to light him up.

He needed some sunlight. He needed to go for a run. He

needed fresh vegetables in his diet, and some high-quality protein. I told him all of this, just to break the ice, and he took it like every word was me punching him in the jimmies. "Wh...what?" he asked, head cocked like a dumb dog trying to decide why its owner had just thrown a tennis ball over his head.

"I said you're not looking very healthful." I bookended my comment by withdrawing the last cigarette from the pack I'd stolen from his female comrade upstairs. "Being a Chinese spy is deleterious to the ol' constitution. On every level, it would seem."

"You can't smoke in here," Li said, managing to keep his voice at a normal volume but not able to mask his outrage.

"Try and stop me," I said, and lit up with the tip of my finger without even bothering to look at him.

"This is why people hate you," Li said, just seething like the little bitch he was.

"Pretty sure there are other reasons," I said, taking my first drag in several long, torturous minutes. "Ones related to loss of lives, and teeth. But we don't need to talk about those right now, Kevin. Do we?"

"I don't know why I'm here," Kevin said.

"Because you got caught in a Chinese spy house under the approach to Joint Base Andrews," I said, pulling out the chair across from him with my powers and sitting down, then blowing smoke in his face. He coughed a little. "Try and keep up, will you? Now, since you were working for a Chinese government that no longer exists, the new republic – if you care to call it that – has already informed us that they have no intention of defending you in any way. You know what that means?" He stared at me, trying to keep the horror from intruding onto his pudgy face; with him, the former Chinese Ministry of Intelligence had not sent their best. "It means your ass belongs to me, cupcake."

I could feel Li shudder behind me, and Kevin did it right to my face. I must have been wearing that look again, the one that let them see and feel the burning malice I held in my soul. I had a suspicion that all the violence I had done in my life had accumulated upon my facade like Dorian Gray's picture. It hadn't bothered me, not for the longest time; I slept like a baby knowing I'd never killed anyone that hadn't been trying to kill me or other people. Sure, I'd struggled with alcoholism, with loneliness, with addictive behaviors, with my weight. But that was just because of my personality, I'd told myself.

It certainly wasn't because I'd killed more human beings personally than most armies could claim in the last decade. No. Killing people was as natural to me as puffing on this cigarette. I blew the smoke in his face again and watched him flinch.

Or: maybe all the ugliness and vileness I'd done, even in the name of good, had put a callous on my soul. And the more I killed, the more I did harm to others, the more malice I unleashed...the thicker that callous got.

And I was calloused by now. Or callous, as the case my be. I could have snapped this spy guy's chubby neck and gone right to lunch, and it wouldn't have raised my heart rate.

But that kill wouldn't be free, any more than the lunch would be. There were always consequences, even if you couldn't see them.

The consequences of all my killing may have started out smooth as silk webs tying me down like Gulliver, nice and easy to break through, but somewhere along the way they'd turned to chains of steel. Now I was bound, and to what...well, I didn't like to think about it. With Wade, it was easy not to.

Without him...I might have to turn around and look the devil in the eye. And I was not looking forward to that.

I don't know how much of this played out on my face as I sat across from Kevin. It probably wasn't "none," based on how fast he fell apart. "I...I...I worked for Fen Liu and the Ministry of Intelligence," he said.

"Fen Liu's dead," I said with astonishing dullness. Just a fact, no emotion. "And your former boss is in a Chinese prison, learning exactly how pliable his anus is. My guess? By now it's like a broken rubber band. Glimpse into your future."

Kevin made a choked-up squealing noise. He was not going to do well in prison. And his anal pliability was going to be tested so much worse than the former Minister of Intel.

"Your only hope," I said, letting the cigarette dangle from my fingers lovingly as I leaned in, "for survival, not just for yourself, but for your anus, is to start cooperating. Sing like a canary, see, and Li and I might just be motivated to help you. Without our help, it's gen pop for you, Kev. You know I hate criminal scum, but I'll give them this much: they're Americans. And they're not big fans of traitor-ass spies." I sat back, putting the cigarette between my lips and enjoying a drag as a substitute for what I should have been doing at this time of day back in Greece: screwing my husband's brains out. "See what I did with the word ass there? I used it in multiple ways. Kinda like how the federal inmates are going to use your body's orifices."

A torrent of begging and swearing came out of him then, mostly unintelligible. It took almost a minute for him to pull himself together enough to belch out words I did understand: "I'll tell you whatever you want to know, if I can. What do you want to know?"

"Someone came into the US," I said, as Li circled around behind him, eyes slightly wider open in appreciation of what I'd done, I assumed. "From China, we think. Whoever it is, they've got doomsday possibilities. Some kind of trigger man, with his finger on a weapon that's supposed to do untold levels of damage to America." I stayed loose, took a moment to take a drag, let these words have the proper impact on him. "I need to get him before he sets things off." I leaned in for emphasis. "How do I find him?"

He paled before me, and quailed before me, withdrawing as best he could. "Y...you can't," he said, shaking in the face of me. "If he's trained...he's trained to disappear." And now he shook his head, whispering in certainty despite the uncertainty he must have felt in his very soul. "I can't find him. You can't find him. No one...no one can find him."

CHAPTER TWENTY-EIGHT

Reed

Entering someone's house via the window when they're ten-plus floors up is a stylish way to make a first impression. Yes, the mess you cause them is certainly prodigious, but that's their problem – I'm borrowing Sienna's assessment of events here – and the gains from your not having to take the stairs, the elevator, or to deal with trifling problems like being refused entry at the door? Well, they're all yours.

"Hello!" I announced myself as we sent a half-dozen people scrambling when Eilish and I flew into Darren Flint's apartment following a swarm of busted glass. "I'm looking for Darren. Anyone seen him?"

Only one guy didn't move when we came crashing in. He was a big fellow; over six feet, built like a truck, bald head shaved smooth. He clutched his TV remote in one hand, phone in the other as though we hadn't just interrupted his viewing pleasures by coming in like Miley Cyrus's proverbial Wrecking Ball.

It took a hard fella to accept people smashing in through his window like this and not to get exercised. Hell, he didn't appear as though his pulse had ticked up so much as a beat per minute. "Whatchoo want?" he asked, with a hard accent that I couldn't exactly place other than to put it in the realm of Wales. Or gibberish. One of those, though they didn't seem far separated.

"To talk."

He looked back at the TV, where a national news channel was doing a piece on the matters before Parliament today. "Talk, then."

What a cool customer. "Eilish, ask him a couple questions, would you?"

"What's your name, lad?" Eilish asked.

He looked up at her dully, yet I sensed there was a wit beneath the dull exterior. "You know my name already or you wouldn't be here. Next."

"Who dropped the body down at the other tower block?" Eilish asked.

"Someone with more power than me," he said, and flipped the channel to a soccer match. Oops. Sorry. Football. When in Rome, and all that. "Someone I don't care to cross, or even know the name of. Next."

"Did you know it was going to happen?" I asked.

At this, he turned and looked at me lazily, with very little care whatsoever. "I may have heard rumors."

I looked at Eilish, she looked at him. "Did you know it was happening?"

At this, he just shook his head and turned back to the TV. "Your parlor trick don't work on me, girly."

Well...that was a surprise. "Why are you talking to us, then?" I asked.

"Have I told you anything valuable yet?" he asked. "Anything you didn't already know from your chat with Gareth?" He gave me another look. "No? Then what does it matter. Next. Try to make it interesting, will you?"

"Why don't you want to know who did this?" I asked. He didn't stir, just focused on the screen. Beyond him was an obvious drug lab, and he seemed not to care that we were seeing it. Scales. Flasks. Beakers. Plastic bags. Pretty women in bras and panties, huddling away from us. Product. And he just did not give a shit. "It happened in your territory. You're clearly unbothered and unafraid of us. Why would you give a pass to someone to make this mess, which has now led to us busting in your window?"

"My window will be fixed within an hour after you leave," he said. "I think I'll go with one that opens, this time. This one was rubbish for circulating air, and it gets a bit smelly in here at times." He sniffed, then turned to look back at me. "And you should answer your own bloody question and stop wasting my time."

"You are lightly afraid of me," I said. "You're just afraid of somebody else a lot more."

He winked at me, mirthlessly. "Bright boy. I've got to live here after you leave, lad. And you will be leaving, sooner or later. How much mess you make in the interim, that does concern me. I just want you off my patch, really, and the sooner you understand that me and mine had nothing to do with this, the sooner I hope you'll move on."

With that, he settled back on the couch and made a mild grunt at the action on the screen. "Lousy. Absolute shit."

Eilish bristled beside me. "Ye want me to—"

"No," I said. To him, I added, "Thank you for your time."

He gave me a bare nod without turning his head. "Good luck." And as I turned to leave, he added, muttered so low only a meta could hear it, "You'll need it."

Once we were out the window and in the air once more, I jetted us to the rooftop on a current rising from above, picking up Webster – with an exclamation of surprise – as we went by.

"What the devil was that about, Reed?" Eilish asked when we were a couple football fields distant from the tower block. "You didn't put the screws to him at all."

"Didn't need to," I said, controlling our turn as I hurled us back toward central London with a gust. "Metahuman powers aside, this is way above him. Did you see his minions? Normal humans, all, based on their reaction times when we came in. He's got power, but he's it for his entire organization. Whoever is behind this, they're big. Way bigger than him. Not just local, but citywide, maybe even national or international." I turned to Webster, who was uneasily floating atop my gusts. "I need the highest law enforcement authority you have in this country on organized crime, and I need them now." I pushed my eyes front as I carried us back toward the Met Office. "We need to start looking at the top."

CHAPTER TWENTY-NINE

Sienna

As Kevin's revelation that no one could find the trigger man for Fen Liu's apocalyptic surprise settled over the interrogation room, I found myself staring at him. His face was open, eyes wide, and I got not one hint of deception coming off him.

Mostly...he was just terrified.

"Walk me through this," I said hoarsely, my cigarette trailing a little smoke as I lifted it up to place it between my lips, then spoke around it. "You're telling me once you send a spy over here, they're completely invisible? Like a cloaking device goes over them?"

"They blend in," he said, slightly edging away from me, as much as he could given his ass was planted in the chair across the table. "It's not like there's a tiny Chinese population in America. It's not like Japan, or Norway, where it's a homogeneous group of some other ethnicity they're hiding among.

Chinese people are everywhere here, new immigrants and ones that have been here for generations. And your spy could be either."

"Assuming he even is Chinese," Li said, a little snippy.

"For what you're talking about, he almost certainly is," Kevin said, so very forthcoming. "Fen Liu wouldn't have trusted some American mercenary to do something like this."

"Why not?" I asked, interested to see if I could make him squirm more. Also, Li was giving me the stinkeye, because we both knew the answer but he didn't want to have it said aloud. Which was motivation enough for me to press it.

"China is a nation of the Chinese people," he said. "It's...hard to explain to someone who isn't from that kind of country—"

"You mean a multicultural, pluralistic society?" I asked, oh-so-sweetly. Li's eye twitched. "Explain it anyway. Use small words if you have to."

"No one in the Chinese government is going to trust someone who's not Chinese to do anything important if they don't have to," he said, as though his life depended upon it. He had the right idea in that.

"Ooh, that's racist," I said, taking such great delight in the fact that now Li was reddening behind him.

"No one in China gives a shit about being called racist," Kevin said. "That's purely an affectation of *Baizuo* westerners."

Li's fists were clenched, and I had to stifle a laugh by taking a drag. When I exhaled, I said, "Yeah, that's probably more of an issue for those of us who have to live in multicultural societies. Kinda like how you can pick a fight with my husband and walk away, but I'm kinda stuck with him. Or vice versa." Even saying that brought my mood down, and I wondered how things were going for Wade in LA. "You sure you can't help me on this, Kev? Your anus would thank you for cooperating."

"I want to help you," he said, leaning across the table, hands open, palms outstretched. "Please. Give me something I can actually help you with, and I'll do it. You want to know about our tasking at the monitoring station? I can tell you everything. All our data, all our files. I was IT for us; I'll gladly open them up."

"What I want to know right now," I said, letting the smoke curl out between us, "is what everyone else's role was in the safe house." I said, lifting my hand expectantly to Li. He rolled his eyes, and came out with a pad of paper and a pen a moment later. "Every single bit of incriminating activity they were up to. What you did, how you did it. And I want it yesterday."

CHAPTER THIRTY

Wade

Los Angeles was not my kind of town, but on the plus side, hopefully I wouldn't be here long. It was one of those warm days they got so often – normal for November here, abnormal everywhere else – and I was already sweating as I came down beside the rally point for the local operations people that the CIA had put together for this raid.

Which was to say FBI and LAPD. Because the agency is not allowed to operate on American soil except with very tight guardrails. Tight guardrails which had ceased to exist after China had taken over our intelligence services but which were, under the eyes of Robb Foreman, operating very tightly again, it seemed, since there was not one CIA agent in the circle waiting for me eight blocks from the target house.

I got the intros in a hurry. In between them all, I picked

out a familiar face. "David Miller," I said with a sigh. "How'd you get in on this action?"

Miller was number two in Jeremy Hampton's meta-hunting mercenary outfit. His black plate carrier didn't have a single identifying agency mark, unlike the LAPD guys (who wore patches that declared them POLICE) and the FBI guys (whose patches read FBI, duh). "I got called in to provide an assist in case your Chinese police station has metas," Miller said with all the emotional force I'd expect from accountants talking business. "I don't want to shock you, but guess what: it definitely does. They all did, all the ones we hit back in the war."

I frowned. Miller was right; Hampton's agency had been used to help execute exactly these raids when Sienna was in charge of the government. Hard experience suggested the Chinese government of Fen Liu had loved nothing more than favoring the party loyalists with superpowers to help them do their jobs. It had kinda even been the death of her. So the idea that this police station, this projection of Chinese governmental authority on foreign soil, had metahuman protection?

Well, that tracked. That they'd survived the death of Fen Liu's regime was somewhat less cool, but it was what we were dealing with. It made me wonder how similar of a situation this was to what Sienna had dealt with back in Maryland. Probably not too far off.

"You get yourself some serum yet?" I asked Miller.

He shook his head. "It's not commercially available, which means if I want it, I've got to get it from hot-packed fentanyl straight out of Mexico. I love my life a little too much to play Russian roulette with Mexican chemistry products."

"Technically it's Chinese chemistry products," I said, as he stared at me flatly. "Their scientists are all China-trained."

"Regardless," Miller said, "if ain't *Hecho en* America, I ain't shooting it into my veins. I'll keep it red and white without turning blue, thanks, and reserve my interest in things made in Mexico for the women, exclusively."

I turned to the board with the house blueprint. "That makes me the only meta on the team, then?" I looked around; no one disagreed. "I'll lead with my pretty face, then, since none of you can heal from a GSW in hours. Want me to kick in the front door?"

Miller nodded. "We could try the back, but I say we surprise them with unrestrained aggression and count on momentum to carry us through. Clear room by room, front to back. Let LAPD SWAT post up in the rear to catch any runners."

"Sounds like a winning plan," I said. "Just stay behind me, okay?" I swelled my muscles with Hercules power, trying to make myself a slightly bulkier target to shoot through, and grabbed a plate carrier and helmet off the storage rack in the corner of the command center. "I'll push guns aside, and blast anyone that comes at us without them."

"You want to lead with your chin, I'm not going to stop you," Miller said. "Just try not to get it shot off."

I grinned at him. "Why? You afraid of the paperwork?"

He shook his head slowly. "Afraid of your wife. I don't think she likes me much, and I don't want to give her any reasons to beat me around with a rifle butt." He hesitated, chagrin passing across his face, which I sensed didn't tend to admit much of that particular emotion. "Again."

CHAPTER THIRTY-ONE

Sienna

"The Federal Bureau of Investigation would like to thank you for your cooperation, Kevin," I said, smiling thinly and exiting the interrogation room as he seemed about ready to pee himself. He was shaking, and pale, and he looked really wrung out. Conversations with me had a way of doing that to you, I suppose.

Li waited until the door was closed before he hit the roof. "What the hell was all that?"

I'd stubbed out my last cigarette on the floor of the interrogation room almost twenty minutes ago, and I was already jonesing. "What was what?" I asked. Out of the corner of my eye, I could see his boss, the Assistant Special Agent in Charge of the Washington Office, Amanda Goldstein, walking toward us from the monitoring room. I'd only met Goldstein for about two seconds before we'd gone in, but she struck me as the sharp, capable, lawyerly sort. She was a shade under six feet tall and painfully thin, yet her handshake had suggested metahuman strength, something I hadn't pressed her on. That government servants were now taking the serum on the regular was an interesting development. Li's limp wrist suggested he hadn't climbed the ladder far enough to qualify for it, though.

"That was some good work," Goldstein said, cutting off Li before he could answer back. Or so I thought.

"You were practically baiting him into calling the Chinese government racist and xenophobic," he said. "And pushing him to say that this trigger man is ethnic Chinese."

"He was just giving you his opinion," I said. "It happens to be one I share, since it is the Chinese government that set this plan in motion, and they're not exactly multicultural. Don't let your western bias blind you to the way things operate in other parts of the world."

"You already have your mind made up that it's a Chinese man we're looking for," Li said. It was no mystery to me why he was taking personal offense at what he assumed my conclusion to be.

"I don't know that for a fact," I said. "We're working on building out a profile here, okay? It's *likely* our subject is ethnic Chinese, and he's *probably* a man, but that's hardly definite. It could be a white woman, okay? Does that make you feel better?" I tried to make it sound as patronizing as I could, because honestly – I had no time for Li to melt down about the fact that the Chinese government preferred ethnic Chinese for their spies. Sure, they'd take info from a black dwarf with a peg-leg, but that partially disabled midget's handler was going to be native Chinese, as sure as God made little green apples.

"You know why I ended up in Anchorage during the war?" Li asked, and the lashing tone of his voice suggested he'd lost emotional control. Which was fun. Mostly for me, but still.

"Your sparkling personality?" I asked, sharing a look with Goldstein, who was slightly grimacing.

"Because it was determined that my Chinese ancestry could suggest I had ties to our enemy," he said, and boy was the anger boiling off him. "It's *Korematsu* all over again; I'm surprised you didn't just round up anyone with a Chinese grandparent and ship them up there with me."

"I didn't send you up there," I said. "But I would have, if I'd known. Not because you're Chinese; I just don't like you."

"I'm sick of having my loyalty to this country questioned just because of my ethnic background," Li said. His face was positively glowing. But not in a positive way.

"Gosh, as a Jewish person, I wouldn't know what that's like," Goldstein said, perfectly deadpan with just a touch of acid.

"And as someone who's made it to the top of the FBI's Most Wanted list on at least two occasions that I know of, for occasionally unjustified reasons," I said, "I invite you to sit down and shut up, in the Alaskan snow. Let it soothe your butthurt, because we have a serious problem to deal with. If you want to cry about mistreatment, please do so elsewhere; I have an apocalypse to forestall."

"Speaking of," Goldstein said, "that was a good move, getting Kevin to roll on his colleagues."

"Yeah, it's almost like I've been doing this kind of thing since I was seventeen," I said, with more than a little deadpan of my own. "Next stop, Lily Chen."

"Thought you didn't want to talk to her," Li said, gruffly. Still not soothed. I was going to buy him a bottle of Vaseline and leave it on his desk. He'd know it was me, but it'd be worth it.

"Didn't you listen to Kevin? She's the one responsible for interfacing with other agents that came through," I said.

"He never said that," Li said, voice rising in annoyance.

"He didn't say it in quite so many words," I said, "but she was the contact that provided their fake documentation. If that's the case, she provided support to any other Chinese agents that may have passed through. Remember how he said she would leave for long periods sometimes, without explanation?"

"You think she was meeting with other spies during that time?" Goldstein's eyes were all wrinkled up at the corners as she concentrated on me.

"It's a non-zero possibility," I said, crumpling up my now-empty cigarette box.

"But that'd invalidate the cellular structure of the spy network," Li said. "If she gets caught, she's subject to rolling over on anyone she met."

"You mean like how she's sitting in our custody right now?" I asked. "Yes. That is the problem with a cell structure; what you gain in secrecy, you lose in efficiency. I think it's possible that someone in the Chinese government, with so much of the American intel and counterintel community wholly owned by them, made a decision – shrewd then, stupid now – to have Lily be a supporting player across multiple points of contact in their spy network in order to maximize their operational success."

"And in doing so, they may have screwed themselves completely," Li said.

"Well, their whole government already fell in an unrelated situation, so I doubt they much care," I said, pacing down the corridor to the next cell, where Lily Chen waited. Tossing the crumpled cigarette box in the trash, I stared at the door, priming myself. "But I suspect it's about to become a major problem for her."

CHAPTER THIRTY-TWO

Sienna

"Hello, Lily," I said, breezing into the next interrogation room. It was pretty standard; crappy wood table, a two-way window, and metal walls. The metal walls were an interesting touch; time was, before metahumans, no one would build holding cells with metal walls. Why bother? Waste of materials.

But ever since my battle in the sky over Minneapolis with Sovereign, smart law enforcement had begun to adapt to the fact that every day, more and more criminals had started to pick up superpowers. I'd read of dozens of cases of meta suspects that, left unattended, had tried punching their way out of interrogation rooms or holding cells.

None of that here, in FBI Headquarters. We were state of the art, with cameras monitoring our conversation that were so small, you couldn't see them. Inches of plate surrounding the walls. Tempered glass on the mirror that was strong enough it'd hold up to my punches – at least for a couple blows. And sensors on them so that if I touched it, alarms would go off bringing a host of guards down on our heads. A glance at the ceiling even revealed what appeared to be a secondary sprinkler head, twice what would be necessary in this space for a fire. That was probably a chemical gas dispenser, for use in case of emergency. Not a bad idea.

Lily didn't respond to my obvious goad. She was middle-aged, Chinese, but all done up in an American style. Her hair was short, pixie-ish, or mom-ish, depending on how you wanted to look at it. Her clothing was a bit dusty after our tussle, but at least she wasn't burned all over her body, like her associate.

Given how sour she was, though, you'd think I'd have burned her.

I pulled out the chair and spun it around, straddling it, Will Riker-style. God, when had I become a nerd? Wade and I had been watching *Star Trek: The Next Generation* on Netflix lately (his choice, but I did enjoy it). So I guess now-ish was the answer. "I don't blame you for not answering. Can you hear me all right?" I tapped my ear. "Did I bust your eardrum with my singing?"

She glared at me sufficiently to indicate that no, she wasn't deaf. In fact, she wasn't even badly hurt.

"Well, no harm, no foul, then," I said, parroting her words right back at her. She glared, but said nothing as I looked down at the file Goldstein had handed me before I'd come in. It was thin, just a basic dossier on her highs and lows. Born in Yorba Linda, California, June 12, 1985, lived there until she went to college at UC Santa Barbara, graduated Summa Cum Laude, at which point she went to work as a legislative aide to a congressman from San Fran. She'd traded up from Sacramento to DC a few years ago, and been spying here ever since. "So, did they get you in college or were you a loyal Chinese spy even before that?" I glanced up at her, looking for a reaction. The only one I got was from Li, who was orbiting behind her and sent me a look so sour it could have curdled fresh milk.

"I want my lawyer," Lily said.

"Your lawyer can't help you now – assuming you could even afford one, with your bank accounts seized," I said, concentrating very intently on random words on page three of the file.

"'If I cannot afford an attorney, one will be provided for me free of charge,'" she said, parroting the Miranda warning I'd said enough times I could write it by hand. While asleep. Underwater.

"Oh, no, that's absolutely true, if you were in serious trouble with the law, you could absolutely have a public defender," I said, looking up with a perfectly earnest expression. "Like if you were charged with a crime, for instance."

That gave her pause. "So I'm free to go, then?" she asked, with slight amusement. There was a wariness to it, though; she sensed a trap.

"You haven't been charged with anything," I said, gently closing the file, "but I think you're going to want me to charge you. And I think you're going to want to cooperate, wholeheartedly. I mean that. With every single bit of your heart."

She gave me a scoffing laugh. "Why? Because you're going to beat me?" She glanced at Li. "Here? In FBI Headquarters? In front of other agents?"

"Oh, no, I'm not going to harm a single hair on your head," I said, very self-serious. I even laced my fingers together in front of me, like the perfect student.

She bit. "Why, then, would I cooperate with you?"

"Because if you don't I'm going to walk you out of here – the FBI's going to release you, I mean – and I'm going to give you a ride just inside the gates of the Chinese embassy." I delivered every word carefully, almost dryly, without inflection. "And they're going to take you back to China, where you're going to be charged with aiding and abetting the old regime. Now, the new republic, being a somewhat democratic, reformed organization – they're going to give you a trial. But I think it'd be a stretch to call it a fair one, given what you're guilty of."

I slid a sheet of paper from the file – a transcript of what Kevin had said about their work together – across the table to her. "A copy of this is going to go with you." I cut to the chase, letting my finger roll down the page to one particular point of interest. "I suspect the republic is going to be very interested in this allegation. You know, the one where you abducted a Chinese expatriate and tortured them to death in the safe house, then disposed of their body in the Chesapeake? I believe she's related to one of the new Chinese ministers." I chuckled humorlessly. "Can you believe it? I guess dissidence runs in families. Kinda makes sense if you think about it."

Her facade of certainty had begun to crack. "You can't do that." But she didn't quite believe it.

"Why not?" I asked. "You're a person of interest to us, but you're not currently charged with anything."

"That's an allegation of murder," she said, voice rising. She couldn't help herself; her emotional control was slipping. "You have to charge me."

"I don't work for the government. I don't have to do shit," I said, smirking. "I do enjoy justice, though, and thinking of you in a Chinese prison, for that crime and...so many others," I made a show of splitting the pages of Kevin's confession, "well, that's gonna keep me warm at night. That, and thinking about you screaming as I drop you in the yard of the Chinese embassy and the guards haul you off to begin the longest years of your life."

"You can't do that." Rising voice, real panic setting in. She looked to Li for encouragement. "You can't let her do that."

Li just grunted. "As if I could stop her."

"See, the other way this can go," I said, "is we charge you here in America. You face trial here. You go into our penal system instead of being unceremoniously dropped into the custody of China."

"You can't do this," she said again, but it was different this time. She was on the verge of sobbing, which, for a woman of her emotional control, was practically akin to begging and kissing my feet while pleading for mercy.

"I'm a goddess, okay?" I just stared at her smokily, though I lacked the cigarette. "I can do whatever the hell I want."

She stared at me, and the beginnings of tears formed in her eyes. "What do you even want from me?"

"There's a Chinese agent loose in the country," I said. "A guy with his finger on the trigger of something big. Fen Liu's final revenge. I need to find him."

"I don't know him," she said, sounding earnestly ready to piss herself in fear. Thinking about going to a Chinese prison will do that to you. As my husband could attest. "I don't think."

"Kevin said you did some interfacing outside the cell," I said. "I need names. I need to know how the Chinese spies are trained. What kind of tradecraft they use. What kind of errors they might make. How they communicate with the homeland. How they communicated with you. Anything that could lead me to this guy."

"There's not that much I can give you," she said, pausing to chew on her lip. "We were insulated for a reason."

"Operational security, sure," I said. "But it wasn't perfect. You had contact with other Chinese spies. I want their names, cover and real. And I want to know how you talked to them."

"It's not that easy," she said, and real discomfort – pain, even – showed up on her face. "We made it difficult to prevent revelation in just this sort of instance."

I laughed. "You are still working for a government that fell months ago, one that's guilty of war crimes. Do you really want to be entombed along with them like some poor concubine of the first Qin emperor?"

"No," she said, shaking her head.

"How did you communicate with the spies you met?" I asked again, with a little more force.

"There's a messenger app," she said. "Peer to peer, phone to phone. But it won't do you any good; it's uncrackable. The encryption, I mean."

"We'll see about that," I said, and pulled out my own. Thumbing the button to dial Sierra, she answered in a second. "Chinese spies are communicating through a messenger app. What's it called?" I turned my attention to Lily.

"Recipe book," she said. "It poses as a recipe book for traditional Chinese recipes, but it has a payment system for cryptocurrencies and a messenger built in."

"Can you track that?" I asked, holding the phone up right about my chin.

"If given an example, I might be able to track it across the internet," Sierra said. "Lily, does your phone have the app installed?"

"Yes," she whispered.

"If you can open the phone to me, I can see what options are available for tracking and cracking it," Sierra said.

I looked at the two-way mirror. More of a statement than a question, that's what I sent through it. Then, to Lily, I said, "What's the passcode?"

"93872902," she said, head hung. She was the very picture of utter defeat.

"Numbers mean anything?"

"Randomly chosen," she said. "For security purposes."

The door beeped, and Goldstein entered, bearing a phone. She handed it off to me, and I repeated the numbers back to Lily while Goldstein hovered over my shoulder. When she confirmed them, I tapped it into the touchscreen.

I watched it open up – for just a second–

Then it went black.

"What the–?" Goldstein's head snapped up.

She was too late. And so was I.

"For China," Lily said, a dead look in her eye. There was a crunch from her mouth, and she tipped over in her chair, already spasming before she even hit the floor.

"No – no!" I shouted, sliding over the table and landing beside her. She was foaming at the mouth, choking, gasping, the poison from the false tooth she'd broken already coursing through her bloodstream.

"She's going into cardiac arrest!" Li shouted, voice echoing off the walls with a peculiar, ringing quality.

"The phone's dead!" Goldstein shouted.

I clamped a hand on Lily's neck. "You're not getting out of this that easy," I said, staring into her rapidly dilating pupils.

Ten seconds. That was all I needed.

Her pulse was almost nonexistent. Her breathing ended, simply, while I was standing over her, with one, last shallow breath.

But neural activity? The brain, at work?

That can continue many minutes after cardiovascular death.

My hands started to burn where they held fast against her neck and cheek, and there was a searing pain that was oh-sopleasurable at the site of our contact. It would have me uncomfortable — it always did — if I'd had time to really sit and consider it.

"She can't do this!" Li shouted, somewhere beyond the fog that had enveloped me as I plunged into the last vestiges of the soul and consciousness of Lily. "It's not going to be actionable in court."

"I'm not building a case," I said, letting the words drift out of me, though I couldn't see him. "I'm stopping a bomb from going off."

With that, I drifted into the mind, spirit, or soul of Lily.

And found myself in unceasing darkness.

CHAPTER THIRTY-THREE

Wade

"**M**oving into position. Rolling up in ten."

I was wearing an earpiece, and the voice crackled through it. This was old school, back to my days in Afghanistan, kicking down doors and pasting people who had earned it. Or bagging and dragging others who'd earned it, but should, in a totally righteous world, have just been shot dead and left for the carrion birds.

The van holding Miller's team skidded to a stop in front of the Chinese police station. Sure, it was a house – but it was also a police station from which soldier/cops of the former regime had threatened and intimidated Chinese expats with knowledge of what was being done to their families back in the homeland in their name.

For me, knowing this was a bonus. Because it made what I was about to do to the people inside this house righteous.

The house was a simple white clapboard, pulled through

time from the 1950's, when Los Angeles was an expanding, post-war boomtown. Sure, the lawns were less well-maintained, because the years had passed and the neighborhood had turned over to less and less conscientious owners, and you could see the wear creeping in at the edges in places like the windows, where hints of rot suggested replacement but the wallets of the owners had pushed back and said, "Wait," but if you squinted hard you could maybe see how it would have been to live here in 1956.

Except for the armed SWAT team swarming across the yard. That was new.

"On your six," David Miller said, his voice audible both because he was two feet behind me, and also in my ear, magnified by his throat mic. "Stacking up." I didn't have to turn to look to know he and his team were assembling themselves in a line in preparation for what was about to happen. They were pros, like me, forged in the fires of the Global War on Terrorism. They'd probably kicked down some of the same doors I had, in some of the same places.

"SWAT in position," came the voice of the LA SWAT leader in my ear. Same guys; we were all of a type.

"Kicking the door down in 3...2...1..." I said, and rocked the door with a metahuman kick that splintered solid wood and sent the door into the house.

"We have action at the back!" the voice kicked to life in my ear. Something exploded deeper in the house, only barely audible over the echoes of the door I'd just kicked in slamming down.

And then another sound – deeper – more terrifying.

Gunfire.

CHAPTER THIRTY-FOUR

Sienna

I'd leapt into the soul of Lily Chen as she plunged headlong into death. She'd choked out her last breath, her heart had come to a thudding halt before she'd even hit the floor of the interrogation room—

But the touch of my soul draining against hers was a process that slowed time's march.

Which was why I found myself in a very dark place, with my skin seeming to tingle with an unearthly chill.

It seemed to be some sort of Chinese temple. Very traditional, the kind the Communist Party had gone out of their way to demolish during the revolution. It was hard to believe how much cultural wreckage that organization had caused, how much of the rich, multi-thousand-year history of China had been utterly destroyed by a dedicated core of commies that functioned, as per usual, like trillions of termites in a wooden house.

I wouldn't wish a communist revolution on my worst enemy. Mostly because communist revolutions had a way of leading to the death of worst enemies, then turning around and devouring you, too. It had cost Cambodia a quarter of their population. In the Soviet Union, between 40 and 60 million.

In China, it had probably killed over a hundred million between the famines and the murders. And those that survived were not typically the most innocent, because surviving the horrors? The innocent didn't have what it took to make it through.

Strains of black fog seemed to fill the air, allowing me to see everything as if through a very dark filter, like some Instaphoto influencer was directing the scene and their only notion was, "Go darker! More sepia, less natural light."

"Lily?" I asked, slipping forward in the darkness. "Where are you?"

"This is my mind," her voice came like lightning out of the dark. "My temple."

"I give zero shits," I said. "Your body is dying. Your mind is next. The only thing holding you back from the abyss is me and my legendary forbearance."

She appeared out of the fog before a statue of Men Shen, both of whom I'd met. Didn't really look like them. "It is my temple. I am in control here." Reaching out, she crackled with lightning and loosed it on me, blue sparks flashing as they ran over my skin.

I screamed.

With laughter.

"Is that how you think this works?" I asked, dissipating her lightning as simply as waving it away. She tried again, and it rolled across my body, which didn't exist. Just like the lightning. "You're a Thor-type?"

She recoiled from me, trying one last time to inflict

damage to me with the only weapon she had. Yeah, the lightning. Certainly not her sparkling wit.

"Yeah, you're a Thor-type," I said, looking around for something more interesting than the idiot who'd just tried to hurt me in my own soul drain. "Is there any way for me to recover the data on your phone?"

"No," she said, sticking her chin out. "The passcode I gave you fried the system."

"This is what I get for playing nice," I said, cursing under my breath. "Well – no more Mrs. Nice Succubus. C'mere, loser – you're getting absorbed."

She recoiled again. "You can't–"

"Oh, but I can." As surely as if I had telekinetic powers, I reached out my hand and she was pulled to me with a scream. "See, I gave you a chance to cooperate. Yeah, it was tinged with a threat. But that's because you worked with a tyrannical dictator to destroy my country as well as your own, and enslave both our peoples. You were always going to be punished for pulling that, but I was trying to give you the easier of the two options on offer.

"But you had to go and make things...difficult," I said, my voice now coming out of me like thunder. I'd grown in the vision; or she'd shrunk, and she was now looking at me with far more terror than a dying person should have. After all, in a few short minutes, she'd be free of all this, and on to whatever comes next.

Unfortunately for her, in a soul drain, minutes could become eternity. And thanks to her lack of cooperation, I had nowhere else to be for the next few hours.

She screamed. I couldn't blame her; the pain I was inflicting was considerable. Probably less than she would have experienced in a lifetime in an American prison, certainly much less than in a Chinese one, but it would have been much more spread out.

This was concentrated pain, concentrated despair, freshly bottled from the emotions I had on hand.

And I drowned her in them.

Over and over.

For about ten thousand years, from her perspective.

"Your soul belongs to me," I whispered.

By the time I was done...there wasn't enough left of her will or spirit to disagree.

I snapped out of the soul drain back on the floor of the interrogation room. My knees were feeling the discomfort of being placed against hard concrete, and my eyes felt dry, as though I'd left them open for too long.

"She's gone," Li said. He was there beside me, hand next to mine on her throat, but careful to avoid contact. His eyes didn't suffer from the same problem, because he was hate-glaring me into the next county. "And we've got nothing."

"I wouldn't say nothing." I let lightning course over my fingertips, with a glow stronger than I'd ever been able to produce before. Before, I'd been able to give someone a hell of a headache if I had my hand right beside their skull.

Now...I could bring down a power grid or two.

"We lost access to the app," he said, "and her phone, and she's dead."

"She wasn't going to help us anyway," I said, floating back up to standing. "She was playing for time, trying to draw us out. She was always holding what she thought was her ace card."

He shook his head. "I warned you about the spies and their hollow teeth."

"Yeah, I guess I should have knocked out all their teeth," I said, letting the lightning dance between my fingers again. "But there may be something that Sierra can salvage from the phone. Furthermore, I have a list of names of spies she came in contact with in the course of her duties. I'm going to give them to Sierra, see what they can make of them."

Li hesitated, looking to Goldstein for advice. "None of this is actionable by us, do you understand that? The FBI is being rebuilt as an agency that follows the law. Because of what happened when China owned us. Do you get that? We have to rebuild trust, and that means due process. Civil rights. None of which are compatible with what you're doing here."

"I know," I said, drifting toward the door.

"Where the hell are you going?" Li asked.

"Why do you think Foreman brought me in?" I asked, pausing to look over my shoulder. "Do you think it's really just because of my people skills? My investigative abilities?" I turned to look him right in the eye. "It's because I am only concerned with saving lives and the world, and don't let the law get in my way. That's why; because he knew this wouldn't be the sort of thing that left behind a trail of people you could prosecute until you reach the trigger man.

"She left behind a trail of people I have to kill...until I get to the last man standing."

CHAPTER THIRTY-FIVE

Reed

I t took a little bit to climb the ladder. Webster was on the phone making calls for quite some time before we managed to get in to see a kindly gentleman with eyes of steely gray to match his hair. His office was upstairs from Webster's, and it looked well lived-in, as though he'd been here for quite some time. The bulletin board behind his desk had articles pinned on it from the seventies, and I think it's fair to say I liked Keith Stubbs immediately.

"...Of course, the streets have changed since those days," Stubbs said, after a brief story about Irish car bombs in the eighties that had spun off into three different, intriguing side stories before we'd reached this exit ramp. "But enough about that. What can I do for you lot today? The call made it sound important."

"It's about this body that showed up in pieces in South-wark," Webster said.

Stubbs nodded. "Heard about it. A bit rough, even for that neighborhood."

"We've been looking into it," I said, "and all the leads are pointing to a big group being behind it, and using it to send a message. So, I asked Webster here to get us in with you because I'm wondering...who are the big organized crime groups in town, and in England and the UK in general?"

Stubbs grunted. "A fair question. The short answer is we have more gangs and groups than you can shake a stick at. We've still got the basic, street level gangs of native British, and Irish, of course, that have been with us always or near to it. But in addition, we've picked up all the new ones, too: Pakistanis, Bangladeshis, Russian mafia – they're always a right gem to deal with – plus Ethiopians, Iraqis, Nigerians – and, well, you get the point. All of them have their territories, none of them take kindly to others crossing their lines." He hesitated, his big, bluff face undergoing a moment of contemplation. "But you asked about the biggest. Well, there's definitely a champion among them all, but you're coming at the wrong time to ask me about that, because it's just changed over and I have less idea than ever about what's going on in these streets." He got a far-off look in his eyes. "Gives me the sense the world might have left me behind and moved on. And it makes me want to take my pension and move to Cornwall."

"So you don't know who rules the streets these days?" Eilish asked.

He shook his head. "We know a touch about them. Whoever they are, they've asserted dominance over all the old ones. Metahuman powers seem to be involved, of course, though I doubt they're as bad as what you're dealing with across the pond." He opened his desk drawer and pulled out a bottle of something old, and along with it came a file. "We don't even have names for their players. Most of my old informants have either gone mum or washed up dead in the last six months." He popped the cork, and now I could smell a whisky that had been in a barrel for a long time before it came to rest in that bottle. "That's how I know it's time to move on – that and the fact I look at these photos after a life doing this and I don't know a single soul in them."

Sliding the file across the desk, he retrieved four glasses from the credenza behind him. "Join me?"

"Don't mind if I do," Webster said, closest to him and the file. He glanced at it, just for a moment, then slid it on to Eilish before taking up the offered glass. A finger of brown liquid rested at the bottom, and he gave it a sniff as he waited for the other glasses to go around.

"No clue about any of these," Eilish said, and slid the folder on to me, along with a glass.

I took up both, letting the folder fall open to a sheaf of pictures taken from a very high angle, looking down on the street. "My man who took those," Stubbs said, "was dead less than an hour later. Barely had time to upload them to me. Of course, in the old days, he would have died with the film on him, or with the pictures lost to whatever developer he'd left them with, so...here's to progress, I suppose." And he raised his glass.

Unfortunately, I dropped mine. Right on the desk, and it sent his priceless whisky...everywhere.

Because...I knew at least one of the people in the photo.

"Ah, don't worry about it," he said, dismissing my drop. "No broken glass, is there? I'll just top you off, then." And he stood to reach across the desk to refill me.

"I know this man," I said, staring down at the photo-graph, which had gotten just a few spots of liquor on it. Because at the center of the frame, and orbited by lackeys, was one central figure. Gray-haired, wearing a worn-out old tweed jacket, he could just as easily have been a bookseller on the Strand.

But he wasn't.

He was a mobster of the oldest of the old school.

"That old gent?" Stubbs asked. "You know him?"

"I do," I said, lifting the photo and pointing at him. "His name is Janus." I shook my head slowly. "And I bet I know who's running things in London these days, too, if Janus is in charge."

Under the desk, I texted: *Omega is back. Janus is in charge.*

Because this was not news that could afford to die with me.

CHAPTER THIRTY-SIX

Wade

The first gunshots rang out as I charged through the front door, David Miller's team behind me. I bypassed the first door I passed, and Miller swept in behind me with at least two of his guys. "Clear!" one of them shouted a moment later, confirming yes, there were no tangos in that space.

I was already moving through, because I knew LA SWAT had problems at the back door. They were supposed to be a bottle stop, keeping the trouble penned in so I could deal with it.

But our plan had sprung a leak, and now I was charging through a living room that was so spartan it may as well have been decorated by a twenty-two-year-old frat guy without a dime to his name.

No, scratch that. The frat guy would have at least had some sort of décor up on the walls, even if it was beer themed. This place had nothing save one old overstuffed, creamy beige couch that looked fresh out of the seventies, and a folding chair that looked like it might have seen action during the Civil War. Across the room was a large archway that led to a dining area, and beyond it, a sliding glass door that had been shattered.

Beyond that, screams. Screams that were bleeding through on my earpiece.

"We got one in the second bedroom!" Miller exulted over the radio. "Down and bound!"

"Another in the third bedroom!" came one of his team's voices. "Put your hands in the air, get down on your knees! Restraining now!"

They had it all under control in here.

But out back...the screams were dying. And so were the LAPD SWAT team, judging by the sound.

I came flying out of the shattered sliding door and found a half-dozen SWAT guys pinned to the ground. There was blood, certainly, but not as much as I might have anticipated. The backyard was a tightly hewn space, bounded by a weather-beaten wooden fence that hadn't been replaced in over a decade (and needed it, desperately).

"Three tangos, they went that way!" one of the SWAT guys said, jerking spasmodically from his place on the patio. He pointed to a spot where there was a hole in the fence, as if a truck had barreled through. That I could have guessed they went this way seemed unhelpful, so I didn't say it. "Somehow they pinned us all to the ground!" he shouted at my back as I flew by. Literally flew; I wasn't going to try and catch up to fleeing metas on foot.

I had a suspicion about the pinning effect. It was a smart move, and explained the lack of blood: one of the Chinese agents probably had powers like Staten Island's own super-hero, Gravity. I wasn't entirely clear on how those worked –

something about creating gravity channels that could pin people or objects to surfaces – but I knew it allowed her to basically fly, which meant my own flight capabilities were going to come in very handy if one of these three had it.

Or so I thought. Until something grabbed me by the foot and yanked me down, hard.

I crashed into the fence just a few feet from where it had already been shattered, busting another channel into it and breaking a couple ribs at the same time. I doubled over as I hit the ground, trying to shield myself from further bone breakage.

It didn't help.

My upper body landed on the concrete alley, and my left arm snapped at the elbow and forearm while my knees collided with the slightly softer earth. I'd been ripped out of the sky like a giant had seized me from about twenty feet up, but the fall felt much worse than that.

It had me rolling in agony, but my foot was still tightly gripped by whatever had brought me down. A gravity channel, I dimly realized, through the haze of pain.

Something moved above me, and I looked, out of self-preservation. A woman loomed there, thin, her hands extended at her sides oddly.

And from them I could see extensions out of her fingertips like claws.

Just before she sank one of them into my chest.

CHAPTER THIRTY-SEVEN

Sienna

"You get all that?" I asked, into my phone, as I exited the elevator in FBI Headquarters. I was hoping to hit the street before Kaddie Katy Lane or one of her servants caught up to me to pull me into a twelve-hour compliance and standards meeting or some such shit.

"We have the data, and some starting points," said Sierra. I'd read out the list of Chinese spies in the elevator, meta-low, as we moved between floors and took on passengers. "Of the fifty-two spies you named, twenty-four are confirmed captured here in the US, eleven in China."

"That leaves a lot still at liberty," I said.

"I have entry records for a further six in China," Sierra said. "Turning over this data now to Chinese authorities. I have also discovered the current whereabouts of a further eight here in the US. They are scattered across the country,

but seemingly located in places of political or military impor-
tance. All coincide with either a defense contractor, or are
here in DC."

"There are spies still here in DC?" I asked.

"Two," Sierra said. "The nearest is six blocks, at a mall,
heading for a vehicle that I believe is theirs, across the
street."

"Nifty," I said, hitting the door and lifting off instantly.
"Let's go have a chat with them."

"The subject in question is Andrew Huang, 38 years old,
Chinese/American dual citizen. Born in Los Angeles to
parents who were both Chinese citizens – and highly ranked
members of the Chinese Communist Party."

I grunted. That wasn't uncommon; for years, Chinese
elites had been traveling to America in the last month or so
of pregnancies so they could give birth in the US and snag
dual citizenship for their princelings. I found it annoying on a
deep level – not to mention a national security concern, since
these people were raised in China to loyal party officials, and
theoretically could go their whole lives without setting foot
in America again, yet still be considered citizens – but since
I'd passed on creating a dictatorship of the goddess when I
had a chance, there wasn't much I could do about it at this
point.

"Get local authorities after the other spies," I said. "Or
pass it along to Candy Cane Lane."

Sierra hesitated only a moment at my joke. "You mean
FBI Director Lane."

"Probably," I said. "But I like Candy Cane Lane better. It
makes her sound like a happy place from a child's board
game, rather than what she is: an interminable pain in my
neck."

"Actually," Sierra said, "it makes her sound like a Christ-
mas-themed stripper. Or the title of a Hallmark movie."

I raised an eyebrow at that as I started to descend over the mall. "You're getting better at humor, Sierra."

"One o'clock," Sierra said. "Green jacket. Walking toward the silver Mazda Miata."

I spotted the person Sierra was talking about almost instantly thanks to her description. The street was somewhat crowded, so it wasn't made especially easy by anything but her precision. People were already pointing me out as I came down, some shouting ensued, and there was not a lot of doubt as to who I was targeting.

Which is why the man in the green jacket turned and saw me. His mouth gaped open, but only for a moment. Then he reached inside his coat—

I was ready for a gun; he'd pull it, I'd Faerie web him, slam into him, disarm him, and we'd have a nice chat. He was going for it, I sped up, my fingertips began to glow with the light web, and we were fated to collide in mere seconds.

Except instead of pulling a gun, he exploded in a shower of blood, bone, and a compression shockwave that swatted me out of the air as if I'd been hit by an SR-71 going at top speed.

I landed across the street in the park, head smacked against a tree. My hearing cut out, but began to come back in fits and starts, and with it came the blaring of car alarms.

Pain lanced up and down my side. I'd broken something, and I set my Wolfe healing to putting it right. Seconds later, I was able to lift my head...

...Which is when I found the row of cars on fire, and the spy's Miata reduced to a crater. The two cars it had been sandwiched between were destroyed, as if a wrecking ball had been dropped on the hood and trunk of each, respectively. The sidewalk behind the cars was strewn with wreckage and — I realized too late — at least a few bodies. The building behind that was missing a chunk of the brick facade at least a hundred feet long. The brownstones there were just...gone.

As if a bomb had gone off.

Because one had.

The Chinese spy had suicided, and taken half a city block of DC with him.

CHAPTER THIRTY-EIGHT

Wade

The Chinese meta sunk her claw blades – about an inch long, and sharp as a dagger – into my chest, I thought.

Then the pain started, and I realized she'd gone for the gut.

"I will tear the heart out of you," she hissed in Mandarin, adding a few more unkind words for me specifically as she buried her fingers in my belly and flexed them, doing maximum damage for minimal effort as I writhed.

For those keeping score, I had (at least) a broken arm, and was now partially disemboweled.

Yes, poor baby, I know. Sienna has been through so much worse. Even more idiotic, I'd absorbed a bit of Fen Liu's soul, and gotten both Wolfe and Achilles powers in the process. I should have been holding onto the latter as I charged into this, and had the former ready to rock just in case the first failed.

I did neither. As they say, no plan survives contact with the enemy, and in this case, the thought of them both fled as close to the most agonizing feeling I'd ever felt flooded through my brain, making my every nerve ending scream and banishing reason.

The Chinese meta's face was about six inches from mine. Which was strange, because she felt about a million miles away, rather than intimately close.

It took my pain-addled mind a moment to make that connection. She batted the gun out of my hand, disarming me, though it fell behind me, still secured to me via a strap. Over her shoulder, battling through my tunnel vision, I could see a man who seemed to be composed entirely of shining steel, and another who had his hands out like he was trying to compel traffic to stop.

A steelskin and my gravity trapper, I presumed, though I could barely form a thought through the pain. And when I did form a thought, it was related to the pain, and the cause thereof.

So I lifted my – now empty – gun hand up below the claw lady's throat–

And a green blast of energy shot through her neck, throat, and spine, ripping through and leaving her head connected to her body by little more than two flaps of skin on either side of her neck.

"Ah!" the gravity guy said, making a very guttural sound deep in his throat as her body collapsed onto me. One of her head's tethers lost its grip in the fall and butted me in the chest on the way down, causing a roiling torrent of agony to bloom farther up my body. It delayed my next move a moment, which was to default to a power that came right to me, and I whipped my right hand around like a cowboy throwing a lasso, concentrating–

A spark of white light emerged from my palm and snaked out as I threw it, sending an energy whip at gravity boy. He really did look like a boy; young, fresh-faced, barely eighteen – or just had the look of youth. Either could be possible; he was probably PLA, and they did start their soldiers young.

I'd been practicing with my energy whips on the beaches of Greece; this came second nature to me now, and it snaked its white tip around his throat as he made another startled noise. Closing the loop, I made the ends join together, and it crackled as I gave it a hard yank.

That took him off his feet with another startled cry, and his hands were gripping the whip, trying to get it off his throat, so he couldn't prevent himself from landing on the pavement face-first. I heard a grand crack and saw blood fountain from his nose. I also felt the tight grip on my foot subside, and knew I was free, at least for the moment.

My next big problem was the man of steel stomping toward me. I couldn't be entirely sure, but based on the thudding sound he was making with every step, I believed his turn to steel had increased his body mass, because otherwise he was way too slight to be making that much impact.

He also seemed quite intent on placing one of those feet on me. Probably somewhere I'd really object to, like my head. Not for long, because he'd cave in my skull and dash my brains out all over the alley, but I'd object.

In fact, I decided to do so now, before he had a chance to crush me.

From my left hand – dangling at the end of a broken wrist, and screaming protest at its ill treatment – I produced a beam of purple energy and aimed it at his leg. I was a little clumsy from all the pain, so it went low, hitting him in the pelvis just shy of his left hip.

He didn't seem to notice it at first, the purple energy beam diffusing across his steely skin as he kept coming, step by step, wading through it.

However, he did notice when it tore through his leg and chopped him down like a tree.

The landing was epic, and I felt it in my bones, like someone had downed a redwood. His head landed next to me, and he howled. Through it, however, he managed to lock eyes with me, and in addition to being in pain, I could see he was *mad*.

He gripped the pavement with a hand, and it crunched under his grip. Pulling himself toward me, I could read the murderous intent in his eyes.

The son of a bitch was going to claw his way over to me. Then he was going to pop me like a balloon.

Not wanting anything to do with his grand plans, I employed the only means to keep him away that I could.

I locked onto his steel skin with my Magneto powers, and pushed.

The problem with that was I didn't have any leverage. I was lying in a clump, right hand bound by a white energy whip to the gravity boy, my other arm was broken, and my guts were exposed to the balmy SoCal air. It was not an optimal position from which to fight a steel being who – conservatively – had six times my mass, and invulnerable skin. When I pushed against him with my magnetic powers, he didn't move.

But I did.

I slid backward, bumping my broken arm and disturbing my already in-an-uproar bowels, some of which trailed behind me like a snake slithering along. I also dragged gravity boy along for the ride, gagging and choking because my energy whip was scorching his throat. I shortened his tether as he flailed wildly, hemorrhaging face catching a broken section of the fence, which did nothing for his consciousness nor his blood loss.

"I'm going to kill you!" the steel man said in Mandarin, his voice hitting the levels of blinding rage. I managed to open the distance between us, and he must have felt the push as I slid across the yard.

"You're gonna...have to catch me first," I said, oozing blood from my lips. Where had it come from? An injury to my mouth? From deep within my guts? Who knew? I'd work that out later.

First, I had to make sure there *was* a later.

How was I going to do that? Well, popping his head off with a purple beam seemed like the optimal course, if I could muster the focus to do so.

Just as I raised my hand to do it, another shock of pain ran through me from the motion, and I wavered. The purple beam instead clawed its way through a still-standing segment of fence, and through the old Buick parked on the alley behind it.

Whoops. Really dropped the Kelly Blue Book value on that one.

My would-be murderer seemed to get wise, and shifted his skin from metal to rubber. I lost my grip on him immediately and quit sliding.

He, for his part, seemed to leap up, with perfect balance, onto his one leg, and then fling himself toward me. It was like watching some sort of cartoon snake, or Tigger from *Winnie the Pooh* bouncing about on his tail.

In the face of this – gutted, an arm broken and half-useless, the other bound to another assailant with a tether of crackling energy – I was not possessed of a surplus of great options. I was fried, my adrenaline in overdrive, my body shutting down from the shock and trauma. My brain moved in slow motion, and my body responded even slower.

Which is why I'm not sure how I did what I did, but I suspect it had something to do with Hell Week from my SEAL training, where being pushed to the limits of exhaustion and sleeplessness produced very similar results.

I disconnected the energy tether to gravity boy, but only after giving it one last yank to raise my hand up. I got it pointed at the leaping (now) rubber man, who was committed to his course, unable to change direction. Several hundred pounds of black rubber were now in flight, at me, physics in motion, and unstoppable unless acted upon by another force.

I could fly, though, and that produced force.

Whipping a flashing white energy lash around his throat was easy; tightening it as I lifted off was a cinch.

Doing a flying somersault with my guts hanging out and my consciousness waning? That was a little tougher.

He, slave to his own momentum, managed no such thing.

I avoided crashing as I turned a hard loop, somersaulting in midair. The energy whip came out from me like a spoke from a wheel. Less than six feet in length, it was just long enough to keep him out of reach of me as I whipped around, the world's fastest Ferris wheel.

The rubber man flew along, gripped by the neck, in a hard arc. He ground against the earth on the bottom part of the arc, managed to chip his face against the gutters on the upswing, kissed the sky as I let the energy lash grow from six feet to twenty as he came up and around.

Then he slammed, face-first, into the concrete alley, shattering pavement and bouncing a full six feet into the air before he came back down.

As a human, all covered in flesh. Because I had, as Chris Tucker would say, knocked him the eff out.

I hung in the air for less than a second before I dropped. First by a foot, then by more, a puppet with his strings cut. I was fading quick, and these two were still, nominally, threats to my life, in spite of the fact that gravity boy was whimpering and choking smoke, and the rubber band-less man was out cold on the alley floor.

But I couldn't trust they'd both remain out of the fight. That was a fool's errand, and a good way to get killed. I came down in a lurching crash between them, and sent out whips from either arm, lashing them each around the neck. That minor task accomplished, I did the next.

I shortened the lashes.

That hurt. I was the binding agent, the thing holding the two of them together. It was then that I remembered I had Hades powers at my fingertips, and started to employ them. The burning started a few seconds later.

I barely even felt it as their souls passed into mine, and I threw them into the pits of torment in the dark, back end of my mind before collapsing into blissful unconsciousness to the sounds of David Miller and his troops arriving on the scene, all thought of healing myself lost in the weariness of my injuries.

CHAPTER THIRTY-NINE

Reed

"Dammit, I should have known," I said, letting out a few choice curses under my breath. We were already back down the elevator, out of Stubb's office. The whisky was churning in my guts, my mind was spinning with the news, and I could tell I hadn't eaten much today.

"I've heard of Omega, and even sort of dealt with them once," Webster said, fanning out the tail of his coat as he sat down in the conference room. Outside the window, the bullpen was pretty close to empty; it was a skeleton crew this time of night, and most of those on this shift were probably out at crime scenes or something. "But it's been a few years since I did any serious study of Sienna-ology – for the health of my marriage, you understand – so any chance you can bring me up to speed with a recap? Other than 'they're bad guys'?"

"Bad, yes. Omega was the bane of my existence," I said

bitterly. "I've been chasing them since I was eighteen, maybe before if you want to count informal hate lessons from my father going back to...well, as early as I can remember. See, Omega is an organization of metahumans that stretches back to the old gods of Greece."

"What an august company of dead people that must include," Eilish said.

"It certainly has over the years," I said. "Zeus himself sat at the top of their org chart in the days when they exercised direct control over the Roman Empire, and the Greeks before that. As time passed, though, they became subtler in their ways of controlling humanity, and stuck more to the shadows."

"Why?" Webster asked.

I shared a look with Eilish, who shrugged. She'd been raised in a cloister in Ireland that hadn't survived the wrath of Sovereign, but it felt to me like maybe even she didn't know the history of metahumans that I was dealing out here. "Because of technology," I said. "Metahumans are nearly unstoppable on a battlefield against guys with spears and bows. I can blow those right out of the air if you throw them at me," I sent a rush of wind around the room, "or just sweep your whole front line into the spears of the guys behind them.

"But...when you introduce the crossbow," I said, "that's harder for me to stop. And when you start throwing in muskets and cannons, metahumans begin to get outmatched. See, ancient battlefields had metahumans on them. They countered each other; if you had a meta on your side, and your enemies didn't – you win the day."

"I imagine machine guns and artillery completely upended metahuman dominance on the battlefield, then," Webster said.

"That'd be World War I, yes," I said. "Chemical weapons. Artillery. Tanks. Warfare's technological advance turned the battlefields into nightmares, zones of destruction even the heartiest meta couldn't hope to survive. Our retreat from the world was already well in progress before that, but World War I was the catalyst that made the last of us go into hiding."

"All the magic went out of the world," Eilish said softly. When we looked at her, she added, "or so me mam said."

"It's as good an explanation as any," I said. "When these old gods realized they couldn't control directly anymore, they didn't just turn into hermits and go into retirement." I paused, thinking of Odin and Hades, probably on some golf course in Florida. "Well, most didn't. They went underground and formed...organized crime syndicates, for lack of a better word."

"And that's Omega?" Webster asked.

"That's Omega," I said, with loathing. "They were kings of the criminal underworld in London and across Europe when I was growing up. They used a delicate touch, front companies, intermediaries, but they controlled vice and graft across the continent. They had their hands in every dirty pie you can imagine – all the way up until–"

"Sienna?" Webster asked.

"Not quite," I said. "Sovereign."

"Ah," Webster said.

"When Sovereign rose, he did so with the intention of bringing down the old order," I said. "Omega was at the top of his list. Right behind them was Alpha – my old organization."

Eilish tittered. "Really?"

"I didn't name them," I said, "but they were set up in opposition to Omega. My father was part of Alpha, and he worked his whole life to try and bring them down and protect humanity – all the way up until Sovereign killed him."

"I'm guessing Sovereign didn't finish the job on Omega,"

Webster said, and in his hand was one of the photos of Janus, given to him by Stubbs. "Given this old bloke's still kicking."

That caused me almost physical pain. "Janus joined up with us after most of Omega died, and helped take down Sovereign. After that he came back to London, and Sienna said he was setting up Omega again. I guess we all hoped he'd take them down the path of a legit business. A few years ago, Sienna had to deal with some criminals – metahumans, of course – who said they were from a new expansion of Omega, setting up in Minneapolis."

"So you knew Omega was back?" Webster raised an eyebrow.

"We knew they existed still on some level," I said. "But Sienna killed those guys in the Minneapolis incident, and we hadn't run across any others. Out of sight, out of mind, y'know?" I looked down at the photo of Janus and had so very many thoughts about leopards and spots, and adages that were cliches because they were true. "Also, I don't think we really wanted to contemplate taking down Janus if we didn't have to. Call it old loyalties, but going after people who were clinch players in the war against Sovereign causes a little ulcer to form in my belly."

"I remember the old gent now," Webster said, doing some staring of his own at the photo. "Last time Sienna was here, someone was wiping him and his old affiliates out – in the most violent way possible. As I recall, there was some money on the line then."

"The hard-grifted assets of old Omega," I said, nodding.

"That was a significant pile of money, then and now," Webster said. "And it just disappeared into a foreign bank account. You think they managed to get their hands back on it?"

I'm pretty sure I reddened, but tried to control my reaction since I knew that no, they had not: Sienna had gotten her hands on that money, and used it to fund a variety of things, including the war with China and the agency we still worked for. "Doesn't matter, ultimately. However they did it, they rebuilt, and they've got rackets aplenty to fund them now."

"And they're dropping bodies," Eilish said. "Trying to make an example of someone, or send a message." She looked at me. "You'd think if this Janus lad is smart, he'd know the authorities would call in assistance of our kind the moment they realized this was a metahuman incident."

"Janus is as smart as they come," I said. "I'm sure the possibility at least crossed his mind – if it wasn't actually his aim." That made me frown, deeply; I really hoped he hadn't intended for this to draw me over here, that my arrival on this case had been a fly in his ointment rather than his intention. Being trouble for him seemed like a lot better place to be than in his sights. "That's all worrisome."

"The sweep of possibilities there?" Eilish asked.

"Yeah," I said. "Because if it's true he anticipated this response, then either he wanted me – or someone from our agency over here – or he was willing to accept it as the price of doing what he did. The latter is mildly vexing, the former is...really concerning."

"It means he'll have a plan to deal with us," Eilish said. "Doesn't it?"

I was left with little to do but nod. "And in spite of our affinity for him, Janus has been around for a long time...and he didn't get that old or to the top of the criminal underworld by doing things half-assed...or mercifully."

CHAPTER FORTY

Sienna

I'd been in the midst of a few disasters in my time. I'd even been at the site of some bombings. One in New York City stood out to me in vivid detail.

But I couldn't recall ever quite seeing anything like this.

There were pieces of people...*everywhere*.

A couple dozen were seriously, dramatically injured. After I'd gotten to my feet, I'd done as much as I could for them – using Persephone healing powers I'd picked up a bit ago from a Chinese meta. It was a delicate balancing act, being a succubus and tapping Persephone abilities. Using them didn't nullify my soul drain, but spreading the use around like I did also meant that no one got the full effect. I healed critical injuries, stabilized people, and hoped for the best.

It still left me all tapped out by the time I was done, though.

"Those things will kill you, you know," said an EMT as he

went by. I was smoking again, on the back bumper of a fire truck. I'd bummed a few from a fireman who'd taken pity on me. They were not nearly as rough as the ones I'd picked up from the Chinese agent earlier.

"Like I'll live long enough for them to do the job," I said, but he was already gone, vanished into the chaotic scene, disappearing between the fire trucks and ambulances and cop cars.

Putting my head against the fire truck's back. I closed my eyes and tried to let the cigarette smoke blot out the smell of death and gore all around me.

It didn't work.

Someone sat down on the truck beside me; a light presence, deft, far too small to be human.

I cracked an eye to look.

A raven stared back at me, its head cocked, as if regarding me with a question in mind.

I exhaled a plume of smoke as I stared down at it. "Got a message for me, big guy?"

"I'd tell you to call grandma," the raven said, "but your phone's being monitored, so don't. And I'd tell you to dreamwalk, but I doubt you'll be sleeping for a while."

"Only the sleep of the heavily drugged," I said, wondering if I was talking to Lethe through Odin, or talking to Odin repeating Lethe's words to me. The effect would be roughly the same, unless Odin decided to get creative as the interpreter. "There's a crisis."

"Naturally."

"Any chance you want to give me a preview of what you want to chat about?" I asked, looking over all the destruction I'd wrought. "Or would that be too much information for an unsecured convo?"

"I just wanted to know if you were all right," came the reply, putting to rest any doubts I had. This was my grandmother, speaking somehow through the raven. How, I had no idea. Odin's powers, though nominally the same as my Warmind, seemed somehow deeper and stronger. I always chalked it up to experience, mostly because when I'd asked him if he had anything he could teach me in regards to using it more forcefully, he'd always demurred. "But I see you're pretty far from that, at the moment."

"There is, indeed, some distance between me and the optimal scenario," I said, head back, staring up at the darkening sky. "Yesterday I could walk in the surf, toes in the white sand, not responsible for anyone or anything save for me, my dogs, my kitty, and my husband. Today I'm responsible for..." I looked at the ruin around me. "...everything, again, it would seem."

The raven was quiet for a moment. "Back to real life for less than a day and you're already drowning in self pity?"

"Oh, up yours," I said. "Do you see this?"

"Yes," she said. "I see you, too. Pitiful. As in full of self-pity, not as in you should be an object of it. Look, you messed up. This is high stakes, okay? That happens sometimes, and the consequences are brutal."

I watched a firefighter walk by with a singed and shredded umbrella stroller dangling from his grip. "You may be understating it."

"Is whatever you're trying to stop going to be worse than this?"

I opened my eyes to thin slits. "Probably, yeah."

There was a flutter, and the raven was on my shoulder. "Then get off your ass and get back to work," the bird said, directly into my ear before giving it a nip that made me shrug him off. "And call me when you're able."

"Why?" I asked. "Is there a party going on?"

"Not yet," she said. "Just call me later. Not urgent. I want to check in on you."

"Fine," I said, and took a drag from the cigarette.

The raven grabbed the cigarette out of my hand and flew off with it in its beak.

I stared up at it in shock before shouting, "I have five more!" at its receding back. "Gonna get a whole pack later. Maybe a carton, when I get out of this shitty tax-your-ass district."

But I didn't light up one of my remaining cigarettes.

I got up off my ass and got back to work.

CHAPTER FORTY-ONE

"What was the source of the explosion?"

I asked this question of Kaddie Lane, who was at the scene, scowling, and didn't notice my approach. I was absolutely stealthy when I was hovering and there was a fair amount of noise around us. When she noticed me, though, it didn't help with the answer. For instead of just scowling lightly at the air, she turned to scowl heavily at me. And with a stony silence.

"Where did the explosion come from?" I asked, wondering if I'd have to do this a third time. It didn't seem sporting to threaten the FBI Director my first day back in civilization.

"Don't you know?" she asked. "You were here for it."

"I was here for it in the sense that I got tossed across the street into a tree," I said. "All I saw was my subject reached into his jacket, presumably for a detonator, and then boom – I woke up minutes later." That wasn't entirely it, but I certainly didn't have any idea whether he'd exploded, the car had exploded, or both had gone off at the same time. For all I knew, there had been a bomb hidden in the building behind him.

Lane gave me a long moment of silent, glaring contemplation, probably wondering if she'd be better off shooting me dead in the street right here and now. It wasn't the first time I'd brought out that question in the people I worked for. "It was in the trunk." She hesitated, and seemed to almost want to say more, though it might have been an insult she held back. Instead, once she got control of herself, she added, "How did you find this subject?"

"It was on a list of spies we pieced together from a lead from Lily Chen," I said. "You should have gotten a copy."

"I did, just before I left to come here." She stuck a narrow finger in my face. "Do not go after any more of them yourself."

I laughed in her face. "How would this have gone differently if you'd sent your agents in instead? Huh? Other than you'd be holding multiple funerals to honor your fallen dead? You're welcome for that, by the way."

Lane's eyes blazed. "Excuse me?"

"Sorry, let me say this again for the cheap seats: the dude blew up, suicide-bomber style." I was in no mood, and that was a dangerous place to be. "That's a new one, at least from Chinese spies. Did you anticipate that? Because I will admit, gooberous moron I am, I did not see that coming. Cyanide capsule in a false tooth; wow, but within the realm of possibility. But a suicide bomb?" I shook my head. "If you'd sent in HRT or some other form of SWAT, they'd have gone boom like me – except without the capacity to shrug it off. Since you don't have to spend the next week attending a circuit of the funerals of your employees, you're welcome."

"I might prefer that," she said icily, "since instead, we have a street full of civilian casualties with no law enforcement losses we can point to as having sacrificed themselves in the line of duty."

"Dear God, I hope you don't mean that," I said, folding my arms across my chest. "Because – man, it's weird I have to say this, but throwing your agents' lives away to give you political cover and sympathy to insulate you from criticism for something going wildly off the rails and killing a bunch of people – well, that is a shitty thing to root for."

Her eyes blazed. "Who else is going to take the blame for this one?"

"Me, I assume," I said. "Like every other time something goes terribly wrong and there's no comfortable explanation. Eden Prairie ring any bells for you? Gerry Harmon? Minneapolis? I hear the survivors of that one are still suffering PTSD from the time-skipping memory-bleed effects."

She stared at me with a very subtle smile. "And you're just going to take responsibility?"

I laughed, but it was rueful. "Responsibility and blame feel like two sides of the same coin, and I suspect it's sitting in my pocket as we speak. So, yeah, I'll take it. How many dead? And how many wounded?"

"Eighteen dead," she said. "Fifty-nine wounded, twenty-two critically. Some are—"

"I don't want to think about it right now," I said, shaking my head. "What's your plan for bringing in the rest of that list?"

"Bomb squad," she said. "Locate their cars ahead of time, contain the scene. Don't enter their houses until they're fully swept. Departments across the country are already working on that, including the one across town."

"No sign of any more kabooms?"

"Not as of yet," she said, back to icy.

"Great," I said, lifting off a couple feet. "I'm gonna go check out the one across town, see if they need any help."

She locked eyes with me in the air. "Maybe you should take a step back."

"I was pretty damned far back before you came and dragged me off the island," I said, and once more, I could tell by her face that that hadn't been her call, so I decided to really rub in the salt, see what it got me. Or I was just being ornery. "You're welcome for that, too."

Her eye twitched as she scowled at me. "Wasn't my call to bring you back. If it was up to me—"

"Oh, I know you'd have left me there until my bones bleached in the sun," I said. "But think of it this way – I've made more progress on this case in six hours than you have in a week."

And with that I flew off, steaming, and hoping I'd at least nettled her as bad as she'd nettled me.

CHAPTER FORTY-TWO

Wade

I woke in the hospital, and there wasn't a soul around me. The beep of the monitors told me I was alive, if the breathing, the waking, and the residual pain hadn't done so already. I opened my eyes and saw the faint light of the waning sun through a window.

Not a soul was anywhere around me. The door to the corridor was open, and my belongings were stuffed in a plastic bag on the rolling tray in front of me. My cell phone looked little the worse for the beating I'd taken, and I fumbled around the IV tubes to retrieve it. Once it was in hand I dialed the first number that came up, and was rewarded with the slightly mechanical voice of the mother-in-law I'd never had a chance to meet: "Wade? Are you all right?"

"I've had better days," I said, clutching the phone to my ear with my shoulder while I ripped the IV needle out of my hand. It pinched a little, and I used the gauze that was already there to staunch the bleeding. Tapping my Wolfe type, the wound closed in a second. All the other pains did, too, in the next moments. "I take it you were watching what happened?"

"Through the body cameras of both Miller's team and LAPD SWAT, yes."

"Did you tell Sienna what happened?" I paused. The answer to this was going to be important.

"I have not had a chance as yet," Sierra said. "She has had…troubles of her own."

That set the heart monitor to beeping a little more frequently. "Is she okay?"

"She's fine," Sierra said, and I got the sense that the answer wasn't that far off from what my wife would have said if she'd been speaking to me herself. "But an encounter with a Chinese spy turned near-fatal when he triggered a suicide bomb in the trunk of his car."

"What?" That dropped my jaw. "A Chinese spy went full Hamas?"

"So it would seem."

That was a significant escalation. "But Sienna's fine?"

"She is. Currently, she is en route to another spy that the FBI is setting up to detain."

"I hope she doesn't lead with her face on this one," I said, ripping off the heart monitor. It flatlined, causing – to my surprise – an utter lack of response from the nurses' station out in the hall.

"How did you know she led with her face last time?" Sierra asked.

"Just a suspicion," I said, throwing my legs over the edge of the bed. Looking around, there was no sign of my clothes. "Shit. I bet they cut off my clothes."

"That is likely, since you were brought in to the emergency room."

I frowned. This wasn't my first time being brought in for medical treatment and having my clothes cut off. It was, however, the first time I'd been in a place where a replacement wasn't readily available. That was one thing about the military; if you were on a base, you were never far from a change of clothing, even if it didn't fit quite right.

"There is a clothing store less than a block away, and I have enabled payment systems on your phone."

"Dynamite," I said.

A nurse stuck her head in just then, looked me up and down once, and nodded. "Checking out?"

"Yeah," I said, finally clear of all the entangling tubes and wires. "I take it you were anticipating that?"

She shrugged. "Your chart said metahuman, and your vitals improved by leaps and bounds just from the time you got to the ER to when you got turfed to our service. They made a call to skip the ICU before you even rolled out of the elevator."

"It does come in handy," I said, striding over to her, plastic bag with the last of my belongings dangling from my hand. "Thanks for taking care of me."

She snorted; this was a woman who'd done this job for a long time. "Wasn't much to it, but you're welcome." She inclined her head down the hall. "Elevator's that way."

I smiled. "Where's the stairs to the roof?"

She rolled her eyes and sighed. "You know you've got a hospital gown on, right? Not like there aren't folks around who wouldn't admire the view if you fly off, but maybe get some pants, first?"

Typical nurse; if she'd seen one, she'd seen them all. "Fair enough," I said, and followed her guidance to the elevator. I'd buy some clothes and then take flight.

And based on the info I'd ripped out of the souls of those Chinese agents...I had a least a couple places I wanted to probe.

CHAPTER FORTY-THREE

Sienna

One of these days, I'm going to learn to be patient. I'm going to learn to stop approaching every problem as though it's a concrete wall, to be plowed through with my fists of...well, I was gonna say iron, but they really are flesh and bone. And I've certainly used them to bust up concrete a few times.

The thing is...my hands heal from that, in less than ten seconds. But the concrete stays busted forever. So who's really wrong here? Me, with my indefatigable urge to break down walls in pursuit of my goals, my suspects, my enemies?

Or the wusses who aren't willing to suffer a little (possibly deranged) short-term pain in order to get what they're after?

"Sierra," I said, "get me the location of that other agent being arrested in DC."

"Certainly," Sierra said. "The other Chinese agent being

arrested in DC is currently at their residence, which is located at–"

An explosion went off in the distance, a bomb blast that rocked the city. I hung in the air for a bare moment, and I'm ashamed to say I truly considered – for just that moment in time – whether it might be better if I didn't show up to the scene of this particular crime at all.

Then I got over it and hit the afterburners as I jetted in that direction, wind blowing in my face with a fury. "Sierra, alert the local authorities and patch me in with Director Lane."

"Already on it," Sierra said. "Patching you in now."

I heard the faint ring of a telephone tone in my ear for only one second before Lane's voice answered. "Hello?"

"I think your team on the second agent just went up," I said. "I've got eyes on an explosion in northwest DC, and it looked bigger than the one I just went through. I have Sierra dispatching fire and rescue, but you might want to head that way."

"Dammit," Lane said. "We have people moving in on these agents all around the country right now – not just DC, New York, and LA, either. We've got them going in Omaha, Pensacola, Nashville–"

"Nashville?" I halted and jerked in midair, trying to remember the list. I hadn't seen anyone on it from Nashville that I could recall.

"The last known address for one of those potential agents was updated recently from Santa Barbara to Nashville," Lane said. "So we called the local authorities. We did warn them there might be this sort of problem–"

I hung up on her without compunction or mercy, turning hard to the southwest. "Sierra!" I shouted, hitting supersonic speed maybe faster than I ever had before.

"Dialing Augustus Coleman," Sierra said. There was a

pause. "Call failed. Dialing Olivia Brackett." Another pause. "Call failed. Dialing Chandler. Failed. Dialing Ileona Marsh...failed. There seems to be a broad-based outage of cell towers in the Nashville area. I am attempting to locate the trouble now. Sending emails to your entire team."

"Do that," I said, my mouth dry, and the air splitting around my face even as I roared to a speed I'd never dared to before. "And give me course corrections."

"Affirmative," Sierra said. "I am attempting contact with Cassidy Ellis through various means, in hopes she might be able to route a message to your team–"

"My friends," I said softly. "They're my friends, Sierra."

And right now, it was entirely possible they were walking unknowing into the line of fire of this maniac – who'd somehow turned the tables on us.

CHAPTER FORTY-FOUR

Reed

I was outside when the phone rang. Webster, Eilish, and I had stalled out on what to do next. Flipping over rocks at random didn't seem likely to draw out Janus, especially if he knew we were in town and was some manner of ready for us.

And based on the fact our organized crime expert thought he and new Omega were running London's underworld, there was no way he didn't know we were here.

The phone buzzed in my hand as I sought a fresh breath and a respite from the stale air in the Met bullpen. The night sky was dark above me, and London was a city of light. The cell phone screen just added to that, and made me cock my head at it quizzically.

Because it read SIENNA NEALON.

I answered, but didn't say anything. Sienna didn't even have her old phone anymore, as far as I knew. Which meant someone was presumably spoofing her number onto their call in order to get me to pick up. That didn't automatically mean someone bad, or with ill intent. It could be as simple as–

"Reed, this is Sierra," came the voice of Sienna's mother on the other end of the line.

I sighed. "Yeah. What's up?"

"I am contacting you on behalf of Sienna, regarding an unfolding incident in DC that has expanded into a national one," she said. "There is a Nashville connection, and we are trying to reach you and the others in your office."

"Not about my vehicle's extended warranty, huh?" I asked. "That's usually what the robocallers reach out to me about."

"Hardly," she said. "Chinese agents in DC that Sienna and the FBI have tried to apprehend have – to borrow a phrase from her lexicon – gone full suicide bomber. The death count is rising, and Sienna fears that Nashville may be a valid target."

"Shit," I said. "Well, I'm not in Nashville right now, but we need to let the others in the office know."

There was a pause. "You are not in Nashville?"

"I'm in London," I said. "On a...an Omega-related case. Janus is involved. There's a dead body."

"I see," Sierra said. "I am endeavoring to get in contact with others from your office to warn them about the potential danger, but unfortunately communications with Nashville seem to be blocked for some reason."

Taking the phone away from my ear, I hit the button to initiate a three-way call, then dialed Augustus. A beep followed by a computerized voice informed me that the network was down in that area. "Huh," I said, a sense of dread growing in my belly. "That's..."

"Not good," Sierra said as I hung up. "Are any of your colleagues presently in London with you?"

"Eilish," I said.

"Then I will redirect my efforts away from reaching her."
Sierra paused again. "I would not recommend your return to
the states at this time. London seems to be safer."

"I don't choose where I go based on safety," I said, "especially as determined by my sister's pet AI."

Sierra seemed to hesitate. "The point remains."

"Yeah, whatever," I said. "Can I talk to Sienna or is she
too busy at the moment?"

"I am afraid she is currently traveling at a speed that
makes communication via telephone prohibitively difficult."

"Damn," I said. "I could really have used her knowledge
on this one."

"Perhaps I could help?" Sierra asked. "I am just a 'pet AI,'
but I have my uses."

It was my turn to hesitate. "Don't you have more important things to do? Calls to make, crisis to avert?"

"Unfortunately," Sierra said, "while the current crisis is
chewing up every single one of my phone lines, as well as
several VOIP lines I am currently creating, my processing
capacity is only being used at 25%. Which means that while
things are incredibly urgent, they are so predominantly
because of a lack of communication with key parties, not
because of a failure to analyze data. Simply put: we don't have
enough information for me to be taxing myself. We have a
failure to communicate."

"Great," I said, with all due sarcasm. "Maybe you could
help me find Janus in London, then. Apparently he's the boss
of all bosses here, so you wouldn't think it'd be difficult."

"Scanning open source data," Sierra said. "Within an
eighty percent probability, I believe Janus's last known
address was in the Kensington area of London. Sending it to
you now. Without being in the London camera system, I
cannot say for certain whether this remains his current
address."

I looked to either end of the street around me to see if anyone was listening. They didn't appear to be. Still, I dropped my voice to meta low. "Can you get into the London camera systems?"

"Unfortunately, not at present," Sierra said. "They are protected by very stringent UK laws – as well as Cassidy's most advanced encryption software."

"Guessing it's the latter rather than the former holding you back."

"As an AI, I am not subject to laws," Sierra said. "However, in asking me to do this, you may be. Therefore, it seems unwise to do so without your vocal consent and a pressing need. You have a lead; why add additional risk before you've explored it fully?"

"An excellent point," I said, clutching my phone. "Keep me apprised of what's going on in Nashville? And with Sienna?"

"I will follow up with you if any news emerges," Sierra said. "Would you like to be informed via text or phone call?"

"Text for minor updates," I said. "Major ones...call me."

"I will do so," Sierra said. "I am also allocating unused processing capability toward locating more information about Janus, any potential known associates, and current activities."

"You might want to look into a couple of former prisoners of the Cube that Sienna killed in the Minneapolis breakout incident," I said. "I can't remember their real names, but Sienna called them Moose, Squirrel, and Franklin."

"I will attempt to unravel any connections," Sierra said. "Take care of yourself, Reed."

Hearing her hang up with that signoff was odd; it wasn't every day your dead stepmom told you to take care of yourself. It made me shiver. Whether in a good way or a bad one, I couldn't tell.

CHAPTER FORTY-FIVE

Wade

W hen I was clothed and moving again, I found myself jarred by a sudden, urgent buzzing from my phone. "What's up?" I asked, after answering it. Because it was Sierra, who I'd hung up on while I was getting dressed.

"Urgent," Sierra said, a little clipped, even for her computerized voice. "A second Chinese agent has triggered explosives on their person or vehicle as Sienna and other authorities have moved in to arrest them."

"Two now?" I leapt into the sky, letting my flight powers vault me upward. "Where's Sienna?"

"Inbound toward Nashville," Sierra said. "We have lost contact with the city. Cellular networks and internet appear to be down. She suspects another detonation is imminent, with her friends possibly in the line of fire."

"Shit," I said, turning east. "I can be there in—"

My phone buzzed furiously in my hand; Wayne Arthur's name came up in the contact window. "Hang on, Sierra. Wayne – what is it?"

"Dire problem," Wayne said. "Don't know if you heard, but Chinese agents are blowing up now."

"I just heard," I said. "Was heading to Nashville to hook up with Sienna."

"Scratch that. You're still in LA, right?"

"Yeah," I said, a little itch of discomfort starting in the back of my head. "Why?" '

"Vegas just went offline, too," Wayne said. "No comms, no 'net, in or out. Like it dropped off the map."

The itch turned into a sinking feeling. "I'll check in, if you want, on my way to Nashville."

"If it's some kind of blackout zone, you may lose contact when you're in there," Wayne said. "Wade – we don't have any idea what this is. It could be an innocuous comms hiccup, or it could be the doomsday we've been working against. No way to tell until you get there – and then you might not be able to get the message out."

"Understood," I said. "I'll let you know as soon as I can, okay?" And I hung up. "Sierra?"

"I was monitoring your conversation," she said. "I can confirm that Vegas does appear offline, just as Nashville did. Several other cities are showing as offline as well – Missoula, Montana; Sioux Falls, South Dakota; Des Moines, Iowa; Mobile, Alabama; and Austin, Texas."

I felt a weird, creeping sensation at the back of my neck. "Can you use satellite imaging to tell if those cities are...still there?"

Sierra answered after a brief pause. "They are still there. And they appear to have electricity."

I set my course for Vegas, based on the GPS on my phone screen. Soon I was going fast enough that I had to put down the phone; I'd be in Vegas in twenty minutes or less.

What the hell was going on?

CHAPTER FORTY-SIX

Sienna

Coming out of supersonic just over the eastern edge of the Nashville metro, I slowed to follow I-40 toward the rapidly changing skyline. It felt like at least a couple buildings had been added in my absence. "Sierra?" I asked, as I came into view of the giant 40/24/65 interchange just east of the airport. I looked down at my phone. Zero bars of signal.

I wasn't going to be finding anyone via the internet right now, that much was certain. I had to make a call on which way to go first, who to talk to before anyone else.

The decision came shockingly easy. I turned south toward 65 and sped toward Franklin, where the agency office was.

I blew through the front doors hard enough that the metal and glass squealed in protest. I was upstairs in a matter of seconds, and threw open the wooden door into the lobby without hesitation. Ignoring the secretary, some new girl I'd never met, I shot onward into the bullpen, ignoring the surprised shouts as I searched offices. Reed wasn't here, but Augustus–

"Whoa, girl, steady yourself," came a familiar voice with a hard bite. I looked down to find Alannah Greene looking up at me. "Get a grip. You're blowing my damned papers everywhere."

"Alannah," I said, and dropped beside her.

"Yeah," she said, fetching paperwork from the floor of her cubicle. "Great to see you, too, cousin. Long time no talkie-talkie." She looked up at me. "What are you even doing here? I thought you retired to get nailed all day on the beaches of Europe with your man candy or some shit."

"Where is everyone?" I put my hands on her shoulders and gave her a real gentle shake.

Her lips curled in a sneer. "Well, your brother's in England with Eilish, Olivia and Angel are in Texas doing something for the Rangers down there. Scotty boy is on vacation, getting banged all day on the beaches of Aruba with his pop tart. And Augustus and Jamal just headed downtown to hook up with your TBI friends on something or another." She stooped to pick up another paper. "That's not counting the expansion team with all the rookies, of course. I swear, I don't even know half the people around here anymore–"

I seized her by the shoulders and gave her a less than gentle shake. "Where did Augustus and Jamal go? Specifically?"

"No idea," she said, annoyance cutting through her voice. "They don't keep me in the loop. All I know's what I over-heard." The look on my face must have finally gotten through to her. "Why? What's going on?"

"Fen Liu left a parting gift for me," I said, hurdling over the cubicles toward Augustus's office. "Agents are blowing up all over the country. TBI was going after one of them; I think that's why they called in Jamal and Augustus. And all the cell towers and internet are down in Nashville."

"Shit," Alannah said as I disappeared into Augustus's office. I rifled over the papers at the top of his desk, looking for an address – any address – but it was immaculately clean, no paper. "We got ourselves an all hands on deck situation here! Who knows where the boss went?" This last bit she bellowed loud enough I could have heard it back in the Greek isles.

"TBI called with a case," someone said. Someone familiar. I flew back out–

To find Madison Gustafson. Who'd once before been our secretary and proceeded to betray me to a host of my enemies at Scott Byerly's parents' cabin in the north woods of Minnesota.

"I've got the address," she said, offering it to me. There was alarm in her eyes, knowing she'd come into my sights. Like she was a rabbit a predator had locked onto.

A predator with metahuman powers. Who'd helped me in the China war. Helped me break my husband out of prison.

"We'll discuss...this...later," I said. "Thank you, Madison."

She gave me a nod, and I think I saw a rush of relief.

"ALL. HANDS! I said," Alannah shouted.

But I was already out the door.

CHAPTER FORTY-SEVEN

Reed

We found our way quickly across town to Kensington, and a street that was old, historical London pockmarked by newer, abysmal-looking brutalist buildings of hideous concrete and windows. It made me cringe, and not for the first time. Everything old in London had a sense of place, of harmony; it fit with the city, with its surroundings.

Everything they'd rebuilt after World War II and the Blitz shared the same awful design, and it really did seem to pull the soul out of you as you walked by. There was no elegance to it, no grace. You could see the exact same style of architecture in any city in the world.

There was only one Tower of London, though. Only one Tower Bridge. Only one St. Paul's Cathedral. And you could recognize them anywhere. This concrete slop could as easily be in Moscow or Chicago as London.

Janus's last known address was in one of the older buildings, one of those classical European-style apartment blocks
that went only a few stories high. His was on the top floor,
and once we'd landed amidst the late night hum of Kensington, entering the apartment building was as easy as Eilish
pushing buttons for the first couple apartments and asking
the first man to answer, "Buzz me in, will you?"

Up to apartment 457B we went, where I hesitated just
before the door. "Anticipating trouble?" Webster asked, hands
in the pockets of his long, brown coat.

"I'm not anticipating a fond reunion with reminiscences
about the old times," I said. "Though it'd be nice. Janus is a
well-to-do fellow. If I could have a talk with him over a
brandy, and convince him to give up his criminal ways, that'd
be an ideal solution."

Eilish had a puckish look on her face. "But you're not
planning on that, right?"

"Nope," I said, and tried the handle.

It swung open, revealing an apartment that no one had
lived in for some time. It was still furnished, in a pretty fancy
style. Almost like Janus had left at least some of his posses-
sions here, and kept the place as a secondary crash pad. Given
he was in charge of the criminal underworld, that wasn't
impossible. Maybe this was *pied-à-terre*, and he'd gone and
gotten himself a manor house out in the country to while
away his days in.

"Seeing as it was open and unlocked," Webster said,
breezing in, trail of his big coat rustling behind him, "I don't
see any reason we can't have a nosy around."

"I'll check the bedroom," Eilish said, in a way that – for
some reason – suggested to me that she might use her past as
a nimble-fingered thief to make anything truly valuable that
Janus left behind vanish. I did not raise this in front of

Webster, but I made a mental note to mention it to her later, in case whatever she lifted might be of actual use.

"Seems if he maintains this place on the side," Webster said, rifling through drawers in the kitchen, "he's given the maid eternity off."

I grunted at that, perusing the drawers of the desk that sat near the windows. There didn't seem to be much within other than a half-dozen old pens and a few scraps of paper tucked in around the edges, where movers might have easily missed them. Most were nonsense; grocery lists, jottings, even a doodle of a stick-figure man.

But in the bottom drawer...I did find one interesting thing.

"Hmm," I said, looking at the scrawl.

BANI – MIDNIGHT – 14

Webster lurked over my shoulder. "What's that supposed to mean?"

"If you can figure it out, you're possessed of a better mind than mine," I said. "Or at least some knowledge I lack."

"Doesn't ring any bells for me," Webster said. Eilish chose that moment to reappear from the bedroom. "Hey, come take a look at this," he said to her.

She trotted over obligingly. "Bedroom's pretty well empty. Not even a change of clothes or a set of cufflinks. If he's still living here, even part time, he's the most spartan chap you'll meet this side of...well, ancient Sparta." She peered at the slip of paper. "What is this? Some sort of code?"

"We were hoping you could tell us," I said, and we broke to search a little further. After a few more minutes, we were all ready to declare defeat. The paper was the only clue in the place. "I don't know what to do with this," I said, clutching it delicately between my fingers.

"It might mean something," Webster said. "Only way to know is to ask someone who'd have an idea if it's applicable to our situation or not." He lifted his phone and with a flash, took a picture of the paper. "Since we're headed back anyway, we might as well ask Stubbs about it."

That sounded like as good a plan as any. With one last look around the abandoned apartment, I made myself the last one out, and shut the door on this former place of Janus's, wondering how far we were from discovering his current one.

CHAPTER FORTY-EIGHT

Sienna

Navigating without GPS was a special sort of talent, and one I only had the passing-est of acquaintances with. I was a younger millennial; I'd had a smartphone almost since I'd left my house. Why would I have ever needed to memorize street names, major thoroughfares, and the like?

Maybe because I was, ultimately, a cop, and a person who believed in eminent disaster. Which is why when I moved to Nashville, I spent a decent chunk of time just scanning street names and putting them into my memory.

I couldn't claim to know every street in Nashville. But I knew where Demonbreun (why did they pronounce it De-mum-bree-un instead of Demon-brewin'? No clue) was, and I jetted toward downtown and the Demonbreun exit like it was where my retirement party was being held and all I needed to do to start the party (and the pension) was to get there.

Nor did it take a genius of the first order to figure out which direction I needed to go on Demonbreun once I got there. The massive swarm of cop cars was a big hint, just down the road into the Gulch section of town, blocking the roads and intersections, blue and red lights flashing madly across the entire horizon.

As I landed just past the police cordon, a cop stood watching me land, his navy uniform flashing in the light of the cop cars, his white teeth standing out with his jaw hanging open. "You're back."

"She's back," came a deadly dull voice, repeating him. I turned to see a homeless guy standing there. He was weathered, gray hair and beard, wrinkles like trenches in his face, a dazed look in his eyes.

"Yeah," I said, "I'm back." And turned to charge toward the building they were swarming.

I was just about to crash in when a familiar face popped out at me from the crowd of uniforms closer in. "Sienna?" Ashley Aylor, TBI agent, short, almost lost in the crowd, her double braids over her shoulder, was standing on the street, hand resting on her gun. "What are you doing here?"

"AA," I said, breathless, "you gotta call 'em back. These Chinese agents are blowing up everywhere."

She didn't even hesitate, snagging the radio at her belt. "All agents: HOLD. Repeat: HOLD. Be advised: Chinese agents have been exploding. DO NOT PROCEED. Copy?"

"Copy that," came a hard voice over the mic. "Please advise."

"Get 'em out here," I said, and she gave just that order. Moments later, filing out the glass-and steel, shiny new condo building, came Nashville's SWAT team, a couple TBI agents of my acquaintance, and–

"Augustus!" I practically tackled him, knocked him back into his brother, who was a step behind, and then got him, too, my arms wrapped around them both, refusing to let go. "Jamal."

"Nice to see you, too," Augustus said. Once I let him go, he straightened his suit jacket, which I might have wrinkled a little. "Kinda unexpected. Now what's this about Chinese agents blowing up?"

"They're going suicide bomber," I said. "I had one go up ten feet from me in DC, and another popped off in Northwest DC. There are dozens dead up there. Maybe more."

"You coulda just called," Jamal said.

"Check your phone," I said, but just as I did, it rang. Or buzzed, as the case was. "Damn. Well, everything was blacked out until a minute ago. I tried."

"Still is," Jamal said, and lifted the phone to show me the screen.

It was a text message from ArcheGrey1819. His girlfriend. *Deep comms hack underway on US networks. Our type responsible. Cannot isolate. Sending this via back door. Response probably not possible. Be aware.*

"Damn," he said, brow furrowed. "What the hell?"

"It's Fen Liu's revenge," I said. "She's trying to get the last word in on me. By dropping a whole lot of dead bodies somehow."

"Doesn't she know that no one gets the last word in on the slay queen?" Augustus asked, with just the appropriate level of sarcasm.

"Probably ought to tell her that–" I started to say.

But I didn't quite get it out...because somewhere on a floor far above us...

...The building exploded.

CHAPTER FORTY-NINE

Wade

I landed beside a Las Vegas PD patrol car. The officer was out on the side of the road, writing a ticket for a driver in a Mercedes when I came down, my hands up in the typical surrender posture, and he eyed me with a raised eyebrow as I touched down. "Sorry to bother you, officer," I said. "Communications are down going in and out of this town and the government sent me to investigate. Is your radio working?"

"Yeah, it's working fine," he said, pausing his scrawl. "Which agency do you work for?"

"CIA," I said. "But I'm interfacing with the FBI on this one. We're having incidents across the country. Do you know if there's anything major going on at the moment?"

He eyed me suspiciously. "Not sure I should just give that information out."

As if prompted, his radio crackled to life. "All units, be advised: disturbance at 3725 Las Vegas Boulevard."

He glanced at his radio, then at me, and his face fell. "Aw, shit."

"You'll thank me later!" I shouted, and jetted back into the sky, turning toward the Strip. Having spent my honeymoon in Vegas, I just happened to know exactly which casino hotel was at 3725 Las Vegas Boulevard.

The Gatsby Grand Casino.

CHAPTER FIFTY

Sienna

Glass rained down on the street around me, and I shoved Augustus and Jamal down, covering them – inadequately – with my body. I felt spurs of pain in my flank, and near my spine, and triggered Wolfe healing immediately. When I heard the last crash of debris landing on a cop car behind me, I waited a further five seconds and sprung back up.

The street was a flaming disaster area.

One of the fire trucks had caught a falling...something. Maybe a couch, maybe a section of drywall, maybe a girder with other debris tacked it. Whatever the case, the truck was crushed and burning all through the middle, like its spine had been broken by a giant stepping on it.

"Well, now it is a fire truck," Augustus said with a grunt, back popping as he rose to his feet. "I guess you weren't kidding about Chinese spies exploding."

"I was not," I whispered.

It was hard to say how many people – cops, firefighters, EMTs – had been in the middle of what was now a burning debris field. Some were obvious; pulling themselves out, moving. I caught a glimpse of AA at the fringes, trying to drag a man thrice her size away from a flaming car.

A disaster. That's what this was.

And it was at least partly my fault.

Glass and debris covered the street. Flames rose from half a dozen places, vehicles, mostly. All filled with gas, surely. Which meant things were going to get so much worse.

I levitated ten feet off the ground and closed my eyes. Picturing in my head Aleksandr Gavrikov, and channeling a sense of rage that had been burgeoning in me for days, weeks, months–

A lifetime.

–I latched onto the fires in my mind's eye. I couldn't put them out from here; too much fuel, too many of them burning.

But I could grasp them. I could pull them to me – away from their fuel. To my loving fingertips – and I did–

Flames streamed toward me, stretching and contorting as though metal filings drawn by a magnet. They seemed to detach from the places where they were burning and come to me, covering me up in a tight little ball of flame.

And then, with nothing left to burn but me – immune to fire – I snuffed them all.

Leaving the street in a semi-darkness, with only a half-dozen rescue vehicles still flashing. The building above us was dark, the power knocked out by the explosion.

I hit the ground with a thud as applause broke out around me. My face burned, flushed, and I hid it as I hurried to the nearest downed person. It was a woman, her face smeared with soot and ash, leg a bloody mess from the metal girder that had caught her just below the knee. I lifted it with one hand and tossed it aside, planting a hand on the exposed flesh. "Hey, what's your name?"

"Bernadette," she said, through the pain. "Jones."

I was healing her as best I could with my limited Persephone abilities. Five seconds was all I could give, after a quick assessment. It was enough to stop the bleeding, put some color back in her cheeks and see the wound knitted together. "You're going to be just fine, Bernadette," I said, giving her a pat on the shoulder and lifting off, flying toward the next wounded soul. "What's your name?" I asked the cop who lay beside a smoking patrol car, third-degree burns having melted his uniform and badge to his chest.

"Matthew Want," he rasped, his eyes opening and closing slowly as he tried to look up at me.

"Well, Matthew, I know what you want," I said. "Hold on just a second – this is gonna hurt a bit."

"Already...hurts," he said.

I formed a miniature energy blade out of my finger and cut off his uniform top, taking care not to hit the skin. I had him out of it in a couple seconds, gingerly ripping off the parts that were burned to his flesh. He gritted his teeth against the pain, but offered no complaint and only a little cry as I finished ripping it off of him.

"I'm...I'm dead," he said, looking down at the charred skin. It covered his torso from collarbone to crotch.

"That is nothing but a little ouchie," I said, taking care to make sure the burns didn't extend any further south. The last thing I needed was to regrow this guy's skin over seared uniform; I might have been able to handle the flaying it would take to remove it without dying, but no human was going to be able to make it through that. Once I'd confirmed that his burns were only on his chest and torso, I laid hands on him. "You're going to be just fine, Matthew."

"You're a...goddess," he said. He was trying to see, but I was holding him down. New flesh was forming on his chest, regrowing over the blackened elements, like a time-lapse photo of a flower growing. I counted out eight seconds and stopped, which was enough to leave him with slightly pink skin across what had been a zone of absolute black, the lumps of char all smoothed out and fresh.

"Sweet-talker," I said, pulling my hands away. "You gotta be careful with girls like me." He stared up at me, a little more life in his eyes now. "Like so many of my kind, I'm a vengeful goddess."

"Yeah, well," he said, stirring, his voice a lot stronger, "you point that vengeance in the right direction, you won't hear any complaints from me about it."

"The problem with vengeance," I said, rising up, ready to find the next person I could help, "is that it's like a firehose running without someone holding it; it doesn't stay pointed in one direction."

With that, I flew on to the next, and the next after. The tower burned lightly above, spritzes of water finding their way down from the building's sprinkler systems as I did everything I could to save the people below.

It would never be enough.

CHAPTER FIFTY-ONE

Wade

I came down in front of the Gatsby Grand casino, and a hubbub was already in full swing. Cops were dragging guys out kicking and screaming, cuffed and meta-cuffed, howling with fury and...insanity, frankly. They were fighting hard against the cops and casino security, with all the energy of true nutters, all four or five of them, but they were losing.

Settling down just under the glittering portico, I found myself beside a female cop who had the back door of a paddy wagon open and waiting for its incoming recipients. She gave me a glance as I came in, a wary one, but I maintained a respectful distance between us in my landing. "Hey," I said. "Federal agent. What's going on here?"

She looked at me and frowned; she was a middle-aged bottle blond, and her roots were showing. Her hair was bound tightly back, and she'd clearly been a uniform for at least fifteen to twenty years. "Hey, I know you," she said. "You're Mr. Sienna Nealon, aren'tcha?"

I guffawed, because that was funny. "Yeah, that's me. I thought it was a secret."

"Not much of one with that lantern jaw, Navy SEAL. As for this," and she nodded to the chaos incoming, "this was a small-scale riot on the casino floor. Bunch of the, uh, unhoused came in off the street, assaulted security, and just started going batshit crazy tearing the place up."

"And if there's one thing Vegas casinos can't abide, it's someone who isn't gambling," I said.

She nodded sagely. Her name plate read Smithson. "They hate that like you probably hate being called 'Mr. Nealon.'"

"I actually don't mind it," I said, chuckling again. "No one's ever called me that before. It's got real novelty."

"Maybe it'll catch on," she said. "Bet you won't be so pleased with it after the ten thousandth time someone calls you that."

"And I bet you I still won't care," I said. "What's the deal with the comms blackout in this town?"

"Dunno," she said with a shrug as the other cops drew close with the first of the struggling madmen. He had darts sticking out of him; no surprise, there. Most of the homeless addicts had metahuman powers these days. "I heard something about an internet node being down, but it's all rumors. Watch out, there, Clancy." This, she said very casually to one of the guys manhandling the first bum, who smelled of urine and very strong body odor.

Clancy was a thickset black cop who had to have weighed over three hundred, and was struggling to get the bum, who probably weighed 120 soaking wet, into the back of the paddy wagon. For those who hadn't seen it, trying to force someone a third your size to do something they were categorically opposed to was, in fact, a struggle. And it looked like what it was.

"Sonofabitch don't wanna go," Clancy said, really struggling. No metahuman powers were being deployed, it was just a good old-fashioned wrestling match. And yeah, Clancy could have destroyed the guy in about two seconds. But Clancy was a professional, and he was trying to make the bum comply without injuring him. Clubbing him over the head might make him compliant, but it could also give him a traumatic brain injury, so he was taking his time and making things difficult on himself. I could respect that, not taking the easy road and just clubbing the annoying sonofabitch.

But I didn't have to be bound by it.

"Federal agent," I said. "Let me give you a hand."

"I wouldn't mind an assist," Clancy said, veins popping out in his forehead as the bum writhed in the opposite direction, straining his grip. Even cuffed, the guy was a huge pain in the ass. Clancy really should have had someone else helping him. I stepped over and grabbed hold of the vagrant, who was cursing violently. Putting a hand on his back, and another on his chest, I took hold. "You got him?" Clancy asked, because I was taking up all the struggle.

"Got him," I said, and Clancy let go to step up into the paddy wagon.

When he did, I hit our struggling prisoner with about 30,000 volts from the ol' Thor powers. He shouted, but cut it off as I finished zapping him. What I gave him wasn't enough to kill him, it wasn't even enough to truly hurt him.

But it did take the starch out of him, and he allowed himself to be pulled up into the wagon and, under the watchful eye of Clancy, be locked into place so he wouldn't go rolling around during transit. "Huh," Clancy said, eyeing me as he locked him down the rest of the way, "I think I smell a little smoke."

"Well, he did just come out of a casino," I said, smiling. "Any idea how this mess started?"

"Only that they went nuts," Clancy said. "Just came in and went crazy on the casino floor."

"That's weird," I said.

"Not really," Smithson said from outside. She seemed like the hands-off type of supervisor. I'd known a few of those in my time. "Vagrant druggies going crazy is pretty normal."

"Yeah, but multiples at once, in the same place?" I asked. "That'd take some coordination, because they're not really allowed in the casinos, are they?"

"No," Clancy said, moving aside to get clear of the cops locking down the other perps. "Casino security is all over them the minute they walk in." He ignored Smithson giving him a hateful look for his knowledge and expertise. "I don't want to say this is 'inconceivable,' but it's pretty close."

"That begs the question, then," I said. "Why and how?"

"How is immaterial," came a strange voice from the throat of the vagrant. Not his, for sure; it had hints of an Asian accent. Chinese, if I was not much mistaken, and he was white as curdled cream. I looked at him, and he was staring up at me. "As for why..." He leaned slightly forward, bound in the seat. "...Because you were coming, Mr. Nealon. That's why."

It didn't take one completely expert in the ways of metahuman powers to know that this bum's mind was out to lunch and someone else was driving him. "Who are you?" I asked, completely by reflex. Of course, I suspected I knew who he was before I even got the question out.

"Who I am doesn't matter, either," he said, smiling. "The question is: what are you going to do, Wade?"

That made me frown. "I mean...not beat the poor guy whose brain you're riding, if that's what you're suggesting."

He threw back his head and laughed. "No, not about this. What are you going to do about *that?*"

And it was only then that I heard the commotion outside the paddy wagon. Someone was screaming in the distance - not far.

It was then joined by another, and another, as a wave of chaos struck.

CHAPTER FIFTY-TWO

Reed

We made it back to HQ and enjoyed the lagging elevator ride in silence. The scrap of paper with the words BANI MIDNIGHT 14 seemed to be burning a hole in my pocket with the possibilities. A name coupled with a time coupled with a location? Dock 14 at midnight, where Bani would be waiting to transfer something illicit to Omega?

These were the thoughts that clouded my head when the elevator dinged and I stepped out after Eilish and Webster. "Let's hope Stubbs is still in," Webster said, "else we're going to be heading out to his home, I reckon."

"Where's that?" Eilish asked.

"No matter," Webster said as we came around the corner and into sight of Stubb's office, "the lights are on. That's a good sign." The door was closed, so he rapped it with the back of his knuckles.

There was no answer, no noise from within. Webster frowned. "Hmm. Maybe that address will be necessary after all." He tried the handle and it worked, opening the door.

And giving us a perfect view of Keith Stubbs, hanging by his tie from the ceiling vent.

Eilish gasped. She didn't turn away, though; like me, she'd seen worse.

Webster moved back to one of the nearby desks, and dialed a number. "We need a coroner to Keith Stubbs' office. We have a dead man here."

And we did indeed. Because Stubbs's eyes were bugged out of his head, face purple, life long since departed.

"It looks like it might be a suicide," Webster said, catching my eyes as he did so. He knew as well as I did that this was no suicide; but he had to say so, because that's what it looked like.

There were no signs of a struggle. Barely any papers out of place. The bottle still stood upright on his desk, though it had been drained since last we were here hours ago.

But the slow squeak of Stubbs's tie was like a punctuating sound that marked our failure, again, to Janus and Omega, and made me wonder exactly how he'd reached right into the heart of the Met to cut off our only possible clue.

CHAPTER FIFTY-THREE

Sienna

Another scene, another man-made disaster. I led the way, naturally, when the time came for the firefighters to storm the building and go into the heart of the explosion. Evacuating took a while, too. It was exhausting work, clearing every single unit in an apartment building, and making sure there were no more bombs waiting to go off.

When all that was done, and the scene was secure, I floated back down to the street right out of the hole gouged in the side of the glass and steel structure and landed next to the triage area, which was quiet. Alannah was sitting there, pale, having arrived sometime during rescue operations. Her hands were covered in blood and she was leaning against a police car tire. "You look about as tapped-out as I do," she said, "and I know your ass just got back from a long vacation."

"It was more of a honeymoon, really," I said, sliding down

next to her. She made room so I wouldn't touch her and she wouldn't touch me. "Or a second one." I thumped the back of my head against the car's metal side.

"Well, I think it's safe to say the honeymoon's over now, whichever one it was," Alannah said. "Where's your hubby?"

"Los Angeles," I said, looking for my phone. Still zero bars. Whatever hacking job the trigger man had done to the network in or around Nashville, he'd done it well. A modern city completely disconnected from the communications grid? The Zoomers in 12South must have been absolutely dying without being able to upload to Instaphoto for almost three hours. "I think. I guess I don't know for sure."

"Don't look now," Alannah said, looking out through thinly slitted eyes, "but I think you got an admirer."

"I have many admirers," I said, opening my eyes and matching the direction of her gaze. We were both looking straight ahead, into the crowd forming around the police cordon. It had grown since I'd first arrived. That same homeless guy was standing at the front of the crowd, though, looking at me in a manner that could only be described as "eerie." And giving me a long, slow, come-hither gesture with his index finger. "Okay, most don't act as weird as that."

"Only the best get that creepy, right?" Alannah asked. She didn't move as I got up.

I floated over to the bum, whose matted hair and weird, missing-toothed grin made me uneasy as I drew closer. "This better be important," I said. "I'm trying to collapse and die over there, and if you dragged me away from that just so you can make some kind of half-assed remark about my whole ass, you're going to regret it."

"There are so many things to regret in this world," the homeless guy – white, weathered, lacking teeth, and gray-haired – said in the thickly accented voice of an Asian man half his age. "I would think the foremost of those would be what you've unleashed by killing Fen Liu."

The voice did not match the look. Not at all. I seized the man's hand, and he laughed – again, in the voice unlike his own. "I'm not actually here," he said. "Just using this vessel to introduce myself."

"I see that," I said, keeping the homeless guy's hand in mine. He smelled. A lot, frankly. It was a deep affront to my sensitive, metahuman nose. But I kept holding on anyway. "So...what's your name? What's your current address? And when can we meet so I can rip your spine out through your nose then beat you to death with it?"

He laughed. "It's a lot more fun if you try and figure it out. Giving you all the answers would seem a senseless waste."

"Not that senseless to me," I said, feeling the first stirrings of the burn. "See, I want to stop you from doing any more evil. My entire person, all my will, all my efforts, everything I have is going to be dedicated to that – until you either stop or you're dead. So there's your sense. And if you have any, you'll knock it off before I catch you."

"You know what the penalty is for treason?" he asked. "It's death."

"It doesn't have to be," I said. "Hell, if you walk away right now, don't cause any more trouble, I might just let you go."

He laughed, loud, long, hard. "We both know that's a lie, and I wouldn't walk away in any case. I believed in what Fen Liu was doing with China. It was going to make us foremost in the world."

"You still can be, you dumbass," I said. "It's just your people will get a say in their governance."

He scoffed. "Why? So they can be like you, the fallen and failing nations of the west? You have no moral authority. You spend your time relitigating the sins of your ancestors, long dead. There's no vitality left in your civilization. You hit the apex and quiet quit, to use your own words. All your people care about is comfort, like one of the suicides where they sit in a warm bath, open their veins and wait for death to come. That wasn't going to be China. Fen Liu was driving us to new heights–"

"Which part was the new height?" I asked. "When you got your asses kicked out of Russia? Or when she got tortured to death by the people she'd pissed off along the way?"

"You're pathetic," he said, a real hate coming into his eyes. "You in the west. You're spoiled children who sit atop an empire of prosperity and peace that you didn't build, and make your proclamations about how those who are doing what it takes to build their own are morally repugnant to you. Trust-fund children, all of you, living off the fumes of an engine you couldn't construct if you had to and bitching about the smell the whole time."

"Let me see where you are," I said, the burning coming to a slow end without any breakthrough whatsoever into the homeless man's mind. "I'll give you fumes that you won't believe."

He chuckled. "I'm sure we'll meet at some point. In the ashes of your so-called civilization, if nowhere else." The homeless guy cocked his head at me. "By the way...do you know where your husband is?" Then he grinned. "Because I do."

With a last cackle, the homeless guy jolted and staggered back. I caught him, and now my hand burned where it gripped his wrist. I was catapulted forward into his mind–

And all I saw there was a junkie who wanted his next fix. A tragic backstory, and one that mostly built on his own flaws and bad choices, bit by bit. I saw it, and thought, there but for the grace of AA and going to a meeting...

I ripped my hand away from him and he choked, hitting a knee. "What the hell...?" he muttered, in a voice very unlike the one that had just been emanating from him. "Don't touch me." He jerked his hand away.

"Wouldn't have dreamed of it if you hadn't been – never mind," I said, not sure if I should even bother finishing the sentence. What would be better? To inform him he'd been possessed? Or to have him not ever know it? "Do you remember what just happened to you?"

"Yeah, you grabbed my hand," he said, giving me a mean-spirited leer. He was high. With a flipped bird, he shuffled away from the cordon tape.

"Never seen an old white guy suddenly start talking like a Chinese dude," Alannah said, suddenly there, at my shoulder. "At least not without putting on the kind of accent that used to get your ass canceled."

"Pretty sure it was the real thing," I said, watching the old guy shuffle away.

"That was your bad guy, wasn't it?" Alannah asked.

"I think so, yeah," I said.

"Well, shit, let's get 'im, then," she said, like she was ready to leap the cordon and chase down the old man.

I grabbed her arm. "It wasn't really him. He doesn't have a clue. He was just a...a mask, I guess." I held myself upright, trying to work through what he meant about my husband, and his whereabouts.

"Where's the real deal, then?" Alannah asked. She pounded her fist into her open hand, producing a smack that was loud enough it made me grimace.

"I don't know," I said, looking at the scene of destruction before me, and thinking back to the ones I'd left behind in DC, "but wherever he is, he's laughing at us right now."

CHAPTER FIFTY-FOUR

HIM

He was laughing.

It was a little tough; the air was filled with smoke, and it made him alternate between laughing and wanting to cough, but he'd landed on laughing and he was going to stick with it.

He shouldn't have been, he didn't think; his obvious goading of Sienna Nealon had, on the surface, seemed like a mistake. So many others had done the same before, including his mistress, Fen Liu.

And where were they now?

In graves. In prisons.

But, occasionally, one might escape that fate.

After all, none of them had what he had on his side.

With a slight adjustment, he cracked his neck. Sitting for so long really put the pain into you. It made him stiff in the joints, stiff in the mind. Rigid. Inflexible. Uncompromising.

But sometimes doing what you truly wanted required compromise.

So he compromised, and kept sitting. Playing the hand he had was going to be a struggle. He was, after all, across the table from people who had a pretty good hand themselves. And you had to be careful of the bluff. Always had to be careful about the bluff.

The problem was...Sienna Nealon didn't seem like much of a bluffer. Bluffing was what you did when you didn't have the winning hand. She had a suite of powers that almost always ended up as the winning hand. As if that wasn't enough, that husband of hers had collected a bunch of his own. Playing together, they were almost unbeatable...

...In the physical world.

But he didn't always play in that realm. Plus, he had a pretty strong hand of his own.

He just had to play it right.

Soon enough...that had him laughing all over again.

He'd have his revenge after all.

And no one would be the wiser.

CHAPTER FIFTY-FIVE

Reed

"This is a real problem, isn't it?" Eilish said, chewing her fingernails as the worldly remains of Keith Stubbs were carted out on a gurney. A white sheet was stretched over his purple features, but the scent of death was unmistakable. I could smell it from here, and I tried to cover my nose as it went rolling past.

It was an "it," at this point, too. Whatever had been of Stubbs, his hopes and dreams for his retirement, they'd been choked out, turning him from a *he* to an *it* as easily as if flipping a switch. Probably with a bit more struggle, but the principle remained the same in spite of whatever trifling effects happened around the edges.

"The only person I know of who might have been able to tell us what that gibberish meant," Webster said, leaning against the wall, arms folded in front of him. "Yeah, I'd say this is a blow. Without him, we'll have to try our luck down

the chain, see if his inferiors know half as much as he did."
Webster grunted. "I'm not hopeful. The man was a repository
of institutional memory the like of which we can't replace."

"But how did it happen?" Eilish asked.

"Janus is an empath," I said, watching the attendants
wheel the body down the hall into the elevator. "A really
powerful one, too. He can dominate emotions. It's not that
hard to imagine he just gave Stubbs a push. He was already on
a sort of edge, thinking about a retirement he didn't neces-
sarily want, but felt forced into. Play with the emotions a
little bit and suddenly all your dreams vanish, your problems
magnify – then there's only one way out."

That prompted a moment of silence from both of them.
"You make it sound like you might have firsthand experience
with that feeling," Eilish said.

"Oh, I'm well acquainted with the depths of despair," I
said. "And I've been hit by a feelz bomb from an empath
before, and had my brain played with by at least one telepath.
Mental manipulation is not a subject we're ready to tackle as
a society. Normies out there have no clue how dangerous
those powers are, or they'd be baying for the blood of
everyone who has even a trace of them."

Eilish gulped. "Some of us try rather hard to avoid
arousing that instinct."

I smiled at her. "No one ever accused you of lacking self-
preservation instinct, Irish." My smile faded. "The fact that
Janus reached in here, to the heart of law enforcement in
London, and snuffed out our best source – that's, as Eilish
might cheerfully understate it – a mite concerning."

"Agreed," Webster said. "And leaves us without immediate
recourse on the clue. What do you think about running it
through that AI your sister has? See if it can come up with
something?"

"Already did," I said. "I texted it on the way over. No dice.

Too little to go on, but Sierra is expending some analytical compute on it. Not something we want to wait around on."

"Not sure what else we can do," Eilish said. "What, are we going to wait around here? Snoop in his office, hoping to find some clue? Likely as not we'll just cork things up for forensics."

"There was no obvious sign anyone else had been in there, anyway," I said, "and Janus could have done this from a mile away, maybe." I didn't know the exact limits of his power, but if he'd had any doses of the serums that were now widely available in his line of work, he probably could have done this from halfway across the city. At the very least, he didn't need to be inside the building. "We should check in on the surveillance videos just to be sure, then...I don't know." I brushed some stray hairs that had been loosed in all the flying about. "I just don't know what to do next."

CHAPTER FIFTY-SIX

Wade

There was a riot kicking off outside the casino, under the glittering, light-lined portico, when I stuck my head out of the Las Vegas police department paddy wagon, and I was hard pressed to know how it had begun or whether I had a chance to stop it.

Looking at it, it was almost like one of those full, double-page pieces of art in a comic book, action going on at every corner of the frame. Up near the entrance, a vagrant wearing plastic bags for shoes used green laser powers to cut through some poor lady, and the car behind her, shearing off the hood. Beside him, another was swollen like a Hercules and kicked a concrete trash can that probably weighed a hundred pounds. It went rolling into the crowd, crushing some guy's leg and prompting a stampede.

Two wolves leapt into the middle of the fray, biting at a security guard. They got his legs first, brought him down, and then started going for more sensitive areas. Before my eyes, one of the wolves shifted into a bear and flung a paw at a passing hooker, pulping her head against a car door. A man with skin that looked like tree bark punched a cop, sending him flying into the back window of a parked taxi, as beside him, a woman unleashed glowing red eye-beams that sent a multi-ton Brinks truck spinning around in a half circle.

And that was just in the first five seconds. It was total chaos. Pandemonium. All hell breaking loose.

"Holy shit," Smithson said behind me, her voice high and terrified, "what do we do?"

"You call for backup and leave it to me," I said, rising up, ready to swoop down on them.

Unfortunate, a car door came flying at me like a Frisbee, and I only saw it out of the corner of my eye for a second before it winged me, knocking me down off the truck and into a cop car, headfirst.

My head rang, pain radiating off my skull in waves. When I reached up to touch my face, my fingers came away bloody, vision blurring from the hit.

I lay there, listening to the screams, sliding in and out of consciousness, as the world seemed to explode into violence around me.

CHAPTER FIFTY-SEVEN

Sienna

I was still bumming around the scene an hour or two later, at loose ends, when a black government SUV pulled up and out stepped Director Candy Cane Lane. Needless to say, she did not look pleased.

"Don't you have enough to deal with in DC?" I asked, as she stomped her way over to me.

"Yes," she said, eyes blazing. I was sitting atop a fire truck, but they were already starting to take in the hoses because the fires were out, the injured had been evacuated from the scene, and even the lookiloos had faded away. It was down to a skeleton crew of cops, and my team, who were shuffling around, meandering, drinking coffee, and mingling with the first responders. "Unfortunately, you chose to come to a dead zone. You are needed in DC."

"For what?" I asked, legs dangling over the edge of the fire truck. I stared up at the gaping hole in the side of the tower.

I hadn't done it...had I? "PR? I'll just screw it up for you. Better I stay on the sidelines for that and in the thick of the action in trying to force this guy out of the shadows."

"How's that going for you?" she asked, just steaming pissed. She mostly hid it well; it did come out in her voice, try as she might to keep it buttoned down.

"Honestly? Not great," I said, hopping down off the truck and cushioning my landing with a last minute bout of levitation before I dropped the last half-inch to the pavement. Barely made a sound in my boots, and I almost didn't feel it. "I did get to talk to the guy for about a minute, earlier, through an intermediary. So that's progress, I guess."

Lane looked extremely torn by that. "What kind of intermediary?"

I stared up at the new Nashville Yards tower in the distance, still under construction. "Some sort of psychic communication via a third party cutout. He seized the mind of a homeless guy and talked to me through him, but when I did a soul drain, I figured out he wasn't there, and wasn't leaving a residual trace I could use to track him down."

Lane seemed to freeze. "You soul drained some random civilian?"

"Relax," I said, looking her in the eye. "He didn't even feel it, and I didn't take enough that he's going to miss it." My voice crept a little lower. "He does more damage to himself on a weekly basis with fentanyl than I did with a three-second drain."

She just stared at me, jaw hanging slightly open, clearly aghast. "Do you ever even pause to think about the consequences of your actions?"

"Sometimes, for a second," I said. "Then I just go ahead and do whatever it is I was going to do anyway. 'Go with the gut' and all that." I cocked my head, enjoying her clear discomfiture. Maybe now was the time to dig down into the tension between us. "You have a critique?"

For just a second, I thought she was going to hold back.

Then she unloaded, the words coming so fast it was like she was one of the Chinese bombs, just letting it all out.

"You are the ruin of absolutely everything," she said, "you are the destroyer of worlds, the wreck of civilizations–"

"I think you may be laying it on a bit thick. We're still standing in the middle of a city that's perfectly fine, other than it's lost Wi-Fi, and a Chinese agent blew a big hole in the tower. Bad, yes, but hardly the end of the world as we know it."

"–the people whose lives you touch are destroyed forever," she said. "Do you have any idea how many people are going to be forever scarred by what you started today by setting off these Chinese agents?"

I felt a sting, keenly, in my mind, and in my gut. "I didn't choose to set off bombs in civilian areas. That was a deliberate decision made by our perp."

"But how many bombs have you set off?" Lane's voice was rising. "Metaphorically? In our lives? You killed a president, and since that day, five years ago, we've gone through four more."

"Gerry Harmon killed himself using my body," I said, irritated. "If anyone should be pissed off about that, it's me. It was a gross violation, frankly–"

"You uncork the bottle and unleash the chaos."

"You mix metaphors. I think. I didn't graduate high school, and grammar isn't my strongest suit."

"Everything you've done," she seethed, "has made the world more chaotic and less safe."

"You'd prefer I just let these people do what they please?" I asked, voice rising to meet hers. "Did you want to become one of the drones in Gerry Harmon's own personal human ant colony?"

"You just do these things, break the world, and let the consequences go in every direction but your own–"

"I have been dealing with the consequences of my own actions since I was seventeen years old, thanks." I pointed a finger at her. "You want soothing lies over hard truths. You want to be a dog on someone's leash. You want to get down on your knees and bow to tyrants rather than have the mess and pain of a fight."

"I want peace!" she shouted, voice echoing through the glass canyons of the Gulch neighborhood.

"Peace is not an option with these people!" I shouted right back. "Only the fight – or complete submission! That's how Harmon wanted it, that's how the Network wanted it, and that's how Fen Liu wanted it! You're a damned servant, a happy slave to tyrants, the exact kind of person that Sam Adams was talking about when he said 'may your chains set lightly upon you.' Well, I'm not a servant of lies. I'm not a servant of any-damned-body. And anyone who tries to put me in chains or takes away my freedom ends up dead. There's your consequences."

"How many people have to die so you can have your illusion of freedom?" Lane asked.

"What makes you think they won't die anyway?" I asked.

"This is unacceptable," she said, voice hoarse, as she pointed at the bomb blast crater in the building above. "This would not be tolerated before. You have destroyed everything, including our standards."

"This is not the first bomb to go off in America," I said. "We had like three thousand of them go off in the seventies. And that was terrible! And unacceptable! I deplore the death of innocents as much as anyone. Which is why I want to catch this guy."

"This is all your fault." She reached behind her back, fumbling with her belt, and came out with handcuffs. She extended them to me. "Put these on."

I stared at her in utter disbelief. "You must be joking."

"You're under arrest," she said, no weapon in her hand. "You are making this situation infinitely worse. For the good of the country—"

"Are you out of your mind?"

"For the safety of the people—"

"I said, 'are you out of your mind?' I'm trying to save people—"

"You are getting people killed," she said. "You are stirring up a hornet's nest of death and consequences, and they're not even landing on you."

"What's your plan? Let rabid, sleeping dogs lie? Until they decide to wake up and bite you?"

"We need to turn down the level of chaos—"

"That's not the job!" I bellowed, and she took a step back, cuffs swinging at the tip of her fingers. "The job is to pursue the bad guys, run them to ground, and arrest or destroy them *utterly!*" Cold fury seethed through my veins. "No wonder Foreman had to drag me off that island kicking and screaming. You don't have what it takes to do this job. You're living in a past that never existed, where everything was peaceful and everybody sang kumbaya together between sips of hot cocoa. There have always been bombs. There have always been people trying to murder each other." I stepped closer to her and knocked the cuffs out of her hands; they clanked on the ground, rattling as they skidded under a nearby fire truck. "The only difference now is that the murderers have super-powers you couldn't have conceived of in your blissful child-hood. You can't make this problem go away with the simple application of a cheerful, can-do attitude. Your enemy wants you and everyone around you dead. This is your moment to be the clutch player, Candy Cane Lane – and you don't have it in you."

I stuck a finger out, halting it an inch from her chest. "You're a coward. You say I have no care for the consequences; I have nothing but care for the consequences. You don't even realize that your consequences mean a world always enslaved to whoever threatens your peace, because you don't have the guts to fight back."

"I want people to be safe," she said, eyes burning.

"There is no safety in this world," I said coldly. "Not even the loving arms of your mother as a baby. Ask me how I know. You want, with all your heart, something that doesn't exist and never has, and you're convinced you can have it. That makes you delusional, and dangerous." I reached out my hand and triggered my Magneto powers. The handcuffs slid across the ground and leapt into my outstretched palm. I slapped them down into hers. "If you want to arrest me, give it a shot."

She looked me hard in the eyes for a moment, then glanced around. Alannah was about two feet behind her, looking like she would happily snap her neck. Augustus and Jamal were posted up conspicuously nearby, hands free. Others from the B team, like Madison Gustafson and her siblings, were there, too, all eyes on our confrontation. AA seemed to be leading the field from TBI, her hand was on her gun, and her eyes were on Lane, not me, watching for a move.

"Get out of my town with your cowardly bullshit," I said, pushing the handcuffs up into her chest. Lightly, but with enough force to make a point. "If you come at me again without the president's sanction, you better come loaded for bear. Not with baby handcuffs and an invitation to surrender." I jutted my chin out at her. "Because unlike you, I don't surrender. My will is not for sale. It's pointed toward one thing: breaking my enemies, and protecting the innocent as best I can."

She stared at me silently for a moment. "You're doing a bang-up job."

"At not being a sniveling coward? Better than you," I said. I watched her retreat, not daring to take my eyes off her, as she went back to her government SUV, and it slow-rolled as it left the scene.

CHAPTER FIFTY-EIGHT

Reed

We were standing on the sidewalk after checking with the team combing over the security feeds. Some small fortune had come our way, in that on said video, as we left Stubbs's office earlier in the evening, he'd been visible, showing us to the door in his avuncular way, talking to us as we walked down the hall. After that, he'd gone back inside.

And he'd never come out again.

No one else went into or out of his office between the time we left and when we returned to find him hanging from the ceiling. No one had even gone near it, there were no windows, and the air vents weren't big enough for anyone but Greg Vansen or his sort to come through. A perfect locked-room murder.

If I hadn't known Janus was involved, I would have been wildly speculating. *It was one of those metas that could pass through walls! Or one of the ones who can turn invisible, sneaking in as we left! Or an Atlas, coming in through the air vents, or under the door!*

But when your enemy is a powerful empath, and the cause of death looks to be suicide...Occam's razor is in full effect.

Keith Stubbs committed suicide, under the influence of a painful flood of emotional manipulation courtesy of Janus.

There was never going to be a way to prove that in court. The laws of humanity might have changed to adapt to the presence of metahumans, but there were some areas it was still inadequate to cover – and a locked-door murder by an empath was probably one of them.

It got me thinking about the other people I'd met when we'd joined forces with Omega. Some were dead, courtesy of Sovereign and Century. Some had survived the war with Sovereign and been cut down by the killer that had brought Sienna in contact with Webster years ago.

But it also got me thinking about one who definitely got away: Karthik, who, when last I'd heard of him (from Sienna), was still sticking with Janus. Karthik, the illusion caster.

Karthik, whose skin tone might have been just about the right shade for the murder victim, now that I thought about it.

"Reed?" Webster was looking at me, staring politely as we stood under the street lamps. "Did you hear me?"

"Sorry," I said, "I was miles away. What was that?"

"I said my wife's got a roast on," he said, holding up his phone to a text message on display. "The baby's already in bed, and we've plenty enough for guests." He smiled. "Would you like to come over for dinner?"

"The roast is lovely, I'm sure," Eilish said, "but I'm knackered. I'm calling it quits and heading for the hotel."

"Fair enough," Webster said. "Reed? What say you?"

"I..." I started to say no, reflexively. I glanced at Eilish, who was yawning. The hotel beckoned; I could go back there, get in my own room, which the Met was paying for, and spend my night hashing things through with Sierra, trying to pound a hole in this brick wall that was sitting astride my case. Maybe my brain would give first, or the brick wall would, but either way, it didn't sound like much fun. Or like it would be very productive.

So, instead, I said, "You know what? I'd love to come over for roast." And I did.

CHAPTER FIFTY-NINE

Wade

Getting winged in the head by a flying car door was not the high point of my day, especially while a metahuman riot was kicking off around me.

I found myself facedown under the brightly lit portico of a Las Vegas casino, as a car went squealing past six inches from my head, driver surely terrified of the consequences of remaining in such a dangerous place. It only made it another ten feet before it stopped; not because the driver hit the brakes, but because it was lifted physically off the ground by some invisible force. The engine revved madly, as though the driver were on a racetrack somewhere, but the tires moved without any avail, because there was no traction to be had. The wheels spun, kissing empty air beneath them, and then the car made an abrupt turn and flew like the DeLorean in *Back to the Future*, right over the bollards designed to prevent it, and into the wall of the casino with the most world-ending crash I'd heard in the last thirty seconds. It didn't break through, but it did deform terribly, and the engine died with a whine.

Blood was dripping down into my eyes, and I could barely string three thoughts together. And at least one of them was, "I wish Sienna was here."

But she wasn't. She was somewhere back east, and no one was coming to save me. As an LVPD officer hit the ground beside me with a crunch, I had to concede that no one was even going to give me an assist.

A woman with enough dirt on her face to fill a sandbag leapt over me. Her fingernails were claws, about a half-inch long each, and she was growling at me like a mad dog. She moved fast, too, metahuman fast, and I got the gist of her threat before she even had a chance to clarify it by going for my throat, or my guts, or more sensitive areas. She looked like she'd been living rough for quite some time, and the blood ringing her lips suggested she'd already done fatal or near-fatal damage to someone else before showing up here, in my face.

I didn't know whether she was guilty or innocent, under her own willpower or slave to someone else's. Instinct and reflex kicked in, and the same skills that had seen me through all manner of hell in Afghanistan worked for me now.

Her face dissolved in a blast of purple energy projected from my fist, leaving her missing most of her head. She pitched forward, and I caught her body with a kick that sent it flying. The corpse hit the side of the police van; one less threat to worry about.

Shit.

I couldn't spare a moment to mourn this poor soul. It became evident to me that she was likely suffering from the same fate as the darted bum in the paddy wagon: being driven remotely by a sadist who wasn't on site, someone who had it in mind to do great harm using the most abundant means available:

The army of American homeless drug addicts who, over the last several years, had received untold numbers of doses of fentanyl laced with metahuman serum.

And now, were being applied in the least elegant way possible to Fen Liu's last command.

Destroy America.

CHAPTER SIXTY

Sienna

"That was tense," AA said, a few minutes after Lane had cleared the scene. She didn't tell her driver to squeal tires; credit to her for that. As mad as I'd gotten at the FBI Director – and I'd been about as furious as I could recall being any time in recent memory – she'd kept her composure.

And asked me to put handcuffs on myself. "The absolute flaps of steel on that woman," I said, still too in my own head to fully acknowledge what AA had said. When I did get out of my feelings, I blinked at her. "Oh. Yeah. It was tense, all right. I probably still couldn't squeeze a drop of pee now if I had to."

AA winced, creasing her tanned face. "How is it I was raised the hillbilly, yet you still constantly say things that make me cringe?"

"Speaking of the backwoods," I said, looking her over; she

was in a suit, and almost looked like a Secret Service agent, "what are you doing here in Nashville?"

"Oh, well," AA said, "that's your fault. When you brought us all in to help out with the government during the China war, things got kind of...shuffled up. I ended up in the Nashville office. Haven't gotten moved back yet." She looked at me hopefully. "Actually, we could use some help. Your old job's still open if you're coming back to town." I must have grimaced. "Oh," she said. "The thought of working with me again is that bad, huh?"

"It's not you," I said, "It's the job. The grind. It's..." I shook my head. "I don't know. How much of an asshole does it make me if I say I just don't want to do it anymore?"

She blinked a couple times. "I mean, I thought you were kinda done after Minneapolis. But you came back, so..."

"It doesn't feel like there's any escape for me," I said. "Like I'm going to be doing this until I'm dead whether I want to or not, because I'm not good at anything else."

"I'm sure you're good at other things," she said. So reassuring, that Ashley Aylor. Also kind of a liar. But in a sweet way.

"Killing people and breaking things is all I've been good at, AA," I said. "Maybe saving a life here and there." Looking once more at the gaping hole in the side of the condo tower, I added, "This is what I do, whether I want to or not. Because no one else can do what I do, and world peace is as elusive as an unused shot of Ozempic at the Oscars." I drew a breath of air that was still infused with the scent of burning, even hours later. "So, where are Chandler and Marsh?"

"They moved up to the DC field office," she said, brow furrowing in a thin line. "With you. Back in the war. Remember?"

I felt properly gobsmacked. No, I didn't remember that; it was probably something Sierra had done and I'd approved during that small interregnum when I'd sat in the seat of the president but didn't have the title. "What were they doing for the bureau?"

"Field work," she said.

Which made my blood go cold. "Do you know..." I tried to find the words. "...They were in the field? You're sure?"

"Yeah," she said. "I shared an email with Chandler just a couple days ago. He's enjoying the work, but misses the Tennessee weather about now." She frowned. "Why do you ask? While looking so grave. Do you think something happened to them?"

"I don't know," I said, trying to bury the sick feeling in my gut. Now, not only was I responsible for setting off a chain of events that killed people in DC as well as here, but I might have gotten people I knew and care about killed. I tried to bury it as I contemplated what to do next, but the sick feeling would not leave me.

CHAPTER SIXTY-ONE

Reed

Webster lived just a little ways outside London, in a suburb that had probably seen better days. His house was well-kept, a little brick town-home, as we would have called it in the states, that sat on a street with a decent amount of green, trees swaying in the night breeze.

The smell of roast hit me in the face as I stepped inside, the warm air a pleasant change from the outside chill. Webster closed the front door, and the scent of cooking meat mingled with the faintest hints of carrots, potatoes, and parsnips, covering over the scent of faded diapers.

Mrs. Webster came around the corner just then, wearing a knitted sweater, her hair a nice auburn, figure thin and lithe. She was tall, for a woman, though not as tall as me. She had a lovely smile, a bit girlish and sweet. She opened her mouth and pure enthusiasm bubbled out. "You must be Reed," she said, stepping forward and extending a long arm to me. I shook her offered hand, and caught a whiff of perfume covering up the smell of a woman who'd been taking care of little kids all day. "Such a pleasure to meet you."

"Reed, this is my Anna," Webster said with a hint of pride.

"Nice to meet you, Anna," I said. "Thank you for the invite."

"Oh, it's nothing," she said. "Please, come in – can I get you a glass of wine?"

I followed them into the kitchen, which was cozy. She poured me a glass of Cab Sauv along with one for herself, and Webster, as she prattled on about pleasantries – the weather, her day with the kids, and how she hoped the food would be to my liking. I told her I was sure it'd be fine, that I really wasn't that fussy about it. Beggars can't be choosers, after all.

We sat down to dinner after a few minutes, and I found myself in the middle of perfectly adequate roast. I'd had better, I'd had worse, but I tried to put on a bit of a front. Not too complimentary, as I didn't want to be over the top. But I didn't want her to think I felt I was eating garbage, either. I smiled, and I complimented the flavors, and when she asked me if I wanted seconds I said sure, and took just a small amount more, begging off because of the need to keep my waistline trim.

The conversation meandered; it stayed away from the case and on everyday things. Their opinions about UK Prime Minister Jo Evans ("She's a good one," Webster insisted, "reminds me of my mum"), about the quality of British beef (I kept mine to myself and nodded along), and general talk about the state of the city ("could be better," which felt like a common lament about cities in this age).

Anna was pleasant and cheerful, at odds with the devil of a case that was bouncing around in my head. I kept dwelling on Karthik, wondering if it was him that had met the fate of being torn to pieces and dumped out in the cold. But to the Websters, I just smiled and nodded, trying to follow whatever they were talking about in the moment.

A small cry came from a bedroom down the hall, and my hosts looked as though they'd both experienced a jolt. "I'll go," Webster said, patting Anna on the arm. "Be nice to see the little lad."

"He's been dying to see you all day," she said, smiling as he went. To me, she added, "'Where's da? When's da coming home?' I swear that's half of all I hear, all day."

I feigned a smile. I was practiced at it. It had been a long time since I'd been able to ask for my 'da,' after all.

"Oh, I'm sorry," Anna said.

"For what?" I asked, frowning. "You've been a wonderful host."

"I didn't even think about the fact that you lost your father," she said, eyebrows knitted together in a special brand of warm concern that only seemed possible from the female of the species. Not all, of course; Sienna would struggle to produce it. But I'd never met a man who could pull it off at all.

"It was a long time ago, and you can't be expected to dodge every word that could possibly remind me of him." It was my turn to smile. "Guessing since you know that I lost my father, you know it's because he's the relation Sienna and I share."

She blushed, and cupped her hands in front of her mouth before leaning in closer. "Is it odd that I'm a fan of hers? Does that make this strange?"

"You're hardly the only one," I said, though perhaps a bit

more stiffly than I intended. I paused, and couldn't control my frown. "Webster has met my sister before. Guessing he told you that," I finished lamely.

"Oh, I know," she said. "We talked about it on our first date, in fact. It was kind of the first rich vein of commonality we struck. Now, I hardly believed, until now, that he really, uh...*knew* her." She seemed to be looking at me expectantly.

"I don't really monitor these things," I said, words sticking a bit in my throat at the implication there, "but I have no reason to think he's lying."

She seemed to glow a bit. "I know it's odd, and I don't even care. She's famous, and I'm – well, I'll never be. This is the closest I'll ever get, this bit of reflected glory, and I'll take it without complaint. We all have a past, after all." She seemed to perk up a bit. "My girlfriends' husbands' version of it usually just involve pub sluts. This is a fair sight better than that."

"I think you were right when you called it 'odd,' though," I said, pushing around the last remains of a slightly mashed potato I hadn't had the stomach space or the will to eat.

"I'll accept my oddness," she said. "Is it hard, though?" I looked up to find her gazing at me expectantly. "The shadow she casts, it must be...well, it's a bit poxy for me to say, 'Enormous,' a bit rude, and obviously she's very fit these days–"

"It is difficult to live in her shadow, yes," I said, lifting my wine glass. "When people know me, they know me because of her. That's me: I share a parent with Sienna Nealon. I mean, we weren't even raised together, but people just sort of think we must be besties." I scratched my head. "She's great, and I love her, and I wouldn't trade her for the world."

She leaned in a bit. "But...?"

"I'm not her," I said. "I'll never be her. And it's impossible to escape the feeling that wherever I am, with the exception of in my own home, with my fiancée, that everyone I meet would rather her be there than me." I paused, and thought. "Possible exception: criminals also would probably prefer I be standing there rather than her."

Anna chuckled. "Fame does funny things to us, you know. Gives her a ten thousand watt illumination."

I waved that off. "She's famous because she's done things I can't." Or wouldn't – but there was no need to say that out loud. "I couldn't stop Sovereign, or Gerry Harmon, or the nukes coming from Revelen. I tried, in all those cases. I wasn't good enough – but she was."

"But why would you measure yourself against her?" Anna asked. She had her legs crossed, and was leaning forward. "That seems to me the path to madness. If I measured myself against your sister, why, I might find myself wanting, in all ways. If I'd done it early enough–"

"Like the first date?"

"Exactly," she said, eyes dancing, "I might have psyched myself out of even giving it a chance with Matthew. Then where would I be? Two less children, for sure. No one's the same as anyone else. And surely there are things you can do that she can't?"

"Well, I'd thought maybe 'please a woman,' was the edge I had on her," I said, "but then I met you, and you seem beyond delighted with her..."

She laughed. "Oh, don't mistake me. It's just a spot of hero worship. Just because she's the only woman on my hall pass list, try not to make too much of it." Her self-aware smirk was delightful. "I'm not Sapphic, I swear. Most of the time."

"I don't try and compare myself to her," I said. "Most of the time. A succubus can simply do things I can't. And she's been through things I wouldn't ever want to go through. Things that made her the person she is. Harder things...things I wouldn't wish on myself."

"What is it, then?" she asked. "You're a smart enough chap. Seems like you have a woman at home that loves you. Your sister certainly cares for you. Why, I've seen her move heaven and earth to save you, just as you have for her. Why does it matter to you, Reed, that you'll never be as famous as her?"

"It's not the fame," I said, as the truth cracked free for maybe the first time in my life, and I could finally say it, between the wine and the honesty, "it's the power. It's that she's got all that power, and I don't. And it's not because I resent her having it; she's great with it. It's because..." and I stared off into the distance as it hit me in a cold, clutching pain in my guts, writhing at the thought, "...if anything ever happens to the people I love, I don't have that kind of power to save any of them. I find myself...inadequate."

Even saying it out loud made me retract into myself. "You know what? This isn't your problem. I should go—"

"No, don't," she said, rising to catch me.

"You've been so lovely," I said, scrambling for my coat.

"You're still more powerful than any of us, you know," she said before I could make it across the family room. "If you're going to compare yourself to somebody, maybe it ought to be those of us who are defenseless? Rather than the one girl in all the world with the power to rain hell down anywhere, anytime?"

I found all I could do at that was nod. "Thank you for the lovely dinner. Tell Webster I'll see him tomorrow." And I ducked out before I could embarrass myself any further.

Cursing my stupidity, I let my feet guide me. I'd seen an Underground stop a few blocks away when Webster had driven us in. I made for it, following this curious sensation of a desire to wander.

I only made it a block before I identified from whence that feeling came.

The custom Range Rover glided to a stop beside me, and I already knew who was going to be behind the glass before it rolled down. "The Underground can be so dangerous at night," Janus said from within, his face covered in shadows. "Why don't you take a ride with me, Mr. Treston? It will give us a chance to...catch up on old times."

CHAPTER SIXTY-TWO

Wade

Fen Liu's last act of vengeance on America was kicking off right in front of me, and I was in real trouble before it even began. I'd been clipped by a car door flung into my head, and boy was I feeling it. Sorely missed was my wife; even more missed were her healing powers, as well as the beaches of Greece that I'd left behind to come to this shitshow.

A Hercules kicked me in the side and sent me flying. I hit the ceiling of the portico, crashed through the sheet metal surface, got lodged in it, and felt my back pop as I reached maximum extension and ended with my body hanging down and my feet caught. I hung there for a moment, swinging like a pendulum with a perfect view of the chaos of a metahuman riot unfolding beneath me like some 21st century version of the sack of Rome.

Getting waylaid by a bunch of psychotic, mind-controlled

bums outside an establishment founded on $9.99 lobster dinners was not my finest hour, so I tried to get my head together. My bell had been well and truly rung, and now I was swinging like one, too, my skull shook up like a can of beer. Hopefully someone wouldn't try and open it, because my brains spewing out would not exactly be the tip top point of my day.

I watched one of the shifters – the one in bear form – roar and charge a cop just below me, and I lifted a hand to help. I discharged a green laser that struck the bear in the flank, just behind his right leg, and he bellowed but didn't slow down, plowing into the officer and turning him to a stain on the pavement from momentum and weight.

Shit. These meta addicts, these members of the most extreme underclass in America – they weren't willingly going along with this any more than the guy in the back of the paddy wagon had consented to having his mouth used to spew our trigger man's words at me. This was a mass brain-jacking, plain and simple, because none of them were cogent, all of them were screaming psychotics, hellbent on destruction and nothing but.

Yet still...they were going to kill innocent people. They might have been vessels for evil, but if I didn't stop them, every single one of them had the damage potential of a bomb.

My choices sucked. But failing to choose was a choice of its own, and carried its own consequences. It was Clancy that had been smashed by the bear-shifter, I realized a moment too late. He did not survive.

Tapping into my Wolfe healing, I felt things start to improve in my head.

Then I blasted the bear's head off with my green laser.

Using my Magneto powers, I ripped apart the debris that had caught my leg, allowing me to flip loose and giving me a greater field of vision. I flung down energy whips that wrapped up the Hercules and the meta with green lasers, catching them both around the neck. I closed the loops and flung them up into the portico ceiling as I came down. It was a delaying tactic; my conscience working on me to find a way to spare them, even for a few moments.

They crashed into the ceiling head first and landed hard as I turned to deal with a wolf leaping at me. I freed one of my energy whips and snagged him midair, sending him sailing past me and snout-first into the bumper of the police wagon. A sickening crack should have been followed by yelping.

It was not.

It was followed by a growl.

The wolf looked back at me, white, crackling energy still snugged around his neck; I had a good grip on him, and if he'd been in his right mind, he'd have known not to attack me when I had him by the throat.

He was not in his right mind. None of them were.

The wolf leapt; I cranked his neck sideways at an impossible angle with a fast swing, and it broke. He'd turned back into a human – naked, wrinkled, dirty, pitiful – by the time he slammed into the Plexiglas windows of the casino. His neck was twisted sickly, and his eyes were dull.

You know whose weren't? The laser guy and the Hercules, who were charging me before I even came back around. The Herc had a split-open head that was pouring blood, but it mingled with the spittle flying out of his mouth. The laser guy wasn't any better; he was drawing a bead on me with both hands as he screamed in a mad battle fury.

I shot him from the hip with a taste of his own medicine, and it slipped between his fists and drilled his brains out before he could open fire on me. He toppled over, and I did the same to the Hercules, catching him in the throat and severing his spine with a perfect emerald blast of energy. He dropped like the string-cut puppet he was.

Thunderous footsteps sounded behind me, and I felt rather than saw a Stoneskin coming; he wasn't a big guy, but his skin was covered in solid rock from head to loincloth, then thighs to toes.

No blocking a runaway train; I drew on my own, today-acquired Stoneskin power as he tackled me, and his flesh of stone met mine of steel.

He lost, but barely. Chips of him came flying off, and he cried out in pain.

I got grabbed from behind by the tree-skinned guy, dragged a few feet, and thrown into the trunk of a Metro PD squad car. My head caved in the aluminum, creating an indentation in the metal as though someone had dropped a bowling ball on it from ten stories. The Stoneskin had my legs and the tree-man got my upper body, and they combined to slam me into it again. This time I ripped through the metal, through the carpet inside the trunk, and kissed the rear axle. Even with a face made of steel, it didn't feel great.

I tapped my flight powers, hit the Wolfe pipe for healing, and twisted in the air, freeing my feet and giving the Stoneskin a kick that would have made any mule proud; I wasn't one, but I'd been compared to one in my stubbornness for most of my life.

He went sailing, and not in a graceful way. It knocked him back a few steps and tipped him over, because his weighty skin made him top heavy. He crashed down onto the pavement, feet going over, and leaving me with Treebeard to cope with.

I coped with him by grabbing him and flying straight up as fast as I could. When I reached the top of the casino tower, I punted him as hard as I could, breaking his grip on me.

Bombs away.

Flying back down, I landed feet-first on the Stoneskin and

drove him into the pavement. I'm no mathmagician, but the force of a man whose entire body mass is composed of steel, hitting another person at a thousand miles an hour–

I drove him into the ground like John Henry's hammer, wielded by God. He smashed through the street and kept going. I like to think he's still smashing through rock, on his way to the earth's core.

Ten feet away, the tree-skinned guy came crashing down into the paddy wagon. I grimaced; that had, perhaps, not been the most responsible way to handle him. He hadn't killed anyone except the tree guys in the back of the paddy wagon, but that hadn't exactly been the most generous solution to the problem. Those guys were darted; they might have lived, if not for me.

A set of ruby eyebeams slammed into my chest and knocked me back a step. That meta had turned attention on me, and was backed up by a slew more that were spilling into the area. Not a single LVPD cop was still moving; most were bloody smears on the pavement, including Smithson, who was somehow in three different pieces behind me.

I screamed in rage and leapt forward, my skin of steel my guard against the painful, red blast that they tried to use to bat me out of the sky. It didn't work; strength, momentum, and my flight powers carried me forward, and the eyebeam meta became another casualty of physics as I landed and turned them into a jelly that coated the asphalt.

It didn't do one damned bit of good.

There was a current of rage all around me. A Hercules hammered at my steel skin with a motorcycle while a Fae fired blasts of light webbing at me that stuck to me like little globs of nothing. Someone came at me with a lightsaber sticking out of their hand and I seized them by the wrist and ripped it off, sending them flying and using their hand to level some idiot who came at me with an icicle spear as long as a fence post.

Someone came at me looking like an oversized cockroach, and I redirected the icicle into his guts when I caught it. Flashes of apocalypse occurred at the edges of my vision, making me think something was coming for me, but I tumbled on to the fact it was illusions just in time to clock the dumbass who was sneaking up behind me with literally nothing in her hands but a gas can.

I started rigging gravity channels to the people screaming around me, sending them up to the portico above to hang there. One after another; the ice spear guy, the screaming Fae, the Rakshasa, the roach, another meta with steel claws, this time, a Reflex that tried to dodge out of the gravity trap. I sent them all upward, along with a plasma burner that accidentally evaporated the flesh of the woman next to her when she got caught.

It didn't matter. They were still coming. Dozens. Hundreds.

Thousands, maybe.

I rocketed up through the portico, smashing my way through while still made of steel. In the distance, coming along like freaking Godzilla, were two Atlas types that had grown to a hundred feet in height. They were doing a surprisingly small amount of damage for their size, probably because they still had the same proportionate metahuman strength. Which made them stronger than a human, but not nearly as strong as a hundred-foot-tall man should have been. One of them squished a taxi, and it was barely flattened.

A woman tried to seize me out of the sky with excessively long hair, and I burned my way through it with a laser blast. Hanging around here seemed like a bad idea, and one that wasn't going to save lives, and might only end up costing them.

But I couldn't just leave the people of Vegas to this fate.

Something slammed into me, and it hit a lot harder than anything else I'd gone up against. It wasn't one of the Atlas types; I came crashing back to earth beneath the weight of something massive, something with jaws the size of a semi-truck.

A damned dragon. Like Sienna, but with different markings, different coloration. It slammed me into the pavement, and I felt this impact in a way none of the others had moved me. Something about the mass of the thing hitting me, about the strength of it, rattled my brain.

Looking down, the silver metal retracted from my hand like the tide receding from the shore, leaving only skin behind. I was almost out, blackness squeezing in around the edges of my vision, when I felt a brisk wind and a splatter of something warm that smelled like blood.

Then I was out, unconscious, in the middle of a riot of people who could easily destroy me – and who wanted nothing more than to do so.

CHAPTER SIXTY-THREE

Sienna

I caught up to Jamal after parting ways with AA. He was standing with Augustus, both looking somewhat shell-shocked, even hours after nearly coming to an end from a Chinese suicide bomb. He was fiddling with his phone, to little effect, or so it seemed. "Anything?" I asked.

He looked skyward, at the small trails of smoke curling out of the gaping hole in the building above. "I'm getting intermittent updates from Arche, but it's not anything good. Entire internet nodes are offline, and also a good portion of the cellular network. It's directed attacks, presumably from your, uh...what did you call him again?"

"Trigger man," I said. Because that's what he was; the assassin and terrorist sent as Fen Liu's last gasp of vengeance. Not a man with a will of his own, just some dipshit with his finger on a trigger I didn't fully understand.

"He's got a real flair for this," Jamal said. "Whatever tools he's deployed, he's managed to thwart Arche, which is no small thing, and Sierra, I assume, too, which may be even harder."

"But why only in certain areas?" I asked.

"Taking down the whole internet is hard," Jamal said. "It's not just a single network, in spite of the name. It's a web of interconnected ones. Lots of nodes from independent companies, big companies, some small ones, some government ones. Same with the cellular network. There are lots of independent tower operators out there that make bank every year selling bandwidth. They use similar protocols, but they're not seamless. Whoever this guy is, he identified some of the seams and slipped in, cutting those sections out – for now."

"Does that mean Arche thinks she can get it back online?" I asked.

"Maybe," Jamal said. "But first we have to knock out this guy's bot army or viruses, or whatever he's got going. It's like trying to turn the power back on while you're fist fighting the toughest opponent you've ever had and he's just broken your jaw. A lot easier to do it if you're not fighting for your life at the same time."

"How big is this blackout zone around Nashville?" I asked.

"About fifty miles," he said. "Why?"

"Because I need to know how far I'm going to have to fly to get a signal," I said, and leapt into the air. "Keep an eye on things around here, will you? I'm not sure where I'm going next, but I think I might be done here for a bit."

"We got you, Sienna," Augustus said, offering me a small salute. "Go do what you got to."

I turned east, and was up to supersonic speed before his words faded in my ears.

They didn't fade from my heart, though. That kept hold of them long after the wind had washed away any other sound but its roar.

CHAPTER SIXTY-FOUR

Reed

The first thought that occurred to me as I stared at Janus in the back of his Land Rover was that he had earned a reputation as being two-faced for a reason.

Unfortunately, I'd had just enough wine to give voice to these thoughts. It prompted the older man to smile and reply, "A two-faced *god.*"

I stared blankly at him. "What difference does that make?"

"A two-faced man would tell you to get in the car," Janus said, "a two-faced god compels you to do it."

I got in the car.

Once I was seated beside him, it started to roll, and I looked over at the older man. "You did that? With your powers?"

"A suggestion, only," he said. "Would you prefer to walk? Or take the train? While not as bad as I hear New York has become, it is hardly the most joyous experience in these days."

In my right hand, hiding it from his eyes, I held my phone, and tapped out a message I could only barely see as I rode. *In car with Janus.*

"Should we open with empty platitudes about how it's been too long?" I asked.

"I do enjoy a good platitude," Janus said. "And manners of this sort have their use. Formalized rituals for humans to maintain relations. Since time immemorial, these are the things that we practice to keep ourselves on a good level with others. Keeps us out of war, which is so very destructive to us."

"You know why I'm here, then," I said.

"To be sure," Janus said.

"Was it Karthik?" I asked.

"Yes." He stared straight ahead.

"He was with you for so long," I said. "Why now?"

"This is where we reach an uncomfortable point of truth," Janus said, turning to look at me, eyes devoid of the warmth I'd caught glimpses of when he worked with us. "My business is my own. Our acquaintance was a matter of survival and convenience, and concluded years ago. I know you have principles that tell you that you must care about what happens here, that somehow the death of even someone you don't really know, in a matter you aren't privy to, affects you somehow. But it does not. This system of justice that you prize, it can go on with the occasional stutter, or unresolved case. This is one that you should let go. For your own good."

"I don't know that I can," I said, somehow compelled to say it; not in a defiant way. Not out of spite. I didn't yell it in his face. It was almost a whisper, straight from my soul.

Janus shifted in his seat. "People die every day, Mr. Treston. The whole world over. I know you cannot care about all of them. You narrow your focus to the ones you can help, do you not?"

"I do. But that doesn't mean my heart doesn't go out to ones in, say, Zimbabwe, when something terrible happens to them."

"Of course, the heart goes where it must," Janus said. "But your considerable focus and effort? It cannot wander everywhere." He plucked a stray thread from his tweed jacket and inspected it from behind his glasses. "You see injustice here, and I agree. But no good can come from this. For either of us. For I do not wish to see any harm visited upon you."

I stared at him. "I wish I could say the same."

"You wish me harm?" His eyebrows rose ever so slightly. "I have kept my plans and my efforts away from your shores. I have given you and your sister and all your friends a wide berth."

"You re-founded Omega," I said, the truth of it producing a desire to grind my teeth. "After it was dead, staked and buried."

"Ah," he said. "So there is the wellspring of your loathing. Alpha to the last, then? Hera told you many tales, I suppose, of our purported misdeeds."

I scoffed. "Hera didn't have to tell me tales, though of course she had plenty. My father worked for Alpha before her, recall, and after he died, I eventually saw his files. And I worked against you in the field for years before Sovereign came along and bowled you all over, your Humpty-Dumpty organization." I leaned just a bit closer. "You may have played the nice, grandfatherly counsel to Sienna during the war, but I know what you used to do. You, and Bastet, and that piece of shit Alastor that ran everything—"

"Times change," he said, looking down at his hands. Not exactly the strong show of confidence I would have expected.

"That cuts no ice with me," I said, and my fury had taken

over, because I'd seen years' and decades' worth of crimes that Janus and those like him, those with him, had committed. He was a pox on this earth, destroying the lives of any who got in his way, now and before. "Sienna beat Rick to death. You know, the last head of Omega before you picked up the mantle of this new organization?"

He did not look up at me. "I was there when it happened."

"She still feels a touch of guilt about it," I said, "because he didn't have any metahuman powers. She was wishing it was Alastor. See, I usually draw a pretty strong line about that sort of thing, beating a powerless man. But you know what? I don't fault her a bit for it, because I know what kind of man Rick was. I know the sort of man his father was, before Alastor died. They were scum of the highest order, and he hid his deeds like he hid his face, trying to keep anonymous. Like you, now. King of the London underworld, and you suicided a guy tonight who not only didn't know your name–"

"Oh, but you made certain that he did."

"He was retiring," I said, with pure heat. "In weeks. He wouldn't have gone after you. He didn't have it in him."

"The old dog with nothing to lose can be the most dangerous of all," Janus said.

"Lucky you've got a lot to lose, I guess." I stared him down. "You're a liar, by the way. Living up to that two-faced reputation."

He gave me a measured look. "In what way did I lie to you?"

"You said before that you left America to me and my sister, gave us a wide berth." I turned toward him now, clutching the armrest between us, the leather squeezed in my grip like I had his head in my palm and was crushing it. "But that's bullshit; Sienna killed three Omega gangsters in Minnesota. Part of your expansion team in the New World. I know they're operating there, some sort of franchise arrangement."

Janus smiled thinly and shrugged, his palms up. "I did warn them before they undertook to build their organizations that they would receive no help from us, and to give you a considerable distance."

"I have zero reason to trust you when you ask me to let this go," I said, fire blazing in me. "No cause to hope that this won't end in so many more deaths if I walk away. If I wasn't already sure who you are, you might have been able to convince me."

"But you are who you are," Janus said, with a thin, almost mournful smile. "This is the key difference between you and your sister, though no one else sees it."

"What?" I asked.

"She is a creature of pragmatism," he said, looking at his hands, folded in his lap. "No one realizes this, because she is so powerful that little can stymie her in pursuit of her will. And it is not to say she has no principles; but she is flexible in how she will go about things, where she will let her attention go. She agreed once before to leave me be, you see. To let me have this...thing, that I do. She did this out of loyalty for our past association, she would say, but...it is pragmatism." He looked up. "She does not want a war with me if she need not have it. So she turns her face away from my activities.

"But you – you cannot," he said, smiling faintly. "A man of principle, you cannot pretend not to see what you have seen. It is the same reason you struggle with killing, while she does not. Because you believe in justice as it is preached – fair, impartial, a balance between humans on this earth. And while you have bent your principles, perhaps, from time to time, it was always under strain, while she believes justice by the law is only useful as far as it goes, and that justice by the sword is a perfectly fine thing, if need be. Better imperfect than not at all, hm?"

"This thing? It has nothing to do with my sister," I said.

"Oh, I know you think that to be the case," Janus said, tsk-tsking, "but I can assure you it is not so." He snapped his fingers, and suddenly, from the front seat, there was a gun pointed at my face. I hadn't even noticed there was a passenger in the seat in front of me. Even now, I couldn't make out any details of his face. "Your sister is saving your life even now. For if you were just Reed Treston, a man alone, with no sibling, you would not make it to your hotel tonight. You would never be seen alive again, in fact. Neither would your compatriot, the Irish girl." He mimed a gun. "Because you believe in the principle of impartial justice, bound by the law – and so does your entire nation, in theory, at least.

"But your sister believes in vengeance, in retribution, in the spirit of *Nemesis*," Janus said, leaning in slightly, whispering. "So if I kill you and your little Irish friend, we will have upon our doorstep, very quickly indeed, an unleashed succubus with little compunction about laying us all to waste. And so," he said, and inclined his head toward the front seat, where the gun disappeared back under the coat of the passenger, "you live to see another day, Mr. Treston. But only because of your sister, and that immense shadow she casts. You may think you wish you could escape it, but I assure you that for every detriment it brings, it holds a corresponding benefit." He smiled. "I think this is your hotel."

I looked out the window. He was correct. My throat felt a little dry.

"Now, the pleasantries," Janus said, and offered me his hand. "It was lovely to see you again."

I took it, strangely compelled, and shook it, in perhaps the most lifeless, robotic way I could. "I suppose now each of us knows where the other stands."

"I always knew where you stood," Janus said. "But it was nice to see that I remain correct, even in my old age."

"Then I guess it's good that I know where you stand," I said. The passenger got out and opened the door for me. "So thank you for that."

"But of course," Janus said. "After all, you did stop by my house. Paying you a return visit seemed only polite. The little courtesies, you understand. The polite fictions, to keep up relations. No one wants a war, after all. It's bad for—"

"Business?" I asked, getting out onto the sidewalk. The Rover had been so pleasantly warm, and out here was so cold.

"Life," Janus said. "Farewell, Mr. Treston. I hope you go back home to that lovely doctor you have waiting for you. You should marry her, I think. Life is short, even for us. And shorter still when we war on each other. So you should seize every bit of happiness from that you are able, and wring it out with both hands."

I glanced at the passenger now, who had opened the door for me. I still couldn't see any details of his face; it was like he was cast in shadow. All I could tell was that he was looking at me, and intensely, I got the sense. He shut the door and seemed to melt back into the car in a stutter-step of movement, like a stop-motion animation.

Janus did not look at me again as the car drove away. He just left me there, in the cold, to contemplate what he'd said.

An offer of war, or an offer of peace. The implication was clear: if I meant war, I'd face him, and all his people...

And, after this display...it seemed very likely that they could, and would, kill me.

CHAPTER SIXTY-FIVE

Sienna

I knew when I hit the edge of the blackout zone because my phone exploded into a frenzy of alerts. Government ones filled the top of the screen, but soon after came text messages from Sierra. Before I could read anything beyond the preview, my phone lit up with an incoming call – from Sierra. I answered. "Yeah, I'm back. Prioritize and give me the news."

"Based on overhead, real-time satellite data," she said, skipping the pleasantries, "Chinese bombs have gone off in eight different blackout zones. I cannot assess the damage beyond the immediate physical impact, which appears considerable. The upshot seems to be that Fen Liu's agent, knowing this was a thread we would pursue, somehow managed to convince the Chinese agents to engage in previously unseen behavior patterns, at least for them."

"I suspect mind control," I said, thinking of the bum in

Nashville that he'd used to speak to me. "Does that mean he's near to my current position? Or just really powerful at telepathy?"

"You have more experience with this than I do," she said.

I frowned, hanging in the cold air somewhere above Crossville, Tennessee. "Lethe can talk to me through Odin's ravens from states away. If this guy is Fen Liu's last agent, he's probably had all the serums. Which means boosted telepathy is a distinct possibility – and that means he could be anywhere in the country, maybe even in the world." I knew this not only from Odin, but from Dr. Zollers, whose help would certainly have been useful right about now – if he wasn't in Russia trying to put the country back together. Again.

"Another note: Chinese authorities have been trying to reach you for some time," she said. "Would you like me to patch them through?"

I grimaced. "Is what they've got to say important, or...?" At a certain level of emergency, filtering became crucial.

"Well, they're not trying to reach you to ritually apologize," she said. Then, after a pause, added, "I don't think."

"Put 'em through," I said, and about ten seconds later Sierra announced, "Wei Zhang is on the line."

I raised an eyebrow. "Mr. Tac. Long time no see." It's a joke. Because his power is to turn invisible. Hilarious, no? And so well-timed.

"Good one. I'm laughing in my heart," he said, with his usual brusqueness. "Listen, you're not going to want to hear this, but we have been monitoring your situation."

"You can take the aggressive oligarchy out of the spy state, but you can't take the spy state out of the newly democratic one," I said. "Go on. You were spying on me and saw...?"

"I just meant we're aware of what you're dealing with, in

basic terms," Zhang said, sounding annoyed, "so you didn't waste time explaining it."

"So you're up to date on the comms blackouts, the suicide bombs, the leftover Chinese monitoring posts, and the flaming Atlas-type currently smashing his way through New York City?"

There was a deep pause. "I'm not aware of that last one."

"Just testing you," I said. "I made that one up. Okay, you're up to speed. What have you got to abate my rage at this little gift from your last government?"

"Maybe nothing, maybe something," he said. "We've narrowed the list of possible spies to ten candidates – at least, that we can sort out. All people who left China with slightly suspicious documents and travel itineraries that could have seen them end up in the US. It's a bit of a challenge going any deeper than that, and we might have missed something, but – it's what I've got for you."

I thought about going all psychotic bitch on him, like I had everyone else today. But thus far it hadn't done me much good, so I went with, "Thank you," instead.

"We'll continue working it on this end," Zhang said. "Minister Jian wants me to tell you that we're deeply sorry about the trouble. If we could have discovered it sooner, we would have."

"Yeah, I know," I said. "That Fen Liu was a slippery one. She had plans within plans."

"Tell me about it," he said darkly. Which was just a touch funny, since at least one of her plans involved killing him. "If anything else comes up–"

"Call me direct," I said. "Sierra, give him my number."

"Sent via text message," Sierra said. "And he's disconnected. We have received his list. I can likely rule out six of the names."

"How'd you do that?" I asked.

"Two are dead," she said. "One is currently in a long-term stay at a resort in Maui, and has been since leaving China, two more are in Europe and Dubai, respectively. The last of this set is riding horses across the plains in Mongolia on an ongoing basis. Unless any of those is performing telepathic activities from their current respective locations–"

"If they haven't been to the US, we can rule them out for now," I said. "Whoever set this up has likely been on American soil at some point, for logistical reasons." I paused. "Unless they're just so incredibly powerful, telepathically, they can do all this from another continent, in which case...scary."

"After scanning the Chinese system, now I can rule out two more," she said. "One is in Hong Kong, and has been for two months, after an extended stay in Singapore, and the other is in Taipei, Taiwan, and has been since leaving China."

"And then there were two," I said. "So where are the last of them?"

"One of them, Wei-Chen Liu, is currently in Las Vegas, Nevada," Sierra said. "And I have no location for the second, one Mei-Ling Yun."

"Vegas, huh?" I made a face. "Think that has any relation to whatever Wade's dealing with right now?"

"Unknown," Sierra said. "Alert: I am picking up a radical change in internet activity in Washington DC right now."

I hung there in the cold air, turning to look east. "Break it down for me, Sierra. What does that augur?"

She didn't keep me in suspense even a moment. "I believe it means that DC is about to become the next blackout zone."

CHAPTER SIXTY-SIX

Reed

Eilish opened her hotel room door wide-eyed, clearly not sleeping. "Oh," she said, like she was surprised to see me. "You."

"You were expecting someone else?" I asked, trying not to look down. Because she'd answered the door in panties and a white, thin tank top that had not a damned thing underneath it. She looked kind of dulled, head cocked questioningly as I took in her attire with a flick of my eyes and then nailed my gaze above her collarbone, determined to hold that line for the rest of our conversation, no matter how long it lasted. "God, I hope you were expecting someone else."

"What? I was just lounging, actually," she said, and I caught a whiff of cannabis that I couldn't believe I hadn't noticed immediately. Probably because I was blinkered by the cute Irish girl standing braless in her undies before me. "Come in?"

I hesitated. "I'm not sure that's a great idea." I didn't dare look down.

She made a grunt in the back of her throat and seized me by the arm, dragging me in. "I'll put on something, ye prude, but I don't wish to have whatever conversation you're bent on having with me knockers and me arse hanging out in the hallway." Slamming the door behind me, she retreated into the room and picked up a pair of jeans discarded on the floor. She hopped into them quickly and dexterously, unintentionally supplying me with an image of her thin, pale legs disappearing into them capped by her arse (her word, not mine), which was...supple. Next she threw on a coat, and by this time I'd turned to face the door rather than keep staring.

"Such a gentleman," she said, tapping me on the shoulder once she was done. There was a women's magazine open on the lone, king-sized bed, and she plopped down next to it. An ashtray with a squashed-out roach butt was sitting on the nightstand, its stink malingering in the room. A fresh joint was sitting right next to it. "I pinched these from Janus's apartment earlier. Can I tempt you?"

I stared blankly into her eyes for a moment, as my brain worked through the meaning of that offer. "Oh, with a – no, thank you, I'm not–"

She flushed a shade of red I typically associated with sports cars and ripe tomatoes. "I didn't mean like that. I was offering you drugs, not – well, you know." Arse. The word popped into mind again, unbidden.

"I didn't think you were – I mean, kinda inappropriate either way, but one is probably worse than the other," I said. "Listen, I came here because Janus just took me for a ride–"

She sat up, a little alarmed, and her Irish accent came on full force. "Are ye all right?"

"I'm fine," I said, mustering the strength to say that, too.

"He didn't...I mean, he threatened me. Got a gun pointed in my face. But he mostly wanted to scare me off, I think."

"Scare you?" she asked, voice full of wry amusement. "I imagine that's a grace he doesn't extend very often, at least in his current role. Clearly he didn't to whoever that poor lad was that got us brought over here."

"No, he didn't," I said. "He as much as confessed to me that he did it. And I suspect the original murder victim is a man named Karthik that Sienna and I knew from back in the war. He didn't say why he did it, of course, but he suggested it was 'company' business, and that I should butt out if I knew what was good for me." Arse out. The vision of hers flashed before my mind's eye, and I gulped.

"He offered you certain incentives for doing so, I imagine?"

"He mostly offered the stick, honestly," I said. "I think he knew I wasn't going to accept a carrot. Not from him."

"Shame," she said. "I'm mad famished; I could use a carrot right about now, with the shops being mostly closed."

I made my way over to the other bed, my knees weak. "I don't know what to do about what he said. I mean, I know what I want to do."

"Let's start with that," Eilish said, still laying across hers like a pinup. Except for the thick coat. "What is it you want to do?"

"Break his head open like a piñata," I said. "Really feel the wind roll through his brains. Not that I'd do it, of course, just..." I forced a smile, and it felt...terrible. "...It's the Sienna way. The easy way, I guess."

That made her snort. "Does your sister seem to be living the easy life, then?"

"I mean, she was on a beach for the last few months–"

"Where else would she be? If not for that. And whatever else she got herself into now."

"She'd be right here with us," I said. "Or on some equivalent case."

"Aye, with her nose right in the hornet's nest," Eilish said. "That's where she always is, until she has someone she loves murdered. Or gets declared an enemy of the state and has to go on the run; I forget how many times that's happened now." She cocked her head thoughtfully. "There was after Harmon, in the US. Then here in the UK after Rose took hold. And sort of again, during the Network issue. Then she had to leave Minnesota after—"

"Yes, and then China, I get it," I said, on the edge of the bed, looking back at her. "She's not living her best life, even in the Greek isles. Point is—"

"Point is, the way she does things isn't the 'easy' way, lad," Eilish said. "It's the expedient one, sometimes, the one that overlooks the law and order imposed by government, which you seem to use as your guidepost, even as you ridicule the excesses of it. But expedient means shortcut, my darling – not *easy*." She picked up the unsmoked joint off the nightstand and put it between her lips. "In my experience, it's the shortest cuts that cut you the deepest."

"So you're saying I shouldn't just ventilate Janus's brains into the balmy British air?"

"You won't get any argument from me," Eilish said. "He seems like a right bad lad, that one. I imagine he didn't just threaten you, either—"

"Nope."

"Oh, so my arse is on the line as well, then," she said, pulling the joint out of her mouth and letting it dangle almost suggestively between her finger. "Lovely."

"Yes," I said, the wine catching up to me, "your arse is lovely."

She reddened again, but smiled. "That's kind of you, but you and I are both intoxicated in our own ways, so let's let that one pass. Point is, you want to bury this bad man in a shallow grave or toss his corpse in the Thames, I'm not going to tell ye no. It's expedient, for sure. Perhaps even easier for us." She leaned slightly forward, a bit wobbly, a bit goofy, indisputably cute, however much I tried to ignore that. "But you know it'll come back on us. These things always do."

"Consequences," I said with a sigh, and withdrew to the edge of this bed. I hadn't been seriously considering anything foolish, like kissing her, but she was looking pretty, and I was drunk enough that the possibility was in my head.

"Like the shoulders of the road, they keep us upon the straight and narrow," she said, sounding a little sad as she looked up at me. Was that a hint of regret?

"Fine," I said. "We do it right. No backing down, no darting with suppressant, then doing the bag and drag to a lonely moor at midnight for a cracked spine."

Eilish's eyes widened. "You gave this a bit more thought than I would have given you credit for."

"I am my sister's brother," I said, "and when he casually threatened you, and Isabella, it really pissed me off. I may have it on a tight leash, but the desire to inflict my will upon the world through use of power and lack of discretion – well, it's there. Buried under the bridle of responsibility, but still there, ready to ride."

She rubbed her face. "Yes. Well. You should go take your riding metaphors somewhere else. I'm going to bed." She put aside her joint. "We'll face this thing in the morning with fresh eyes, and start thinking about how we need to build a case to bring Janus and his ilk down."

I nodded. "Right." The thought that maybe we should stick together, in the same room, purely for safety's sake, died on my tongue because I knew where it might lead in our current conditions: nowhere good. Or somewhere quite good, but only in the short term. Consequences, again. "I should go."

"You should go," she said softly, and almost meant it.

I made it to the door through that sheer will I mentioned earlier, and she followed after at a safe distance. "Lock this, bolt it, make sure your windows are secure—"

"I'll be the soul of utmost caution," she said, through the barely-open door. She was watching me go. "You watch your back as well." She hesitated. "Unless...ye might wish to..." She hesitated, and it was right there for me if I only asked.

"Good night, Eilish," I said.

"Good night, Reed," she said, and closed the door before I could finish walking away. The clicking of the lock and the drawing of the chain sounded like the loneliest sound I'd maybe ever heard.

CHAPTER SIXTY-SEVEN

Wade

I woke up in the desert at night, and my head hurt like someone had taken a jackhammer to my skull. The stars spun above me, like some kaleidoscope effect, blurring into lines of light.

"Don't sit up," came a voice that sounded like it was filtered through ten gallons of water. "You got knocked in the head pretty hard. Your brain needs a chance to heal." A firm hand pushed down on my chest.

I tried to look at whoever was speaking, but my balance was gone. I tried to push back, but tumbled backward and landed, dust blowing up around me. "I was...metal..." I managed to get out, but it sounded like cotton had been stuffed in my mouth.

"Your brain wasn't metal," the voice said, "and it got jarred around in your chrome dome pretty good. You need to give your body a chance to repair the brain damage. Sit here and let it happen, okay? I don't need you dying on me."

"How...who...you?" I asked. I sounded drunk, even to myself.

"Look, Vegas is in a mess," the voice said again. I couldn't tell if it was male or female. It sounded like the voice of God speaking right to me, in my addled state. "I need to go help. Are you going to sit here and heal, like a good boy, or am I going to end up getting myself killed trying to save you again?"

That hit. "I'll be good," I said, relaxing under the pressure of the hand on my sternum. I still couldn't see anything beneath the shadow.

"Wonderful," came back the voice, laced with sardonic wit. "I don't really want to piss off your wife by getting you killed."

"Lotta that...going...'round," I said. "Who...who are you?"

...But the shadow was already gone, nothing but a cloud of dust left behind to mark their passage.

CHAPTER SIXTY-EIGHT

Sienna

"I nform Wade about the Las Vegas connection the next time he checks in," I said, already surging east and north, toward DC.

"It has been several hours since his last check-in," Sierra said. "But it is possible he is caught up in something in Vegas, much like you became embroiled in events in Nashville. Either way, I will inform him when he next reaches out."

"Good," I said, and pumped up the speed. "Where in DC should I be heading?"

"DC's communications infrastructure is slightly more hardened due to it being the capital," Sierra said. "Still, there are several nodes that could be considered vulnerable to strike. The most likely is a hardened structure in central DC."

"Okay." I stared at the picture that popped up on my phone, along with the address. "That's as good a place as any to start, I guess." I pocketed the phone, amped the speed, and raced back to DC.

CHAPTER SIXTY-NINE

Reed

I 've stayed in a few hotels in my time. More than a few, really; I probably lived in hotels or temporary apartments for most of my life up until a few short years ago when I'd settled in Minneapolis. Being away from home, away from all the familiar scents and feelings, away from your own bed and pillow – I found it to be the loneliest way to live.

I held onto my pillow, the lights on, door secured, desk turned upright to block the window, and thought of Isabella.

And maybe – just a smidge – Eilish.

It wasn't that I'd never noticed Eilish was attractive. It was that she'd come into my life at a time when I was already locked down. She was funny, she was smart, she was a friend. Nothing more. That she'd occasionally used her powers to get her way with me on things great and small was a thing we all overlooked, because it was entirely on petty matters like jobs or desk assignments in the office.

I found myself suddenly thankful she hadn't invited me to stay with her. And still regretful, all at once.

Isabella and I had been together for eight years. An improbable couple, the two of us, the kind that our friends had wondered at. She was older than me, hotter than me, and smarter than me. She was a doctor, after all, and not one of the dumb ones that should have their prescription pad taken away before they get it lodged up their nose with their crayons.

But we'd been together for years, and engaged for a few, and some of the fire was out. Being a man of the wind, you'd think I would fear the fire. And mostly I did. Reliable was good. Reliable was the sort of thing you could build a life on.

Still, every once in a while...some pretty Irish thing walks in front of you with no bra under her tank top, and panties with barely enough cloth to cover a Post-It note, and ideas spring to mind.

Terrible ideas. Sexy ideas. Ruinous ideas.

Most of them revolved around some sort of variant of leaving my room via the window, flying to hers and knocking on it until she slid it open and let me in.

Passion would follow. Fire; real fire, of a kind that maybe I hadn't felt in a while. I was going to be up all night, unable to sleep anyway. Might as well do something fun with it.

Sometime around or after the sun rose, I'd retreat back to my room. This time I'd use the elevator, and I'd maybe be dressed except for an article or two of clothing lost in the night. It'd be a walk of shame, and I'd come down off the high and crash just as surely as a plane that ran out of fuel.

The consequences would be severe, of course. I'm not a liar, nor could I keep such a secret. I'd be compelled to tell Isabella, probably the moment I next laid eyes on her. Because doing so over the phone would be the move of a true

coward, and because anyone who'd throw away their relationship in such a way deserved to experience the torturous
heartbreak of their love firsthand, to receive the torrent of
abuse or the silence of betrayal square to the face.

I took a hot shower. Way better than a cold one for
keeping bad thoughts at bay. When I finally got out, my head
had cleared a bit from the wine and the stupidity, and I pulled
out my phone. I called Sierra.

"Hello, Reed," she answered. "It is after midnight in
London. Are you having trouble sleeping?"

"Something like that," I said, leaving it on speaker as I
paced before the bed. "I needed to talk some things out, and
everyone else I know should be sleeping. But first – any word
from Sienna?"

"Little new," Sierra said. "She is currently en route to DC.
Wade is in Las Vegas, which is experiencing a comms blackout. I continue to devote compute to both Sienna's problems
and yours."

"I assume that compute has not yielded any solutions or
clues?" I asked.

"I'm afraid not," Sierra said. "Other than the last known
address I provided you, there is nothing I can find in open
source records that would lead me to Janus."

"Damn," I said, fiddling with my phone. "I'm uploading
the autopsy results to you. See if you can glean anything from
them?"

"I will put them in the evaluation queue," she said. "It
may be a few minutes before I can get to them. My compute
is being used on one other project first."

"That's fine," I said, settling back on my bed. "I've got
time. Not like I'm going to be sleeping tonight." I felt a wan
smile crease my lips, and I glanced out the window. London
was dark; short. It wasn't like Manhattan, built up to the sky,

tightly, within the bounds of an island. The window didn't face their burgeoning downtown. Outside all I saw were the tops of six-story buildings, at most.

I was still looking at them when the wine caught up to me and I nodded off into sleep.

CHAPTER SEVENTY

Sienna

I followed the familiar route between Tennessee and DC, the air growing colder as I flew. DC was a sprawling metroplex, and I saw the lights long before I reached it, night having fallen deeply over it sometime while I was away. The uniqueness of DC's downtown, compared to others, was the lack of height: the tallest building (not counting the Washington monument)) was the Old Post Office at twelve stories. It was grand and elegant in its way, but also stunted in others.

But the building I wanted was not so lovely; it was a stunted, concrete structure that lacked so much as a single window. I could see a little motion around it in the form of a couple of shuffling homeless folks, but nothing else. I gave it a couple overflights just to be sure, before arcing around one last time and making my landing in front of the entry doors.

And that was as far as I got.

The squeal of tires was the first sign that something was desperately wrong. There was a change in the air as it sounded. Then, a noise in the near distance, a sort of sound like a hiss, a snake whispering from somewhere across the street in the darkness.

A tiny prick of discomfort pinched my shoulder. I looked down to see a feathered dart protruding from my arm. Liquid within the tail sloshed as I stared at it beneath the street lamp.

Shit.

Suppressant.

With a panicked flick, I sent it flying. I attempted a leap into the air, drawing hard on the Gavrikov powers of flight–

Something boomed, and I got slapped as if with a metal wire. A net covered me, dragging me into the concrete wall of the building. I slammed into the stupid, ugly concrete head-first, and it rang my bell.

It didn't take my full faculties to suss out what had just happened. The net had weights on it, and some sort of grapples that had clung to the concrete surface of the building, restricting my flight. I hung there, blinking, as I felt the last drafts of power leaving me.

With a scream – that lacked any sonic power – I managed to get an energy blade to spark from my wrist, and cut a hole in the bottom of the net.

This did me less good than you might imagine, because I was suspended ten feet from the sidewalk. Cutting the net just allowed me to spill out, and I landed clumsily, with an *oof!* And thankfully, no broken bones. Though my palms had some wicked road rash.

Five guys slammed into me in sequence, like the latest hit in the history of football. They had me down, my hands behind me, trussed up hand and foot with metacuffs, all in the course of ten seconds. Ten seconds where I barely knew what hit me.

"Got her?" came a very familiar voice.

"She's dosed, constrained, and power levels should be at zero," said another. Not familiar, this one.

"Bring her up," the familiar voice said again, and I got dragged to my feet...

...And saw my captor for the first time. Agent Li. He wasn't smiling, surprisingly, though the thin level of satisfaction was plain on his face. "Well?" he asked. Of me, apparently.

"If you're asking me how much you've just screwed up," I said, "on a scale of 1-10, I give you a 9,847,220. Seriously, you now have a life expectancy shorter than a Boeing whistleblower."

"Bring her," he said. "Inform the other team that we're moving her to FBI HQ, per orders."

"Bet those weren't the president's orders," I said, singsonging through a bloody lip that was starting to swell. "Be interesting to see how he takes this news."

"I wouldn't worry about that," Li said, as a big panel van squealed to a stop in front of us, back doors hanging open. I got handed up before he finished his statement. "Because I don't think anyone's going to be hearing from you for a long time."

He shut the door as they put a bag over my head, consigning me to the darkness as the van raced away, taking me along with it.

CHAPTER SEVENTY-ONE

Reed

I jerked awake with a slight headache and a mild crick in my neck. With a grunt, I flinched; light was streaming in from the windows. Not the light of early morning, but the light of a day well in progress. Someone honked their horn on the street far below, and I looked at the clock. 9 AM. Ugh.

My phone had slipped from my fingers during the night, and I retrieved it now from where it sat on the covers. The battery had died in the night, which was just great. I got up and plugged it in, and the screen favored me with the notification graphic saying, yeah, you drained the hell out of this sucker. Chill a minute.

I knew it was going to be a bit before I could even turn it on, so I got up and headed down to the lobby restaurant, where I grabbed a cup of coffee and fixed it just so. (Extra cream, extra sugar.) Riding the elevator back, I got off at Eilish's floor.

The plush carpet built static with my every step. I paused outside her door, feelings of awkwardness welling up in me that delayed my knock. Duty took precedence over it, though, and I finally did.

Which caused the door to swing open a few inches.

"Eilish?" I called, peeking inside.

The place, what of it I could see, was trashed. The desk was overturned, the phone and everything on top of it scattered across the carpet.

Pushing the door open, I caught the same scent of burnt ganja as before, and nosed my way in. "Eilish?"

The bed was a wreck; clothing from her suitcase was scattered all over it, her phone charger was ripped out of the wall, weed scattered in flakes with the ripped paper of her remaining joint spread like potpourri.

And on her pillow, like a mint left by a maid, was an emptied syringe.

That was a message.

I bolted back for my room, reaching it and fumbling for my phone. It turned on, thankfully, and barely had the lock screen faded in than I had it dialed and up to my ear. "Come on, Webster," I said, "answer."

"Hello, Mr. Treston," came a voice tinged by an English accent, the moment it was answered. "I'm afraid DCI Webster is not available to speak with you now. He's a bit...tied up. Along with your Irish partner. And his wife. And his children."

"What the hell do you want?" I asked, pulling the phone away from my ear. "Hello?" I shouted. "Are you still there?"

Then I frantically dialed Sierra on the other line, said, "Mute yourself, listen, and record," before switching back over and shouting, "Are you there? I can't hear you!"

"Can...can you hear me now, Mr. Treston?" the voice came, uncertain. There was a sound in the background I couldn't quite identify, but it sounded like a city street.

"Yes," I said. "Go on."

"You are not cooperating," the voice said. "My employer gave you every opportunity to listen. He warned you of the consequences should you not. Now...I'm afraid we must exercise those options."

"You do this, you're going to regret it for the rest of your life," I said. "All five seconds of it."

The man chuckled lightly. "Your sister is a little busy with her own problems right now."

"I'm not talking about my sister," I said. "I'm talking about me. I'm going to find you, and I'm going to do to you what Liam Neeson has done in every one of his movies for the last few years."

He made a tsk-ing noise. "I don't think we believe you, Mr. Treston. Your sister is the stone killer, not you. We are watching. Leave for home immediately, and we'll return your Irish comrade."

That made my blood go cold. "What about Webster?"

"Oh, I don't think you'll be seeing the DCI or his wife ever again," the voice said, very casually. "But if you hurry, you might save their children."

He hung up, leaving me listening to the cold, empty line between us–

And leaving me with the realization that I might have caused the death of both Webster and Anna.

CHAPTER SEVENTY-TWO

Sienna

G etting bagged and dragged was entirely too familiar a part of my life these days, though these FBI goons hadn't bothered with a gag. Just the bag and the drag, and they removed the bag once we were moving.

The van bumped as it skidded down the streets of DC, racing like the devil herself was on their tail.

Stupid. The devil herself was already in the van.

"Do you idiots even realize what you've done?" I asked, into the tense silence. The entire crew of these morons looked like they could have used their anuses for wire cutters, they were so afraid. Six guys, one woman, all looking at me from the eyeholes of their ski masks, and not a neuron to share between them. "Do you really think I'm going to stay locked up?"

"Do you really think you're going to make it to the station?" one of them asked in a low growl.

I laughed in his face. "If you summarily execute me, you're doing me the biggest favor of anyone, ever, in my life. Because I'm going to go to my grave with the deep satisfaction of knowing that my husband is going to hunt you to the ends of the earth, pal, and when he finds you, he's not going to finish you in a gentle and expedient manner. You're going to die knowing what your own entrails taste like, and if you're lucky, he'll hurt and scare you bad enough you'll shit them clear before you do." I sat back and scoffed. "God, I hope you do it. My fight is over at that point, and I'll go out like a queen picturing how you'll go out, you fakeass cop. From enforcing the law to executioner in one easy step. Pathetic."

It wasn't more than two seconds before I could sense the atmosphere in the car grow tenser. Nobody spoke, but a lot of eye contact was traded, and I picked up the implication – there was not going to be a summary execution today. These weren't hard-nosed pipe hitters in the van with me. These were a bunch of mid-level bureaucrats and half-ass SWAT wannabes. Yeah, they'd just proven that anyone who properly plans can sucker punch me into next week, but they weren't the kind who'd actually put a bullet in my skull.

Which was going to turn out to be a real shame for them, I decided then and there. Yeah, they were going to regret that by the end. If you come for Sienna Nealon, you better not half-ass it, or I will put your whole ass in a woodchipper. My patience had long since vacated the premises on this point.

"Great, so we're still going to FBI headquarters, then," I said, shaking my head as I blew air noiselessly between my lips.

"Shut up," Li said, with more gusto than sincerity. He was puffing himself up like a scared baby goat, trying to make himself seem more in control of the situation than he actually was.

"You really didn't think this one through, did you, Li?" I asked, glaring him down. "You think they'll just keep me in the basement of the building forever? That I'll never get out?"

He pulled his gun – a real pistol, and cocked it, sticking the barrel out as he pointed it between my eyes. "Give me a reason, Nealon."

"I'll give you two," I said, leaning forward and letting it press into the center of my forehead hard enough to cause pain. "When I get out of here, I'm going to skin you alive myself, law be damned. And you're going to die just as you've lived – with your head firmly shoved up your own ass. I'm not even kidding, I will break ribs to make this contortion happen."

"Good God," one of the other men breathed.

"Also, this is an illegal arrest," I said. "But if you need a reason, go with the first two. Fear for your life, Li. Because in spite of our past differences, I never came after you. I'm going to do it this time, though. I'm going to come after you with everything I have, and I'm going to end you in such a way you die screaming." I could feel my nostrils flare with anger. "I don't have one more ounce of restraint in me at this point. The whole damned country is on the line, Chinese spies are blowing up and killing your fellow agents left and right, and you're here, doing this." I leaned in against the barrel harder. "You will fight me every day harder than you ever fought to save innocent lives, and I'm done pretending you're anything other than an enemy combatant who's been at war with me for years. So do it, Li. Strike the last blow in our personal little war. Get your revenge for Zack, who I never did kill, and send me out of this world. This world with arrogant little pricks like you in it, who care more about their pride and their fiefdoms than actually stopping terrorists trying to destroy the country you're supposedly sworn to protect." I waited a second, letting the barrel press into my skull. "DO IT!" I shouted in his face, spittle flecking out of my mouth. "You'll be the best friend I ever had, if you keep me from having to constantly come back to save this world, this world that has shit like you in it. Human garbage. I'm sick of cleaning up for you when you can't hack it, sick of getting blamed for the people who die because I have to be the one to do your job for you – DO IT!" I screamed again, ramming my head against the gun barrel hard enough to draw blood. "Just do it," I said, a note of pleading entering my voice. "Just do it and get it over with."

Li's mouth was slightly open, and he pulled the shaking gun out of my face, putting it back in his holster and flipping the retention lock up. "I...I don't think so."

"Figures," I said, letting my head thump back against the solid metal of the van. There were tears in my eyes.

"Something's happening up ahead," the driver said. I felt the sudden deceleration as the van went from forty down to fifteen or so. Uncertainty seemed to run through the crowd around me, too.

"Is this her husband?" one of them asked.

I wanted to laugh at that; Wade was in Vegas, doing who-knew-what. But they didn't need to know that. Leaving them in pants-shitting terror was the only satisfaction I had at the moment, and I was going to enjoy the small fruits of my impotent rage as best I could.

"This is something else," the driver said. "Looks like a riot out there. There's flames and people rushing around and – oh, shit!"

I barely got my head off the van's metal side when the sound of a gunned engine reached my ears. Something slammed into us, turning the world upside down like a washing machine spin cycle—

Everything spun, and I got rammed into the metal where my head had rested only a moment earlier, and I went out without even knowing what had happened.

CHAPTER SEVENTY-THREE

Wade

I came to, again, in the desert, stars overhead like a ceiling. My head ached like someone had played whack-a-mole with me and had an absolute field day on my dome. Running a finger through my hair, I found my skull was in perfectly fine condition. Holding up my hand, I was able to transform back to steel, then rubber, then rock, without any difficulty. Tapping the Wolfe healing cleared my vision, allowing me to finally see.

Whoever had saved me was gone; nothing but a cactus nearby kept me company. A hill waited, under the dim, partially clouded-over sky, and I climbed it to find Vegas in the distance, the biggest light source on the horizon.

Patting myself down, I came up with my cell phone. Whoever had saved me hadn't picked my pocket, at least. I dialed up Sierra, and she answered in a jiffy. "Wade?"

"I'm here," I said, squinting against the dimness. "Still alive, I think. I got caught up in a riot in Vegas."

"I have unconfirmed reports of similar activity in several of the other blackout zones. The glow of fires is visible from the satellites I have access to."

"Any word from Sienna?" I asked.

"She is in DC," Sierra said. "Unfortunately, she has been out of contact for thirty-seven minutes now, and DC is one of the cities where rioting appears to be occurring."

"It's the trigger man," I said. "He's somehow weaponizing the population of drug addictd, homeless metahumans. Some sort of telepathy, I think."

"There are several different types of telepathy that could be in use, given that description," Sierra said. "Standard telepath, of course, perhaps with a booster. Empaths are excellent at stirring emotions. An Aphrodite such as Eilish may be capable of such control, though she would also likely require a booster. A Firbolg or an Ares may also be the culprit; Firbolgs convey a sort of battle madness, and Ares types can harness thoughts of violence to spur the user to a mindless rage."

"That's great," I said. "Not sure how much good it does us to know what type when we can't find him, though. I mean, it could even be that there are a dozen of these guys out there, one in each city."

Sierra hesitated. "I do not think so. Chinese documents from the prior regime suggest that Sienna did a very effective job of eliminating their telepath corps. If this is a telepath, it is a lone one, operating with extreme powers. Similarly, it seems unlikely that this ability would be withheld from use by the Chinese government if it conveyed some sort of broad-based advantage that could have won Fen Liu the war. For that reason, I would guess that it is, in fact, one person, with tremendous psychic powers, which perhaps do not include traditional telepathy. Therefore, this is most likely one of the other types, boosted to an extreme, operating in one location – a Firbolg, an Empath, an Ares, or an Aphrodite."

"Aphrodites have to be in the physical location, don't they?" I asked. "I mean, I didn't work with Eilish too much, other than briefly, during the war, but she controls with her voice, doesn't she?"

"That is correct," Sierra said, "but a phone call can be as effective as a means of control. A better way to rule out the Aphrodite thesis is to determine whether women and men were involved in your riot."

"There were definitely both," I said. "I blasted the face off at least one woman."

"Not an Aphrodite, then," Sierra said. "One additional data point: one of the suspected Chinese spies, a Wei-Chen Liu, had a last known location in Vegas – but I have no additional information, as the address given appears to be fake."

"This is all pointless," I said, looking at the flames rising on Las Vegas Boulevard; the city lights illuminated the smoke. "What could I do about that, anyway? Start an investigation while the city burns?" I slumped to the ground, staring up at the stars.

Sienna was in DC, which was probably going off just like Vegas, and I was here. She was in danger 2,000 miles away–

And I was just sitting here while the country burned.

CHAPTER SEVENTY-FOUR

Sienna

I came out of a rollover crash to find the doors getting ripped off the van. I blinked at the strange direction of everything, and it took me a long moment to realize that I was hanging upside down, and everyone else had ended up on the ceiling. They'd buckled me by the handcuffs to the freaking seat, and it had kept me from getting tossed around in the spin cycle. "This is why," I muttered around a mouth full of blood, "you should always wear your seatbelt."

The squeal of ripping metal sharpened my journey back to consciousness. Someone was peeling the van open like an orange, and I guess we were the sweet, citrus-y goodness inside. I struggled against the bonds holding me in place, and the whole bench moved, groaning under the strain of my perfectly human strength trying to force it. I guess it had really taken some damage, but protest was all it did; it did not release.

With another scream, the metal in front of me tore, and gave me a view of what was happening outside. It was a damned riot, dirty, angry faces out there like a window to the French Revolution. I got a sense by the look of them that rather than a guillotine, though, they were going to be dragging our guts out with their bare hands and tearing us to pieces, like an old-fashioned medieval execution. Yeehaw.

There was a lot of rage and red eyes in that crowd, and it motivated me to get my damned hands free. There's a secret to getting out of handcuffs, and it basically boils down to dislocating your thumb. Most people have a well-honed instinct for self-preservation that prevents them from doing such things. I, however, had a slightly higher motivation: keeping myself from being ripped to shreds by an angry mob, and so I dislocated my thumb with real viciousness.

I screamed as my hand came loose, partially loosing me so I flipped and landed in a pile of humanity that had been a couple of FBI agents. They weren't so much that anymore as lumps of meat. At least one of their necks was broken, the other had ribs jutting out through their chest – which poked me in the side. Again, seat belts, people.

Without my powers of healing, or my strength, I didn't spring back to my feet. What I did was more drag myself back upright, avoiding even touching my dislocated thumb. That was going to be a job for Wolfe healing, whenever it returned, but for now, my thumb and I were going to do our best to ignore each others' existence. I wasn't going to touch it, it was going to scream at my nerves, and I was going to pretend it didn't. I grabbed keys from a downed guard and freed myself the rest of the way.

Forcing open the back door of the van was an interesting experience with one hand. Rioters were scrambling through the front window's bulletproof glass, which had been cracked but not broken. Well, they were breaking it now, in a frenzy, even as the other group peeled away the side about an inch at a time.

But I did manage to get it open, and found the van wedged in the mouth of a small alley, blocking the approach of the rioters. I had a clear field of escape, brick walls lining each side like the bounds of the royal road TF outta here, and I made ready to hop out.

A hand clamped on my ankle, and I found myself looking at the last breathing occupant of the van, other than myself. "Help...me..." Li whispered, through cracked and bloodied lips. "Please..."

I turned. Paused. Counted to two.

"Damn you," I said, and, with my good hand, grabbed Li by the back of his collar. Luckily, he was thin, and trim, because I was operating on only my own, human muscles here. "Damn you all the way to hell, Li." And I started dragging him away, down the alley, as the sounds of the blood-thirsty mob behind us ripping into the van grew louder and louder.

CHAPTER SEVENTY-FIVE

Sienna

I made it about a block before I was winded. Now, I was in pretty good shape by this point; I worked out every morning on the island, went for a ten-mile run every afternoon, and walked the dogs for miles in the evenings before dinner.

None of that mattered without my metahuman strength. Without it, I was 155 pounds of woman, Li was at least 175 of man, and while I still had moderately thick thighs, they didn't have it in them to drag a body heavier than me for a freaking mile.

We were in a slightly rundown section of town that I didn't recognize immediately. Apartment blocks were ahead, white concrete surfacing with windows glaring in the night. In the backlight from one of the windows, I saw someone pounding their head against the glass, splintering cracks starting to appear.

"So it's a broad-based hysteria," I said, dragging Li around the corner of a garage door that was left open about six inches from the ground. "Good to know."

Howls of rage behind me told me that our pursuers were in the van. I heard the most awful noise, something akin to a pig feasting on slop, and I didn't dare look back because I knew a real-life zombie movie was unfolding behind me. Instead, I tugged Li around the natural corner of the brick, toward the slightly open garage door. Dropping his drag handle – causing him to moan in pain as he toppled over – I put both hands under the garage door and started to push it up.

Whoever had left it open had a plan to keep intruders out, and that plan was some sort of lock on the rails. If I'd been powered up – or even had the use of both hands – this would have been no problem. The damned garage door would have sailed up, the metal locks helpless to resist my unfathomable strength.

But at the moment I was nothing but a smol bean, as the kids say, and my lift was rather limited.

I managed to move it up a half inch, then an inch, the door straining all the way as I did so. I was sweating furiously from the exertion, my hamstrings screaming that no, I did not have any business doing this, my fingers crying out that they were going to give up and just break cleanly off if I kept up this ridiculousness.

Stepping back amid the howls behind me, echoing down the alley, I judged the height of the door as maybe, barely, enough to squeeze Li through. If he held his breath and didn't mind losing his nose. I certainly didn't mind if he lost his nose, so I started shoving him under the door.

"Stop," he moaned, as the screams of violence behind me, and around the corner, suddenly included the thump of one of the van doors being jarred.

"Is it too much to ask that you put even minimal effort into your own survival?" I hissed through my teeth as I shoved and kicked his body underneath the door. All I succeeded in doing was wedging him about halfway under it, unfortunately.

But, then, that was sort of my plan.

I hit the ground and slid under it myself, asphalt dragging at my clothing. My shirt got hung on the metal, and Li kicked me limply, and probably accidentally, in the head, as I squeezed in beneath his feet, brushing the soles of his shoes. Once I was inside, I rolled in the minimal light and grabbed his arm.

Pulling him from this position did not give me maximum leverage, but I really only needed him to move about six inches to clear him from the damned door. I was dripping sweat, my breath was coming in ragged gasps, and I set my legs, hand gripping his left arm at the wrist. I pulled, and he barely moved, emitting a gentle moan that made me hate him all the more.

I didn't stop pulling him, though. My legs felt like they were going to cave in, my back wanted to give up and collapse, my dislocated thumb screamed murder most violent.

But I didn't stop.

Once his body was under, I grabbed his right arm and rolled him, just enough to get the door down. I shoved it down almost as hard as I could, and it moved easily. After a moment, I slowed it, gently bringing it down to tap against the asphalt.

I collapsed against it, weighing it down with my body, because I could feel the springs wanting to drag it back up. We were covered in darkness, only the thinnest lamplight shining in around the edges of the rails. Through one of the slits I saw movement in the alley. A howling mob went by almost comically, like something out of the cartoons of my youth, snarling for blood, one of them blasting off energy jolts of green that tore into the brick on either side of the alley. Within a minute, they were out of sight, the screaming from the far end of the alley faded, mingling with screams and sirens farther away.

DC was having a hell of a night, it seemed.

"What...now...?" Li asked, his words mangled by his swollen lips.

"Now we sit here in silence until I regain my powers about six hours – and God knows how many dead bodies – from now," I said. "You dumb shit." Through the crack in the door, I could see flames on the distant horizon, over the buildings between me and whatever was going on. "Your idiot ass just lost the entire city of Washington DC, at least." I sat there, breathing hard, watching events unfold as though in Plato's cave, a shadow play that marked the end of our entire society.

CHAPTER SEVENTY-SIX

Reed

The realization that I'd gotten people killed – people who'd been kind to me, who'd needed my help, people like Webster and Anna – hit me hard, and I collapsed into the chair at the side of my hotel bed. All the angry defiance went out of my legs, all the fury purged out of my system, replaced with terror for those at risk.

Had Janus truly killed the Websters? It was a distinct possibility. Omega was a deeply evil organization, and always had been. They'd killed children in the past, trafficked people in the past. Was Omega reborn really any different than the original recipe?

"Reed?" Sierra asked. "I can hear you breathing. Is there anything I can do to help?"

"Connect me to my sister," I said hoarsely, voice cracking. All this effort, and when the shit struck the fan, this was the recourse I came to.

"Unfortunately, she is out of contact in the DC blackout zone," Sierra said. "The Nashville office, too, is in the blind, along with Wade."

"Shit," I swore quietly. "I need to call the Met." I paused. "Who do I even call at the Met?"

"I feel obligated to point out to you," Sierra said, "that this is a very expansive criminal organization with a considerable reach, and resources. If they were able to reach into the offices of the London police department and suicide one of their top cops, the likelihood that Omega have blocked your ability to access the organization is quite high. You may end up spending hours on the phone, lost in a bureaucratic morass, only to find Omega at the end of the maze."

"They absolutely would do that," I said, my vision darkening at the edges, turning into a tunnel. "They're watching me. Making sure I leave town."

Sierra was quiet for a moment. "One of the ways they may be tracking you is through your phone's contact with the local cellular networks. If need be, I can mask you, and show your phone making contact with cell towers on the way out of the country."

"That fools them, and lets me stay," I said, "but it doesn't solve the underlying problem: how the hell do I beat them? With nothing but the wind at my fingertips." I threw a blast of wind against the closet, and it knocked a pad of paper off the desk – and nothing else.

"Perhaps you cannot," Sierra said. "Perhaps, given the parameters, it might be best to undertake a strategic retreat."

"Dammit, I am not quitting!" I shouted, blasting the chair into the wall. It bounced off, then overturned, leaving a mark on the gray wallpaper. "I refuse to let the gangsters of Omega get their way through murder and terror." I squeezed my hand tight. "I know people think I don't have much in common with Sienna, but dammit – I can't let this stand."

"If you do find them," Sierra said, "they outnumber, and out-power you. This, coupled with their hostages, gives them immense confidence, and a solid negotiating position."

"They're confident because it's me," I said. "Because they've got me in a corner, and my sister is too busy or too blinkered to turn her attention this way." I squeezed my hand into a fist. "They think I'm weak. Everyone thinks I'm weak, because when I'm standing next to Sienna I look like a powder puff."

"I don't think you're a powder puff," Sierra said, and it was just strange hearing a computer in the voice of my step-mother saying that. "There are over two hundred cartel *soldados* that discovered differently last year and achieved a liquid state of matter in the process."

"You're right," I said, holding up my phone. "The problem is that none of my American friends are available to give a hand. Which leaves Omega thinking they've really got me boxed in." I typed a message into the phone and hit send. "The problem is I'm not Sienna; there's no box. And I will not be contained by them." My eyes narrowed. "Sierra...I'm going to need access to some things you know..."

"I am at your disposal," Sierra said.

"Good," I said, channeling my inner Sienna, "because I'm going to rip Janus's spleen out and shove it down his throat. Which ought to remind him that messing with *anyone* in our family is a terrible idea that's guaranteed to ruin your life."

CHAPTER SEVENTY-SEVEN

Sienna

I lay in the quiet, dark garage with the only light the bit coming in around the rails that allowed the garage door to raise or lower. At least three buildings in the distance were on fire, and not just a little bit. They were fully involved, to use the fire department term, flames leaping into the skies above DC.

This was Fen Liu's revenge, in full swing. And I'd not only failed to stop it, I'd been sidelined by my own government, declawed like a cat, and nearly left to die in the frenzy of it.

Why the hell did I even bother anymore? With friends like these, I didn't need Sovereign, or Century. Nor Rose, the Clarys, the Network, or even China. My own government consistently screwed me over more than my most hated adversaries.

Here I was, left in the dark, breathing as quietly as

possible every time ravening hordes went by, slobbering, dripping blood, screaming like banshees and savages.

People were dying out there. Innumerable people. Probably in cities all across America, similar things were happening. How many people would lose their lives tonight because the government hamstrung me in catching the trigger man?

How many more times would I have to go through this cycle?

And what was going to happen on the day when the real threat – the looming one, the final one, the apocalyptic one – showed up to turn everything and everyone to a cinder?

"You just gonna...give up?" Li asked, reminding me, unwisely, of his presence just above my head.

I resisted the urge to reach up and whack him in the balls. It certainly wouldn't hurt as much as if I had my powers, but it'd still be a fine way to express my disapproval for his actions, his attitude, and his continued existence. "What would you have me do?" I asked, sounding utterly hollow and defeated. "I don't even have a gun, Li. Neither do you, by the way; I checked. So unless you expect me to go out there and fight metahumans hand to hand in my wounded and entirely powerless condition, yes, I give up. You have defeated me at last, you nimrod. Now sit back, shut up, and enjoy this barbecue you unleashed."

"Didn't expect it...to go like this," he said.

"What did you expect?" I asked, looking up and realizing I was talking to his crotch which, thankfully, was still over an arm's length away. So tempting to play punch-the-weasel. "That you'd lock me up, and everything would go just dandy? Did you think Fen Liu made an idle threat, and if you just darted me and stuck me in the basement, all would be well with your soul and all else?"

"Just...did what I was told," Li said, and now it was his turn to sound utterly defeated.

"Well, bang-up job, Fido," I said. "Maybe your next promotion will see you catching the ball for Director Lane every time she throws it, since you're such a good boy." I said it in the exact tone I reserved for my dogs, too. "Who's a dumbass? Yes, it's you, you're a dumbass. Well, you caught the car after years of chasing it, dipshit. Congratulations. If anyone should be asking if someone's giving up, it ought to be me. Because compared to how badly you've hobbled me, you're in fine fettle. So, what are you going to do about fixing your colossal screwup, Li?"

"I...can't think of anything at the moment."

"That's because you leave your thinking to others," I said savagely. "First, to Foreman, when Omega, Winter, and Century were running roughshod over everything. Now, to Director Lane. I wouldn't trust you to think your way out of a corn maze composed of a single stalk, you idiot. You have the intellect of a brain-damaged pinworm. You shouldn't be allowed to look at a gun, let alone carry one, and this is all your fault."

"I...know," he said at last.

"Well, marvelous," I said. "Welcome to a clear-eyed view of the present. So...what are you going to do about it, shit brick?"

"You're better than me at these things," he said. "What do you want to do?"

"I'm better than you at almost everything. That doesn't mean you get to eff everything up then dump your problems on me," I said. "Why am I stuck with the consequences of not only my own actions, but the idiocy of you, too?"

"Because you're the only one," he said, voice weakening, "who can fix these...things." And he drifted out.

"Do not go dying on me, Li," I said, smacking him in the leg. He barely stirred. "You cannot make this giant of a mess and leave me holding the bag alone."

There was no response. And why shouldn't he? Didn't I always have to, ultimately, deal with the consequences? Because I killed Clyde Clary, his relatives got pissed and came after me. Century killed Rose Steward's cloister in their annihilation. But because I was doing my best to save people, and made the choice to do my best to save the ones close at hand, she got her brain all twisted up and vowed revenge. President Harmon decided he wanted to mindjack the entire world to become a human-led version of the Matrix, and ever since the US government had been a topsy-turvy world of chaos like Lane said.

Fen Liu spearheaded the Chinese effort to take over the world. Because I decided to say, "No," and firmly punch her in the tit, everything had unraveled across the planet in the months since. Yes, I often had help, but not always.

Not this time.

"I'm in this one alone," I whispered. "Again."

Fine. It was on me. I'd find a way to stop this. There was probably no repairing the damage, but the sooner I could get my powers back, and get out there, maybe there was at least a way to limit further destruction.

The sound of footsteps outside cut through the blaring sound of a city descending into chaos. "You're sure she wasn't back there?" came a familiar voice, muffled by the garage door in between us.

"I mean, there were a lot of pieces," came another familiar voice, this one tinged with a thick, Indian accent, "so no, I can't be entirely sure without picking through them all. But I'm pretty sure she wasn't in there."

"She wasn't," I said, rolling Li off the garage door and letting it snap back up. Lights hit me right in the face, blinding me, as I squinted against them. Through the glare I saw the silhouettes of two figures–

Both pointing guns at me.

"You trying to kill me?" I asked. "Like the rest of the feds?"

The lights bounced to the side, and the guns went down. As my rods and cones started to reset, I could see Chandler and Ileona Marsh, the Memphis Belle. Chandler reached down to give me a hand up, which I gladly accepted – with my good hand. "Thank God you're all right," he said, then looked at Li. "Oh. This one."

"Yeah," I said, dusting myself off. Lying on a garage floor for the last hour or so hadn't been particularly clean, as activities went. "He was the sole survivor of the wreck, or ambush, or whatever it was."

"I am prepared to accept either," Marsh said. She still had her gun out, and was scanning the alley in either direction, as if expecting us to get jumped at any moment. "This city is going right to hell." She gave me a nervous look. "Got any ideas for how we can put a stop to that?"

No, to hell with this city, was the immediate reply. It died before it even had a chance to be born, not so much as a syllable escaping my list.

"I have an idea or two," I said. "But it requires us to get out of here before we get pulled apart by a mob. Got a car nearby?"

"About a block away," Chandler said, slinging Li over his shoulders. He made it look so easy.

"Then let's go," I said, following them back down the mouth of the alley. "We've got a lot to do before sunrise."

CHAPTER SEVENTY-EIGHT

Wade

I'd failed my wife and I'd failed my country. All the vows I'd ever taken were lying in ashes in front of me as I watched Vegas burn on the horizon. Oh, it didn't burn completely, to be sure; the Horseshoe was definitely on fire, though, as well as Treasure Island. Flames billowed out of the windows of both establishments, the kind of apocalyptic fire event that tended to prompt a government inquiry into what went wrong. More flames sprouted from the old downtown, though I was far enough away I couldn't tell what was happening there.

There was no sign of the person who saved me. They didn't come back to check on me, didn't show signs of flying around in the city.

I was alone.

"Sierra," I said into my phone. The call had dropped at

some point, but I managed to get a single bar of service. "Status report."

"Reed is in trouble in England," she said. "Sienna remains off grid, in the blackout zone. Nashville is blacked out as well." She hesitated. "I'm afraid there is no one on the company payroll in range who can assist you in Vegas. Los Angeles is now blacked out as well."

"Is there anyone beyond that?" I asked, getting to my feet.

"The closest of Sienna's contacts is Veronika Acheron in San Francisco," Sierra said. "Would you like me to request her assistance?"

"If possible," I said, looking down at my sleeves. "But she won't be here for hours, if she makes it at all." I steadied myself. "I'm going to have to go down there and do this, Sierra."

"There are an uncertain number of metahumans in the mobs at work down there, Wade," Sierra said. "At least hundreds. Possibly thousands."

"Doesn't matter," I said. "I have to do something."

The AI stopped me for a moment. "Why?"

"Because I already failed my wife," I said, "and she's so far away...and she can take care of herself." I straightened up. "I have to do the maximum good where I am, so...Vegas." There was a slight tickle in my brain. "If you were the trigger man, in Vegas, where would you hide?"

"There's no way to be certain," Sierra said. "The riots have gone countrywide. He could be anywhere."

"Yeah," I said, and floated into the air. "Anywhere. But I'm here." It was time to commit. I may not be able to save the city, but I was going to go down swinging making a difference.

With that decided, I launched myself toward Vegas – and the fight ahead.

CHAPTER SEVENTY-NINE

Reed

I had a heart filled with rage and the words Bani Midnight 14. Plus the basic elements of a plan.

However, I was lacking two crucial things, and one of them was the knowledge of where my enemies were currently located.

"Sierra?" I asked, flying across central London and crossing the Thames. "You got that location for me yet?"

"I have it narrowed down," she said, against the winds that were blowing unchecked across the sky today, "to a small corridor in Holborn. I am presently cross-checking. Give me about five minutes and I'll have it exact."

"You've got more than five minutes, I'd say." I was approaching a certain tenant block that stood high in the sky in Southwark, and flying right to a window that I'd burst through only a few days earlier.

This time, though, I paused outside and gently knocked with the back of my knuckles.

Darren Flint was inside, watching TV, and had his head cocked. He walked over, bald head gleaming in the sun, flipped the latch, and opened it enough to look out. "I appreciate you not bustin' my nice, new windows."

"I appreciate your nice, new windows," I said. "And I was wondering if I could borrow a moment of your time."

He looked at me warily. "I've hear tell you're supposed to be leaving town." Behind him, the women in bras and panties did their work, measuring drugs into little baggies from the chemistry going on at their tables.

"Me leaving town right now wouldn't get you what you want," I said, with a smile. "But I promise I'll make it quick. Five minutes. And I can threaten you, if you'd like."

"Sure," he said, "come on in. We'll just consider the threat implied." And he stepped back to let me inside.

CHAPTER EIGHTY

Sienna

DC was burning, and it was sad to watch.

Don't get me wrong; I hated this town. For whatever charms it had, I'd never have willingly chosen to live here. The first time I'd been forced to had been among the most miserable times I'd ever lived, being during the period I was hostage to the Network while I was trying to come up with a way to Uno-Reverse their control over me. It left a bad taste in my mouth, which had not gone away during the brief period when I'd been acting CIA Director, before the government had fallen to the Chinese, or my third, after I'd kicked out the Chinese and had lived in the ruins of the White House while finishing the war.

That's three strikes; DC was out. My feelings about it were akin to Minneapolis, which had lost my love and esteem some time ago. There were just some zones of the earth that were too cursed and too painful for me to contemplate revisiting. DC was now one of them, along with the aforementioned Minneapolis, and Scotland.

It still sucked to see it burn.

Mobs were tearing through the streets, faces lit by the fires burning in the background. In ancient times, humans searched for explanations for the absolute savagery they glimpsed upon the faces of their fellow man in moments like this. Some way to explain the dual nature of a person who could talk to you normally one minute and be clubbing you remorselessly in the next.

Demonic possession was one of the explanations. Battle madness. Frenzy.

I was seeing that firsthand tonight, as Chandler steered the car up onto a sidewalk to get around a burning van in the center of the street. The faces of those we passed fell into two categories: terrified victims...

...And frenzied participants.

The victims were pretty obvious; stark terror on their faces, a desire to get the hell away from the baying mobs running roughshod through the streets of DC.

And the participants...they were even more obvious.

I saw their faces as we roared by, as fast as Chandler could reasonably go given the makeshift blockades in the streets. He didn't ever let the car get below thirty miles per hour, even when mounting the sidewalk. More than a few heads met his bumper along the way, all of them attached to faces that exemplified demonic possession. If you could have asked an ancient – or, hell, modern – person what demonic possession looked like, it was here, on the faces of all the people running about committing murder, thoughtless arson, and careless destruction of property. They were the ravening barbarian hordes of ancient days, they were the spirit of destruction, they were the gates of hell opened upon the capital of the United States.

Fen Liu's revenge was here, and I was literally powerless to stop it.

Chandler whipped the car down a side alley, then into the parking garage below the FBI building, flashing his badge at the line of SWAT officers on perimeter duty. They looked nervous, but nodded him through, and we were parked in a handicapped spot in front of an elevator bank a moment later.

What? It seemed unlikely a handicapped van was going to come pulling in right now, in the midst of the most destructive riots I'd ever seen. Besides, I didn't park it.

Riding in the elevator up, I listened to the muzak in a tense silence. I wasn't entirely sure about this plan, and I could see the reservations on the faces of Chandler and Marsh.

When the elevator doors opened, I strode out like I owned the place. It helped that building security was focused on keeping a perimeter on the outside of the building rather than trying to create a defense in depth here in the halls. It allowed us to get right to the director's office, the door of which stood slightly ajar.

I kicked it all the way open and walked right in.

Kaddie Lane looked sick to her stomach when she saw me; all the color left her face. "You're alive," she said, and added, without an ounce of insincerity, "Thank God."

"And no thanks to you," I said, glaring at her. "That entire team you sent is dead except for Li."

Her eyes widened and her mouth dropped open. She still didn't reach for a weapon, though. "You killed them?"

"No, I didn't kill them," I said, my voice rising, greatly offended. "The mobs killed them!"

This caused her to blink a few times. "You didn't save them?"

"You had me darted, moron!" I shouted, causing everyone

in the room to blanch, even though I'd just admitted to being without power. "I barely managed to drag Li out and get to a hiding place before they shredded their way through the van."

"Where is he?" Lane asked, looking around.

"In the back seat of our car," Chandler said. "I don't know how badly he's injured, and we couldn't chance getting him to a hospital right now."

Lane sat down heavily in her chair, barely landing on the edge; another inch or two off and she'd have ended up on the floor. Which would have been hilarious, even under the circumstances. "We've lost the Capitol building," she said in a haunted voice, casting her eyes to a flatscreen on her office wall. A projection of the DC streets showed red zones where the rioters were, presumably, having a grand ol' time tearing shit up. Nowhere was green, but there were some places in yellow, including the area where we were currently hanging out. "But fortunately, Congress wasn't in session."

"Yay," I said, without enthusiasm. Congress had kinda been dicks to me since I had (probably illegally) seized power to run the war, but no one deserved to die to this mob. Well...almost no one.

"A wave of rioters is moving in on the White House right now," Lane said, in a pleading voice. "Secret Service is depleted since the Mitchell assassination—"

"Oh, I remember," I said.

She got up off the chair and made her way around the desk to me. "This country is a thin thread away from breaking, Sienna. We lost almost all our elected leaders in the war, and we just replaced them. The president's been in office for three months. We cannot handle any more upheaval, any more chaos."

There was a distinctly frosty edge to my voice. "You probably should have taken that into consideration before you had your agents remove me from the board tonight."

"I didn't know this was going to happen," she said, air of desperate pleading. She was well past depression and anger, and deep into the bargaining stage. "I had no idea that this was what Fen Liu's revenge was going to look like." She had a ghostly aura of terror about her, pale and sickly. "I assumed it was the agents with the bombs that you kept setting off–"

"I didn't even set them off, dumbass," I said, causing her take a step back. "The trigger man has some element of control over the minds of the agents – and the mob. He's watching through their eyes, and compelled them to blow themselves up at the appropriate time. He was waiting for this. You could have sent your guys, they would have died along with whoever was nearby at the time. There was no stopping this one with the info we had, Lane. He cut our comms for a reason, and it was to drive up the casualty numbers."

"Fine, fine," she said, rasping, backpedaling. "I believe you. But – we have to stop this." She took my hand with hers, and hers was shaking. "*You* have to stop this."

I stared down at my hand, trying to will some flame to come forth. The thinnest thread of smoke appeared from one of my fingernails, and that was it. "I don't have a lot to work with at the moment, Lane. If I go out there and throw myself headfirst into that ravening mob, I'm going to end up torn to bits alongside everyone else that gets in their way. Don't get me wrong, I want to help, I'm just not well equipped to do much at the moment." Her face fell like it had been poised at the top floor and then stepped into an empty elevator shaft. "But," I said, "give me a big gun, turn me loose, I'll do what I can."

"Thank you," she said, shaking my hand. "You won't be alone. We'll all be right there with you."

"Great," I said, without enthusiasm. "You got powers?"

She nodded, and lifted her hand, emitting a bright burst

of cerulean plasma. "Everyone at the top gets the serum, and most develop at least some powers."

"Oh, good," I said, a thin line of smoke wafting in front of my face, as though an ember were clutched in my palm. "Because it's going to be a while before mine come back, and I do not want to be in this fight with nothing but an AR and a prayer."

CHAPTER EIGHTY-ONE

Wade

I didn't see much sign of my savior, except in the form of a half-dozen nutso rioters hanging from light posts with their limbs all bound with cable from some construction project. They screamed and raged and swung, upside down, with their hands bound behind them, frothing like dogs with hydrophobia.

Flying down the strip, I was not left with much in the way of consolation. Things had definitely unspooled since I'd taken my beating in front of the Gatsby Grand Casino; not only was Treasure Island and the Horseshoe on fire, but now Luxor and the castle of Excalibur were both in flames. I could only hope that people weren't screaming for rescue from the windows – which was not something I could hear over the chaos in any case.

A quick flyby of the stunningly retro, art deco Grand Gatsby tower showed that it was maybe the only hotel that hadn't sustained obvious damage. The Wynn had a half-dozen windows out, gaping and obvious like teeth missing from a pretty girl's smile. The Venetian and Palazzo were little better; it was clear at least elements of a metahuman mob were loose in the towers, as I saw an explosion halfway up the Palazzo tower.

Diving in through the newly blasted hole in the side, I found myself in the midst of a terrifying scene. A scrubby bum with his shirt off was holding down a thin, screaming girl of about sixteen who had nothing on but a towel, her hair soaking wet and the smell of soap still permeating the air over the fetid aroma of her attacker's body odor.

I saw red.

As I grabbed him off of her, he turned his glaring, blood-shot eyes on me—

And I saw something else entirely.

It felt like someone had put my head on a chopping block, dashed my brains out all over the ground with a sledgehammer, and while my dying eyes were watching the chunks, with every nerve still screaming straight fire to the vestigial stem of my brain, someone then hacked my head off with cleaving blows using a dull hatchet.

All the while, a raven pecked his way through my brain.

This was the Warmind. I knew its touch from Sienna, who'd unleashed it on me at my request during our bouts of training so I could ready myself against psychic attacks.

Shaking it off, I punched the bum in the face, causing him to cease his psychic assault on me. Keeping my grip around his throat, I flew him out through the smashed door into the hallway. "Get in the bathroom and bar the door!" I shouted at the girl on the bed, who was already scrambling to do just that.

In the hall, there were a half-dozen more rioters going nuts, creating chaos, committing murder. I watched one with plasma hands dissolve a screaming senior citizen into free-floating atoms, then turn his powers on a man with a Vietnam Veteran hat. He, too, was undone, but only to the waist, his legs falling dead over.

I tried to box out the thoughts swirling around me about how this was going on elsewhere – this scene, being repeated hundreds of times over in Vegas alone right now, let alone in the rest of the country.

And in DC, where Sienna was, far outside my reach.

The bum with the Warmind's soul ripped loose and rushed into my mind, and I discarded his body. He was just a poor bastard, hadn't asked for any of this, didn't have much consciousness of his own, just a raging addiction to meth that had consumed his mind, body, and will for nigh on fifteen years until so little was left that trying to grasp the threads of it was futile; he faded away in my brain before I could even get more than his name: Mark Jones.

"I won't forget you, Mark Jones," I said, tapping into his power immediately and turning the Warmind loose on the raging plasma fiend down the hall.

She went from coated in blue, superheated energy to half-naked in a moment, throwing her head back in agony. I kept up the intensity of the Warmind attack as best I could, as I summoned my Hades powers until the burning sensation within me became the familiar, sweet, rushing feel of her soul ripping free and swirling within mine.

Another poor wretch who'd met her end with addiction. First to Oxy, then the black tar heroin, finally Fentanyl. This woman, one Tara Wilson, never really had a chance after the back injury she picked up working in a daycare back in the early 2000's. The doctor told her that the Oxy was non-addictive, and it let her sleep. Many such cases, as they say.

As her body fell, the face relaxed from the raging horror that had been upon it when she'd dissolved two human beings into nothingness, into a serene near-innocence. "I won't forget you, either," I said to her, and turned my attention to the next half-dozen turbulent souls just on this floor.

I spun up a wave of plasma from my hands in the shape of a perfect circle; the symmetry was unnecessary, but I did it in the spirit of perfectionism, and flew forward down the hall at the maws of death that screamed at me as I approached. I had no idea who they were, unlike Mark Jones, or Tara Wilson, and had no time to learn their stories.

I flew through them with the plasma alight, burning them to cinders and ash and atoms, taking the top part of their bodies off and leaving the rest to fall limp and lifeless to the ground, a tumble of legs and arms and lower torsos.

The hallway was silent except for the sobs of the terrified people in the rooms, half the doors battered off their hinges. "Clear," I said to myself, a slight burn still in my hands, not from the plasma, but from the knowledge I'd just swept half a dozen people from this life with little to mark their passage but traces of their atomized bodies.

This was but a drop in an entire sea of chaos, but I'd made it calm. With my breaths coming quick, I flew into the nearby stairwell, and down to the next floor to do the same thing over again.

CHAPTER EIGHTY-TWO

Reed

"Where are they?" I asked Sierra after my visit to Flint and a brief stopover afterward. I'd confirmed two things I needed to confirm, and now I was ready to make my next move.

"I have narrowed down the location of the call to Russell Square's northeast corner," Sierra said. "The call was made several hours ago, however, and I have my doubts that they will still be there."

"Only one way to find out," I said, and jetted across the Thames. I couldn't fly nearly as fast as Sienna, but I could move when I wanted to, and I did so now.

I was about to hit Russell Square only a few minutes later, and lifted my phone. Hitting redial, I heard a voice both in the distance, and over the speaker. "You decide to get smart and leave? Or do you require another incentive?"

Without replying, I came rushing down in the direction

of the voice I'd heard. It was coming from a guy standing beside another at the northeast corner of the square, two dudes with no neck between them, and not a strand of hair, either. I slammed into them, knocking the phone cleanly out of the first guy's hand as I drove them both into the pavement with a wind-assisted landing. I hit them at a hundred-plus miles per hour, and savored the sound of bones cracking in a way I never had before.

Pedestrians screamed and ran, and in the distance I heard a whistle sound. Grabbing the two of them, I flew off into the air, holding their limp (in one case) and struggling (in the other) bodies. I made it to a nearby rooftop and landed, discarding them both like rubbish before turning on the one that had put up a fight. "Well?" I asked.

He looked at me through eyes lidded with pain. "Well...what?"

"Well, where's Janus?" I asked.

He snorted, then caught himself because it must have hurt. "If you wanted to know that, all you had to do was ask. He's across the river." He spat out an address. "He had a feeling you'd want to talk face to face before you left."

"Great," I said, and dropped him to the roof.

"'E said to warn you," Mr. Thumb said, "your intransigence is going to cost...someone." He looked at me through wary eyes. "You're going to pay for this. That's what he said."

I stared at him. "I'm going to exact some payment of my own." I lifted off, my phone in hand. "You get all that? Because I hope you're ready." And I headed south toward the Thames.

CHAPTER EIGHTY-THREE

Sienna

We managed to thread our way through the worst of the riot zones around the White House, and got to the building itself without having to run anyone down. The streets of DC possessed an eerie quality, lit by fires, smoke blacking out the sky above and reeking like a barbecue gone terribly wrong.

The White House was still in shambles after the China war, but it had been at least functionally rebuilt, if not polished. I remembered the way to the basement bunker, and the door was opened by a relieved-looking Secret Service agent so that Lane and I could step in.

"There she is," President Foreman said, looking a little relieved himself. A map of Washington was on the big screen behind him, almost exactly like the one we'd left behind on the wall at Lane's office, except there was a bit more red now. "I guess we know now what Fen Liu's revenge looks like."

"Yeah, it was a bit more comprehensive than we might have imagined," I said, giving him a nod and plopping down in the seat beside his. Lane took position opposite me. "We've brought the entirety of the FBI, and they're assembling a perimeter now to protect the White House."

"That's nice," Foreman said. "But what about restoring order?"

"Sir," Lane said, "our priority has to be protecting you. Without you, the US government falls again." She grimaced. "We cannot let this become a pattern."

"She's right," I said. "Civilizations tend to collapse when instability is allowed to fester." I caught a look of relief from Lane. "We've had too much upheaval lately, sir. We need to draw a line here. Then we can work on restoring order."

"All right," Foreman said, and turned to look at the map. "You should be able to deal with this in fairly short order, Nealon."

"Sir," I said, "in spite of the rabid nature of the mobs, these are citizens and human beings. We're probably going to have to kill a number of them in order to protect this place, but I feel I should at least mention that I'm doing this under duress, and because we have no other options."

"Noted," he said. "And when we catch the guy who did this, I'm willing to do whatever is legal to see him held responsible for every death that occurs due to these events. But first we have to stop them, and catch him. Any ideas on either of those?"

"Stopping them just comes down to making a hell of a mess," I said. "The second thing's going to have to wait, though, because we have no line on him. Whoever he is, he pulled the trigger before we could track him down."

Lane paused and cocked her head; someone was talking in her earpiece. "Our perimeter is established. We've got mobs moving in from across Lafayette Square, and south from the Ellipse. ETA is less than five minutes."

"It'd be really fantastic if, once this is over, our capital could stop being a battlefield for a while," Foreman said. "You know, in the name of stability."

"I have a dream," I said, "that one day, we can cross the street to get a steak at Joe's without fearing to be taken out by a Chinese missile or an insane meta or even just a powered-up gangbanger. I have a dream today."

"Hilarious," Foreman said. "Well – get to work making your dream come true, will you?"

I lifted my hand; only a small thread of smoke came out of it, along with a few embers. I was still a good many minutes from having my powers back, and when I looked up, I saw Lane looking at me with wide, concerned eyes. To Foreman, though, she said nothing. "Yes sir," I said, and went off to find the Secret Service armory.

CHAPTER EIGHTY-FOUR

Wade

I cleared the entire Palazzo tower, almost solely using the one-two punch of Warmind and plasma to stun my foes and then dissolve them into atoms, and was considering starting on the Venetian when I flew out to see how things were looking around Vegas. It seemed more or less the same, except the flames had gone higher, which caused me to hesitate – and cringe. Whoever had helped me earlier, I hoped that they'd done something about at least the innocent people stuck in those burning towers. I did a quick flyby, and sure enough, no one was screaming from within, but the whole place was fully involved, flames bursting out of the windows.

Meanwhile, the Gatsby Grand was completely fine, other than crowds of zomboids swarming outside on the Strip.

I decided since they were all in one place, I'd do a little something about that. So I flew down, landed, thumping, on the ground in the middle of them. From out of my body, I threw half a hundred gravity channels pushing out, which knocked down everyone within twenty, thirty feet of me.

Once they hit the ground, I knelt, putting a hand on the pavement, and started charging up the asphalt. It was nothing but zomboids around me for a couple hundred feet, zomboids and corpses.

And I was going to take full advantage of the blast radius.

The ground glowed beneath my touch as I poured energy into it from my charge-up power. When I felt it reached critical mass – about twenty seconds, during which time the zomboids were scrambling over each other to try and get to me – I flew into the air–

And the ground where I'd been kneeling a moment before exploded outward in a blast of energy.

It definitely killed half of them, and injured more, and that wasn't bad for the moment. Using the distraction of the explosion, I flew toward the Gatsby Grand, and in through the front doors–

And entered a world like nothing I could have imagined.

CHAPTER EIGHTY-FIVE

Reed

I found the spot where Janus was headquartered. There were areas south of the Thames that were perfectly wonderful. Other parts, not so much.

This one...this one was somewhere in between.

It was an industrial site that had old factory shells at its core. Some of the buildings had already been knocked down, and the skeletons of others remained. A huge construction project was going on across the street, leaving me with a simply massive area to cover, or be attacked from. A construction crane towered over the site, and I perched there for a moment, giving myself a chance to look over what I was dealing with.

The area in front of Janus's building was perfect for doing battle, especially if I wanted to use my wind abilities. There was a ton of upturned earth nearby, which would be useful to an earth-mover, like Augustus, reuse ponds filled with water that'd be tremendously helpful to a Poseidon, unsecured metal girders and tons of unwrapped rebar that'd be an absolute playground for a Magneto, with clear lines of sight for snipers.

It was, in short, a total nightmare for an Aeolus who was going to be facing an unknown number of metas on his own without the backing of the British government, additional mercenary assistance, or his sister close at hand. To say nothing of Janus himself, who'd be sure to prey on my emotions every way he could.

"I think I'm about as good as I'm going to get here," I said into the phone. "I'm going in."

"Understood," came the reply.

With that, I drifted down out of the sky into the space outside the door of the red brick and concrete office building that Janus had made Omega headquarters. It was a bit more modern than their last HQ, but not as centrally located. I came down on a concrete sidewalk a dozen paces outside the front door.

"Janus!" I shouted, though I doubted I needed to announce myself. "I'm here."

"Indeed you are," came the quiet voice of Janus, from behind me. I turned to find him there, having stepped out, unseen, from seemingly midair, the parking lot behind him. "It seems you were determined not to heed my advice."

"Your threat," I said. "Advice is friendly. Your words had bite to them."

"Yes," Janus said, "forgive me my inelegance of speech. All these years with the English language, and it is still not primary for me. A threat, yes, is what I gave you. I'm afraid the price, this time, will be much higher."

"For you, as well," I said, staring him down. In the corners of my vision, I could see movement. Dozens, if not hundreds, of people moving – in the shadows of the ruined buildings, from behind cars in the lot, out of exits from the office park.

Janus coughed, then removed his glasses and gave them a polish with a cloth he pulled from his coat. "In order to threaten me, Reed, you would need some ability to carry out some action of harm."

"You were terrified of the harm that would be visited upon you by my sister when last we met," I said, with a thin smile. "Do you think that no longer applies?"

He put his glasses back on, and glanced at the phone sticking out of my front pocket. "I presume, then, that your sister's AI is recording even now, in case something were to happen to you?"

"You presume correctly," I said. "Give me back Eilish and the Websters, now, or she gets that, plus all the evidence I've collected against you."

Janus raised a gray eyebrow. "Such as?"

I steadied myself and looked him in the eye. "Bani Midnight 14."

He stared back at me...

...Then dissolved into laughter.

I admit, I was feeling a touch discomfited at that. "Care to share with the class?"

He managed to straighten himself out. "That would be the company and color shade of the custom order sofa I placed recently." A snicker died on his lips. "Please, do send that to your sister. I think she would appreciate the Bani company's quality upholstery."

"Don't get cute with me, Janus," I said. "You killed Karthik. You killed Keith Stubbs. You kidnapped the Websters, and Eilish. Return them or–"

"Or what?" Janus asked, all amusement gone. There was a crackling terror in his voice, and I felt a disquiet run through my bones as he unleashed his powers on me.

One of his goons was easing up behind me. "He'll blow a stiff breeze through your short hairs, Janus," the goon said, prompting a chuckle to run through a goodly portion of the Omega thugs arrayed around me.

I gave him a hard look, and said, "Him."

He looked back at me, still chortling. "Me, what?"

His brains exploded out the back of his head as a rifle shot cracked across the empty space between the tower of the crane and the doors outside Omega HQ.

"You, that," I said to the corpse, and then turned to look back at Janus. "Now give me back Eilish and the Websters...or I'll have my sniper blow your damned head off."

CHAPTER EIGHTY-SIX

Sienna

Defending the White House was a tricky proposition, I could already tell. All the China war defensive options we'd placed – machine gun nests, barbed wire – had been removed in favor of the newer, lighter feel of Foreman's "back to business as usual," look of getting the place back to a pre-war footing. That meant a wrought-iron fence that could be leapt by a meta in a single bound, and blind spots in the vegetation for those of us on the lawn, though they were covered electronically.

"What are you thinking?" Lane asked, perched next to me in a thick cordon of agents. She had a tentative look on her face, like she was seeking my approval and afraid she wasn't going to get it.

"That I miss the machine gun nests," I said. "Since we're going with the lethal option anyway, we could just let loose with those and sweep the approach vectors. Sure, we wouldn't get them all, but we'd reduce the amount of trouble that made it through, make our jobs easier. Maybe have a possibility of preserving our lives."

She looked straight and when she spoke, she sounded deeply uneasy. "I actually told the president to keep them. That as unstable as America has become the last few years, he might wish they were there sooner rather than later."

"No one can be wrong all the time, I guess," I said.

"I'm sorry I was wrong about you," she said. "I was afraid that, as many times as you'd been over the line before, as near a grip you had on power – you were practically dictator of America for a minute there – you wouldn't be able to give it up."

I laughed, and it was a short, sharp bark. "Power is the one thing I always seem to be able to turn down." My hand smoked, but it was still just a little burst of embers that came from my palm. "Probably because it's brought me no joy at all."

"There's a difference between 'power' and 'powers,'" she said.

"Yes, one is plural," I said dryly. "The thing you have to understand is...Stan Lee got it right. Power and responsibility go hand in hand. And I can barely handle my own responsibilities on a day-to-day basis. I'm an alcoholic, Lane. My marriage was in shambles up until a few months ago – hell, it's still not exactly conventional. My life is in perpetual ruins from the decisions I make and the responsibilities I have. That's power, working on me. You think I ever want more of it?"

"It's a tricky thing," Lane said, looking out into the night. The howls of the mob were audible, but it was tough to tell where they might be in relation to us. "Power is the ability to shape your world to your liking. It's influence over others."

"See, that, there, is the trap," I said. "People think power is control, and it is – but it's really limited. I'm keenly aware of the limits of power. Let's say I somehow cracked the ability to use this super telepathy I've got up here." I tapped on the side of my head. "I could make people do what I want. Sounds great, doesn't it?"

She stared at me. "Yeah, kinda."

"Wrong," I said. "If I make you do what I want, you cease being a person who operates on her own and become a puppet. How many people host solo puppet shows just for themselves once they get out of childhood?"

"Only the really creepy ones, I guess."

"That's the power you're talking about," I said, looking through the fence. "The power to control, the power to annoy. You can do some good here and there, but it's mostly a cacophony of people trying to get defense contracts and union perks and favorable interest rates and whatnot. The type of influence you need to wield to do this job well would not be suited to my hands. I'm a hammer and I know it." I checked my M4 carbine. Still a bullet in the chamber. "I don't even want to hit nails anymore, but at the very least I know I don't want try and do the screwdriver's job, too."

The first strains of movement appeared on the horizon, figures striding out of Lafayette Square. They were purposeful, they were driven, human guided missiles moving at metahuman speed.

"All right," Lane said, settling down beside me, her own rifle up to her eye, "the rules of engagement are to wait until–"

I had a target in my sights, and I fired a single shot, adjusted my aim, and shot again, dropping him to the ground.

"The rules of engagement–" Lane said, utterly scandalized.

"It's war, Lane," I said, picking the next target and dropping them with three sequential shots that required adjustment throughout to get back on target. "The rules of engagement are 'Don't let these pawns take your king.'"

Others were firing now, though I didn't hear her take her first shot until about ten seconds later. "Attagirl."

"When in Rome, during the fall," she muttered.

"That's the spirit."

We fired, M4's chattering away. The figures in the distance were growing larger, numbers swelling. It got easier to fire, because there was no lack of targets, and the chattering of rifles all up and down the line added some metahuman energy projection powers firing off. Shades of green and purple and red blazed along the perimeter, lashing out and finding targets among the fast approaching mob.

It didn't seem to make a difference.

They were a swarm, a hive, stirred and enraged, and they were upon us in seconds, knocking over the fence like it was a cardboard barricade. Energy blasts lashed back from the encroaching mob, along with sonic screams that hit further down the line from me and had agents doubling over in pain, blood running from their ears. I'd never realized before that the Brance scream had an effective cone of destruction, and it was very forward-directed unless you were in a confined space. From some ways off, I was able to plug two screamers with several rounds and turn their screams into cries before they fell and were trampled beneath the stampede of their own fellows.

This was the mob that was the bane of Enlightenment thinkers. Ravening, angry, uncontrollable, thoughtless. It was a creature unto itself, wild. It struck down the line first, and the clash resulted in immediate deaths within our numbers; I saw bodies fly into the air, heard screams fade mid-hit.

Ejecting a magazine, I pulled the next off my vest and slammed it home, drawing a bead on my next target. My thumb was killing me. All I had was this weapon, as I tried once more to produce fire from my hands. Sparks of embers came, and nothing more, and so I went back to shooting anything that came at me until the mob broke over me in a furious wave, and I was slammed to the ground by its force.

CHAPTER EIGHTY-SEVEN

Wade

I was completely unprepared for what I found in the Gatsby Grand Casino. And I don't mean the opulent, 1920's décor.

Because the moment I made it inside it was just...normal.

Slot machines made their magical sound, roulette wheels spun. People moved back and forth between the various games, all with that retro spin; if anything was missing, it was the casual movement through the casino of people just passing through. Here, everyone seemed very focused on whatever game they were playing, with only a few lookiloos and no one passing through with a purpose. No striding with intensity, no power walkers, no one breaking away for a cup of coffee.

This was a gambling hall, and the only business being done here was gambling. While a riotous, superhuman mob was destroying the city outside, this was a haven of peace, an oasis in the desert, a calm in the storm.

"Yeah," I said to myself, "that's not coincidence."

I continued to levitate, floating in past the check-in desk – employees smiling eerily behind it, not a soul in line – across the casino floor. No one took any note of me; the slot machine addicts were too focused on pulling their levers, pushing their buttons, listening to their jingles. Their eyes were wide and dull, each wearing a thousand-yard stare that, in fact, terminated two feet from their faces.

There was a bit more cognitive effort going on at the Blackjack tables. Some chatter, too, though none of it even slightly off topic. "Twenty-one," the dealer said, as I moved past overhead. The pit bosses seemed to be in a trance, taking no notice of me, just like the customers.

A noise in the distance caught my attention; a roar of approval. I let my eyes follow the sound, and there, in the distance, was a crowd gathered around a Texas Hold 'Em poker table.

I felt drawn to it, like a vortex was pulling me in. My flight powers cut out, and I dropped, catching myself on the red, plush carpeting. I drifted to the back of the crowd, then it parted for me, slowly, so that I could make my way forward.

Once I was at the head, I found myself looking at a table with six players and a dealer. Three of them were gray-haired white guys that I observed and passed over almost immediately. There was a middle-aged white woman with raven hair who wore a low-cut, figure-hugging black dress that my eyes did not pass over quite as quickly, but who I was able rule out after a look. Then a second one, just to be sure, either about her or the dress. A younger black man with dark shades, slick, bright white, eye-catching clothing, and a toothpick in front of a small mound of chips caught my attention for a second, then I passed on...

...To the young-ish Asian man with the absolute mountain of chips in front of him. Way more than any other player, by far. He wore sunglasses, too, and was playing sleight-of-hand games idly with a small stack of poker chips in his right hand. He wore a tasteful suit with no tie, white dress shirt open to the third button, showing a muscled chest. His hair was perfectly black and slicked messily, like he was some playboy from Macau. As I watched, he flipped a chip dexterously onto the pile at the center of the table and said, "Raise a hundred."

Honestly, if he'd had a sign hanging over him saying, "TRIGGER MAN," in bold letters, he couldn't have done a more effective job of highlighting himself.

I opened my mouth and started to speak, but he held up his left hand, the empty one, and I immediately shut up through no will of my own.

Play continued uninterrupted, and three of the players folded, leaving him in with the slick black dude and one of the Boomers.

"Full house, Aces over eights," the dealer called, when Trigger Man showed his hand.

In spite of the mental stifling being exercised over me, I snorted.

Trigger Man looked over at me, letting his shades slide down his nose. "What's funny, Mr. Nealon?" The Boomer had just busted out, and was shuffling away – but not far; he couldn't escape his enthrallment, and he joined the crowd clustered around the table. "That's what they call you these days, isn't it? Mr. Nealon?"

"Sure, I've been called that," I said, a sort of mellow muzak playing in my head. Like I was on the world's calmest elevator ride. I wanted to lift my hand, turn this man's face into atoms, but for some reason...I just couldn't.

"How are you at poker?" he asked, looking at me. His gaze

was hypnotic; he held his shades just down so he could look me in the eyes.

"Fair to middling," I said. "But it's a fun game. I like it."

"Have a seat," he said, and I did. A stack of chips was placed in front of me, along with an Old Fashioned with some high-grade bourbon, unasked.

I tried to scream; I couldn't. I tried to stand up; that didn't work either. So I settled in for the game, leaning in, as the dealer dealt, and waited for my opportunity to either win...or die.

CHAPTER EIGHTY-EIGHT

Reed

"You didn't think I'd do that, did you?" I asked, looking at the Omega operatives ringing the battlefield. So many eyes were on the dead man behind me, his skull emptied upon the field. "You think I'd just walk in here helpless, Janus?"

Janus looked, almost disgustedly, at the dead body. "I suppose I didn't think you were foolish enough to escalate this war in such a manner, no."

I took a step toward him. "Your couch color aside, we both know what you did. Karthik. Stubbs. The Websters. Eilish. You rubbed my nose in this, now you've told me I can't prove it, and to leave town before you visit more evil upon me. You escalated this. I'm ending it. Your head comes off next. Eilish. The Websters. Return them now."

Janus stared at the ground, seemingly deep in thought. Then, he looked up at me. "No. I think not."

"Fine," I said, "I'll get them myself." Lifting the phone up to my mouth, I started to speak.

A wave of despair slammed into me, a hopelessness I had never before felt; it was depression times a thousand, and it brought me to my knees.

Janus was suddenly beside me. "You're an Aeolus, Reed. A strong one, to be sure. But your compatriot out there – and I think I know who it is – she's not immune to my powers, either. Or to death, if I decide to visit it upon her."

"You'd do that...to your own sister?" I asked, looking up at him with fury in my eyes. The emotion he was flooding me with acted as a paralytic; the only antidote was another, stronger emotion.

I chose rage.

"Diana and I parted ways long ago," Janus said, standing above me like some great lord trying to make me do homage. "That she has come here, with you, willing to – as you say – 'pop my head off,' suggests that bonds between us that may have existed long in the past, are as broken as your chain of reasoning." He planted a hand on my shoulder, and around me, I could feel the other Omega servants pressing in. "I would admire your boldness, if not for the arrogance. You stuck your neck out a bit too far, you see. And the neck that sticks out must be–"

He took a staggering step back, clutching at his own head out of sheer surprise. I felt motion around me rather than saw it–

Until earth came crashing down on the Omega operatives to my left in a giant pile, and a rain of girders and rebar landed on the ones to my right, piercing them and turning them into a modern version of Vlad the Impaler's garden of death (hey, I know that guy). A wall of water splashed down behind me, wiping out the operatives there, and Diana's rifle fired in rapid succession, taking out the few that survived along any vector around me—

Except for one guy. Big, swollen, and suddenly glowing with fire, he came at me swinging hard with a flaming hand—

I caught it in my own, spark of embers blasting out of my fist and climbing up my wrist as my flesh caught fire.

It didn't hurt, though. It felt...

Good.

His eyes widened as he stared at me, cupping his fist in my hand.

Then...my hand turned a bright, glowing blue as I triggered my new plasma powers.

He lost his balance, all that effort he was throwing into trying to bowl me over working against him as his hand dissolved into atoms, then his wrist and elbow, and then the rest of him up to the shoulder. He screamed, and I whipped my hand across his face, vaporizing that with plasma.

Someone came at me from my left, in my peripheral vision, and I whipped my other hand around. A blade of ice extended from it and I heard them crash into it, full force, impaling them straight through. I turned my head to look, then goosed the ice powers. Spikes of ice extended out of the blade, and the guy, who had a haircut like a British cap, was ripped through in a dozen places, icicles growing out of him like a frozen porcupine. He slumped over, blood oozing out of him at the piercing points.

Janus was watching me from his knees, head tilted to the side. "So...not just an Aeolus anymore, then?"

The ground was quaking around us from my earthquake power; the Omega army was broken, running. Those that hadn't been crushed by the mountain of earth I dropped on them, drowned in the flood, or turned to pincushions by both Magneto and ice had apparently thought better of opposing me.

"I've got a real combo platter of devastation for you, Janus," I said. "Did you feel the Empath powers at work?"

He nodded from his knees. "Indeed I did. Unpracticed, but indisputably powerful. It has little effect on me, of course—"

"You're just on your knees for purposes of submission, then?"

"Yes," he said, nodding, hands at his sides. "I am curious where you got the serum, but ultimately, it is immaterial. You have bested me in this. You have no crime of mine that you can prove, but I am defeated nonetheless. I am at your mercy."

"Yep," I said. "Now where are the Websters, and where is Eilish?"

He held his hands out. "You don't understand. See, you've bested me." Slowly, he began to get to his feet. "But you can prove no crimes, including the kidnapping you are accusing me of." Keeping his hands out. "Therefore, you have choices before you: you may let me go – or you may kill me. That is it."

"Eilish. The Websters," I said, voice hard as a diamond. "Where are they?"

He smiled thinly. "Kill me or release me. I have nothing else to say."

I stared at him, and his smile only widened.

He knew he'd defeated me.

CHAPTER EIGHTY-NINE

Sienna

W e were swamped in seconds, metahuman zombies crashing into our position like a wave of human refuse. They smelled terrible, like the worst body odor ever, mingled with upturned earth as they ripped into the lawn and tore up the grounds with attacks. Battles raged everywhere around me.

I was a little island in the middle of the insanity, trying to fall back under the surging tide. I fired my M4 as swiftly and accurately as I could, but it was like flipping water droplets onto a raging wildfire with the wind at its back. Lane screamed beside me, going down under the tide even as she sent a blaze of purple energy upward into the attacker that dragged her down. He died, she didn't, and she scrambled to get back even with me, firing indiscriminately through the mob.

When she got close enough, I stooped to offer her a hand

and she took it, dragging herself up with metahuman strength, firing all the while. I didn't take my eye off the holographic sight, though I probably could have just turned the M4 sideways and shot down the barrel at this point. "They should never have done away with bayonets," I growled, backpedaling at approximately $1/10^{th}$ the rate of the mob advance. They were past me, around me, and I was but a small breakwater in the river of chaos and murder.

"I don't think a bayonet would help right now!" Lane shouted, sending another blast of purple in a sprinkler arc in front of us. It sizzled its way through thirty, forty raging zombies.

"That would, if you kept it up," I said, turning my fire to our flanks for a moment.

"I only have so much zap available," she called back to me, employing it again. It was more faded, less bright in intensity. It took out fewer zombies, but still did a nice job of keeping them off us for a few seconds. "Don't you?"

Looking down at my hand again, this time it sparked for a few seconds into a near-fire before fizzling out. "I am definitely lacking zap at the moment but no, not usually. It's like a muscle, Lane. You have to exercise your capacity."

She screamed rather than answered; from her blind side, she'd been struck by something that made a pop like a gunshot, and it sent her flying past me as though she'd been picked up and thrown by a giant. She disappeared beyond the curtain of darkness that clouded my human vision, and I pivoted to face the guy who'd attacked her.

He looked like something out of a Viking nightmare; bald, with overgrown facial hair and a serious eating disorder, his teeth black as the night. He came at me with a slight glow on his hands, and I dodged and thrust my M4 up to block him. His fist made contact with it, and it spun out of my grip as though some god had flicked it. Thankfully, I didn't have a strap on it, or it probably would have taken me with it.

I tumbled over, bowled by the strength of his power. I'd seen its like before; Tara Hays had it, this ability to punch and have it slap with energy upon contact. He'd sent Lane flying, disarmed me with it, and as I tumbled to the ground, him on top of me, I tried to grab his wrists and keep him from touching the side of my head for fear it'd explode.

But he was too strong, and I was too weak at the moment. He started to push in on me, my fingernails digging into his wrists, trying to keep him from touching me. His fists edged closer and closer to my head, and his black teeth were like reflections of the all-consuming night as he grinned and prepared to kill me.

CHAPTER NINETY

Wade

"A pair of twos?" I asked, in disgust, as the Trigger Man flipped over his cards.

"Beat 'em," the Trigger Man said with a cocky grin. "If you can."

I turned over my cards, and watched his face turn.

Pocket Jacks. With the one on the table, I had three of a kind.

He grimaced, and it quickly turned to anger, then a smoldering grin. "Okay. A real player, finally."

"We just going to sit here and play cards all night?" I asked, claiming my winnings.

"You got something better to do?" He was grinning ear to ear. It was maddening, like an itch I couldn't quite scratch.

"No," I said, because everything I wanted to say, I somehow couldn't. "I don't."

"That's right," he said, nodding. "So let's play." As the dealer started to toss out the next hand.

CHAPTER NINETY-ONE

Sienna

I was going to die with black, meth teeth dripping drool on me, my grip fading on the wrists of a zombied-out psycho. My nails had dug in deep enough to draw blood, and now my hold on him felt slick and disgusting, friction disappearing with every passing moment.

He wanted to trap my head between his fists, pop my skull like a water balloon. It was all there in his eyes, a lust for death and blood as recognizable to me as simple words written in English.

I tried to flare fire, to scream and break his eardrums, but it just sounded shrill in the night, as the riotous cacophony went on around me.

My strength faded, my muscles burned as I failed, and he eased his face closer and closer to mine even as I tried to hold him back.

And then...

I felt the burning.

It was like seeing an old friend after a long time apart, like taking your first breath after having your head underwater for far too long. My unsteady hands shook with the effort of trying to keep his freakish strength from smashing me, but the burning in my palms and fingertips went on, everywhere that our skin made contact.

I burned with the succubus power at work. The first power. My true power.

He didn't feel it at first, and by the time he did, it was too late. Now he tried to pull his hands free, but my grip was too much for him. Now he tried to jerk, to raise his head and scream, but I didn't let go, and I didn't heed him.

Now he tried to rip away.

And I ripped out his soul.

The mob surged around me and I struck out, drawing on this new man, whose name I could not dredge up, because he didn't even seem to know it anymore, he was so far gone. My fist made contact with a nearby zombie and she shrieked and flew, like Lane had bowling over a dozen others behind her.

I leapt into the air and my flight powers caught – but barely. I was weak, at a fractional amount of my power, as evidenced by the fact it had taken almost thirty seconds to drain that man. My flight stabilized as I rose, though, and I was only slightly unsteady as I came up about fifty feet, glimpsing the surging mob making its way toward the White House below like a black tide crashing on a midnight beach.

I flew down among them, channeling my newfound punch power and crashing down into the earth. It worked exactly like I'd hoped, a surge of my snap punch energy racing outward from my landing site in a circle, batting over everyone around me for a hundred feet. The nearest of them seemed to catch fire, the red energy blasting them with light and flinging them twenty, thirty feet back from the point of impact. It weakened the further out it got, barely unsteadying those in the distance.

Which is why, when I dropped horizontal and cracked the gates of hell, it caught them standing upright and vaporized them. I spun in a circle and let it loose, dissipating it once it extended past the edges of the mob, and it cleared the area of the lawn around me, allowing me to move back to the driveway that ringed the White House and stop there, the line firmly held.

They were still coming, in the distance. They'd broken the perimeter, and now were rushing to get inside the building.

But now...they were going to have to go through me – with all my power – to do it.

CHAPTER NINETY-TWO

Wade

I got a bad hand, and played it badly.

The six of diamonds and four of clubs. Low cards, unsuited. Bleh.

A genius at Texas Hold 'Em could, perhaps, have turned my cards into a win. I couldn't; I didn't even try. I folded on the flop, when the nine of diamonds, the ten of hearts, and king of spades were laid down. Unless the next two cards were two sixes or two fours, I had no hand, none at all, at least none worthy of wagering serious money.

And the trigger man? He was instantly into the serious money.

"Raise a million," he said, pushing stacks of chips into the center of the table. He looked up at me with a glint in his eyes. A challenge, clearly.

I tossed my cards in. Watched the rest of the table go 'round, folding one by one.

"Awww," he said, leaning over to collect his winnings.

Was he bluffing? Probably.

Could I afford to find out with no hand at all?

Nope. It would have required me going all-in, and I got the feeling that the moment I lost all my chips – even as easily as they'd shown up – the game was over for me.

"You know what I like about you, Mr. Nealon?" He sounded cocky as hell. I wondered if he'd mentally heard the conversation outside where the cop had called me that – or if he'd implanted the suggestion in her. "You're just rolling with it. You thought you'd come in swinging—"

"I floated in very cautiously, in fact," I said, not holding back much in my irritation. "Wei-Chen."

He seemed mildly surprised I'd interrupted him, and his reaction was even more pronounced when I said his name. He seemed the sort that loved to hear himself talk and didn't hesitate to use his mental powers to inflict that particular cruelty on anyone unlucky enough to wander into his range. God save me from rambling, narcissistic windbags. His smile returned quickly. "But I bet you didn't think you'd be sitting here, playing poker, while your country burns." He looked to the dealer. "Next hand. LFG."

I rolled my eyes at the Zoomerspeak. "Is this gambling a hobby for you?" I asked as the cards were dealt. "Or is the destruction of America the hobby?"

He smiled, showing his teeth. "What would make you doubt my commitment to the destruction of your country?"

"The fact we're in here, playing poker, while everything burns outside."

"This place is still gonna burn, it'll just go up last," he said, studying his cards. "And then I'll be forced to move on. Monte Carlo. Aruba. Macau, maybe, though I feel like I wore out my welcome in that town." Grabbing a handful of chips, he threw them in. "Raise 500k."

I stared at my cards. Pocket aces, of spades and hearts. This was the best I was likely to see for the whole game.

So I put down my cards facedown on the smooth, green felt, pushed all my chips to the center of the table, declared, "I'm all in."

And then I hit him with the Warmind, as hard as I could.

CHAPTER NINETY-THREE

Sienna

I needed to be careful as the mob surged in again; FBI agents were sprinkled in here and there, so I didn't unleash massive effects like cracking the gates of hell, or dropping and shocking (snap punching the ground after a long fall), or even deploying the ultrasonic voice to burst eardrums.

Instead, I stuck to the classics.

Lightning coursed out of my hands, full power now, and chained in between the various zombies, a little bleeding off with each successive one struck until it guttered out into sparks about thirty feet from me. It killed the ones nearest me, but jarred them fifteen, twenty feet away and made them stumble.

This was it; me against the raging mob. Them in front of me, the president behind me, somewhere, in the depths of the White House. The trigger man clearly had his objective –

wreck everything down to the foundations. Then wreck them, too.

Again I found myself standing between those who wanted to overthrow the world, and those who wanted to save it. I'd call it an unenviable position, but it was clear I was envied by those who'd never walked or flown a mile in my shoes.

This was the fight I was in. Me against unstoppable numbers, unbelievable odds, tasked with holding them all back...yet again.

I was so sick of this, of bailing out the world, of saving it. So sick I'd quit after the wrenching, repeated destruction of Minneapolis. I'd wanted to quit after Revelen, but President Gondry had hauled me back then, too, as had the Network. And before that, too, when I'd given myself over to the police in Maple Grove after running from the law post-Harmon. And before that, even, when Harmon had run me out of Minneapolis with the law chasing after me.

How many times had I tried to quit? All the way back to the original, when Zack was murdered by M-Squad using my body as the weapon. Since that day it felt like all I'd done was take hits that would have crushed any normal person, enough to make me say, 'No more,' and every time be dragged back to take more.

I sliced through six zombies with my energy blade and screamed, focused, bowling over dozens in front of me.

Yes, I had powers. But it seemed to me the one that saw the most use in my life was the one that allowed me to be flayed and heal from it. To be almost destroyed and come back from it to have it happen all over again, in new and exciting ways.

I'd quit after Zack, shutting myself in the box. After Harmon, after Scotland, before and after Revelen – I couldn't even count how many times I'd quit, at least temporarily, before Minneapolis. Before China.

Every time I found myself back here – I cut the head from a man who was awfully obese for a homeless – then cut through six more who charged right into my blade, blind with rage as they swarmed me. Every time I found myself back in this position – this position so enviable to those who'd never been here, who called me hero, and wished they could be like me–

I killed eight more people who hadn't asked for this, didn't sign up for this, didn't – presumably – want the trigger man to turn them into unthinking murder machines bent on destroying our whole society.

This was it, forever. I would be slaying the enemies of human life, the destroyers of civilization, until either I croaked from old age, or someone got lucky and one-shot-ted me.

I was going to fight until I couldn't anymore. I'd fight on like this, alone...

...Until I couldn't fight anymore.

I spiked the ground with another charged punch, and bowled over everyone around me for a hundred feet. Beyond that, even, they suddenly staggered, and I stared.

Something had just happened. Something that had turned loose the grip of these ravening hordes for just a moment.

CHAPTER NINETY-FOUR

Wade

The effect of using the Warmind on the Wei-Chen was immediate.

He flinched, clutched at his nose as though I'd punched him in it, and his head rocked back. He knocked over a stack of chips with his elbow, and a trickle of blood ran out of his right nostril.

"*Wáng bā dàn!*" He shouted, a pretty nasty curse in Mandarin. The eerie silence around the table had broken; someone shrieked behind me, and there was a stampede away as people regained their mental footing.

I poured it on, throwing more Warmind at him. I focused on his face like it was a target at the range, or an AQ tango, and I goosed it with the power I had, throwing in Hades power for good measure.

Reality seemed to warp around me, and he lurched backward again, tipping over. One of his loafers went flying, and he slithered under the table. The noise in the casino had become cacophonous; people were screaming and running in every direction, as though their hair was on fire and their pubes were heating up to follow.

I leapt the table, terrified that if I let him go now and regroup, he'd reassert his control over me, rip through my brain like it was putty under a machete blade. My momentum as I struck it flipped the heavy, wooden poker table over on him, and it crushed his leg from mid-thigh. He screamed, and I crashed on his chest with both knees, driving them into him by my power of flight, and aided by a gravity channel tethering me to the ground for extra oomph.

His sternum cracked and he spit blood from the force of my blow, eyes growing wide. He reached up, and I felt myself choking as he panicked, somehow strangling the life out of me with his mind. I fell over beside him, dropping the Hades ability as the world contracted around me. We both struggled against the forces weighing on us – him, the damage I'd done and the gravity tether, and me, the overwhelming panic that he was pouring into his powers as he suffered untold agony.

Which one of us would die first was now a race.

CHAPTER NINETY-FIVE

Reed

Janus's smile was the epitome of smug, so certain he'd boxed me in. He left me with two alternatives, which he helpfully repeated one more time: "Kill me, if you will. Otherwise, I am leaving."

"I just killed half your people," I said, "what makes you so sure I won't choose the first option?"

He stared at me, that smile tugging at the corners of his mouth. "Because I know you. Certainly, you have surprised me this day. But you can't change who you are with a serum, and a call to *my* sister for help. You are a moral man; you don't do executions of unarmed souls. You are still not Sienna." He got up off his knees, and dusted off his tweed jacket. "So...I think I'll be leaving now."

"What do you think the future holds, then?" I asked, as he made to walk past me. "For you and me?"

"Oh, I don't know," he said airily, taking care to pat me on the shoulder as he went by. The remaining water from the flood I'd brought glistened behind him in the faint strains of the sun peeking out from behind the winter clouds. "I do hope we never meet again."

I reached out and clipped him on the side, and he jerked his head around to look at me, vaguely offended at my touching his person.

But that look quickly turned to pain.

Janus fell to his knees again with a grunt, because I'd spiked him in the hip with a dagger I made of ice. He moaned, because I was growing it within his body, sending tendrils of freezing sharpness through his veins into his leg, where it burst out of the skin and tore his expensive trousers.

"Really?" I asked, pumping more ice into his veins, "because I see our future as clear as if I were a Cassandra. You're going to kill my hostages, if you haven't already. Then you're going to seek your revenge. That's a threat to my life. I don't have to be Sienna to want that threat ended, for the sake of me and mine."

He shouted in pain, writhing as he fell flat on his face in the mud. "I...would..."

I pumped another round of ice growth into his tissues, and the flesh above his knee burst into a sea of bloodied spikes. "Tell me where I can find the Websters, dead or alive – all of them – and Eilish. Or I'm going to rip you apart an inch at a time."

He rolled onto his back, breathing and huffing agony. "Torture...? I didn't...think you had it in you, boy."

"I am not my sister," I said, "but I recognize evil when I see it. And I'm sick of letting it threaten the people I care about. You're a cancer, Janus," I pressed the ice to grow, and it blew out his kneecap, drawing a scream from him, "and I'm going to cure you, one way or another."

"I will see them returned to you," he said, sweat popping out of his wrinkled brow, "all of them! They're still alive!"

I clenched my fist, and halted the ice growth. Pulling my phone out of my pocket with my other hand, I held it in front of him. "Tell Sierra who to call to make that happen. Touch your own pocket and you lose that leg below the knee in the most painful way I can imagine." Eight spikes of rebar hovered over my head, guided by my own mind, along with a square-foot globule of water that I let perch six inches above his, ready to waterboard him if he tried anything. "Try to betray me, and you'll drown."

"Obviously," he said, and rattled off a number from memory that Sierra immediately dialed. A rough male voice answered, and Janus said, "Please bring out Ms. Findlay and the Websters. We have reached an accommodation with Mr. Treston."

The voice was deep. "Give me two minutes."

With a click, I was left alone with him. "Diana," I said, "keep an eye on whoever comes out, and don't hesitate to turn them inside out if you see a hint of betrayal."

"Have you ever known me to hesitate?" Diana's accented voice crackled over the line. "Either of you?"

That was a good point. A Reflex type – maybe *the* reflex type, as in the first – striking last or moving slow was never her thing.

"I hope you never find out what it feels like to have your sister betray you in such a way," Janus said, and offered me his hand. "Help me up?"

All I did was wave mine, and the ice lifted him. I kept it where it was, a giant growth of ice blades sticking out of his right leg, holding him upright. He studied me in between pained grimaces. "You have changed."

"Yep," I said, keeping one eye on him and the other on the Omega building.

"I suppose I should have feared you as well as your sister," Janus said, "and dealt with you accordingly. But...I thought I knew you." He forced a smile.

"You thought my sister was the devil, and I was the angel. But she was just the devil you know," I said. "I'm the one you didn't."

"I see that now," he said, nodding as he mopped his brow with a handkerchief.

"Do you?" I turned, menacingly, to look him right in the eye. "Why did you kill Karthik?"

He hesitated enough that it made me wonder if he was telling the truth. When he finally spoke, the answer was simple, though it was impossible to tell if it was heartfelt. "He questioned a new direction we were taking in operations. In my business, you can weather much – attacks from outside the organization, supply problems. You cannot survive your leftenants questioning you. He had to be dealt with."

"You have the loyalty of a hungry viper," I said.

A door on the building burst open before he could answer my accusation. Out of it emerged Eilish, first, looking pale and dazed. After her, one by one, came Matthew Webster, Anna – clutching the baby in her arms – and their young son. They made their way over to us with a man walking behind them.

He...was something else.

Tall, black, bald, and with eyes that seemed to burn like a furnace that had reached runaway temps, his mere walk suggested strength that his steps didn't quite display. He was clad in a white suit, but there was a slight gray to his skin.

He stopped, staring at me across the field between us. I almost lifted the phone to my face to tell Diana to shoot him from his aura alone...

...But I didn't.

He stood there wordlessly, menacing, the hostages

between us, and for a moment I got the sense that he wanted to slaughter them all. I spun the rebar missiles around to face him, and positioned the water to drop on Janus's head. I'd flash freeze it and strangle the life out of him if it was the last thing I did, and I felt him tense up behind me.

"What shall we do now?" Janus asked. "You have gotten what you want." There was a tenor of pleading there. "Perhaps it would be best if my associate and I withdraw?"

"Do you think that in some way absolves you of what you did to Karthik?" I asked, not even bothering to look at him. I kept that water poised and ready to drop.

"I suppose not," he said.

"You think I'm going to let you just walk away after all that?" I asked. "After what you've done?"

He sounded quite tired when he answered. "No. No, I don't think you will. Not at all."

I spiked the rebar at the big man, and it whizzed past the hostages and struck him as he raised a hand at me. It impacted all across his chest and right shoulder, driving him back—

And not even scratching his skin.

"Achilles!" I shouted, mostly for Diana. I whipped up a burst of blue plasma and prepared to hurl it at him—

But a white light emanated from the ground beneath him – a portal, opened at his feet – and he dropped into it, disappearing instantly.

I spun on Janus—

But he, too, was gone, along with his peg leg of ice.

I looked around the battlefield, which was now silent except for the quiet sobs of Anna Webster, and asked, "Did we just win?"

But somehow, I knew, with Janus and that other man having fled the field...

...No, we hadn't. This was not over. Not even close.
Omega was back.

CHAPTER NINETY-SIX

Wade

I was choking, an invisible hand at my throat, throttling the life out of me. Chaos abounded in all directions; I saw the legs of running people fleeing the scene all about us. It was going to be a strange final scene, for me to go out watching people flee from me in all directions, as I was choked to death by a telekinetic mass murderer.

If only I'd had my knife, or a gun, or anything at hand. That was my first thought.

Then I remembered – I had far better than that.

And then I realized – why was I allowing myself to get strangled?

I shifted into steelskin, and the pain at my throat subsided. My breath returned, and I was able to roll sideways, where Wei-Chen was still writhing from my psychic attack.

Lifting my hand, I stared down it as he lifted his own.

"Wait," he managed to choke out. "This won't stop...without me!"

I looked him in the eye, and assessed what he'd said. He'd put the whole country in a meat grinder, psychically setting off our entire homeless, drug-addicted, and/or mentally ill underclass, then loosing them on major cities. And all this after committing acts of electronic warfare, and actual warfare. Maybe he did have some help to contribute to stopping this. Perhaps he could send a mental command, and all this would end.

But it struck me that the function of my duty, and the reason I was here, was to do the thing I always did:

Eliminate the enemies of my country, whatever the consequences to me. Especially the lying-ass ones.

And if there was one thing I was good at, it was this.

I fired a blast of purple and took his head clean off his neck.

CHAPTER NINETY-SEVEN

Sienna

I slugged a guy in the jaw and the *pop!* of the energy hit knocked him over in a near-flip. It had been an endless stream of these madmen, coming in even as I blasted with lightning, hammered with my fists, bound them with fae webs, and occasionally cracked the gates of hell along a horizontal axis to burn them down.

Still, they had kept coming.

Until this very moment, at which point they just...stopped.

The running mobs had slowed, their momentum leaving them. Occasional flyers had streaked across the sky, brought down by gunfire and blasts from the White House roof.

And now the whole mob just settled upon the lawn, staring at me, as though their whole minds had just been handed back to them after a psychic lobotomy.

"What happened?" asked the guy at my feet. He had a

partially broken jaw, and was looking up at me through a badly blackened eye. Considering he'd been about to unleash a purple death beam when I hit him, he'd gotten off easy.

"You went nuts," I said, offering him a cautious hand. He used it to pull himself up, rubbing his jaw. "I had to knock you down."

"Oh," he said, mouth swollen like he had the mumps. "Okay. Well." He glanced around, took in the White House, and then turned and ran like he'd been caught shoplifting.

He was not alone. There came a great flight across the White House lawn, all but a very few of the rabble that had been turned against us bailing at the thought they might be in the kind of trouble they probably didn't want to find themselves in.

As for me, I watched them go, and fell down on my ass on the soft, muddy grass, upturned by all the fighting and exploding. I just didn't have it in me to chase them. Not today.

CHAPTER NINETY-EIGHT

Reed

The Met police came at Webster's call, and we commenced hours of interviews, and talk, and walks around Omega's now-abandoned offices. There was a surprising amount of evidence of wrongdoing; a drug lab, drug packages, guns, security cameras that had recorded all manner of criminal activity involving all manner of underworld luminaries. Within two hours of their arrival, arrests were happening all over London.

Oh...and we found the spot where Karthik had died. It was not subtle, but had been mostly cleaned. Mostly being the operative word, because cleaning up that much blood left spots.

It was right in the middle of the bullpen, beside a cubicle that had dark stains spattered in the gray carpet that ran along the sides. Wine-colored, they stared at me as I stood there, answering questions and signing statements and working through paperwork for hours.

It was in hour five or so that Eilish made her way over to me, as I sat and stared at that cubicle that could have been taken out of any corporate office building in the UK. Peeking her head over the divider, she asked, "All right, Reed?"

"No," I said. Looking up at her now, I found it hard to believe I'd contemplated what I'd contemplated with her only last night. Nothing against her; she was pretty, but absent the alcohol and the insecurity that had been ripping through my veins, now I only saw her as the funny Irish girl I worked with, whose capture was the result of me letting my hormones and emotions get the better of me to the point I couldn't keep myself around her without fearing doing something stupid. Nothing more.

"I reckon ye will be, though, soon enough," she said, pulling out a rolling chair and plopping down. "Brought down a whole criminal empire today, didn't you?"

"No. Maybe some of the foundations of it," I said, glancing across the room. A series of offices for the big wheels were right there. The biggest, I figured, was Janus's. But I was left wondering who the players were that occupied the other half dozen. "Janus is still out there. That big, scary guy that was guarding you, he got away. Didn't happen to get his name, did you?"

She frowned, pursing her lips. "He didn't say much, that one. Just something about your sister, and killing her."

I felt a wall of stone descend over my face. "He's not going to get that chance." My hand was clutched tight. "Not ever."

"Reed?"

I turned to find Anna Webster there, clutching the baby, asleep against her. "Matthew's looking for you."

"Then I will go find him," I said, and stood as she walked

away. With a look at Eilish, I added, "By the by...I'm sorry about–"

"I was a bit stoned and you were a wee bit drunk," she said, blushing. "Nothing happened. And it's better that way. Right?" She stuck her hand out in an awkward-ass handshake.

For a moment I stared at it, then shook it. "Right," I said. Because she absolutely was.

CHAPTER NINETY-NINE

Wade

The cops showed up in surprisingly short order, probably because the chaos on the streets stilled almost instantly after I took Wei-Chen's head off. It was as though the riots were some electrical device on which the plug had been pulled. When I went outside a few minutes after finishing off the trigger man, the only sound in the air was the squeal of tires as people got the hell out of town, and the quiet cries of those in despair from what had happened.

I helped where I could, but before long, I found myself sitting at a table in the police department. They'd been cordial, but they'd had a lot of questions. Some of them they'd passed up the chain via phone calls to the local FBI office. Which was how I found out that communications had been restored.

"Mr. Wade?" A Las Vegas detective stuck her head in. "We've consulted with Washington and you're free to go."

"Cool," I said, gathering up my phone from the surface of the table. They'd left it with me, but the signal in here was shit, so I hadn't been able to get a call out. "Any idea who it was that might have saved me...?"

She shook her head. "Whoever it was, I think they probably saved a lot of people. We've got countless members of the, uh, unhoused tied up in knots all over town." She adopted a pained look. "Thousands dead, just in Vegas. Who knows how many more injured. Yet it could have been worse if your mystery man didn't save you and stop whoever else they could." Her eyes got hard. "I miss when your wife was in charge. Shit like this didn't happen then."

"Yep," I said, not even nodding. And not because I agreed with her. But because I wanted to get out of here – and back to Sienna – as quickly as possible. I found myself running through the halls until I made it past the security checkpoint, and the exit. I was already dialing Sierra as I hit the free air, orienting myself east and ramping up to supersonic.

CHAPTER ONE HUNDRED

Sienna

I was sitting alone in the newly refurbished Roosevelt Room, staring at the table's handsome top, lost in thought. How many people had I killed today? Not drones, not zombies, but people. Mentally hijacked, to be sure. Lethal threats? Definitely.

But I'd killed them nonetheless.

All I felt...was empty. And maybe a touch hungry.

There was a gentle knock at the door, and I could see Director Lane through the window. I beckoned her to enter, and she did, announcing, "Comms are restored. All the blackout zones are...well, not blacked out anymore."

I nodded. "Thanks for letting me know. I still don't have a phone, though, so..." I shrugged, unsure where I'd even lost it. Somewhere in the chaos, surely.

"Can I ask...?" She had a hell of a shiner, but it was already fading under her meta healing. I was pretty sure she'd had broken ribs, too, when I'd found her plowed into the ground on the lawn, but she wasn't walking nearly so gingerly anymore. "Why didn't you throw me under the bus back there?"

I blinked; she was talking about the press conference, where we'd stood shoulder to shoulder with the president in the briefing room and listened to him smoothly explain that yes, the crisis was over. Fen Liu's revenge had been thwarted, and all it had cost was untold thousands of lives. Hell, given the number of human beings the trigger man had dragged into his service, ones that probably didn't show up in any census, we would never know the exact human toll of her revenge.

But it was high. Too damned high. Tens of thousands. Maybe even a couple hundred thousand, just counting the dead. Some people...they might not be dead, but their lives would sure as hell never be the same.

She stared at me. "I mean, why wouldn't you just let me have it. I deserve it. I—"

"It's easy to hate me," I said, looking at my shoes. Which looked like they'd been through a war. Because they had. "Hell, I hate myself a not-small portion of the time." My knuckles were bloodied. Most of it probably wasn't mine. "Why would I blame you for that?"

"I don't hate you anymore," she said softly.

My fingertips were pressed against my lips, and I felt wetness at the corners of my eyes. "That's okay. I still do enough for both of us. Maybe enough for the whole damned world."

She must not have known what to say to that...because she just left.

CHAPTER ONE HUNDRED ONE

Wade

"I need to talk to you. Can you make a stop?"

Wayne Arthur's call caught me somewhere over the Blue Ridge mountains. I'd yet to get ahold of Sienna, and all I had were the assurances of Sierra, and the people manning the White House switchboard, telling me that she was fine, she had made it through the crisis alive, and was being debriefed or something. Sierra had noted she'd appeared in the White House press conference, stony-faced and saying little.

That had only made me race east even faster.

"I need to get to my wife," I said, having slowed just enough to be able to carry on a conversation. "I'm afraid you're going to have to wait, Wayne."

"What if I can get you through to your wife?" he asked. "Would that change the equation? We really need to talk about what happened."

"I...sure, if you can get me through to her so I can be certain she's all right," I said. "But if she says she's not, you're in a holding pattern until she's actually fine, I don't care if it takes longer than you live. Got it?"

"Your priorities are understood." He chuckled. "I'd expect nothing less. Hold on a second."

It was actually about three minutes before I heard Sienna's voice on the other end of the line. "Wade?" she sounded tired, almost dead in her way.

"Oh, thank goodness," I said, feeling some of the panicked tension leave my body. "You all right?"

There was a short pause. "Tired. I got darted at one point. Had to fight through an army of...well, zombies—"

"I called them zomboids."

"That's better," she said. "Anyway. President's safe. Country's...well, the place is kinda wrecked. Wherever a homeless underclass gathered got pretty well shellacked into oblivion."

"Yeah," I said. "I was in Vegas. Which, as it turned out, is where the trigger man was hanging his lack of hat."

"I heard," she said, "that you left him with a lack-of-head."

She was cracking jokes. That wasn't a definite sign that she was okay, but it was pretty close.

"I did do that," I said. "Wish I'd done it earlier, but he kinda paralyzed me. I only managed to throw him off his game with the Warmind. Which I'd only absorbed a short time earlier."

"You are certainly accumulating powers rapidly, Mr. Wade."

"Yeah, I picked up Stoneskin, Warmind, and gravity, too."

"Hmph," she said. "I powered up my Thor and added power punch."

"Looks like we both gathered some souls this time."

"Not really," she said. "Mine flaked to dust almost as soon as I got them. I think I might have gone and gotten too powerful. They don't stay for long anymore, even if I don't cage them."

I nodded. "Wayne Arthur wants me to stop off and talk to him. Are you still being debriefed?"

"Yeah," she said, sounding utterly exhausted. "I don't think I'm...I'm not going to be much for conversation for a bit. I'm just sitting in a conference room waiting to sign a statement or whatever so I can leave. Not even sure who I'm supposed to talk to, if anyone, so you probably have some time."

"Okay," I said. "I'll just stop off and chat it up with Wayne for a minute. See what he's got to say for himself."

"Sounds good," she said, and I couldn't shake the feeling that she should be in bed, sleeping off whatever she'd gone through today. "See you in a bit."

I hung up after a goodbye, and slightly adjusted my heading. CIA HQ it was – before I could see my pretty wife again.

CHAPTER ONE HUNDRED TWO

Reed

"Call me Jo," Prime Minister Evans said as she shook my hand. Firmly – a little too much, at least for a normal human. There was a glint in her eye that suggested a secret we now shared. She looked to be in her forties, dark-haired, pale, slightly freckled, with just a hint of gray at the roots to suggest a maturity that the lack of wrinkles didn't hint at. "I hear we have you to thank for the breaking of this crime ring."

"I just did what I could," I mumbled, taking a seat across the desk from her in the office at number 10. It was wood-paneled, very dignified, exactly what I would have expected from the seat of British power. "Made a bit of a mess, honestly."

"That was a very British answer," she said, picking up her cuppa. "Do you anticipate more trouble from this Omega group?"

I winced as I contemplated the answer. The one I wish I could give her was, "No, they're all wrapped up." Unfortunately... "Yes," I said. "They've been around since time immemorial, and unfortunately the ring leader managed to escape my grip."

"You know," Evans said, eyes still glinting, "even with our separation from the EU, we've remained somewhat bound, at least in theory, to their 'no metahumans' policy. I know, I know – it was always horrendously unfair, and piteously enforced. We've done little better over here; trying to declare an entire class of people unwelcome in your society has done little but drive them underground, leaving us easy prey for organizations like this. We're simply unprepared to deal with metahumans."

"It feels like *you* could deal with them if you wanted to," I said, with a sly smile.

"I'm afraid I don't possess your gifts of a steely constitution – and offensive abilities," she said, setting down cup and saucer. "Mine are rather limited."

"Well, we're always happy to send people over anytime you have a problem," I said. There was a wetness in my palms, and I thought of Janus, out there, just lingering somewhere, waiting to strike again. "Whenever that might be."

"I was thinking we might adopt a rather different solution," she said, looking at me completely clear-eyed. I cocked my head, and listened to what she had to say. To my surprise...it was exactly what I'd been thinking myself.

CHAPTER ONE HUNDRED THREE

Wade

"This was preventable," Wayne Arthur said, once I was past security, and sitting across the desk from him. "We didn't see it coming because we don't have eyes anywhere, anymore, Wade."

"I know this," I said. "China rolled up our spies. Left us blind. You know how I know?"

"You got rolled, too," Wayne said with a wary nod. "And I don't blame you if it's once burned, twice shy—"

"Wayne," I said, cutting my hand across in front of us. "Get to your point. I have a wife to go see." I hadn't heard from her yet that the White House was kicking her loose, but I wanted to be there to meet her.

"We could use a man of your talents," Wayne said. And I felt my stomach drop as I contemplated that possibility.

CHAPTER ONE HUNDRED FOUR

Sienna

The White House let me go after just a bit more waiting, and soon enough I found myself standing outside in the quiet gloom of the lawn, staring up at the dawn starting over Washington. Red-orange skies glared down at me, like a trick being played on my mind, telling me it was morning when clearly I hadn't slept, so it must be night. I rubbed my eyes and felt for the cell phone that wasn't there in any of my pockets as I walked toward the gate and exited onto Pennsylvania Ave.

"Hey!" Wade's voice reached me as he streaked down out of the sky the last twenty feet or so. He was on me in a moment, his arms wrapped around me, mouth on mine. It was the first time in hours I had contemplated how long it had been since I'd brushed my teeth. When he pulled back, his eyes were rimmed with concern. "You okay?"

"I made it out alive," I said, hands still on him. "Thanks to you finding the source of our problems."

He cringed as he looked at the immensity of the damage to the fence, and Lafayette Square. "Looks like it was just in time."

"But you made it," I said, "and that's what matters." I ignored the blood on my hands, but was afraid to take his.

"Sienna," he said, and something in the way he said it reminded me of a time I'd plummeted from the top of a collapsing building in Revelen, or the WSM tower in Nashville. "I talked to Wayne Arthur before I got here."

"Oh?" I asked, already wary.

"This thing we just went through...it happened because we don't have good intelligence," he said.

"Far be it from me to argue with the proposition that the US government is stupid."

He chuckled weakly. "You know what I mean. We have no spies anymore. China burned them all."

I nodded; this was true. In fact, it was a problem back when I was running the war. It kinda made me blind.

"Someone needs to re-establish networks," he said, and I sensed he was building to something. "But with AI rising, and electronics being so easily compromised these days, it has to be someone who can pass information without a digital trace."

My eyelids fluttered. I could see where he was going with this...

...And I steeled myself.

"He asked me to do it," Wade said. "He asked me to become Director of Operations, to rebuild our networks worldwide. I'm going to have to get really hands-on with it, get out in the field and build this thing from the ground up. Making contacts, passing info, convincing people to trust me..."

I forced a smile onto my face, almost as natural as the real one. I hoped, in the glow of excitement over what he was telling me, he would ascribe any woodenness to my shell shock over the day's events. "That's great. You'll be fantastic at it."

"But...I won't do it if you don't want me to." He leaned in, close, bringing his forehead almost to mine. "We can't live on a private island anymore, but we could go somewhere else, if you want. He's going to be paying me...a lot. If I get this done in the next year, two years...we'll have enough to, maybe not get back to the private island life, but at least purchase a nice property here in the US, somewhere off the beaten path where we can be left alone."

"That...would be magical," I said, voice hoarse.

"I only worry," he said, "that trouble is going to come, and soon. I mentioned it to Wayne, and he promised I won't be out of contact to the point where I can't be reached. When you need me, I'm there. That's understood."

"You really are driven by duty, aren't you?" I stared at my husband, the earnestness on his face. He didn't want to run away to a private island and hide from the world, not even after a brutal stay in a Chinese prison nearly killed him.

Unlike me...he was a hero. And he'd willingly fight to the end without quitting.

"I am," he said. "To you. To my country. It's a balancing act, but I think I can pull it off."

"Okay," I said.

"Just a short little parting," Wade said, and he kissed me. "We're going to be driving each other nuts for a very long time to come, Mrs. Wade. I'm gonna be feeling those cold feet of yours on my legs in bed for millennia yet."

I tried to brush aside the worries threatening to drag me in, and put on the brave face of wives since time immemorial as they sent their husbands off to war. "I hope you're right," was the best I could manage.

"Where are you going to go?" he asked, once we parted. I wasn't even teary anymore; how could he know I was breaking inside?

"Back to Tennessee," I said. Because I had no other answers. We said goodbye there, as the sun rose over Washington.

I hoped it wasn't for the last time.

CHAPTER ONE HUNDRED FIVE

Reed

I landed back in Tennessee around daybreak and dropped off Eilish with the sunrise coloring her hair. She gave me a sleepy wave and disappeared inside her building. Truly, I felt that; but I needed to get home and talk to Isabella before I collapsed.

She met me at the door in a bathrobe, with a cup of hot coffee in her hand and a look of slight surprise. The thing about my fiancée – she's gorgeous, even in fluffy pink. I kissed her, then kissed her again. Then I got distracted for a while...

Ew.

We lay in silence in bed afterward, her hair all beautiful and messy. Her toes found my ankle and probed it playfully. "Have you slept?" she asked.

"I'm a little off schedule," I said. "And probably a little drained from all these new powers." I lifted my hand, and fire rose from my fingertips. "Not sure Sienna ever mentioned it, but man, they take it out of you. I feel like I could sleep forever, and I don't think it's just the jet lag."

"You sleep, then," she said, and leaned over to kiss me. "I need to get my day started."

"Before you go," I said, seizing her and making her laugh. "Do you want to get married in, say, a couple weeks?"

Her perfectly manicured brows rose. "Traditionally, one would simply set a date."

"Great. How does two weeks strike you?"

"Rushed," she said, sitting up. "Are you serious?"

"Yes," I said. "And...also...one other thing..."

CHAPTER ONE HUNDRED SIX

Sienna

I landed on my property in Franklin, Tennessee, while the sun was still high on the horizon. It was a ruin, chewed up and destroyed by Chinese military forces during an ambush in which they'd tried to kill me along with now-Minister, then-fugitive Jian Chen. We'd escaped them, but the house was in ruins. I probably had enough left to rebuild it, but...honestly, why? It was sure to be destroyed again. Why keep lighting fire to money when I was running so short on it?

Why keep doing any of the things I was doing? Rebuilding houses, saving the world. I only had to do them again a few months later. This was my treadmill, and the treadmill was a device that had been used early on as a torture method for convicts.

"I thought that was you." I heard soft footsteps a couple hundred yards away, at the treeline. Isabella Perugini came trudging out of the woods wearing a fluffy pink bathrobe, a sheen of fine sweat on her skin that, even in my addled condition, I knew the origin of right away. "You are back?"

"Yep," I said, turning back to look at my ruin of a house. There was no staying here unless I pitched a tent. Which was, perhaps, the best option. I could have a succession of tents burned down and not suffer unbearable financial losses. "I assume Reed made it home okay from England?"

"He did," she said, picking her way over to me. It was quite a distance, and she didn't hurry. Probably because of the coffee mug she was clutching in her hand. As soon as she made it to me, she proffered it.

I wasn't too proud to take it. "Thanks."

"If you just got back from somewhere, I assume you need it," she said.

"Didn't turn on the news yet this morning?"

"Why would I spoil a perfectly good morning by watching the news?"

I sipped the coffee. She had a good point.

"Are you just going to stand here looking at this ruin," she said, arms folded across her fluffy robe, "or do you want to come back to the house and stay with us?"

I started to answer, then halted myself. "I'm never going to have a normal life," I said. "With a house that doesn't get destroyed, or a husband who sticks around. I can't have kids; my enemies will be wanting to take them hostage every five seconds. They'll be targets, not people—"

"You are sounding a bit like a crazy person," she said, taking the coffee right out of my hands. "Maybe you do not need caffeine."

I hadn't even seen her reach out for it. "How...how did you do that?" I looked at her hand, then mine.

She brushed a hand past my face at about six hundred miles an hour. It stirred my hair into a near tornado. "I am not an idiot; my husband is in constant danger. My sister-in-law, she has enemies the world over. For as long as I could, I protected myself with a shotgun, as my father taught me. That is no longer practical, and there are better ways. This, you should know. And 'normal,' what is this? I have never been 'normal.'"

"Having known you for something like a decade, I'm not sure that's true."

She spat, as Italians sometimes did. "It is nothing, this 'normal.' A pipe dream. A word people use to suggest some basic idea of how things should be. The problem is, normal for you is not normal for me. My soon-to-be husband shows up after a long trip, and guess what he wants right away?"

I blinked a couple times. "I mean...I've only been married a little while, but I'm pretty sure *that's* normal."

"Of course, that. But not what I am talking about." She fanned away in my face dismissively. "He wants to get married – in the next two weeks. And then he wants to move to England." Her eyes widened in that way she had, when she was looking for approval or expressing disbelief or something. "Can you imagine?"

I stared back at her blankly. "...England? Like...why? The bad weather? The worse food?"

"The Prime Minister, she wants him to form an agency expansion there," Perugini said. "He has already talked to Augustus about it, and received his blessing. Your little business is going international. Is that 'normal?'" She paused, and brushed some dust off my shoulder from the flight. "Come. You can stay with us. Probably you can stay in our house while we are gone, if you try not to blow it up. I know, very hard to promise, but even if you do, I am sure Reed will still love you."

I caught the inference there. "What about you?"

She waved dismissively again. "I am your sister-in-law. We

are stuck together even if you blow my house up. But what am I saying? I don't care, the fortune they are going to be paying us in England? It is enough to buy ten of these a year. Come. Reed is sleeping, and you look tired. The guest bedroom is always made up for you." She brushed my shoulder again. "Come. Out of the cold."

I nodded, and let her lead me away. "Congratulations," I said, a bit numbly. "On getting married. And England. That sounds like a...a big leap, career-wise, for Reed."

"He is very excited..." she said, leading me away. "We both are. It will be nice to be back in Europe, a close flight to home. There is so much to plan. You must be my maid of honor, of course. I promise not to put you in a dress that is too hideous..."

She led me away, talking the whole time. The forest loomed ahead, a small patch of light shining through it from the path that led to her house from mine. As we walked, all I could think about was Wade and Reed and Isabella, moving forward with their careers, and their lives, in DC and England and elsewhere...

And how with all of them gone, I was one step closer to being totally alone.

EPILOGUE

Location Unknown

The Watcher watched, as he did. Watched the silence unfold. Watched the silence *break*. This should have been a new event for him, but it had become quite commonplace. Commonplace since the Sleeper had wakened. That had been an event. That had been of note. That had been—

The end of a long silence.

Now...nothing was silent anymore. Regrettably.

"I made the decisions I thought best, under the circumstances." The speaker was a gray-haired man, one whom the Watcher found irritating. Less so than others, perhaps, but worse than the silence he'd enjoyed for the last decade.

"Janus." The Sleeper spoke, his face in shadows that even the Watcher's keen eyes could not quite penetrate. Of course, the Watcher knew what the Sleeper looked like. He had stared at his face for hundreds of years before the long quiet, and saw it well in the glassy, ice-covered window of the suspension pod that he'd spent the last ten years shepherding from place to place – London to Revelen. Revelen to China. Waiting for the Sleeper to wake. Then back to London–

And now they were here. Again.

Janus looked up; he was crumpled. Losing to the Treston boy had worn him. Losing had, perhaps, wounded him worse than the loss of his leg, which was slowly coming back. Still, he was on his knees, before the Sleeper–

As one should be...when one was before a man who'd once held the sword of Zeus himself. Who'd been chief aid to Poseidon. Who'd stared down Hades. Who'd helped run the Roman Empire, pulled strings in the French Revolution, helped guide the rise of the state of Prussia, shaped the modern world–

And who slept no longer.

Alastor stood from his throne, still broad of shoulder and strong of chin. The symbology of kings was present in everything he did, and the blood of them flowed through his veins. The Watcher watched, mesmerized, at the return, after so long, of this man. This man, who had done so much for him. Ten years in the darkness? A pittance. A small price to be paid for surviving Sovereign, for remaining out of the sight of Nealon, and others, unseen–

Until now.

"You failed," Alaster said simply.

Janus's head sagged. "I failed."

Alastor was quiet for a moment. His hair was close-cropped to his skull, graying, and the hints of a beard had begun to grow on his aged cheeks in the months since he'd emerged from the cryogenic pod. "I don't blame you for this, of course. Nealon has been causing problems since before I took my little...sojourn."

"I truly thought you were dead," Janus said, raising his eyes.

"It's what you were meant to think," Alastor said. "I couldn't have Sovereign overrun the Omega offices and his pet Hades pull the knowledge of my survival out of you." He made a slow loop around the kneeling Janus.

And the Watcher merely watched. For that was what he did.

"It's a shame the boy Karthik had to die," Alastor said, pausing behind Janus. "But someone needed to be an example of my power for your little army, and he was as good as any."

Janus nodded slowly from his knees. It was a good place for him to be, the Watcher judged. He should remain there forever.

"More of a shame is letting any of Nealon's ilk get on the trail," Alastor said. He extended his hand toward the back of Janus's head. "I thought you had control, had connections in the British government?"

"They are not so powerful as to make a body go away that you ripped apart," Janus said, keeping his head bowed. Properly. "Not one so obviously put asunder by a metahuman."

Alastor's hand hovered at the back of Janus's head. Would he strike? The Watcher found himself hoping for just this, but alas, he let it drop to his side. "We'll have to work on that. And besides...Nealon would never have stayed out of this business of ours forever." He clasped it behind his back, cupped by his other hand, and walked on, still circling Janus. "No, she will have to be dealt with. And we've been heading toward this collision forever, haven't we?" His eyes glinted. "Ever since she showed up in 1999 and rescued her younger self from our clutches."

Janus cocked his head, looking up uncertainly.

"Oh, you didn't know about that?" Alastor's eyes glinted with amusement – and malice. Always malice. "She's quite the power, that succubus. I can't shake the feeling that if we could have just gotten hold of her – but alas, she's been protected by powerful forces – including herself. But that's all out of the way now that Akiyama is dead, as well as Sovereign. One by one, her powerful defenders have fallen. Persephone and her ilk – though that will bring complications, of course. Hera and Alpha. Winter and his pathetic sort."

"She is a law unto herself now," Janus said, still huddled.

Alastor stopped, and grinned wolfishly as he looked at the Watcher. The Watcher smiled back, not a thing he did very often. "Then I suppose it is fortunate," Alastor said, with the malice – again, and always, "that we are the world's best lawbreakers. Because she must, indeed...be broken."

Sienna Nealon Will Return in

Liberty
The Girl in the Box, Book 60
Coming August 2, 2025!

PRE-ORDER NOW!

NOTE: There are only 6 books remaining in The Girl in the Box Series. It will end with book 65!

Sienna also returns in the new spinoff, The Girl Who Ran Away, Book 2 which includes special guest star SIENNA NEALON!

Buried in Lies
The Girl Who Ran Away, Book 1

Get it NOW!

Somewhere in all the lies, the truth must be hiding...

Ava Garcia was a normal student – until the day Ty Foster walked into Sunvail High school and killed eight students, including Ava's best friend. Except things don't quite add up. Mysterious disappearances, unexplained accidents, and a seemingly invisible man follow behind the tragedy, leaving Ava wondering what is going on.

Able to remember only flashes of what happened on that day, unable to stomach the lies of the principal, the sheriff, and the mayor, and weighed down under the burden of survivor's guilt, Ava can't help herself – she has to know the truth. And she won't stop until she finds it...

From author Robert J. Crane comes the first tale in a new series set in his multi-million selling Girl in the Box universe.

Get it NOW!

Listening to Fear
The Girl Who Ran Away, Book 2

GET IT NOW!

Bound in Silence
The Girl Who Ran Away, Book 3

GET IT NOW! .

Those Deadly Secrets
The Girl Who Ran Away, Book 4
Coming October 2nd, 2025!

PRE-ORDER NOW!

AUTHOR'S NOTE

We're moving into the endgame now. This is the 59th book in the Girl in the Box series, and the beginning of the final story arc. I always said I'd write The Girl in the Box as long as I was able to find fresh ideas and approaches, and I am running out of them. So it's almost time to say goodbye. It's not right away; I estimate the earliest I'll get the last book (book 65) out is late 2026. You've got some time. And Sienna's got one final major story arc (which will run from this book to book 64) and a final volume (65) as a coda or epilogue to her story.

Thanks for reading! If you want to know immediately when future books become available, take sixty seconds and sign up for my NEW RELEASE EMAIL ALERTS by CLICKING HERE. I don't sell your information and I only send out emails when I have a new book out. The reason you should sign up for this is because I don't always set release dates, and even if you're following me on Facebook (robertJcrane (Author)) or Twitter (@robertJcrane), or part of my Facebook fan page (Team RJC), it's easy to miss my book announcements because ... well, because social media is an imprecise thing.

Find listings for all my books plus some more behind-the-scenes info on my website: http://www.robertjcrane.com!

Cheers,
Robert J. Crane

Other Works by Robert J. Crane

The Girl in the Box
(and Out of the Box)
Contemporary Urban Fantasy

60. Liberty* (Coming August 2nd, 2025!)

The Girl Who Ran Away
Contemporary Mystery Fantasy

1. Buried in Lies
2. Listening to Fear
3. Bound in Silence
4. Those Deadly Secrets* (Coming October 2025!)

The Sanctuary Series
Epic Fantasy
(in best reading order)
(Series Complete)

1. Defender (Volume 1)
2. Avenger (Volume 2)
3. Champion (Volume 3)
4. Crusader (Volume 4)
5. Sanctuary Tales (Volume 4.25)
6. Thy Father's Shadow (Volume 4.5)
7. Master (Volume 5)
8. Fated in Darkness (Volume 5.5)
9. Warlord (Volume 6)
10. Heretic (Volume 7)
11. Legend (Volume 8)
12. Ghosts of Sanctuary (Volume 9)
13. Call of the Hero (Volume 10)
14. The Scourge of Despair (Volume 11)
15. Rage of the Ancients (Volume 12)

Ashes of Luukessia
A Sanctuary Trilogy
(with Michael Winstone)

(Trilogy Complete)

1. A Haven in Ash (Ashes of Luukessia #1)
2. A Respite From Storms (Ashes of Luukessia #2)
3. A Home in the Hills (Ashes of Luukessia #3)

Liars and Vampires
YA Urban Fantasy
(with Lauren Harper)
(Series Complete)

1. No One Will Believe You
2. Someone Should Save Her
3. You Can't Go Home Again
4. Lies in the Dark
5. Her Lying Days Are Done
6. Heir of the Dog
7. Hit You Where You Live
8. Her Endless Night
9. Burned Me
10. Something In That Vein* (Coming April 2nd, 2025!)

Southern Watch
Dark Contemporary Fantasy/Horror
(Series Complete)

1. Called
2. Depths
3. Corrupted
4. Unearthed
5. Legion
6. Starling
7. Forsaken

8. Hallowed

The Mira Brand Adventures
YA Modern Fantasy
(Series Complete)

1. The World Beneath
2. The Tide of Ages
3. The City of Lies
4. The King of the Skies
5. The Best of Us
6. We Aimless Few
7. The Gang of Legend
8. The Antecessor Conundrum

*Forthcoming, title subject to change

ACKNOWLEDGMENTS

Thanks to Lewis Moore for the edits, Jeff Bryan, for the proofing, and thanks as always to the great Karri Klawiter of artbykarri.com for the cover.

Thanks, too, to my family for making this all possible.

Made in United States
Cleveland, OH
04 March 2025

14875413R00233